Sin and Betrayal

Sin and Lies

Book One

Sienna Snow

Sin and Betrayal

By Sienna Snow

Published by Sienna Snow

Cover Design: The Book Brander

Editor: Jennifer Haymore

www.siennasnow.com

ISBN - eBook - 979-8-88535-018-1

ISBN - Print - Paperback - 979-8-88535-019-8

ISBN - Print - Hardback - 979-8-88535-020-4

AI Disclosure

No generative artificial intelligence (AI) was used in the writing of this work. The author expressly prohibits any entity from using this publication for purposes of training AI technologies to generate text, including, without limitation, technologies that are capable of generating works in the same style or genre as this publication.

Tropes List

- Dark Mafia
- Antihero
- Alpha Hero
- Bodyguard
- Boss's wife
- Second chance
- Enemies to lovers
- MMF
- Why choose
- Forbidden Romance
- menage romance
- Suspense
- Off-limits romance
- Hurt you to save you
- Protector
- Spicy Romance
- Forced Marriage

- Forced Proximity
- Billionaire
- Found family
- Girl squad
- Kink/BDSM
- Touch her, and you die
- Hate to love you
- Strong heroine
- First Love

Author's Note

Content Warning

This book is a dark romance with subject matter that may be triggering to some readers.

- Forced Marriage
- Domestic Assult
- Sexual Assault (light on page, discussion of past in graphic detail)
- Physical Assault
- Violence and graphic death
- Body mutilation (not on page)

One

Present Day
Nerine

I finally did it. I finally killed him.

The bastard deserved to die by my hands.

He won't hurt me anymore. He won't hurt anyone anymore.

He thought I was a commodity, a thing to use for power and status.

Big mistake. Huge mistake.

I stared down at my blood-soaked hands. The dark, crimson liquid glistened rich and beautiful, pooling in my palms, still warm, still filled with the essence of the monster I married. Not by choice but force.

Tick, tick, tick.

The grandfather clock in the library counted the seconds since Andraius Fredric Angelos's demise.

Not a true Angelos but a faker, a charlatan, someone who assumed a name to take my fucking throne.

Bastard.

A laugh bubbled up inside me, but my stomach clenched before I set it free. Then chills filled my body, making it seem like I'd never feel warm again.

I dropped my head back against a wall of books, trying desperately to ignore the pounding in my head, and shifted my attention to the asshole.

The handle of the knife I'd used to slice his belly open poked out from underneath him as he bled all over the rug.

A brutal death was a fitting end to the demon who used a blade to carve his punishment into my skin for not meeting his expectation of a new bride.

That was nearly five years ago.

I'd lost count of the number of times since then that he'd threatened to end me, take another, younger wife, and use the inheritance that came if I died to build upon his empire.

His empire.

Fucker. It was *my* damn empire. I was the true Angelos. Not him. Without me, he was nothing. And now he *was* nothing.

He'd done everything to destroy my spark, my confidence, and my youth. And in the beginning, he'd almost succeeded. I'd lost everyone and everything I loved, and he preyed upon it. He turned me into a shell of the person I remembered before he entered my life. Then I realized falling under his rules made him happy and gave him power over me.

That was unacceptable for a girl brought up to fight for what belonged to her.

I decided I'd rather have him hate me. He'd treat me the same no matter how I behaved.

Plus it wasn't as if I'd get back all the time stolen from me.

At nearly twenty-four, most of my old friends had graduated from college. In contrast, I'd spent my time in hell, living as a wife to a man who'd take my family name as if it were his birthright and then wanted to breed me like a mare so he could legitimize his claim.

Thank God the bastard never proved to be anything but sterile. Though he'd never once admitted it. No, it had all been my fault.

As in all cases when men held bigger egos than abilities, they blamed a woman for their shortfalls.

Piece of shit.

Tick, tick, tick.

The clock rhythmically warned me to get moving.

Wiping my hands on my clothes to clean away Andraius's blood as best as possible, I pushed to my feet. Immediately, I gritted my teeth as a shot of pain radiated down my leg.

The fucker always knew how to land those sneaky kicks when I least expected them. But then again, I hadn't expected tonight's attack at all.

I closed my eyes and breathed through the dizziness.

I could handle this.

I'd lost count of the number of times I'd borne the discomfort of his abuse, hidden the bruises, and pretended indifference. Knowing the public knew damn well it was all a fucking lie.

I could admit he'd eased up on his lessons, as he liked to call them, over the last two years. It had nothing to do with him becoming a better man and all to do with me refusing to give him the reactions he craved. It wasn't as much fun for him when I acted the cold, calculating bitch he accused me of being.

By locking down my emotions and acting as if nothing hurt me, I forced myself to die inside, to become the epitome of the venom-filled whore that he'd named me.

It wasn't a part of me I relished. I never expected to develop the persona of a bitter, unhappy woman.

Yes, I'd always spoken my mind and fought for what I believed was right. But that girl, the one from five years ago, saw a future of possibilities.

Who I'd become held a rage that festered and unleashed at specific times and usually in the direction of the newly departed bastard on the floor.

My undisguised hate had kept him away from me.

Well, for the most part. The only exception was when it came to impregnating me.

He hated me but had no problems fucking me. However, when I made the experience as miserable for him as it was for me, he decided to turn to science.

I smirked.

Not anymore, asshole.

With ginger steps, I moved to Andraius's lifeless body and loomed over him.

"All I wanted was one fucking night of peace, without having to think about you, and you couldn't even give me that. Surprise, surprise. I learned a few skills from the very person you thought would teach me how to be a proper wife. She taught me the exact moves I used on you tonight, fucker.

"I believe her husband's version of proper and yours are vastly different. You deserved this and more. I wish I hadn't waited this long to be the person Papa raised me to be. I was never stupid or as weak as you believed. I am ashamed that I let you take so much from me."

The urge to kick him, punch him, mutilate him overwhelmed me. I craved to chop him into tiny pieces as I'd heard he'd done to my baby brother, Linus, and my papa on the day he'd staged his coup.

My heart ached for the eight-year-old boy who'd never been able to live because of this bastard.

Everyone assumed since I had a brother, Papa planned to groom him to take over the family. And because of this, Andraius had targeted a defenseless child.

Fucking bastard never knew Papa wasn't one to follow traditional gender roles, especially since Linus's birth was a surprise. He'd raised me to fill the position of heir. Papa taught me everything about running the organization, informing me of every secret passed down through the generations to how to access all assets. Most of all, he taught me how to be ten times as ruthless as any man since women rarely got a seat at the table.

How could I have forgotten all those lessons? Why had I waited five years to act?

I was an idiot for giving Andraius power over me. I let him rule my life, all because he dangled the lives of my mother and sisters in front of me. Challenging him as a bitter, cruel wife was never enough. It hadn't stopped him from raping me, destroying the legacy Papa created, or spending millions that never belonged to him.

I released a deep exhale, pulling back every instinct to mutilate my disgrace of a husband.

I would survive. I would make it to the other side of this lake of poison I swam in. Logic and a thought-out process was the key.

Touching him would leave evidence leading back to me. The last thing I wanted was for anyone to suspect me. Too many people I loved would pay the price for my mistakes.

No one could ever know. I'd have to take this secret to my grave.

Oh God, but my prints were on the knife he held in his hand.

A piercing cold engulfed my body, and shivers ratcheted me to my bones.

Fuck, fuck, fuck.

Why couldn't I get myself under control?

I had to get myself under control. Panicking led to mistakes.

Think, Nerine.

After a few seconds, I decided I had no choice but to shift his body. Using my shoulder I pushed Andraius just enough to reveal his hand with the blade. With the hem of my robe, I pulled the weapon from Andraius's fingers, and as thoroughly as possible, I wiped the handle. Then using the robe as a barrier, I wrapped Andraius's hand around the hilt and set him back.

Okay. Okay. I'd managed that without making a mess. Well, a bigger mess.

My attention shifted to the clock. Five minutes since the last time I looked.

Tick, tick, tick.

The echo of the gears moving rang in my ear, causing my headache to intensify and nausea to build in the pit of my stomach.

Scanning the room, I searched for anything that pointed to my presence. As far as the household knew, I'd gone to bed.

No one dared enter the library without my permission. Every Angelos family member, soldier, and employee knew this was my sanctuary, and out of respect for me, they kept it off-limits to everyone. I spent hours here at a time, writing, reading, and trying to study everything that was denied to me when Andraius had forced me to withdraw from college following his ascent to the head of the family after our marriage and after he murdered Papa.

My blankets and sweater sat in the exact spot where I'd left them earlier in the afternoon. The room sat almost the same.

Well, except for the dead man face down on the carpet.

I tugged my robe off and cleaned my arms of any remaining blood with quick, efficient movements. Then, I picked up anything that could remotely make it seem as if I'd been in here

—my slippers, my book, and my shawl—and placed them in my dressing gown, tying it closed with the silk belt.

I'd never know how we managed not to knock any furniture over or alert the guards.

Luck, maybe?

One thing I knew for sure was that he hadn't expected anyone in here tonight. The surprise and then rage that flashed on his face told me he planned to search the room for something.

What? I hadn't a clue.

It no longer mattered. Now I'd take the same passageways I'd used to enter the library to guide me back to my bedroom, where I'd pretend nothing happened.

With one last shaky breath, I clutched the robe satchel to my chest, stepped around Andraius, and headed toward the passageway entrance.

I couldn't help but sigh in relief when I saw the slightly ajar wall panel. I'd never been so glad I'd left the hinge open in my life. Usually, I'd go out of my way to ensure I secured it. Only a handful of people knew of the secret hallways in the house, and Andraius and those loyal to him weren't part of that group.

Stepping inside, I rushed through the corridors, up a flight of stairs, and through a narrow walkway to a flat wall outside my bedroom. With a tap of my heel to a groove at the bottom, the panel slid to the side. I rushed inside, paused for a brief second to ensure the wall was sealed shut, and then moved to the bathroom.

The need to wash away the filth of Andraius's blood from my body surged through me.

I had to get clean. There was no choice but to get clean.

I pulled open the shower door and stepped inside, clothes and makeshift satchel included.

I barely registered the ice-cold spray touching my skin before it adjusted to a tolerable warm temperature. All I knew was I had to wash the devil off me.

But instead of following through on my intentions, I slid to the floor and braced my back against the tiled wall.

The pounding inside my skull intensified, and thoughts upon thoughts whirled in my brain.

"Would anyone believe me if I were to tell the whole truth?" I whispered into the silence of the room. I hesitated for a moment as my body trembled with fear. My heart raced, trying to answer the question: would I be strong enough to reveal the truth, no matter the consequences? In the end, I just wasn't sure.

So many people hated him. Would anyone really miss him?

I hadn't planned for this to happen.

Well, maybe I'd dreamed about making his last moments on earth as excruciating as possible.

I still couldn't believe God had granted me this wish, especially since he'd abandoned me in everything else over the last five years. Why now? And what price would I pay?

The consequences were inevitable. All I wanted was to escape, to take my mother and sisters and run, to hide where no one would find us or use us.

Now, my plans were shattered.

"If only one of his enemies had taken him out before this happened." I dropped my head against my knees and whispered, "I defended myself. I have to remember this, no matter what."

He was the one who snuck into the library. He was the one who attacked me from behind. He was the one who planned to put me in a coma and use me as an incubator for his child. I'd protected myself in the only way I knew how.

My palm ran over the now-soaked leather knife harness. I'd have to say goodbye to this beautiful gift.

Just another special item destroyed because of the monster I'd married.

I lifted my head into the heated spray, letting the water pound my face and my clothes.

After a few minutes, I pushed myself to stand, stripped, and scrubbed every inch of my face, hair, and body clean.

Thankfully, scraping the last remnants of Andraius from my skin helped me gather some semblance of control.

Time to prep everything for destruction.

Thank you, Papa. Without your lessons on cleanup, I'd have no idea what to do next.

I sent my words up to heaven and then went about my tasks.

I slowly cleaned up the bathroom, gathering my clothes, scrubbing the shower walls and doors, and ensuring the bedroom had no traces of my departed spouse anywhere.

Twenty minutes later, after a quick trip through different passageways to the furnace room where the family disposed of "unnecessary garbage," I sealed myself in my bedroom and slid into bed.

I stared up at the ceiling of the dark room, with only the sound of my unsteady breath in the air.

Was this real? Maybe this was a dream, and I'd wake up soon.

No. I wasn't sleeping. My body hurt too much.

All of a sudden, laughter and tears bubbled up from deep inside.

"I'm free. I'm fucking free. I didn't have to use my escape plan. I didn't have to run. I—"

After a few hiccups, the humor disappeared. Who was I kidding? I knew better than to pretend otherwise.

Freedom stopped existing the very moment Andraius killed Papa and Linus and took over the organization, and it would never exist again.

Now the real prison sentence began.

More secrets, lies, and pretenses.

I would do it because I finally had started to find myself again. My heartbeat accelerated as a realization washed over me.

According to the succession of power, I'd just inherited the seat back as the head of the Angelos Syndicate.

Oh God, what had I done?

This was the last thing I wanted—more power games. More people set into position, ready to use me.

I knew there was no escape, but now there really was no escape. All my plans, all my effort. Would any of it ever happen?

Nausea settled in the pit of my stomach as Papa's words during one of our lessons echoed in my head.

"You decide your path, cara. You'll fight a war either way. You have to decide whether you're a pawn or a—"

At that moment, a deafening bang echoed through my bedroom as the door shook violently with each pound.

"Nerine, open up, now! Or we're breaking it down if you don't."

In the next second, the door splintered inward, and two dark figures emerged from the hallway, their steps heavy and determined.

They approached me swiftly, and before I could utter a single word, the taller one scooped me up in his arms and held me tight against him before whispering into my hair, "Thank God, you're safe. I don't know what I would have done if anything happened to you."

Then the other one said, "Andraius is dead, Angel. We've got to get you out of here, now."

Two

Four Months Ago
Xander

"Any news on Chicago?" Andraius Angelos, the current head of Angelos Shipping, asked during our regular Monday morning briefing.

The fucker loved his briefings, running this operation as if it were some nine-to-five corporation instead of the twenty-four-hour hands-on syndicate it truly was.

Idiot.

But if that was how he wanted it, my best friend Theo Nephus and I would run it that way. Or let him believe we carried things out in that fashion.

"Nothing yet," I answered.

A frown marred Andraius's face. "How is that possible?"

Under Theo and I, the different teams reported to Andraius what we believed was necessary. Then they carried out what we told them to do. This moron had eroded his power bit by bit, never even realizing what he was doing. As far as this organization was concerned, he was a lame-duck boss, a figurehead, and none the wiser.

Fucker. And he'd done it all to himself, thinking he was so smart.

He'd shipped us off to manage everything internationally the moment he'd slithered into his seat. What dumbass gave near twenty-four-year-olds that much control?

"I have a few loyalists in key locations keeping tabs on things. None of your brothers are sending any of the Stratos collective to challenge your place."

He was a paranoid fucker, constantly worried about the family he'd abandoned for his current position of power instead of focusing on everyone around him.

"I don't trust any of them. The fact we're family means nothing to them. Given the opportunity, they'd stab me in the back as if I didn't notice how Tobias sucked up to me at the party last month. They're trying to muscle their way into the East Coast."

Well, surprise, surprise. He finally figured out that his nephew Tobias was the real power behind the Stratos Family. Andraius's brothers played a minor role in operations while the empire belonged to the children, led by Tobias.

We'd had a run-in or two with Tobias in our youth, and that fucker had no qualms about using every dirty trick in the book to get his way. From what I'd learned of the adult version of him, he followed the same tactics. He ran the Chicago outfit by undercutting and cheating his allies, not realizing he left a trail of enemies gunning for his blood.

I guessed stupidity ran in Andraius's bloodline.

"That boy needs to step out from his father's shadow and take over the organization. He's too old to play errand boy all the time."

Correction, this jackass knew zilch about how the Stratos organization ran.

How the fuck had he orchestrated the Angelos coop? This moron couldn't have been the mastermind behind it.

Christ, I needed a drink to get through this meeting.

"Thankfully, I can count on you two." Andraius nodded as if he'd done something right. "I wasn't so sure about sending you off to represent us, but damn, trusting the two of you with my interests was probably the best thing I could have done. No matter what, I know you have the family's best interests in every decision you make."

As if he'd had any other choice but to trust us. He'd killed all the people who knew any fucking thing about the organization.

No, that wasn't true. Andraius had allowed Pops to live. Somehow, my father had convinced this jackass that our family's undying loyalty to the Angelos family translated to him.

It had taken us a few years, but we'd worked our way through the various networks. First, we'd had to battle the stigma of being traitors, which still gutted me.

Once people saw where our loyalties honestly sat, things

shifted faster than Theo and I could ever imagine. We'd maneuvered and formed alliances to back us when we ultimately set our trap in motion to take down this betrayer.

It was only fitting for us to double-cross a double-crosser. And on top of everything else we'd lost, we no longer had each other or *her*.

"We appreciate the recognition, sir," I responded as I leaned back in my chair and studied the asshole on the other side of the desk.

How Andraius used the word trust and never choked on it always surprised me. He was an interloper. A man who'd changed his name to occupy a seat meant for someone else.

The reasons the people of Angelos Shipping, more widely known as the Angelos Syndicate, hadn't revolted against him all revolved around keeping the true heirs to the organization alive.

We'd let him blow smoke up our asses if it kept the fucker thinking he was the big man on campus.

"How is our progress with the negotiations with the Greek suppliers?" Andraius studied the paperwork on his table.

"Everything is going as planned. Security is in place for your arrival in Cyprus." Theo spoke this time.

After a slight pause, Theo added, "However, I urge caution."

I almost rolled my eyes at the corporateness of this conversation. I fucking missed the days when I could say, "Boss, it's better to watch your back and keep the deal quiet so outsiders don't learn of it and try to fuck it up."

"Meaning?"

"I suggest you reconsider the trip and finish the final paperwork in Boston. The security risks are higher than normal, considering the parties involved in the deal. The Drakoses have an estate in the suburbs outside Boston, and news is less likely to leak."

Andraius considered Theo's words, nodded, and said, "I'll consider it. It may come to that if I don't solve another problem on my table."

I waited for him to drop whatever issue he had waiting for us to handle.

An actual boss showed up to the negotiation tables as the head of an organization, but he let Theo mediate for the family, so we'd go with it.

But fuck. I was tired. And the last thing I wanted was to get on another flight.

Could he give me more than a week in Boston at a time? I'd barely had a decent conversation with Pops and Mama since everything happened almost five years ago.

But as Pops would tell me, this was the role I'd trained for and then inherited as part of my duties to the Angelos family. I came from four generations of Onassis men and women who had never and would never falter in their loyalty to the Angeloses.

Hell, Theo's family had followed the same traditions even longer. The Nephus family went back to the inception of the Angelos Syndicate back in Greece.

Our two families' legacies were to fight with and protect the Angeloses.

Only once had they failed. Not quite five years ago, when

some of our own betrayed us and helped the fucker sitting before us to pull off his plan.

But at least I could say Pops had fought a good fight. He'd come out with nearly fatal wounds as he'd tried to shield little Linus. It had broken his heart to learn one of the bullets had pierced through him and into the kid.

Theo's pop, Theios Mik, hadn't been so lucky. He'd died protecting our Angel and her sisters. He'd stood between them and this bastard before me.

One day, I'd make this fucker pay. No, Theo deserved the honors. He'd lost his only parent that day. I still had both of mine. He'd also lost his three brothers. Even if they weren't close, they were his family. Now, he was the last of his line outside of Greece.

"Let us hear your problem, and we will come up with a solution," I coaxed.

Andraius kept quiet for a few seconds, then shook his head. I knew this whole pausing shit was all for dramatic effect.

This guy represented the biggest cliche in mob life ever fucking described. How had he spawned from one of the most influential organizations in Chicago? This shit truly was a waste of space.

When he finally finished with this, whatever he wanted to call it, Andraius said with a sigh as if he held the weight of the world on his shoulders, "My wife."

Immediately, my back went up.

His wife. *Nerine*

I resisted the urge to clench my jaw.

His wife.

The woman he'd forced to marry him at gunpoint. The woman who meant more to Theo and me than anything on earth.

Our Angel.

The blood heir to the organization.

Anger surged in the pit of my gut, along with guilt and shame. I'd let her down. I let her believe I was the enemy. I'd promised to always stand by her and be her rock, her best friend.

I'd fucking failed her, and this fucker forced himself upon her when I wasn't even in the damn area.

My throat burned as the rage continued to build, and only years of hard-earned training kept me from giving any of my true feelings away or reaching across the desk and bashing the bastard's face in.

"I want you two to watch Nerine at all times, day and night," Andraius ordered. "She's up to something, and I want to know everything she is doing."

Was he fucking serious? He planned to demote the two people who ran his organization while he pretended to be lord of the manor to watch his wife.

Okay, yes, the woman happened to be one of the loves of my life. But this made no damn sense.

A throbbing ignited in my head. What the fuck was he up to?

"She has around-the-clock security teams keeping tabs on her. The reports say she is clean."

Theo and I knew everything that went on in her life. Circumstances had forced us apart, but that hadn't meant we weren't aware of her every move.

Over the last nearly five years, Theo and I had watched the light leave her eyes. She'd become a cold, yet combative version of the spitfire, takes-no-one's-shit person she was before the coup. According to our men, she directed most of her ire toward Andraius. She hated him and had no problem letting him know her feelings. There were no traces of the girl with the wicked humor who laughed easily.

She believed we were her enemies by aligning ourselves with Andraius and becoming his right-hand men. We had seen the anger and the hurt every time we caught her looking in our direction during the first year of her marriage.

I would have given anything to tell her the truth, but giving away our secret would put her in danger.

However, the time of watching Nerine and her sisters suffer would soon come to an end. The right players were maneuvering into position, and then the trap would be sprung.

Then our Angel would finally get the chance to gain her wings back.

Andraius had ripped them to shreds over the years, something I'd never forgive. He had no idea the depth of what I imagined doing to him, inch by microscopic inch.

"She has that team wrapped around her finger, and I don't trust them."

I narrowed my gaze. "My father's soldiers are beyond loyal. He doesn't tolerate deception, and neither do I. And they know the consequences if they do."

"Yes, yes." Andraius chuckled. "No one wants to end up in your Caves. Maybe I should bring Nerine down there to watch you work, and then she'll straighten up. I doubt she has the stomach to handle a discipline session."

I glanced for a fraction of a second in Theo's direction. He kept a stoic expression on his face, giving nothing away. However, I knew what he thought of that suggestion.

Bringing Nerine down to the Caves would only serve to remind everyone who the true Angelos heir was. No matter what Andraius believed, changing his name would never solidify his claim to the seat.

In the eyes of the organization, he'd remain the backstabbing betrayer Andraius Stratos. First, he'd weaseled his way in by marrying Angelos's cousin, and then, when she died in childbirth, he'd decided to stay. After that, he'd pretended his undying loyalty to Peter Angelos, our beloved boss, all the while setting up people to overthrow him.

When Andraius took over, he'd made everyone swear allegiance to the Angelos Family, not him. To us, the Angelos Family were Peter's surviving children. His daughters, Nerine, Christina, Ariana, and Fiona. Giving them our absolute fidelity took nothing from us.

We'd do what it took to protect them and the family's legacy. Theios Peter had named Nerine his heir, even if Greek syndicate practices didn't traditionally accept female leaders of an organization, business, or syndicate. Then again, Theios Peter had no choice but to modernize his views, having had four girls in the family and no sons for most of his life. Even after Linus's unexpected birth, he'd never altered his perception.

"Would you like the visit to the Caves arranged? This way the men will know to expect your wife's arrival," Theo asked, snapping me out of my thoughts.

The glare he shot me said Andraius had been waiting for my response, and Theo had to jump in before he noticed that I'd spaced out.

Theo preferred to watch and rarely spoke unless absolutely necessary.

Well, the only exception was with Nerine. But then again, she'd gotten under his skin when she hit fourteen and he was seventeen. So his teenage way of dealing with his attraction to the then-boss's daughter was to needle her until she tried to punch him.

Enemies to lovers, at its finest.

Then there was me on the other end of the spectrum. The best friend, the one who watched out for her, the one who'd beat a motherfucker to a pulp for picking on her.

She was the one person who saw past my bulldozer exterior and allowed me to care for her. The polished one fought with her nonstop, and the brute cuddled her.

Even before our Angel turned us into a trio, my relationship with Theo went beyond that of best friends. We felt more and wanted more. It wasn't until we hit high school that we acted on it. Then Nerine blew into our world, throwing both of us off balance.

We loved her, and she felt the same for us. Our unconventional relationship worked.

"Yes," Andraius answered with a smirk. "Set it up for some time in the next few weeks. I want to spring it on her. Keep her on her toes."

Fucking manipulative bastard.

"Back to watching her. I want the two of you to take over personally."

He was serious about this.

"What about our duties to you? Aren't those priorities?" I asked.

The last time I'd played any security detail duty, I was in the middle of puberty. By the time I left high school, enforcement had become part of my weekly routine and then turned into my full-time gig by my first year of college.

"You'll suspend travel unless it is absolutely necessary. As for your duties, I know you two are well-versed in multitasking. So delegate things others won't fuck up and handle everything else as you normally do."

Meaning he planned to continue to sit on his ass, take all the credit, and let Theo and I do all the work.

Theo moved closer to the desk. "Is there something you aren't telling us, sir? Is there a threat against Nerine you need us to eliminate? If so, I will have my top men prioritize research and data collection before disposal."

I had to give it to him. He had a way of being diplomatic, even when talking about slaughtering a fucker for information. And the smile on Andraius's lips said he was eating up all the bullshit European genteel training.

I wouldn't say I hadn't learned the same lessons. I just chose not to use them in front of this dick. The ability to fake polish and charm only lasted as long as the means justified the ends. Andraius viewed me as his muscle and strategist.

Being the rough, unrefined one of the Theo-Xander duo worked in my favor.

He'd realize soon enough the calm ones were the people to worry about. They hid their darker sides. When Theo joined me in the Caves, he garnered answers ten times quicker than anyone else I knew.

I played the psycho for Andraius, but the true unhinged one sat next to me.

"Nyx Mykos-Drakos seems to have taken an interest in Nerine."

Good for Nerine. She needed someone like Nyx in her life.

Nyx took shit from no one.

And as the wife of Simon Drakos, the head of one of the largest Greek syndicates on the east coast of the United States, it was either hold your own with the man known as the master of death and fortune or get run over. Nyx was also the daughter of Phillip "the surgeon" Mykos and sister to Tyler Mykos, who ran another large syndicate. The alliance between the two families made them the most powerful group in the eastern half of the United States if not the whole country.

I could only hope Nyx's influence would help Nerine to drop her guard. The shield she wore around herself could only protect her so far. She needed companionship and friendship, something Andraius had gone out of his way to prevent these past five years. He enjoyed isolating her, making her believe she had no one. He believed if he broke her, he'd have a weak, compliant wife to do his bidding. Except what he received was a woman who chose seclusion over companionship and a public facade of unapproachableness.

"I need you to be my eyes and ears whenever they meet."

I held Andraius's stare, letting him know I believed my involvement in this was pointless.

He needed me too much to flip out on me. He knew it as much as I did.

"These are duties our men already handle. They give you a detailed accounting of her activities whenever she is out and about." I paused and added, "Or does this have to do with Simon Drakos?"

Andraius believed his alliance with the Drakoses would truly cement his power over the Angelos Organization. Then he'd no longer have the specter of his predecessor's achievements haunting him.

Too bad, he'd yet to figure out that Simon Drakos only tolerated him.

"Of course, it has to do with him. I want you to make sure Nerine doesn't fuck up all the progress I've made with Drakos by pissing off his wife. I need that deal signed, and Drakos is soft for Nyx. I want Nerine to keep her happy."

I resisted the urge to shake my head and clock this moron. He had no clue about the players of the world.

Anyone with a grain of sense would know Drakos wasn't a man led around by his balls. From the first moment I encountered him, I understood the only way Nyx could influence anything with him was if someone targeted her. Then all hell would break loose.

Outside of that situation, the couple kept their boundaries.

Nyx liked to dabble in things that she'd rather her husband not get involved in.

The fact that Andraius hadn't picked up simple cues would make it so much easier when we executed our plan in a few months.

"Why would she endanger this relationship?" The coolness in Theo's tone came out in his standard unemotional way, but the flash of annoyance in his silver eyes screamed he'd had enough of the digs against Nerine.

The time and distance hadn't lessened his guilt and anger for not being here when everything had gone down. And every slight against Nerine added fuel to the fire.

"My wife is stubborn and prefers challenging me at inappropriate times. I wouldn't put it past her to offend Drakos's wife to spite me." He shook his head. "Of Angelos's four daughters, I ended up with the standoffish, cold bitch of the group. What are the damn odds? I'd wonder if she had a pulse if she didn't have that viper's mouth. I hope she gets pregnant soon. It's like fucking a venom-filled whore with ice in her veins."

Motherfucker.

5, 4, 3, 2, 1.

5, 4, 3, 2, 1.

I continued to count backward in my mind until I calmed down enough to focus without seeing red and then asked, "How do you want us to manage Nerine, sir?"

"You two grew up with her. I'm sure you can get her to let her guard down and convince her to be nice."

"We aren't nice men." Theo's deadpan tone almost had my

irritation leveled out enough to smile. "And we barely knew her. We ran in different circles."

"No matter. You aren't strangers to her. She will be comfortable around you. You can report her activities and, at the same time, spy on the Drakoses while you're at it. It's a win-win."

I released an exasperated breath, noticing Andraius narrow his gaze at me but keeping his mouth shut.

"This is a waste of our time. I'll put a new group of my best men on her. They won't lie. They grew up around her, too. Theo and I have better shit to do than babysit an errant wife."

Andraius slammed his hand on his desk. Guess I pushed him too far.

"You will do as I say. I want her watched. She has her current team wrapped around her finger. They do everything she tells them, and I don't believe they are reporting everything she does. I know she's taking something to keep herself from getting pregnant. They lie for her."

"My men don't lie," I pushed back, matching his ire and daring him to insult my soldiers again. "As I said, they know the consequences. I've already agreed to switch out her team."

Loyalty to my people remained paramount in my world. They put their lives on the line for the family daily, and I refused to let anyone insult them.

Fuck this asshole.

"Then prove it to me and watch her. I trust you two, not them. If your findings are the same, put her original team back on her."

Knowing I no longer had any patience left for the dick in

front of me, Theo set an elbow on the end of Andraius's desk as if no explosion had occurred and stated, "She isn't going to like it. Her preferences for routine and schedules over sudden changes are well-known in the organization."

"She'll do as I say. And if she gives you any trouble, let me know. I'll have a word with her." He flipped through some paperwork on his desk. "Now, let's discuss some information I want you to gather at the Drakos estate tonight."

"Does this mean we are starting our duties effective immediately?" Theo continued his corporate speak.

And thank God because I had no fucks left to give after what Andraius had said about Nerine.

We'd had no choice but to stay away. Pops knew how close we were to her. Well, maybe not the full extent of the relationship, but he believed we were best friends. And he thought if Andraius had gotten one whiff of it, he'd have killed us on the spot.

"Partially. I'll head over with her and my team. You'll come in with the rest of the security personnel and work on the tasks we'll discuss. Then, at the end of the evening, you will bring Nerine home."

"In other words, this is another thing you plan to spring on her." I let the disgust in my voice show. "This isn't going to make your wife like you."

"I don't care about her liking me. I want her to know I can make her life very difficult if she doesn't start behaving."

Fifteen minutes later, Theo and I walked down the corridor leading out into the main foyer of the Angelos Estate house.

"I thought my hate for the bastard couldn't get any stronger," I muttered, pushing down the urge to grind my teeth together.

"Yeah, well. He tends to outdo himself at every turn."

"Pops isn't going to like this." I ran a hand through my hair as we veered into the hallway leading into the security section of the compound where Pops kept his office.

"Has Theios Alex liked anything that's happened over the last five years?" Theo asked. "I'm not sure we can be near her without giving it away."

"What choice do we have?"

"She's not ours, Xander."

"She will always be ours."

"We can't touch her."

"No, we can't." I gripped the back of my neck, closed my eyes briefly, and released a deep breath, hoping he wouldn't avoid answering the question as usual. "And what about us?"

"What about it?" Theo kept his focus in front of him. "It's the three of us or nothing."

"How is this going to work? We can't avoid being around each other for long periods anymore."

"Exactly as it has for the last five years."

"Meaning?"

"Pretend our history with the Angel or each other never happened. You made that call. Now we're sticking with it."

After the coup, it felt as if the world had shattered around me. Losing Theios Peter and little Linus broke my heart, then so many people we loved and cared for. And the worst was we hadn't protected Nerine.

I couldn't handle the guilt, or the heartache. And instead of turning to Theo and talking to him about how we would live life without Nerine, I made the decision that unless we were all together, there wasn't a relationship.

I'd realized the mistake I'd made almost immediately, but the damage was done.

And it seemed Theo wasn't going to ever forgive me even after five years and countless apologies.

Deciding to change the subject, I said, "She's going to give us hell."

"Thanks, Sherlock. As if I hadn't figured that out. She thinks we betrayed and abandoned her. I wouldn't be surprised if she hated us."

"Hopefully, she'll stay calm when Andraius drops the bomb about the detail change." I pictured her face for a moment. "She's going to lose her shit."

"Maybe she'll keep it together long enough to let us explain it was for her own good. That everything we've done has been to keep her safe," Theo contemplated, and then, before I could tell him he was fooling himself, he spoke again. "She'll pull a gun on me if I say that crap to her."

I said nothing, feeling the weight of the last few years settle on my shoulders.

Then Theo added, "She has to love us still, or she wouldn't watch us when she thinks no one will notice. She'll forgive us."

I cocked a brow as if he'd lost his mind. "You know, there is a thin line between love and hate. We can only hope the love hasn't morphed into hate."

Three

erine

"Tonight, you will see how a proper wife behaves in public."

I stared out the window of the limousine. I and the jackass who'd forced me to marry him were going to the Drakos Estate for an evening of hobnobbing and elbow-rubbing. I'd spent the last ten minutes ignoring Andraius as he rambled on and on about my lack of ability to be the type of spouse he desired. He played this monotonous track every time we were near each other, especially on evenings when we attended any event.

My response, as always, was to give him my flat, expressionless face. The image of a woman who felt nothing and gave no reaction to any dig thrown her way. She protected herself with an ironclad armor that no person could penetrate.

The facade was all bullshit, but a girl had to learn a few tricks to survive in her hellhole.

One day, I'd escape this prison. I'd take my mother and sisters and find my freedom. Then, everyone who wanted to take this dynasty could do whatever the fuck they wanted with it.

Destroy it, for all I cared. I wouldn't be in the picture. The Angelos women would disappear, and no one would find us ever again.

Especially this bastard who sat across from me. The one who'd stolen so much from me.

I loved my family history, the long Angelos legacy going back nearly seven hundred years to old-world Greece. But this legacy, this lineage, had cost me too much, and I'd rather have no part of it.

Papa, please forgive me for thinking this. I would rather live and be free of this family than preserve it and stay locked in a cage.

"Don't ignore me, Nerine."

"I couldn't ignore you even if I tried." I glanced in his direction. "We both know you wouldn't let me."

His dark brown eyes held a glaze of irritation, and a few glasses of bourbon. "I mean it. You need to watch and learn. Nyx Mykos-Drakos is the type of wife I need."

He must have forgotten that before her marriage, people called her the Mykos Hellion for being a cutting bitch to anyone who crossed her. There were even rumors that she liked to pull knives on people and threaten to slice their throats.

I guessed marriage to the right man had tamed her wild ways.

"What do I need to look for since you have spent so much time ogling another man's wife?"

"She stands by her husband's side, increases his connections, knows how to conduct herself in public, and occupies her time by doing feminine things like gardening. I believe she will spend the summer developing the new botanical gardens."

The woman has a PhD in horticulture, that's why the foundation invited her to lead the construction of the botanical gardens, jackass.

I'd read about it in the news. Nyx loved plants and studied them, not as a hobby but as a vocation.

Her father and brothers believed in treating her as an equal and sent her to school just like the rest of the family. Something I would have had if Papa was still alive.

Instead, a fifty-year-old man had forced me to marry him at gunpoint and shattered my dreams of a college education by never allowing me to take a single class at Boston College again.

The dumbass thought if he kept me from an educational institution, I'd give up on pursuing my education.

Big mistake.

I'd improvised and used the very library in my family's home as a classroom. Andraius thought I wasted my time reading all day and writing in my journals about my sad life when in fact, I'd enrolled in online classes. I'd never get the degrees I wanted. Still, it hadn't stopped me from taking every available course to achieve multiple degrees. I'd even gained some mentors who taught me skills that weren't on the average curriculum of any school.

Fucker had no idea the shit I could do with a computer. I wasn't perfect at it, but I was getting there. One day, I may even achieve hacker-level status.

I sighed dramatically. "Then it's too bad that she is married to her age-appropriate husband, who she is madly in love with and has the physique of a Greek god."

I lifted my chin in a dare as Andraius clenched his fists. Reminding him of his age and lack of physical prowess was always good.

In all honesty, Andraius was a handsome man. He kept in shape and looked years younger than men his age, but I'd never give him the ego stroke he craved.

"You didn't even give our marriage a chance."

The nerve of this bastard to even utter those words.

"Explain why I would even microscopically consider giving you a chance after you murdered my father and baby brother, forced me to marry you at gunpoint, and then carved *whore* into my body on our wedding night? It's impossible to think of you as anything but a monster."

Ignoring everything but the bits he found pertinent, he said, "Well, you were nineteen. Who were you fucking before you married me?"

The loves of my life.

"It doesn't matter because I never wanted to marry you in the first place."

"My Lisa was a virgin when I married her, and she was twenty-two."

His first wife, my late cousin Alisa, was no virgin on her wedding night. However, the women in our family knew how to keep secrets, and they taught their daughters ways to convince their traditionalist Greek husbands of their purity.

For me, it hadn't mattered.

I smirked. "You keep believing that. Alisa could have fucked all my father's men, and you would never have known."

"Of course, I'd know." A vein pulsed on his forehead. "The rumors would have reached my ears. I'm a fucking Angelos."

"Wrong. Alisa was a true Angelos by blood. You don't have a drop of it. I'm a true Angelos. It doesn't matter who she fucked or who I fucked. Those loyal to the true Angelos descendants will keep our secrets to the grave."

My words held a bit of truth and some lies. The loyal Angeloses would only ever tell Papa all the secrets, others not a chance.

I'd kept my secret from nearly everyone—even my sisters and especially my parents. Yes, Papa believed his daughters had equal rights as Linus when it came to ascending to his seat as head of the Angelos Family. However, he wouldn't have been able to handle the idea that I'd fallen in love with two men and that we were in a committed relationship.

"And hence the reason you will see *whore* marking your body until the day you die."

I shrugged as if I couldn't have cared less.

"It still doesn't stop you from attempting to impregnate me whenever your dick decides to work. What does that say about you?" I tapped my lips. "Ahhh, yes. It says you like to fuck whores. And you can't deny it since you have so many of them tucked away around the city in hopes of getting them pregnant to pass off as my child. Isn't that right?"

Before I realized what he had planned, he grabbed my wrist in an excruciating hold and hauled me toward him.

His alcohol-infused breath wafted over my face. "Listen very carefully. You will behave tonight. You will act like a dutiful wife. You will not cause a scene."

"And if I don't." I clenched my jaw, trying desperately to ignore the pain radiating down my arm. "What will you do to me that you haven't done before?"

"I will kill you," he gritted out through his teeth. "I will replace you with a younger woman who will give me a child."

I laughed, "Go ahead. I die, and my money goes to my sisters. Not to you, asshole. You think Papa was stupid. The Angelos money will never, ever go to a spouse."

"But it will go to a child."

"That would require you to get me pregnant, not one of your whores. DNA, or did you miss that lesson in school?"

He lifted his hand as if to strike me, and I tilted my chin up, waiting for the blow. Maybe my stupid streak had reared its ugly head tonight, but I wanted the people of this ball to see the monster I'd married and what he did to me.

He threw me back onto the bench seat. "You bitch. You wanted me to hit you so everyone sees the bruises."

"Why not? It takes a big, strong man to beat his wife into compliance." I rubbed my wrist, where I had no doubt I'd bear the marks of Andraius's brutal hold.

"Listen, Nerine. All I want is a fucking child. Give me that, and I will never come near you again. Is that too fucking much to ask for?"

I wanted to shout, *"Yes. I will never have your fucking child, you bastard."*

Instead, I said, "Did you ever think that you are the problem? You are the common denominator. You have doctors telling you I'm healthy and when I'm most fertile. Yet still, it doesn't happen. Not a single one of your whores has ever gotten pregnant."

It was a wonder this fucker hadn't given me an STD. Good thing I tested myself constantly with the way he passed himself around.

Disgusting piece of shit.

God, when had I become so bitter?

Oh yes, when I decided it was either break under the weight of my existence or become the very thing he believed I was and fight back.

There was no place for weakness in the world I lived in. The time when I could let my guard down and let my vulnerable side free was gone, along with the two who'd broken my heart.

"You're doing something to prevent it. I know it."

Yes, I am, dickhead. I will continue to do everything I can to keep from carrying your child, even things that aren't detectable through medical testing.

Thank you, Mama, for all your secret, old-school methods of preventing conception.

"Believe what you want. Just know I will never ever claim another woman's child as mine. So don't even think about it."

"Nerine, I run this family. Not you. Remember that."

"Without me, there is no family, Andraius. I'm the true Angelos in this pairing. Remember *that.* You are only an interloper."

"Don't forget what I told you," Andraius warned as we entered the main ballroom of the Drakos mansion on the outskirts of Boston. "I am going to talk to Drakos's family. You find Nyx and kiss her ass."

"I don't kiss anyone's ass. You should know this better than most."

"Use your manners instead of behaving like an animal."

I adjusted my cuff bracelet over the sleeve of my gown where it rested at my wrist and said, "I've attended balls from the time I turned six. I'm well-versed in etiquette. The reason I don't use it around you is that I hate you beyond anything imaginable."

"Nerine, I—"

"However," I continued, cutting him off, "for my mother's and sisters' sakes, I'll behave tonight. Because if I don't, I'm sure you'd find a way to take it out on them, even from across the ocean."

"How the fuck did I get saddled with a bitter, cold cunt like you?" he muttered to himself.

Pausing as I walked away, I tilted my head and answered so he could hear, "Since you have such a short-term memory, let me remind you for the second time in an hour. You betrayed and murdered my father, brother, and countless others who trusted you.

"Then you forced me to marry you in front of a corrupt priest by threatening to kill me, my mother, and my three minor sisters, and to seal the deal, you raped me in front of said corrupt priest. Then to top it off, you mutilated my body. You're the cream of the crop, aren't you?"

With my shoulders back and spine straight, I strolled around the edge of the crowd. They socialized and discussed the latest developments in society and politics while sending me curious glances as I passed them.

I kept to myself, smiling and nodding acknowledgment at those around me but not engaging otherwise. I had nothing to say to any of them.

I'd fight Andraius nonstop in private, but I'd grown reserved and quiet in public.

The partygoers probably wondered what had happened to the outspoken Nerine Nicolette Angelos. Where did the girl who stuck her nose into her father's business when other girls wouldn't dare go? And most of all, tonight's event attendees probably wanted to find out what Andraius had done to get the misfit of the Greek syndicate world to become a quiet mob wife.

A server paused before me and offered me a glass of champagne. After tipping my head in thanks and taking a flute, I scanned the room.

Not far from me stood Simon and Nyx Drakos. Surrounding them were the Mykoses, Nyx's four brothers, and her parents. From the information Andraius had told me to learn, Nyx was the first female born into the Mykos family in over a hundred years, and her marriage to Simon fulfilled some contract negotiated for the previous female in the family.

In my opinion, it was all bullshit. No arranged marriage resulted in the type of affection Simon Drakos showed for his wife. The man had a reputation as an emotionless, cold-blooded killer. Their story went deeper than her giving their marriage a chance, no matter what Andraius wanted to believe.

Simon glanced down at Nyx as she spoke to one of her brothers, and his deep green eyes lit up right before he lifted a finger and traced down the side of Nyx's cheek.

That simple, intimate gesture sent a wave of sadness into the pit of my stomach. I'd had that long ago with someone. Actually, with two someones. As unconventional as we were, it worked for us.

Then it all imploded, and I'd buried it under a mountain of lies and secrets.

It had taken me the first year of my marriage to feel as if I wasn't cheating on them, to accept I'd had no choice, to understand staying alive meant others stayed alive.

"Nerine, it's so good to see you," Nyx exclaimed as she approached me.

She moved toward me in a way only a woman with complete confidence in who she was could pull off. She owned her sexuality. She wore her dark black hair in a one-shouldered style piled to the side, and her long ivory gown accentuated the golden hue of her skin perfectly. She had an ethereal glow about her that made you pause to look.

Then there was her husband, who approached along with

her. To say Simon was gorgeous was an understatement. He epitomized the bad boy vibe but in a very tailored way. However, it was his green, almost emerald-colored eyes that made a person stop to study him. Like a snake, he could mesmerize until one was under his enchantment.

They were a power couple at their finest.

No wonder Andraius wanted me to get in good with Nyx.

I wanted to be like her, but I'd run across hot coals before admitting that to my husband.

And no matter how much Andraius wished it, he wasn't even anywhere in the same vicinity as Simon. He'd never achieve the power, respect, or magnetism that Simon held without trying.

"Thank you for inviting us," I said to Nyx, then smiled in Simon's direction. "It's good to see you again."

"Hello, Nerine." He took my hand and kissed it, which garnered a shake of the head and an eye roll from Nyx.

That definitely wasn't proper behavior and broke a ton of etiquette rules.

For some reason, that one gesture had me relaxing. She wasn't the prim-and-proper wife Andraius made her out to be.

Releasing my fingers, Simon searched behind me. "Where is Angelos?"

"He's probably discussing business with your uncles." I gestured with my chin to a circle of men deep in conversation.

"Too bad they have no sway over you when it comes to decisions," Nyx muttered, or I could have sworn she had.

But her utterly impassive expression made me think I'd possibly misheard her words.

Then a smirk appeared on Nyx's face, and she tucked her arm in mine as if we were long-lost friends. "I've arranged for you to sit with me at dinner. I believe we have a lot of things in common."

I highly doubted that, but okay.

"Wouldn't you rather sit with your family?"

"Believe me," Simon interjected from behind us. "You are far better company than any of her brothers."

Nyx shot him a glare over her shoulder. "I see them all the time. Plus, I fly back to New York every week."

We moved toward a long hallway decorated to give the feel of walking through a garden.

"I have a question to ask you," Nyx said.

"Go ahead."

"When you walked in tonight, were you envisioning ways to slit your husband's throat?"

I just gaped at her, completely dumbfounded.

Nyx laughed. "And my next question is, would you like me to teach you different ways to do it and not get caught?"

What the hell was happening here? I pulled back. "I'm not sure what you expect me to say."

"Behave, Goddess. Let Nerine settle in. She just arrived and isn't used to your sense of humor."

"I wasn't kidding, Simon."

"I know this." Simon set a hand on Nyx's waist and leaned in so only Nyx and I could hear his words. "Sometimes it's better to use a scalpel than a machete."

"Just because you hang out with Papa does not mean you're an honorary surgeon. I like blades."

I felt as if I'd entered the twilight zone. "I don't understand any of this."

Ignoring me, Simon said, "Nyx, until Nerine learns to handle the smaller instruments, you can't give her bigger ones to play with."

"Are you two for real?" My voice shook as I whispered, "Who are you?"

"The question you need to answer is, who are *you*?" Simon's voice softened. "Peter Angelos was part of a small group who stood by me when my Pappos died and my uncle challenged my legitimacy to the family leadership. That isn't something I will forget. You deserve better than what has happened to you."

His mentioning Papa sent a pang to my heart. I missed him so much.

"Play the game with us, Nerine. Don't you want to fight back?" Nyx asked.

"And do what?" I shook my head. "I don't want to take the seat. I want freedom for me, my sisters, and Mama."

"Before deciding who takes the seat, you must remove the person sitting there." Simon steered us into the dining room.

"How do you expect me to do that?"

"It starts with you learning to defend yourself." Nyx sighed and then took my hand in hers, shifting my cuff to expose the bruise forming in the shape of fingers. "If he wasn't who he was and we weren't where we are, I'd gut him for you. Or get you to do it."

"Goddess, she doesn't have the skills."

"Oh, she will."

"Let me guess. You plan to teach me."

Before she could respond, Andraius approached, and she released my arm.

"Ladies, are you ready for dinner?" Andraius offered me his elbow.

"Absolutely." Nyx smiled at him and said, "Oh, I wanted to say how happy I am that Nerine has agreed to help me at the botanical gardens this summer. I hope we can start her training this week."

Surprise flashed across Andraius's face, a hint of pleasure as if I'd finally done something right. "Yes, she is always willing to lend a hand. That is, of course, the Angelos way."

Four

Theo

"Are you in position?"

"Yes, asshole. I know my job," I responded to Xander through my earpiece.

"This is your first surveillance assignment stateside in three years. So I have to make sure you can handle being around this type of snobbery."

"I'm ten times better at this than you are. Hence the reason you're sitting up there on a perch."

"No, I'm up here because my tolerance for the dick down there is at an all-time low."

I could almost visualize the rage still boiling in Xander's dark eyes. He'd impressed me with the length of time he'd managed to keep his cool during the meeting with Andraius. The asshole had tapped out my reserves of calm, so I knew Xander's bordered on desert dry.

Thank God Theios Alex possessed this ability to focus Xander and give him purpose to channel his rage into a mission. Because the moment we'd entered Theios Alex's office, he'd seen the turmoil boiling inside his son.

First, Theios Alex sent Xander to work his magic in the Caves with some less-than-forthcoming snitches, and then he'd worked with us on a plan to handle the next few weeks.

"Did I touch a nerve?" I asked.

"Fuck off. Some of us don't have ice pumping in our veins instead of blood."

We both knew this wasn't true, considering my reaction to his question about us from earlier in the day.

"Are you jealous that it makes me better at work in the Caves than you?"

"You're one sick motherfucker."

"As Theia Brenna would say, pot meet kettle," I said. "Besides, for me, it's a means to an end. Not something I enjoy."

"I swear, my mother likes you more than me."

"You say to-may-to. I say to-mah-to."

"Will you shut the fuck up and let me do my job?" Xander muttered.

"Our job just walked in." I focused on the dining room entrance, where Simon Drakos, his wife Nyx, Andraius, and Nerine walked in.

The couples were deep in discussion. Well, all except the Angel. She observed and listened.

The glow of youth and mischief no longer lit up her features as they had five years ago. Instead, she carried herself with control, caution, and watchfulness.

She probably meant to carry off an understated look tonight with her simple silver gown and minimal jewelry, but nothing could hide her striking beauty.

She'd inherited her mother's model features and height, making her as tall as Andraius at just shy of six feet in her three-inch heels. And then there was her body, curves in all the right places, perfect in every way.

She was a woman born for people to notice.

Although she'd lost weight in the last few years, something I'd seen from afar and couldn't do anything about.

If what Xander and I had with her had become public knowledge back in the day, it would have caused problems with our families, but eventually they would have gotten over it.

Having our past come out now would get all of us killed.

As if sensing me watching her, Nerine's cobalt blue gaze lifted to my corner of the room and homed in on me. Her lips parted for the briefest of moments as that familiar surge charged between us.

Memories of our past filled my mind, her nails scoring my skin, her mouth swollen from kisses, her body writhing between Xander and me, and her throaty moans and sighs. But, most of all, it reminded me of the long nights of talks, secrets, friendship, love, and laughter.

The next second, she looked away, breaking the connection and leaving the longing and pain behind.

"Fucking hell," I muttered, not intending for Xander to hear.

But of course, he had.

"We're playing the long game, Theo." Xander meant his words to bring me back from the pit, but seeing her only emphasized the chasm separating us.

This was why I stayed in the shadows whenever I returned to Boston. I never wanted to chance running into her, especially knowing I'd failed her and was part of why she lived with the man who'd destroyed her family.

Since I had no doubt Xander had secured the line and we were the only ones on com-link, I said, "She's not ours anymore. How am I supposed to get over that?"

She slept in another man's bed. He touched her, took pleasure in her. A fucking bastard thirty years older than her, who'd thought he'd gained a prize to use. He possessed not a single fiber of understanding of how to cherish the incredible woman he'd married.

One day, I'd make him pay for all he'd done.

"She'll always be ours." Xander's words snapped me back to the present.

"Fuck that shit. Until Nerine is aware of this, none of it counts. Or do I need to remind you of when you said without her, there is no us?"

Xander muttered something.

"What was that? I couldn't hear you with all the teeth grinding."

"I fucked up. I said it. Losing her broke something in me, and I took it out on all of us."

I understood regret. I felt it every damn day. But what Xander had done had made an already bleeding wound start to hemorrhage.

"It's too late to change the past. We have to accept this is the road we are on."

"What happened to you spouting that she loved us?" Xander asked.

Resignation filled me. "Maybe you were right."

"I thought I was the glass-is-half-empty guy?"

"Not when it came to her," I said. "You were the fucking sunshine and roses singing at the top of his lungs."

"I truly want to kick you in the teeth right now."

Even with all of the unaddressed issues between us, Xander was my best friend. I wouldn't think twice about taking a bullet for him, and I had no questions that he'd do the same for me. There was nothing he couldn't ask me to do for him.

I focused on Nerine as she sat next to Nyx, still lost in whatever conversation they were having.

However, the moment Andraius interrupted her, she shot him a cold glare, clearly stating she wanted him to be anywhere but next to her.

The feeling is mutual, love.

"I need to ask you something serious."

"I had a feeling you were going to get all philosophical." Xander's bland, know-it-all tone made me want to punch him. "This is your usual MO when doing surveillance, so I made sure to secure and encrypt the line from our crew in case they got nosy."

"You're such an asshole."

"What do you need to get off your chest?"

"Sooner or later, Andraius is going to find out about our relationship with Nerine."

"If he hasn't found out by now, how the fuck is he going to learn about it? We've talked about it enough times over the years to know our people are loyal. They'd rather die than betray her. Hell, Pops still hasn't figured it out. As far as everyone knows, the reasons we and the originals stayed on are for Nerine, her sisters, and her mother. When did you become so fucking paranoid?"

"It's not paranoia when I'm questioning what will happen when we're around her twenty-four-seven."

Or what it was going to be like when Xander and I were around each other nonstop. Nothing could go back to the way it was, and hoping for it was a pipedream.

Xander made it clear that without Nerine there was no future for us. I accepted his decision, and now he regrets it.

Too fucking bad.

"It's not going to be all day and night," he said. "We have a team with us that will take shifts."

"Stop fucking around and answer the question."

"We have to lock it down."

"Is that even possible for you?" I asked. "You wear your emotions on your face when it comes to her."

"I've done it for the last five years, right?"

"That's because you rarely, if ever, occupy the same space as her."

"I've spent more time in town than you have. I'm the one that needs you to answer that question. Nerine is the only woman I've known to get you to lose that calm, iceman demeanor. Think you're going to be able to keep it in check?"

I had to be honest. "No. That's the problem. I already know she will take great pleasure in pushing every button I have. That's her way. The more I ignore her, the more she'll get in my face."

"Yeah, and this time, you can't push her to her knees and shove your cock in her mouth to shut her up."

I clenched my jaw. He brought up our past on purpose. To remind me of what we had together.

"You're not helping the problem. We can't touch her, period. Nerine isn't ours."

"One day soon, that will change."

"We can't claim another man's wife."

"We wait until Drakos, one of Andraius's Chicago family, or one of his other enemies take him out."

Others, meaning one of us.

We'd readied the stage for all three possibilities to come to fruition. The vengeful, sick-fuck part of me craved the pleasure of watching my hands force Andraius to gasp his last breaths.

I wanted to feel his blood on my fingers as he mewled in pain, and I couldn't wait to revel in his death the same way he'd done when he gutted Papa for stepping between him and Nerine.

"Heads up," Xander announced. "His royal highness is scanning the room. I believe he's about to summon you."

I blew out a deep exhale, simmering down the vengeance churning inside me.

I adjusted my suit and waited for Andraius to find me in the crowd. The second he saw me, he nodded, giving me his unsaid command to come to him. I moved from my position on the outskirts of the dining room in his direction.

"I fucking should have taken the perch," I muttered.

"Don't forget you're the more refined and diplomatic of our duo. You have that European sensibility from all your years of dining with royals. I'm the rough meat-and-potatoes guy."

"Meat and potatoes, my ass. I eat more meat than you do, dickhead. I can't believe you even call yourself Greek with all the clean eating you like to do."

"Chicken is meat, idiot."

"You wonder why Theia Brenna loves me more. I eat everything she makes, and you don't. Greek mamas want their sons to eat their food and not complain about it being unhealthy."

"I could beat your ass into next week."

"Like hell you could. Bulk means shit."

"Shut up and go see what the fucker wants."

I smirked and weaved my way through the multitude of tables. Even before I reached the table where Andraius and Nerine sat, I noticed Nerine's back stiffen. Then, when I stopped behind Andraius, her attention wavered between her conversation with Nyx and me.

Nearly five years since we'd been this close to each other.

God, she'd lost so much weight. By my guess, it was at least fifteen pounds, if not more. Her curves were still there but less pronounced, and she carried an air of unapproachability along with a hint of fragility I'd never seen before.

The woman before me wasn't Peter Angelos's Nerine—well, maybe the essence of her was under there, but she was buried deep under an aloof, hard disguise.

I longed to demand she bring back the girl who never hid that she was up to something or laughed and joked about the most mundane things. What I wouldn't give to see the fiery temper that would punch someone in the mouth for getting in her face, instead of this very poised and controlled person she showed the world.

I couldn't understand why she was trying so hard to hide the girl who made me and Xander do our homework and yelled at us to study?

An unleashed fury burned in her blue eyes now, telling everyone around her she wouldn't forgive or forget easily for all that she'd suffered.

The girl with a snarky sense of humor and a heart completely open to expressing her passion and love for others had disappeared.

Andraius set his palm on Nerine's thigh as he turned to face me, and she not-so-causally threw his hand off, whispering, "Don't touch me, or did you forget that I hate you?"

"You'll do as I say."

"Or what?"

Pretending that I hadn't witnessed the exchange between the couple, I waited for Andraius to speak.

"We need to have a quick discussion. Let's go, Nerine." He stood and pulled out her chair.

Frowning, she rose from her seat and followed, only glancing behind her at Nyx briefly as if passing some unsaid communication.

When we reached a quiet area in the hallway among a group of ivy-like plants, Andraius asked me, "Remember the discussion we had in my office?"

"Yes." I resisted the urge to glance in Nerine's direction. "We have everything arranged as you stated in our meeting."

"We will move things up from the end of the evening to now."

In my ear, Xander muttered, "What the hell happened to the order to search Drakos's estate, fucker?"

"And the other duties we must complete during our time here?"

"I'm going to let you two conduct business and stand over here." Nerine tried to move away from us, but Andraius caught her upper arm, holding her in a grip tighter than necessary.

"Stay right here. This discussion is veering into something requiring your presence."

Nerine glanced up at me for a brief second and then asked, "Meaning?"

"Keep listening." He set his hand on the small of her back, and she visibly arched and moved forward as if she couldn't bear his touch.

Then, I saw something on her face that resembled a mix between sadness and shame. When she realized I caught her reaction, she shifted her attention to Andraius, who was completely unaware of anything happening around him.

"Put our previous plans on hold. There are other priorities you need to manage."

"I'm not following."

"Nyx is taking Nerine under her wing, as I mentioned earlier. And from their conversation before dinner, Nerine will spend considerable time at the Drakos estate training to be a proper wife, starting this week."

"Well, well, well," Xander hummed in my earpiece. "I believe Mrs. Drakos is jumping into the game as well. This whole thing is about to get complicated as fuck. I hope Drakos knows that his wife altered our plans and will probably do the opposite of anything and everything he tells her."

Yeah, Nyx scheduling her one-on-one time with Nerine at the estate wasn't part of the original strategy Xander and I'd arranged with Drakos. They were supposed to get Nerine involved in the botanical gardens project in downtown Boston. This way, she would be safely away whenever someone decided to make a move on Andraius.

This monkey wrench meant I couldn't let Nerine out of my sight when she was with Nyx. I no longer trusted anyone but Xander with her.

Maybe I'd become a cynical bastard, but life had made me that way.

Acting as if I hadn't heard anything Xander said, I responded to Andraius. "Understood. Should I inform the team now or after dinner?"

"As of now. I have a few people to visit, and then we will say our goodbyes to the hosts."

"Done."

I stepped back as if to leave, but Andraius stayed me with a lift of his hands.

Glancing at Nerine, he said, "Since you don't like change, let me give you a heads-up."

"What is that?"

"As of tonight, you'll have a new security team."

"What?" Her voice came out a bit louder than acceptable, garnering a glance or two from the people milling about around us. "That's not a heads-up."

The way she shifted, I had no doubt she wanted to peer in my direction. I kept my attention on the crowd through the open doors of the dining room, even though I could see everything happening between Andraius and Nerine in my periphery.

"I didn't have to tell you at all. You could have just had a new group watching you."

"They won't tell you anything different than your current spies say."

Did she actually believe that Theios Alex would assign anyone to her that would invade her privacy? He loved her as if she were his daughter.

No, she had a right to her concerns. In the group were some of the traitors, Andraius's men, he'd sprinkled into the mix. They'd rat out their own mothers.

Every single man from the originals protecting her was loyal only to her. They'd keep any secret she wanted them to keep. But weeding out who she could trust would have taken her time, and the thought of going through that again probably gave her anxiety.

God. We'd fucked up, letting her believe she had no one. And it just wasn't fair to expect Theios Alex to pick up our slack and keep our secrets.

"Then you don't have anything to worry about. Do you?"

"Fine. Do what you want."

"I will. Theo, she is all yours."

Immediately, she whirled in my direction. Her dark blue eyes bored into mine. A storm of emotion swam in her irises. Was it surprise or rage, or worry? Or maybe betrayal?

Keeping my expression locked down as we stared at each other, I inclined my head as any support staff would do. She furrowed her brow and shifted back to Andraius.

"Why would you put your top enforcer on me? Isn't he needed to do you dirty work in Europe?"

So she'd kept tabs on me.

"I have my reasons." Andraius lifted the tumbler of scotch he held in his hands and took a sip. "And you have two."

"Two what?"

"Two enforcers. Theo and Xander. They will be responsible for you, day and night."

She stiffened, narrowing her gaze. "And where will you be? Let me guess, with your whores."

Andraius tightened his grasp on his glass, jerked his other hand as if to strike her, thought better of it, and slid his palm into his pants pocket.

"I plan to do my job by putting the family's interests first. As you are going to do by keeping Nyx Drakos happy."

"As if you'd know anything about putting family first."

Ignoring her jab, he taunted, "You won't be able to hide anything from me now, Nerine."

"Let me repeat, do what you want." Nerine turned and stalked away from us.

I nodded to Robert Lavinos, the head of Andraius's security, who came into view. He followed Andraius as he strolled toward a group he wanted to meet, and then I followed Nerine.

I kept a healthy distance as Nerine headed into the ladies' lounge, where I'd positioned a female team member to watch for any information she may hear tonight.

"So, how mad is she?" Xander asked into the earpiece.

"Between one and ten. I'd say nuclear. Something isn't right."

"As in?"

"It's like she wanted to antagonize him. As if she wanted him to lash out at her."

"There has to be some truth to the rumors."

I clenched my jaw as roaring flooded my ears. "We didn't protect her."

"How the fuck were we supposed to protect her when we were living on different continents and were barely able to see which side was up? You need to let it go."

"I was assigned to protect the family."

"No, Theios Mik was assigned to them. You were nowhere in the vicinity when everything went down."

No, that wasn't how it had gone down.

Theios Alex had ordered Papa and my brothers to watch the five Angelos children so Xander and I could take our fucking finals.

The memories of the blowup I'd had that morning with Papa still haunted me to this day. The old man had raged about having to babysit instead of doing, as he liked to call it, real work in the field. He viewed my time spent studying or teaching any of the Angelos girls anything as time wasted.

He'd never respected me or anything I valued. In his eyes, a college degree had no value in our world. And for the most part, he was right, but he also knew about the promise I'd made to Mama to become the first person on either side of our family to go beyond high school.

Papa only believed in keeping his word for things that benefited him, and I was never part of that equation since he'd hated me from the moment of Mama's death.

Hell, even before that, I couldn't remember a time the man showed me any affection other than the standard nod of the head. It had always been my mother who'd given me any form of kindness or an ounce of love.

My brothers were the ones Papa loved. They were over-macho assholes like him who used brute instead of brains.

Fuck, what the hell was I doing?

I focused back on Xander. "I bet Papa is sitting in hell thinking that if I hadn't skipped out on my responsibilities, Theios Peter, him, my brothers, and countless others wouldn't have been slaughtered."

"I loved Theios Mik, but he was a dick to you."

"It doesn't change the fact the bastard was right in this

case. That degree has done nothing for me, just like he said it would. And in the end, we had to play traitors."

In one afternoon, Xander and I had lost everyone, from our leader and his little boy to all of our siblings and my parents. The only reason Andraius let us live was because we pledged loyalty to him. And we'd agreed to that only because Theios Alex said the only way to protect the Angelos women was to hold our noses and play the betrayers.

I still couldn't understand how Andraius believed we would immediately give him our allegiance. But thank God for small favors.

"Wrong. Without your degree, we couldn't have run this organization without the moron knowing. Now, do you want to ease up on the guilt? I thought it was my job to play the martyr." Xander hummed. "I know you need to visit Father Michael. He'll give you a *komboskini* to pray over as you count the knots, and then all the sinners' guilt will disappear before you finish all fifty-two prayers."

"You're such a jackass."

"The truth is the truth."

"Shut up and come down from your perch. We need to get Nerine home."

"On my way."

Xander had barely finished speaking when Nerine came out of the lounge. From how she moved directly toward me and the ire filling her blue eyes, I'd done something to piss her off.

What the fuck could I have done already?

"Is something wrong, Mrs. Angelos?"

She paused two feet from me. "I do not need someone in the toilet with me. Where the hell do you think I will go in a gown like this? It's not like I can sneak out a window."

"Rebecca will only intervene if your safety is compromised." I kept my tone bland and without inflection.

She cocked a hand on her hip. "My other team lead didn't feel this level of security was necessary. Why is it so important now?"

"Your other security lead wasn't me."

"Or me," Xander added, coming up behind me. "We take our roles seriously."

A flush crept up Nerine's face as that unsaid energy that seemed to flow from the three of us surged. We shared so much history, and it couldn't reach the light of day.

How long had it been since we'd been this close? Almost five years. The night before everything went to hell.

"I'm not a child." She kept her gaze between Xander and me, not daring to look us in the eyes.

We knew this firsthand.

"We have our orders to keep you safe," Xander responded.

"This is all to keep me safe?"

I hoped she read past the words I'd say next. "Everything we've done is to keep you safe."

"Is that right?" She smirked. "Could have fooled me. Fuck off with keeping me safe."

I should have known better, subtle never worked with her.

"Whether you want it or not," I said, "we will make sure nothing happens to you, Angel."

Fire lit her eyes, and for a split second, I thought she'd deck me.

"Never call me Angel again. I'm not your angel. You lost the right." Her attention moved to Xander. "And so did you. I am only an assignment to you. Follow his orders like the good little enforcer lapdogs you are. I've survived on my own so far. I can keep doing it."

Turning, she stalked toward the main entryway of the house.

"That went better than I expected."

I glared at Xander. "We shouldn't have stayed away. She hates us."

"No, she doesn't. She's smarter than everyone around us and knows we had no choice but to keep our distance."

I resisted the urge to smack him on the back of the head. "From where I'm standing, she'd rather gut us than look at us."

"Did you forget how you two started?"

Only an idiot would forget how we'd circled each other as if we were feral cats ready to claw each other's eyes out. It had annoyed the hell out of me that Papa saddled me with babysitting duty for the boss's fourteen-year-old daughter. And she'd felt the same way about me being her babysitter.

After getting expelled from her elite private school with all the debutantes like her and where security was part of the tuition, she'd decided to attend school with all of us peasants instead of finding another institution on par with her social status.

So my job was to keep an eye on her as she navigated her first year of high school.

"That was a lifetime ago."

"Doesn't change the dynamics." Xander's gaze locked with mine, the undercurrent of the unsaid pulsing between us.

Nerine folded her arms, shooting me a glare as she waited for us. The giant rock on Nerine's left hand glimmered with the reflection of the light.

Needing to correct Xander's perspective, I said, "You're an idiot if you think it doesn't. She belongs to Andraius."

"The fuck she does," Xander retorted, his pace growing faster. "She is trapped. We will get her out. Then all bets are off."

"You act as if it is a done deal. We are a long way from that day, and how I look at it, waiting will only make her hate us more."

"It's better for her to hate us now and make it believable than to get her killed."

Nerine glanced over her shoulder as if she wasn't sure if we'd actually followed her and then quickened her pace. Right before she turned back around, her gaze locked with mine for the briefest of seconds, and that fucking undercurrent of anger mixed with longing hit me.

Christ. With the rollercoaster of emotions Nerine and Xander were about to throw at me, this was never going to work without killing me.

"And how will you explain the attraction if anyone notices it?" I asked.

"You're good at playing the emotionless asshole. Just keep doing what you do best."

I scowled at Xander. Not a few seconds ago, he told me that Nerine and I were volatile together. "And you?"

"I'm a flirt." He shot me a bright grin. "Everyone knows this. Andraius will think I'm sweet-talking her into doing what he wants. I've done this shit for him before."

Hearing him talk about himself like that annoyed the hell out of me. We'd become completely different versions of ourselves to survive our new realities. However, the way we'd moved on wasn't a topic I anticipated. Especially Nerine's reaction to the way Xander and I moved on without her.

"We are fucked, and not in the good way. We'll be lucky if we keep our balls."

Five

Nerine

I marched through the Drakos mansion's main hall, feeling my heart thud against my chest as I sensed Theo and Xander's eyes upon me. Their presence seared into my back, pulling at everything I'd worked so hard to lock away.

All these years, I waited to see, needed to see, just one sign that they hadn't rolled over when Andraius took over. And now they were here, looking at me with those eyes that knew me too well, making me remember and question everything I'd believed since the day Papa died.

I'd watched them from a distance, caught glimpses of them doing their duties and running Andraius's empire, but we'd never interacted. Sometimes I'd wondered if they even noticed when I looked in their direction.

Theo's words echoed in my mind.

Everything we've done is to keep you safe.

Had it all been an act?

Andraius had isolated me like a caged bird, determined to keep me away from anyone who could have even the vaguest trace of loyalty to Papa or me.

He kept me trapped and alone.

So fucking alone.

My hands shook as the overwhelming desire to turn around and punch one of them roared through me. They'd let me live with a monster all of these years.

Without so much as a backward glance, I directed, "Please call the car around. I want to go home."

"Nerine, we can't leave without Andraius," Xander informed me in a hushed tone.

"These are your choices, gentlemen. Call the car, or I'll arrange a ride myself. My spouse is planning to fuck one of his whores tonight. We don't need his permission to leave. Tick-tock, gentlemen. The rideshare app on my phone is calling my name."

"When did you become such a brat?" Theo muttered, and I whirled around to face him.

"I'll answer that question," I said through clenched teeth, but then closed my eyes to calm my temper.

I couldn't make a scene here. There were too many people.

"We are waiting for your answer, Mrs. Angelos." Theo

taunted, his tone laced with something that ate away at my ability to hold it together.

With as cool and emotionless a tone as I could muster, I whispered, "When the two men I loved sold me out for an agenda they never saw fit to tell me about."

Theo scowled at me. "Agenda? You're the—"

Immediately Xander stepped between us, shooting Theo a warning glare before returning his attention to me.

"This isn't the time nor place for this discussion," he said, his voice firm and steady. "Let's save it for another location. I will procure our means of transportation to ensure your safe arrival back at your home."

I kept my angry focus on Theo, not saying a word.

Some things never changed. Xander would always remain the voice of reason.

Unruffled and poised.

Though this new refined way of speaking must be a talent he'd picked up over the recent years.

Theo continued to peer at me, making it very clear we were in a stare-off.

Keeping my gaze locked with his and just to annoy him for making the brat comment, I asked, "Well, are you getting the car like you said, or do I need to arrange my own way home after all?"

"I've got it covered." Xander stepped in front of me, blocking my view of Theo.

His dark eyes were just as intense, just as painful to look into. These two men had been my everything, my safe place.

Now I was alone, without a soul to wrap their arms around me to give me even a second of comfort.

Shaking the thoughts away, I pivoted and called over my shoulder, "Okay then, I'm waiting."

Fifteen minutes later, I was seated comfortably in the back of one of the luxurious cars Simon Drakos provided to guests who wanted to depart earlier than their companions.

Xander steered the car down the winding road while Theo sat in stoic silence beside him. I had no doubt they were completely aware of my every movement. We hadn't exchanged a single word after leaving the Drakos estate.

The tension between us lay so heavy, filling the air and weighing down the car. And time felt suspended, as if it had been centuries since we'd been this close, this intimate, without anyone else around.

It had only been a little under five years since I was that naive nineteen-year-old, the girl who loved hard, dreamed big, and planned to change the status quo with these men by her side.

But that person had vanished, and I'd learned to keep my secrets hidden and to trust no one.

I'd trusted the men before me, and what had that gotten me?

Absolutely nothing.

Tonight, so much crashed down upon me. First, Nyx and Simon threw their bomb my way with them wanting to be my champions, to teach me to fight back, to help me destroy Andraius, and now these two before me.

It made no sense.

I wanted to hope, but could I afford to hope?

I couldn't be naive. My sisters and my mother depended on me.

I barely saw them as it was. I couldn't risk those few precious moments by doing anything stupid.

If only my body understood what was at stake. A war played out inside me. One where the memories of the past resurfaced, reminding me of everything denied me for years.

I pressed my fingers to the bridge of my nose and dropped my head back to the seat, closing my eyes.

Shouldn't I hate them for leaving me to fend for myself? Shouldn't I lash out, be the bitch persona I'd cultivated to protect myself?

I'd tried, and it felt so wrong, as if I wasn't being true to the real me.

Not with them

But who was I?

I had no fucking clue.

Opening my eyes, I studied the back of each man. Both had grown larger and more muscular, something I hadn't thought possible. Anyone looking in their direction would know they could handle themselves. Their tuxes gave them an elegant and polished appearance, but when anyone looked into their eyes, only danger peered back at them.

I'd felt the impact earlier when they'd stared at me, taking in every one of my reactions. They'd done it countless times in the past. However, those instances had led to activities full of passion, desire, and dirty sex.

An ache deep in my core that had lain dormant for so long

pulsed to life, and I couldn't help but swallow to ease the dryness in my throat.

Fuck.

What the hell was I doing?

I couldn't go there. I'd locked that box, and opening it would only lead to disaster.

"What are you thinking about so hard?" Xander asked, his dark, penetrating gaze studying me through the rearview mirror, reminding me of those nights when he'd stared at me as if he could look into the depths of my soul.

Keeping my voice as calm as possible, I responded without giving him the whole truth. "The events of my life."

"Such as?" His lips curved slightly at the corners, and for some reason, I could not look away.

The low throbbing deep in my core grew more intense, and my nipples beaded in the confines of my gown.

"You aren't privy to the information." Out of the corner of my eye, I noticed Theo's fist clench on the armrest along the car's center console.

His one tell, when agitated.

He definitely understood the undercurrent of what Xander had asked, even if he hadn't seen my face.

My skin heated, and the thirst for everything I'd given up surged forward as if in the flood of a tsunami.

I shifted in my seat, trying to ignore the two men in the front seats of the car. However, the movement only intensified everything I craved.

The car pulled into the driveway of the Angelos compound, and in a desperate attempt to break away from the attraction between the three of us, I declared quietly, "This can't work."

Theo stared forward as he spoke. "We don't have a choice. Andraius gave us his orders."

"The three of us together is a disaster waiting to happen. People will learn about our past and what we were to each other."

"No one but those we trust know about us, and they have kept it silent so far," Xander countered. "And since we won't touch you, there isn't a problem."

"You have all the fucking answers, don't you?" I growled.

"That's my job," Xander replied.

"Your job." I gritted my teeth and asked Theo, "Since he has all the answers, what do you do?"

"I implement all the plans."

"I'm not a plan." I couldn't hide my outrage as the roaring of my drumming heartbeat in my ears grew to a deafening level.

This night needed to end.

Glancing over his shoulder, Theo chuckled darkly, making me want to deck him and kiss him. "You're the long-term plan, Angel. Get prepared."

"Fuck that shit. I'm not part of any of your plans. I waited for one little sign, one small clue that you two were on my side. But it never came. You left me. So, your long-term plans can go to hell."

Theo shifted to face me, his gray eyes blazing and void of the cool mask he loved to cloak himself with. "Do you actually believe we wanted to leave? You are the fucking air we breathe. We had to keep you safe. He would have killed you if he had learned about us. We barely managed to hide it from Theios Peter."

Grabbing the handle, I pushed open the car door. "Safe? Let me quote a line from one of my favorite movies. I know you're familiar with it since we watched it together. You keep using that word. I do not think it means what you think it means."

Without a backward glance, I strode into the house, feeling the urge to cry for the first time in ages.

As the morning sun slowly crept through my window, I stared up at the intricately designed ceiling of my bedroom. No matter how much I wanted to let the tears fall, I'd kept them at bay. If I opened up that tap, it might never close. Instead, I'd tossed and turned all night long.

Dreams of Theo and Xander had invaded my sleep, reminding me of our times together. Our hours of laughter, long conversations, friendship, and pleasure I'd only ever found with them. They were once upon a time, my rocks, my safe place, the people I trusted with everything.

Then it all shattered into tiny, microscopic pieces.

Since taking my vows, I had trained myself to repress my desires and accept Andraius's twisted form of sex. I'd convinced myself that at least I'd had love and pleasure for a short moment in my life and locked away my needs.

Now that barrier had all come crashing down in one night, reigniting feelings I couldn't have.

Their sheer presence made me want, crave, and ache. A deep throbbing pulsed in my core, and there wasn't any relief in the future from it.

My eyes drifted to the open doorway that led to Andraius's bedroom.

Just the thought of him touching me gave me nausea. He only knew how to take, never to give.

At least I wouldn't have to endure anything from him for another few weeks. He only came around when the doctors said I was at peak fertility.

In the meantime, he'd travel between his variety of women tucked around the city.

I'd say more power to them. I'd happily divorce the fucker and let one of them replace me.

I sighed and tucked the covers more snugly around my body.

His mistresses only saw him as an attractive man who looked younger than his fifty-four years. However, once he tired of their newness, they'd get the full view of the disgusting and ugly monster hidden under the handsome face and designer clothing.

I hated him for taking the suite of rooms that had belonged to my parents. There were so many others to choose from, bigger ones, renovated ones. Still, he'd picked this one because of its significance to me and the organization.

At least he believed the bullshit I fed him about my parents having separate bedrooms and me wanting the same thing. If Papa and Mama were ever under the same roof, they never slept apart. I'd wished for the type of love they'd shared and believed

I'd found it with Xander and Theo, as unconventional as it had been.

Mama used the room I currently slept in as the "I had a bad dream room" for my siblings and me while growing up. The last occasional occupant was Linus.

The pain of loss shot through my heart. I adored that boy. He was the surprise no one expected, full of joy and laughter. He'd completed our family and brought the energy of a volcano into the house.

A lump formed in my throat, and I quickly shoved it back. No, I refused to dwell there.

At least I had Mama and the girls, even if they were far away.

God, I missed them.

I had to remember they were safe and couldn't see first-hand what my life had become. Even with the chaos Andraius caused in our lives, his sending Mama and the girls to Cyprus may have been the best thing for them. They lived freely, doing as they pleased as long as they followed the rules of not engaging with any of the other syndicate families.

Or, we'd made it seem like they'd broken ties with all families. Everyone knew Papa was the eldest son of a boss and had inherited my grandfather's seat, but people seemed to forget Mama was the daughter of a power boss from a province in Greece. No matter what my idiot husband believed, one never cut ties with their blood in the syndicate world, especially immediate family. My maternal grandfather may have passed away, but my uncles were still alive and ran their organizations.

I'd rather deal with the bastard here than let him or his cronies know how my mother or sisters actually lived abroad.

Which included access to the many Swiss accounts where I'd funneled some of the Angelos coffers when Andraius had locked me in the library before he forced me to marry him.

Fucker thought he could keep my Mama on a tight budget and make her beg him for money. I'd let hell freeze over before that day came.

Papa was one of the most intelligent men I'd ever known, and he'd had backup plans for backup plans. I never thought I'd have to follow through on one, but I had. If only I'd had the skills or contacts I possessed now back then. I could have done so much more. Hell, none of this would have happened.

There was no point in dwelling on all of that now. I had other shit to worry about.

Seriously, a whole lot of other shit.

I might as well take a shower. It would give me a more productive way to kill time before I dealt with my two new bodyguards.

Rolling to my side, I rose from the bed and moved toward my bathroom.

Crossing over the threshold into my en suite, I pushed down my worries and finished my morning routine before stepping into the shower.

Bracing my hands against the tiled walls, I lifted my face into the steaming cascade of water and allowed the heat to soak into my skin and relax my muscles.

Ignoring the water pelting my lashes, I focused on the freshly formed bruises on my wrist.

I couldn't help the smirk that bubbled up.

When riled, Andraius liked to lash out like a feral cat. So, I'd egged him on.

Maybe it was childish and a bit reckless. No, it was full-on dangerous. However, at this point, outside of protecting my sisters and mother, I had no fucks left to give.

Andraius wanted to project this image of refinement and elegance. I'd only go so far to play the part. Somewhere along the timeline of the past few years, I'd gone from numb and depressed to full-on cold rage.

The more he pushed me, the more I challenged him.

He needed me alive, no matter how many times he threatened to kill me. His claim to the family came through me, and he couldn't marry any of my sisters because they were still minors.

I'd feared him for the first year of our marriage. He'd broken me and made me believe I'd had no one.

Anger burned bright inside me.

Then, everything changed on the anniversary of Papa's and Linus's deaths.

While visiting the family gravesites, a few of my security team had gone out of their way to ensure I noticed the Angelos crest pin they strategically wore on the inside of their suit jackets. The very pin Papa had given them when they officially joined the organization.

It had healed something in my heart and given me hope for the first time since entering the cage that had become my life. It made me realize they weren't loyal to Andraius at all but to Papa, and now my sisters and me.

Since then, those men had gone out of their way to make my life easier. They took extra shifts, ran errands, or sat with me while I worked in the library. They gave me spare time to linger while out and about town. I had peace of mind whenever they were around, knowing no one monitored my conversations with my mother and sisters.

Although I knew some of the men reported my movements to Andraius, I quickly figured out who they were. Papa had taught me how to recognize people's mannerisms, habits, and body language, so I observed and noted every detail.

And I tested my team by giving them certain pieces of information and seeing if Andraius was alerted. After a while, I knew who sat in my corner and who resided in Andraius's camp.

With the knowledge that some of them were looking out for me rather than Andraius, I was able to gain a tiny bit of my confidence back.

I may never return to being the girl who'd had her whole life planned out and knew who and what she was. But the woman I'd become today had survived and knew going head-to-head with Andraius would help me slowly siphon my power back.

Besides, what more could he do to me than he'd done the day of the coup?

I slid my palm over my flat stomach.

That day would forever remain etched in my memory.

He'd held guns to my mother's and sisters' heads. He'd used the threat of their deaths to force me to marry him, then fuck him. Afterward, when he learned I wasn't a virgin, he carved "whore" into the flesh below my stomach with the same blade he'd used to murder Papa and Linus.

I clenched my fists. One day I'd laugh knowing an enemy of his took him out in as gruesome a manner as he'd done to those I loved. I craved to be the one to do it, but the chances of that were slim to none.

Logically, I knew I couldn't physically overpower him. At nearly five-foot-nine, I wasn't short or a tiny woman, but Andraius's body mass could overwhelm me in a heartbeat. He carried a full eighty pounds more than I did, and he knew how to fight, something I'd never gotten the chance to learn to a level that would allow me to defend myself against a grown man.

Nyx mentioned training me, but in what? And could I truly trust her?

I couldn't wrap my mind around the events of last night.

First, the craziness with the Drakoses, and now, the change-up of Theo and Xander. How would I handle it all?

None of this made any sense—especially my new bodyguards.

Watching me had to be a downgrade from their traditional roles. And considering who they were in the structure of the organization, why had they agreed to the change?

I'd spent the last few years locked away from the family's day-to-day operations. Still, I never stopped paying attention to the things happening around me, especially information about them.

They ran the entire Angelos Syndicate.

I'd often heard how Andraius turned to them for everything, including operations. Sometimes they were referred to as his enforcers and sometimes as his chief lieutenants. But in reality, they were both enforcers who had risen to the ranks of top lieutenants, who'd muscled their way past even those with years more experience than themselves. They gave the impression of carrying out orders without question but were, in fact, the power that controlled the family.

They had made themselves indispensable to Andraius. I wondered if Andraius realized he had little control over the organization he'd commandeered.

And why did Theo and Xander pretend to bow down to a man like Andraius when they already ran the enterprise? What was their end goal?

But if I were to believe Theo's words from last night, why hadn't they given me even a glimmer of anything to convey they were on my side?

No matter how much I wanted to believe, how much I wanted it to be true, allowing myself to fall victim to my naivety would only lead to disaster, not only for me but for my sisters and mother.

And if I went through with Nyx's offer, how would I keep our activities quiet? Could I risk it?

Who was I kidding? Taking the chance with Nyx was my only real possibility of escaping this cage I lived in.

I guessed I had my answer.

Okay, Nerine Nicolette Angelos. Time to face the day and deal with whatever comes your way.

Six

ander

I stood outside Nerine's bedroom, waiting to escort her to her daily workout at the gym. Her previous team lead, Stefano, one of the originals, had given me a rundown of her routine. According to him, every day at six thirty sharp, Nerine left her room for a jog and then a weight training or pilates session in the basement gym.

But of course, today, she decided to change things up.

Glancing at my watch, I scowled.

Five to seven.

What the fuck was she doing in there?

Getting impatient, I knocked and then waited for a

response. When none came, I knocked again and leaned against the doorframe.

That's when the familiar surge prickled down my skin. Only two people ever caused that reaction.

Theo and Nerine.

The former was in a meeting in the city.

Which left my assignment.

Why hadn't my men informed me that she'd slipped out of her room? Weren't they stationed everywhere?

Releasing a frustrated breath, I said, "How did you leave without us seeing?"

"You're not as all-knowing as you believe, Mr. Onassis."

I turned to face her and felt like she'd punched me in the gut.

She wore an old college hoodie with yoga pants that hugged her amazing ass. She hadn't a stitch of makeup on her face, giving her an aura of youthfulness. And the way she had her thick braids pulled into a high ponytail reminded me of the girl from five years ago. The girl who'd been mine. The girl whose hair I had the right to fist and use to bring her in for a kiss.

We held each other's gazes. The weight of so many things we couldn't say sitting so heavy between us. One day, when it all went down, I'd tell her everything. Get her to forgive me.

Her pupils dilated, turning her eyes into rings of blue, and the familiar surge of lust pulsed between us. She licked her plump lips, and her breath grew shallow, hinting at the arousal building inside her.

Fuck. I'd never survive this.

Shaking off the trance, I moved in her direction and asked, "Would you clarify that statement?"

"Nope." She strode away and then called over her shoulder. "Let's go. I want to have breakfast."

Okay, Angel. No matter what version of you that you try to throw at me: brat, diva, bitch, broken, or anything in-between, I can handle it.

I kept a few feet behind her until she entered the kitchen, where I remained on the periphery. There she busied herself, chatting with the staff and preparing the ingredients for her breakfast.

The morning kitchen duty was a tradition she kept up to pay homage to her father. From the time I could remember as a child, Theios Peter would spend the morning with the kitchen staff, preparing his breakfast and learning about them. The short time he'd spent with them gave him a chance to learn different things about the household and any gossip that generally wouldn't reach his ears.

Peter Angelos was known for being as ruthless as they came, but he cared for his people and knew how to run his empire, inside and out.

His one biggest mistake had been trusting Andraius to the level he had. It had cost him everything.

"Eat." Nerine stood before me with an omelet, making me realize I'd spaced out.

"You're feeding me? I thought you hated me."

Something flickered in her cobalt eyes as I took the plate.

Instead of responding to my statement, she said, "It's weird to have you staring at us while we have breakfast. Might as well join us."

I glanced down at my food and looked at hers on the butcher block table behind her. My omelet was filled with sautéed spicy vegetables, the exact way I liked it, and hers had only spinach and cheese. Why would she go out of her way to make something for me?

Then it hit me. It was our thing, too. We'd loved to cook together and make things for each other. I'd taken multiple cooking classes with Nerine under the guise of being her bodyguard while she was in high school.

The pulse of energy hummed between us again. Nerine bit her lower lip, and a flush crept over her cheeks. My body responded, and I'd never been so grateful for the fucking suit jacket covering my now engorged cock.

Fuck. I had to get this under control. This was only the first day.

"Did you make breakfast for Stefano every morning, too?" I asked in a tone meant for her ears only. "Or is this a stroll down memory lane, Angel?"

As if sense came back to her with my words, she closed her eyes briefly, gritted her teeth, and hurried to her place at the table.

The kitchen staff glared at me as if they sensed I'd said something to upset Nerine, but I kept my face stoic. Of course, they weren't part of the originals who worked on alternate days of the week. So, my experience with this group left me questioning their loyalties. Though if I gauged anything by the frosty reception I garnered now, I'd say they loved Nerine and wanted nothing to do with me.

To keep the peace and stay on their good side, I said, "Thank you, Mrs. Angelos. Making breakfast was very considerate of you."

"You're welcome." Nerine lifted her gaze to mine for the briefest of seconds before digging into her food.

"How'd the morning go?" Theo asked as he met me outside of the Angelos library, where Nerine had barricaded herself for three hours following the end of breakfast.

"The forecast ranges between ice storms and Antarctic conditions."

My response garnered chuckles from two team members stationed outside the library's mahogany doors.

"Then I guess I should have worn a heavy coat." Theo gestured for me to follow him. "We need to have a proper discussion with her."

"It's your funeral."

"Since when are you so worried about her temper?"

"Since I realized she harbored a powder keg of rage under that bitchy, bitter facade. It's only a matter of time before she blows, and either we will be the recipients of her wrath, or she will do something that will fuck all of our plans to hell and back."

Theo studied me and shook his head. "What the fuck happened this morning?"

"She made me breakfast," I stated.

Surprise flashed in his gray eyes, and then he probed, "And?"

"Nothing. I stayed in my corner, and Nerine was in hers. I know her, and she is up to something. Andraius may be a paranoid bastard, but in this case, he is correct to have his suspicions."

"She's going to fuck up our plans."

"Undoubtedly."

"That's all we need." Theo charged toward the library door and, without knocking, turned the knob and walked inside the giant room.

Snuggled on a long couch with a blanket tucked around her and a laptop on a portable desk, Nerine scowled in our direction. "It is rude to enter a room without permission."

"We ensure your safety. Where you go, we go," Theo countered.

"You're such an asshole."

He shrugged and then waited until I'd entered to shut the door and lock it. Nerine's eyes widened, and she sat up.

"What are you doing?"

"We need to have a chat." Theo sat across from her, and I positioned myself in an armchair near the fireplace.

"I said all I needed to say last night. Unless this concerns something pertinent to your work for my warden, get lost."

Theo leaned forward, resting his arms on his knees. "Well, Angel. It is about our job. You are our job."

"I'm not your Angel. I'm not your anything," she voiced through gritted teeth, shifting her body to match his position.

"And you can fuck yourself with thinking I'm your job. You're part of my protection detail. Nothing more. Now, what do you want?"

Before Theo could say anything and escalate the situation further, I interjected, "We need a rundown of your daily and weekly schedules. And starting today, we would like for you to update a shared electronic calendar for activities so we can implement appropriate security protocols."

Nerine cocked her head to the side and studied me, and I couldn't help but smirk.

"What? Did you think he was the only one who could use proper English? Just because my assignments weren't in Europe didn't mean I spent any less time with the upper crust."

Nerine's face grew stern. "That's right. You left the country to keep me safe. So explain to me how letting another man put a gun to my head and force me to marry him and then fuck me without consent kept me safe?"

The bitterness in her words felt like a kick to the gut. I'd done that. I'd let someone force her into a marriage.

Fuck. I had to get it together. I bitched at Theo for living in his guilt and here I was doing it myself.

"It was that, or you died, along with your mother and sisters."

"I see. Makes complete sense now." She tapped her finger to her chin. "So you whored me out to save my family?"

Theo clenched his jaw and shifted slightly, telling me Nerine had hit that trigger point for him. He could remain calm in all things but with her.

He'd goaded her by barging into the library, and now she'd pushed back with her words meant to hurt.

"Don't you dare talk about yourself like that." The ire in Theo's voice would have made most men piss themselves, but Nerine laughed.

I couldn't fucking believe it. She laughed.

"Or what? Andraius has done everything possible to me, so I doubt you could add anything new to the list. Oh, wait. You can't touch me, can you?" she asked with fake smugness that pulled at my nerves. "Like at all."

"So it's the brat today?"

She glared now. "No, there is no brat. You might as well forget about that brat you loved. She's dead and gone. I'm a raging, cold-hearted bitch. I became one because that's the only way to survive when you have no one but yourself to depend on."

Fuck. This wasn't how we needed this conversation to go.

"You're not alone. There are many more people on your side than you believe," I tried to assure her. "We had to stay in the shadows until we could get everyone in position."

She shook her head. "Oh, I feel so safe with everyone in the shadows, moving me around like a chess piece."

"Don't you want your seat? It belongs to you."

Fire lit her dark eyes as she stood and moved toward me with a fist and more anger directed at me than I'd ever seen before.

"You fucking bastard. How dare you? How fucking dare you?"

Theo grabbed her by the waist and hauled her against him,

keeping her from attacking me. She thrashed in his hold, trying her best to get free.

When she realized there was no hope of Theo allowing her to unleash her rage, she said in a tone so cold it was as if she were a different person. "Once upon a time, I may have wanted to fulfill Papa's dream, take my seat, run his empire. But that all died with him and Linus. Now I want to escape this hell with Mama and the girls and leave all of you assholes behind. Every fucking last one of you. I want nothing to do with any of you."

"And where would you go?"

She smirked. "As if I'd tell either of you. You're not my knights in shining armor here to protect me. I'm not depending on you. Were you ever the man I could tell all my secrets?"

I grimaced. "I'm still your Xander. No matter what, you can still talk to me."

"That's a fucking lie." She shook her head. "You're not my best friend anymore. Neither of you are. I'll find a way out. I'll get my revenge one day. Let's hope you're not in my way."

"Angel, all we wanted was to keep you safe." Theo spoke against the back of her head. "That's all we still want. You mean everything to us."

I wasn't even sure he realized he hadn't let her go. The lucky bastard got to hold her, even if she was spitting mad at the time.

She dropped her head, and her shoulders sagged. "Theo, I'm not your angel. Please, I beg you. Please stop calling me that. I'm nobody's angel. And how can you keep me safe when the enemy shares my bed?"

"Let us explain."

"No. The time for that has long passed." She settled her attention out the window. "You just stay in your corner, and I'll stay in mine. We will pretend, as always, that our little Theo-Angel-Xander throuple never existed. I'll do my best to curb my bitchiness, and you stay out of my way."

The defeat of her words made it seem as if there was no hope for us in the future.

Fuck that shit.

"Nerine."

She shifted her gaze to mine.

"Do you remember the promise we made to each other? Or the way we described what we had?"

She said nothing, just stared at me.

"Did you forget? Or is it that you don't want to remember?" Theo asked as he released her and stepped away. "If you hate us so much, it wouldn't have meaning. You could talk about it as part of your past, right?"

There he went again, pushing her buttons.

Anger washed over her features. "And what good would talking about us do? It makes no difference."

"Our feelings haven't changed," I informed her. "Unconventional yet permanent. Isn't that how you described us?"

"You two are fucking idiots."

"You'll forever be it for us. We will wait."

"Xander, do you even listen to what's coming from your mouth? I'm married—end of story. There is no happy ending. And if Andraius has his way, it will never change. To gain my freedom, one of us will have to die."

Neither Theo nor I uttered a word in response. We only stared at her. The weight of the statement filled the room.

"You can't be serious," she whispered, then shook her head no. "No, don't do this for me. I don't need you to save me."

"I have no idea what you're talking about, Mrs. Angelos." I leaned back in my seat. "I suggest you work with us on your daily and weekly schedules and let us see if we can come to some compromise so we don't invade your space too much."

Nerine's attention shifted to Theo.

They stared at each other, and then she nodded as if they'd decided to call a truce. Which I knew was bullshit since one or the other would say something extra annoying. But I guessed I'd deal with it when it came.

When the fuck had I become the peacemaker? I was the one who got in people's faces and caused scenes. Shit. When it came to Theo and Nerine, though, I was always the peacekeeper. Fucking Switzerland.

I needed a drink to handle this changing personality with Theo's and Nerine's shit.

"Let me update you with today's plans, and then we can go from there."

Seven

erine

"Hello, Mrs. Angelos. Welcome back to the Drakos estate." Stevie, Nyx Drakos's head of security, greeted me as I stepped out of my car.

"Hi, Stevie. It's good to see you again."

Her stern face softened, turning her into the runway model she'd been in her youth, and a slight twinkle lit her dark eyes. "I hope you're ready for the beginning of your training in plants."

"As ready as I'll ever be," I answered, releasing a deep breath.

I gestured with my chin to the bag on the floorboard, and immediately, she reached inside and handed it to a man waiting behind her. I noticed Theo's scowl—he hadn't seen anything in my hands when I'd slid into the car at home.

Yeah, I had a feeling he'd ask me about it on the way back.

She'd barely glanced at Xander and Theo. Still, I knew she'd taken in everything about them, from Theo's irritation toward me to how Xander scrutinized everything around him.

But the three of them hadn't counted on the fact that I caught the glances that passed between them. They knew each other, maybe not as friends, but they weren't enemies on a deeper level than security for two syndicate heads.

Cara, remember you play multiple games at the same time. You can't focus only on one thing. It isn't fair, but you are a woman, and they will treat you differently. You have to be better than all of them.

Were they working with Stevie on this long-term plan of theirs?

They could go right ahead.

I'd work mine, and they could carry on with theirs.

We'd see who got to the finish line first.

"I'll take you to the solarium. We've prepared it for your lessons."

Stevie led us through the opulent front entryway. Any trace of last night's event no longer existed. Though the way they'd created the living garden indoor atmosphere was beautiful, I preferred how it looked now. This classic, clean with hints of a modern aesthetic, called to me. They'd brought the house up in time with technology and art but kept the original prewar New England style, structure, and coloring.

A warm, comforting sensation washed over me as we weaved through the house. This place wrapped a person in a feeling of love and contentment.

This was a home.

The energy here welcomed a soul.

A pang hit my heart and reminded me of what I'd once felt in the Angelos compound. Those times were long over.

A few seconds later, we stopped outside two thick wooden doors.

"Gentlemen, you are not permitted inside the room." Stevie crossed her arms across her chest in a no-nonsense stance.

"We go where she goes," Xander challenged.

The firm set of his jaw screamed he had no plan to budge on his assignment.

"Wrong. Mrs. Angelos is a guest in the Drakos home. Nyx wants a private afternoon with her friend. She will get a private afternoon."

Theo moved to stand between me and the door, his granite-like stance blocking my way into the room. "As Mr. Onassis stated. We go where Mrs. Angelos goes."

Irritation coursed through me. This whole situation was stupid.

I shoved Theo out of my way. "What the hell is going to happen to me here?"

"You are our priority. Those are our orders."

"Orders? Andraius is jizzing himself right now that I'm here."

"I do not believe he would find that language appropriate." Xander's chiding tone had me ready to deck him.

What he couldn't say was he hated that word—always had, especially when I said it.

What had he expected when I fell for two enforcers and hung out with their crew? I could be as raunchy as the rest of them.

"I'm his wife, not his child. Get a grip or get lost."

Stevie moved toward me. "They can sit outside if that makes them more comfortable."

With an icy glare, I shot back, "No, they can't. I want privacy as well. So go have a cookie or something in the kitchen."

"A cookie?" Theo's eyes narrowed menacingly, and he stepped in my direction. "I swear to God, Ne—"

He cut himself off, pausing his movement, and clenched his jaw, realizing we had an audience. I'd made him break his calm iceman demeanor.

I lifted a challenging brow and taunted, "You were saying?"

Xander stepped between Theo and me. "Go play with your plants. We will occupy ourselves for the next few hours."

He glanced at Stevie, who showed him four fingers in a silent response, conveying the number of hours for the lesson.

"We will see you at six o'clock sharp," he said gruffly before turning and striding away with Theo on his heels.

A throat cleared, and my attention shifted toward the solarium. Leaning against one open door, I found Nyx. A tight bun sat atop her head, and she wore a fitted tank top with slim workout pants.

The curious expression on her face told me she'd heard part of the exchange I'd had with Xander and Theo.

She confirmed it when she lifted a brow and said, "Something tells me those two were much more than bodyguards in your former life. Hmm?"

"I have no idea what you're talking about. I'm a cold-hearted bitch, or haven't you heard the complaints my husband likes to spread about me?"

Nyx gestured for me to enter the room. "Sometimes, the only armor a woman has is her cutting tongue and slicing personality. So I'm going to teach you another way to protect yourself."

"Want me to keep a certain green-eyed busybody away for today's lessons?" Stevie asked.

"As if that is even remotely possible." Nyx gave Stevie a deadpan stare.

"Then what do you propose we do when he decides to supervise? And you know he's going to want to supervise." The annoyance in Stevie's voice made me think she was more of a friend to Nyx than exclusively a bodyguard.

Nyx smirked and scanned me from head to toe before saying, "Nothing. The asshole I love called and said he has to fly to Greece for some emergency negotiations for a shipping contract. He may not be back for weeks."

Stevie cocked her head to the side. "Let me guess. Your brothers are involved in this business?"

"Why would I know anything about my brothers' dealings?" The smirk on Nyx's face said she was well aware of everything going on. "What I do know is that I've got this one all to myself and her husband won't have any objections to lessons from me every day if I request them."

This woman seriously had some balls of steel. She gave no fucks at all.

"What do you think?" Nyx asked as we entered the solarium.

The space gave the feel of an enchanted garden, where the sun shone through the glass walls in beams of light onto the incredible array of plants around the space's edge. But what made this room unlike anything I'd ever seen were the cases of weapons and armor situated at various points around a giant training mat.

"Is this your gym?"

"Almost every other day while I'm in residence."

I studied her, taking in her complete confidence in who she was. She appeared to be the Mykos Hellion turned refined Drakos wife to the outside world. However, everything I'd learned in such a short time told me it was all a guise, and she'd never truly conformed. Instead, she'd just learned to manage her reactions more.

As if sensing my scrutiny, Nyx made a circle with her body, hands out.

"No, you aren't in the twilight zone. And yes, I'm the same person from last night. But, I behave because that will cause the least amount of issues for Simon and my brothers." She shook her head. "The shit a girl does for the people she loves."

"You are seriously like no one I have ever met."

"I can't wait to introduce you to my other friends. They are going to blow your mind."

I gaped at her, dumbfounded.

"No, seriously, those women scare the shit out of even me. But every girl needs a tribe, right?" Before I could answer, she added, "Now, with you in the mix, I won't be the youngest. You are like a baby. What are you, twenty-four?"

"Umm. Not yet."

"You are the baby. Let's hope they don't put a hit out on Andraius before Simon sets his plans in motion."

I decided to sit down as my mind started to whirl.

Sliding to the floor, I stared up at Nyx. "Why are you being so open with me? I don't understand any of this. Nobody is this free with a person they just met. Just put everything on the table. What do you want from me?"

Nyx approached me and kneeled, her almost black eyes peering into mine. It was as if she saw something in me I wasn't aware of myself or maybe had forgotten about.

Whatever it was, my stomach was uneasy, and I braced for her words.

"Do you know what New York society called me as a teen? Hell, they called me that name until I married Simon."

I nodded. "You were the Mykos Hellion."

"There is no *were* about it. I'm still that same girl. I'm just better at camouflaging it."

"And what does that have to do with me?"

"You are the younger, Boston version of me. My brother Tyler mentioned you years ago, so I had to see for myself. And he was right. You took shit from no one. Didn't they call you the Angel with the tongue like a viper?"

My lips trembled, remembering how Papa had told me to use that name to my advantage, to wield it as a weapon since I'd lead the family one day. He'd said angels brought hope and salvation and destroyed and conquered those who stood in their way.

I swallowed the pain of knowing I'd failed at being who he wanted me to be.

"I'm not her. She died with Papa."

"No. I call bullshit on that sentiment. And I'm going to prove it to you."

I held her gaze. "How?"

"I believe you are hiding plans you don't want anyone to know about."

A roaring echoed into my ears. Who the fuck was this woman?

Instead of giving any reaction, I kept my face emotionless.

"Excellent, emotion control." She quirked her lips, amusement evident on her face. "To achieve your goals, the plan isn't the only thing necessary. You need to learn to defend yourself."

"And you're the person who's going to help me?"

"Yep, with a few friends of mine."

Friends? A shiver slid down my spine. "And you're doing this because I remind you of a younger you?"

"A younger me without the brothers and father to back me up. Though I believe those two protective men you have in my kitchen would step in if asked."

Ignoring the latter part of her answer, I said, "I don't buy it. What do you get out of this?"

"Let's say I get to fuck with a misogynistic system that tried to force me to marry a man for a pot of gold."

My eyes widened. "But you're in love with your husband."

"True. I love that asshole and would cut a bitch for fucking with him. But it doesn't change the fact that he held all the power over whether we married or not and used it to his advantage. I had no say in my future because of a decision made a century before by a group of men."

"Are you saying you hate-fucked each other until you fell in love?"

My thoughts drifted to Theo and how much I'd disliked him and his overbearing ways during high school. Though fucking hadn't been part of anything between us. Well, not until my senior year.

That's when things changed with Xander, as well. The attraction and desire sat as an undercurrent of our friendship, but we never acted upon it. Plus, I was well aware of what Xander and Theo had with each other. Then, one night, in the middle of a volatile argument with Theo with Xander trying to play peacemaker, it all changed.

"It coasted more on the lines of blackmail, but that's a story for another time." The mischievous expression on Nyx's face told me she'd enjoyed the situation she'd found herself in. "Are my ulterior motives for helping you acceptable?"

I stared at her as a war of uncertainty battled inside my mind. Trusting her meant putting so many things in the hands of another person—no, not just one person, but many people.

Then again, at the moment, I had very few people to depend on.

I couldn't second-guess myself now. I'd made the call this morning in the shower.

Tilting my chin up, I responded, "I'm not sure I can trust you, but I don't have other options, do I? So until you prove me wrong, I'll give you the benefit of the doubt."

"You're a smart girl." A voice came from the corner of the room. "Never give anyone blind faith. That's lesson number one."

Adrenaline shot through my system, and my heartbeat hammered in my chest as two women stepped out from the shadows and approached us, one Indian and one tall brunette.

I recognized them immediately. They were Devani King, the Queen of Diamonds, the notorious head of a gem-mining conglomerate, and Lilly King, the daughter of Papa's long-time friend, German mob boss Joseph Lennox.

For years, I'd admired Lilly. She'd had the same role in her family as I had. If she'd stayed in Germany, she'd have become her father's second-in-command. Rumors said she was as ruthless or even more so than her father. However, she'd decided to follow an artistic path.

The two women had married into the King family of New York City, known for playing the mediators between the underworld, i.e., various syndicates, and upper-crust society. Though I'd heard they were as heavily involved in the business as their men.

And from the looks on their faces, something told me everything said about them was probably true.

"I take it you recognize our new arrivals?"

I nodded but kept quiet, watching the ladies approach.

"Nerine, let me introduce you to some new friends. Devani and Lilly. They are going to help me train you. In the next few months, you will learn things you would never have learned in any formal education institution."

"Oh, don't look so scared," Devani King almost purred. "I have a secret to share with you. I'm not the bitchy socialite everyone believes."

"What are you?"

"A girl who was a trained assassin by the time she turned fourteen." She gestured to Lilly. "I taught this one everything she knows. And I'm going to teach you some of the same things."

A shiver shot down my spine. Dear God. What had I gotten myself into?

Then Lilly smiled at me, her stormy eyes taking me in. "I'm going to do for you what your Papa did for mine."

"And that is?"

"Teach you how to run an organization. You need to know how things work whether you take the helm or not. Also"—Lilly tapped her lip—"are you going to turn in your assignment? It was due this morning."

"What assignment?"

I stared into Lilly's stormy gray eyes resembling Theo's.

After a few seconds, I remembered. I'd forgotten to turn in my training module from my mentor.

"You're the hacker?"

"Among other things."

"I think I'm going to be sick." I dropped my head into my lap.

Nyx patted my shoulder. "You're going to be just fine. By the time this is over, you may change your mind about leaving."

"No, that won't happen."

"Then you train, and we'll help make it happen."

Eight

Theo

"Where the fuck is Nyx?" Simon Drakos asked someone from a hallway, making me shift my attention from my laptop as I sat at the long prep table in the kitchen of the Drakos mansion.

This was the space Xander and I had taken over as our workstation nearly every other day over the last few weeks. Since the sunroom or whatever they called it was off-limits, we decided to get as much work done as possible during the three to four hours we spent here.

Something in my gut told me this set-up would be coming to an end.

"Why would I know this? I'm your keeper, not hers. You're the one who left her unattended for nearly a month and a half.

Knowing her, she's probably running an underground poker game right now in one of your ballrooms."

I smirked, hearing Drakos's second-in-command, Kasen Alexandros, answer. The fact Simon hadn't killed him years ago for giving him shit right and left spoke volumes about the level of their relationship. Beyond being first cousins, they were the closest friends and told each other the truth, no matter how brutal. It was on a level with how Xander and I dealt with each other.

"You're lucky that you're still alive, asshole."

"No, you're lucky you're still alive because of me. Ask Nyx, and she'll back me up. And remember, you're the asshole."

As they turned around the corner entering the kitchen, both men abruptly stopped.

"Want to tell me why the fuck you are sitting here as if it's teatime?"

I glanced at Xander, who shrugged his shoulders, and then back at Simon before answering, "Your wife has Nerine sequestered in the solarium until six o'clock."

"Doing what?" He moved closer to me.

"Training. The same thing Nyx and Nerine have done every other day for the last five weeks." Xander closed the lid to his computer and studied Simon.

"Training on what?" The clenching of Simon's jaw and the flash of concern in his green eyes had the hairs on the back of my neck standing up.

"What do you mean what? I don't know—plants, flowers, whatever she needs to learn for the botanical garden project."

"First of all, the plants she needs work with are at the

botanical gardens in the city. Hence the reason for keeping Nerine away from her house if anything went down. And second—" Simon set his hands on the long table and loomed over us. "Are you saying you didn't even go in the room to see what they have been doing for weeks?"

"Your security team barred us from the room," I countered. "We don't need to be with her every second of every day."

Simon shot Kas a look over his shoulder and then shook his head. "Just once, I'd like for her to let me know she planned to do it her way."

"In her defense, you probably would have tried to stop her." Kas's response garnered an angry scowl.

"Want to loop us in on this plan? And its effect on what we've discussed?" Xander's tone broached no argument, telling me his temper simmered, readying to blow.

If Simon were playing some game behind our backs with Nerine and kept us out of the loop, not only would Xander lose it, I'd punch the motherfucker in the face.

"Keep your shit together. Nothing has changed with what I have in the works for the fake Angelos. We have everyone nearly in place." He held my gaze. "Could have used your assistance with some of the discussions in Athens, but as you are playing bodyguard, I guess it's forgivable."

I held in the urge to tell him to fuck off.

I wasn't under his umbrella and held no loyalty to his family. Still, his backing and power would give back Nerine her empire.

"So what have you decided to do with the angel behind our

backs?" Xander asked, the irritation still very evident on his features.

Drakos lifted a brow in Xander's direction, giving him the not-so-subtle indication that he needed to toe the line of respect. The shit Xander pulled with Andraius would never work with this one.

Kas answered, breaking the tension. "Nyx believed it was time to teach Nerine how to defend herself. Having Nerine help Nyx with the botanical garden project was a cover. However, his goddess decided to move up the timeline of the plan without telling him why."

"Let's go find out what she's been up to." Simon continued to glare at Xander, who still hadn't backed down. "Xander, I understand your feelings about her, but remember who I am. Our history won't stop me from knocking some sense into you."

As if the words snapped him out of the haze of anger, Xander nodded. "I apologize."

"I should let Theios Alex do it. He'd probably have you scrubbing toilets," Simon said as he strode to the hallway leading toward the solarium.

I noticed Xander visibly grimacing, knowing that was what would happen if Theios Alex got wind of Xander mouthing off to our most prominent ally.

"We're going to go in through the back. Make sure to keep your voice down. This way, my goddess won't be aware of our presence until after the session."

"Stevie will know the second we enter the room," Kas observed.

"That's her job. The point is to stay out of the way until they finish."

Simon led us through a set of double doors leading out onto a terrace and then to a movable glass wall that he shifted to the side.

We all stepped inside and stood behind a lattice covered in thick ivy.

"You've gotten damn good with the balance." Nyx complimented Nerine as they stood in the middle of what looked to be a giant training mat in the center of the room. "Remember to use that to your advantage."

Then someone else added, "It will give you time to counter an attack because your opponent will be too busy thinking they can get a surprise attack on you."

I tried to scan the room to see who spoke, but the woman was in the shadows.

"For the love of God," Simon muttered and gripped the back of his neck. "She has her involved in this? Fuck me."

"Your idea of jumping in to help her is screwed, cousin," Kas responded in a hushed tone and patted Simon on the shoulder.

I looked between the two men. Who was that woman? And why was she a problem?

As if hearing my thoughts, Kas whispered, "Devani King."

He couldn't be serious. Was he even aware of the woman's true identity? Yeah, she may have married into the notorious King brothers' underworld family. However, she was deadlier than anyone around her. Devani was a trained child assassin who proudly wore her reputation of eliminating anyone who got in her way without a backward glance as a medal of honor. I'd only discovered the tidbit of information while visiting an underground poker club in New York.

If Nyx was going to find someone to train Nerine, of course she'd bring in a woman classified as a deadly weapon.

Simon shook his head. "I swear, I'm going to tan Nyx's ass red."

"Did you forget you're the darkness to her night? She likes all that kinky shit you throw her way."

Simon glared at Kas.

I glanced at Xander and resisted the urge to laugh. Simon rarely, if ever, showed a less-than-serious side. Well, except when Nyx or Kas was around. And even that had its limits.

"What the fuck are you two smirking at?"

Xander answered, "The fact you two sound like us. It's refreshing."

"I'm surrounded by assholes." Simon stepped around the ivy and leaned against the wall, making it so anyone who looked in our direction would catch sight of him but keeping it from being obvious.

"Let's go through another round, and then I have a present for you." Nyx rubbed her hands together before picking up a wooden box and lifting the lid.

"You've already had a turn with her. I'm up."

"Are you kidding me, Devani?" Nerine exclaimed. "You'll kick my ass. Last time I could barely sit and had to make up some bullshit about missing a step on a ladder and landing on my butt."

Devani came into view, wearing a pair of workout shorts

and a fitted top, the same outfit Nerine had on. Both women were barefooted, and they circled each other.

"You did land on your butt quite a bit. You kept forgetting height isn't always an advantage. It's the way you handle your body."

"I was trying to keep you from stabbing me. It wasn't a death match, and you acted like it was."

"The best way to learn is if you feel the fear, causing the adrenaline spikes, which forces you to conquer it. I don't want you to freeze if someone attacks you." Devani shrugged and then pivoted. Nerine seemed to expect it and shifted her movement to counter Devani's.

"My two bodyguards knew I was lying through my teeth."

Xander nudged me with his elbow and said in a low tone, "Told you. I even said she was walking as if she had some sparring injury."

Devani pursed her lips. "I'm going to need to teach you how to lie. Fuck. You're too damn pure to be a mob princess."

"Mob wife," Nyx corrected.

"With any luck, that's only a temporary situation." Devani tapped her chin. "Okay, young one. Let's see how this knife wielder has done with your training."

"Well, at least I know from the beginning that you're going for a death match, so I'm ready for pain." Nerine took two weapons from the box Nyx held, inspecting each blade.

Devani selected her deadly instruments. "I'm happy you're thinking ahead."

When the match started, they went straight at it. No preamble, no "go," no nothing. Just a straight-on attack.

Devani charged for Nerine and slid to the floor, ready to slice at her shin. Immediately, Nerine pivoted and jabbed to the left, barely missing Devani's shoulder as she made some back-bend-like move to avoid the hit.

"Holy—" Xander attempted to charge toward them, but Simon grabbed his forearm and covered his mouth.

"Quiet, asshole," Simon whispered. "You're going to stay right here."

When Xander relaxed and made it clear he'd keep his ass with us, Simon released him and spoke in a hushed voice. "For some reason, Nyx has involved people outside our circle in Nerine's care. My wife always has a reason for everything. Devani King is one of the most dangerous women in the world, and if she is willing to take Nerine on as a pupil, she is vested in her. So don't look a gift horse in the mouth."

"Meaning?" I asked, matching my tone to Simon's.

"First, answer this question. Why are you doing all of this? What is it you want after we dethrone the imposter? Are one of you planning to take the helm?"

My temper flared. "You know damn well that's not the plan."

"Then clarify it. The two of you are too invested in Nerine for it to be just about putting the true heir in the seat."

I kept quiet and stared at Nerine as she trekked all over the mat with Devani, countering and then attacking with various offensive moves. She was no match for the assassin but had some basic skills down to keep her from being an easy target.

"Do you think I haven't picked up on the truth by not verbalizing it?" Simon pressed. "All the clues say the two of you had something with her. And for all of your sakes, no one better catch wind of it."

"Nothing is going on. We watch out for her best interests. She will take the helm." Xander's words may have come out quiet and almost low enough to be a whisper, but the way he held Simon's gaze as he spoke, he was daring Simon to challenge his statement.

"She can't take anything if those around the table see her as weak. It doesn't matter if you are her muscle. Everyone would believe the two of you as the true heads behind the face."

"Is that what all of this is about? You went behind our backs to train her to give her credibility?"

"That was the original intent." Kas spoke this time. "However, it looks as if Nyx went behind all of our backs and brought in someone better suited to accomplish this goal."

That's when I noticed Simon and Nyx were holding each other's gazes as if they were amid an unsaid conversation.

Then I caught Xander staring at me, and he lifted a brow and mouthed, "Let's get out of here. We need to have a chat."

I nodded but turned to watch the women sparring for a few moments more. Then as Nerine reset for another round, Devani King lifted her focus up to where we stood and cocked a brow.

It looked as if the only one unaware of our presence was our Angel.

She was in good hands. And these women could give her everything we couldn't—a connection, friendship, belonging.

I thought about everything I knew about Nyx. She'd grown up with a father and four brothers who treated her as an equal, and according to rumors, she'd learned her skills with weapons from her eldest brother, Tyler.

Then there was Devani King. Outside of the fucked-up assassin thing, which I'd yet to figure out the origin story behind, she ran a cutthroat billion-dollar diamond and precious gem conglomerate. If there was anyone who knew how to wheel and deal in a world dominated by misogynism, she did.

Releasing a deep breath, I turned and walked out of the sliding glass door, not caring if anyone followed. But of course, Xander had, and to my surprise, Simon and Kas trailed behind him.

We remained quiet until we returned to the kitchen, then Simon said, "Gentlemen, as of this moment, our business dealings have concluded. Our original plan will go forward. You keep the Angelos women alive and their organization operational. I will do my part to keep others from encroaching on their interests."

"And we will continue to play interference while the Angelos Angel gains her wings back using the Assassin Squad," Xander stated.

"Oh, that was a very astute guess on the name we call ourselves," Devani cooed as she strolled through the hallway leading from the solarium with Nyx and Nerine with her.

The women wore their workout gear and hadn't changed into their day clothing, making it clear that all were aware of our imposing on their training session.

Simon moved directly toward Nyx, stopping right in front of her. "Goddess, we will discuss this."

"I'm sure we will." She lifted a brow and then set a hand on his chest. "How was Greece?"

I shifted my attention to Nerine, who stood behind Nyx. Her focus teetered between Xander and me. The intensity in her dark blue gaze as she clutched an ornate box under her arm completely different from the one with the weapons from her training session. The way she held it made me wonder what was inside.

The apprehension and uncertainty radiating from her pulled at something in me and made me want to shake her and demand how she could still doubt us.

We'd settle this on our way back to the compound.

"Are you ready to head home?" I asked her.

She wiped the sweat from her brow and licked her lips. "Yes."

"Before you take my pupil away, I want a word with the two of you." Devani approached us, handing me a paper. "Here is her schedule. To keep the charade of the botanical garden, Nerine is well-versed in the terminology and will take care of her studies. As for you, gentlemen, your assignment is to supplement her learning with your specialties. Those details are also listed."

Xander pulled the note from my fingers and read.

A crease formed between his brows as he turned to Devani. "Mrs. King, this is quite a bit of knowledge you've procured about us. May I ask who provided it?"

"I never reveal my sources. All you need to know is that you wouldn't have made it back stateside if the intel provider didn't like you." The deadly glint in her black eyes held a warning mixed in with the information.

It looked as if she wielded a lot of power in the organization that had turned her into a living, breathing weapon.

During my year in Europe, I learned that these institutions worked deep underground and recruited their members at a young age. They used an indoctrination of sorts, similar to a cult, where they trained in every combat and mind manipulation possible.

"We don't need threats to protect Nerine." Xander's ability to remain calm had utterly disappeared, and I knew it was time for me to step in.

"Mrs. King, we will do our part and play interference with all necessary parties. Thank you for your time with the Angelos Angel."

A smirk touched Devani's lips. "Very diplomatic of you, Mr. Nephus. You're good at playing interference."

"He's had years of practice," Xander said. "What agency do you work for, Mrs. King?"

"She's the Queen of Diamonds. She runs a gem empire. Everyone in the world knows this," Nerine answered from behind me, and the smug satisfaction on Devani's lips had me shaking my head.

This was just great. In a matter of weeks, she'd managed a master level of influence on Nerine.

"If I were you, I'd get ready for her to do everything in her power to push your buttons, gentlemen."

I resisted the urge to glance in Nerine's direction.

Instead of giving Devani my thoughts on her perdition, I inclined my head. "It is time to return Mrs. Angelos home."

We walked silently to the car, with Nerine between Xander and me. She kept her gaze forward, saying nothing. The steady stream of tension radiating off her said she expected us to demand an explanation.

Once we started our drive back, I waited for Nerine to begin the conversation. However, when I glanced in the back seat, I found her fast asleep, clutching the ornate box against her chest.

Nine

erine

Unbelievable.

That was the only word that came to my mind the second I lifted the lid of the case. Nyx had given me two black metal blades, etched with intricate designs, nestled inside a plush housing. Wood and steel made up the hilts, and if I wasn't mistaken, jewels, maybe sapphires, rubies, and diamonds.

Pulling one out, I studied the handle.

OMG, these were authentic gems. Were these women nuts? They wanted me to practice with knives that had actual diamonds in them. I had to be living in some alternate universe.

That's when I noticed a small lever in the box and tugged.

Underneath sat another collection of weapons, knives of various sizes, two guns, a pickaxe-looking thing, a few other items I couldn't identify, and a note.

No, we don't expect you to learn with jeweled weapons. Give us some credit. That's a showpiece.

You'll practice with the items below. Talk to your bodyguards between lessons if you have any questions. They have instructions. And keep up your studies.

-N&D

I couldn't help but smile seeing the initials for Nyx and Devani. It was fitting since all three of my teachers, including Lilly, were known for wielding a weapon to deliver a deadly message.

I stared at the small arsenal the women had provided me, and a sense of apprehension and awe filled me.

This was actually happening. In the last several weeks, I'd not only started to learn to defend myself but also to believe I could truly pull off my escape.

I wasn't sure when or how it would happen, but my gut said soon.

Yeah, there were people all around me playing their games. I knew it, felt it, and saw it—with Simon Drakos, Xander and Theo, and even the ladies.

But the difference with the ladies was that they had nothing to gain but to help a victimized woman regain her strength and thumb her nose at the world that had taken everything from her.

I sighed. Was I getting carried away and being too trusting and naive?

Well, a girl had to have hope.

I slid the jeweled blades back into place, closed the case, and then hid the entire thing in a secret compartment inside a sliding baseboard panel near the side of my bed.

This house held so many passageways and hidey holes. Very few of the hidden corridors connected to each other, so if a person discovered one, it wouldn't necessarily lead them to others.

The only people currently alive who knew about them all were Theios Alex, my sisters, and Mama. Xander and Theo had learned of the passageways when we were younger but never traveled them to the level I had or could walk them blindfolded as I'd done for the fun of it as a child.

Keeping the weapons case from prying eyes was paramount. This gift meant so much to me.

It symbolized the start of my transition from the girl who'd shattered into pieces to the one who planned to create a new life for herself, her mother, and her sisters.

Deep down, I knew Papa would understand.

Maybe what I wanted was to run away, but I thought I'd earned it. My life here meant I was a commodity. My value came in my body, my name.

As if sensing my train of thoughts, Andraius appeared between the threshold of his bedroom and mine, watching me, lust glazing his eyes.

I released an internal sigh.

Here we went. For the next four nights, he'd fuck me to acquire this baby I'd never let come into the world.

But first, the small talk.

Time to slide on my bitch cloak, or I'd throw up the second he touched me. I should have downed a few shots of ouzo or something, and then maybe this would go easier.

"How are the lessons going with Nyx?" Andraius asked and stared at me with this disgusting interest that made me want to gag and punch him simultaneously.

"Fun. I like Nyx. I may take up some of her ideas for the gardens here."

He studied me as if he thought I was full of it. "What kind of flowers are you interested in planting?"

"Low-maintenance greenery is a better option this late in the season, and then we can consider things for the spring that won't suffer shock with the upcoming cold cycles."

He considered me for a few seconds as if he were seeing a different woman.

Yes, asshole, I do know a thing or two about plants. It was part of my training.

"I was concerned about this association with Drakos's wife, but now I think it's the best type of influence that could have happened to you."

I shrugged. "As I said, I like Nyx and am learning a lot from her. It is nice to have a friend to visit."

"So there isn't any truth to the rumors about her obsession with knives?"

Oh, you mean like the fact she wears one strapped to the

inside of her thigh wherever she goes, and it was given to her by her husband?

"Umm, no," I said, giving him a frown. "Outside of the ones used to prune plants, I haven't seen anything. Besides, gossip is a waste of time. I'd rather give people the benefit of the doubt, wouldn't you?"

He ignored my question and asked, "And what about Drakos? Does he spend much time at the estate?"

"He was in Greece until today. We left around the time he arrived. I believe he wanted us out of the way so he could be alone with Nyx. They are a very affectionate couple."

"You don't know anything. Drakos wanted your security to be out of the house so that they wouldn't spy on him. I can't believe Peter thought you could run the family. You don't have the mind for it."

Ignoring the jab, I decided chitchat time was over.

I cocked my hand on my hip and asked, "Are we doing this? I want to go read otherwise."

"If that is how you want it. Most couples do talk about their lives."

"Couples that have actual relationships or want to be around each other talk. It's not as if you even know how to make me come. Let's just do the deed."

"Fine, remove your robe, and I'll do the deed, as you put it."

With no regrets, I tugged off my robe, revealing the negligee underneath that accentuated the handiwork he'd sculpted into my body. Andraius's face grew red, and he clenched his fists.

"You wore that on purpose."

"What, you don't like seeing how you cherish your wife? I thought this piece of lingerie displayed my body beautifully. I've started a new workout routine. I'm more toned than ever. Can you tell?" I pivoted side to side as if I were modeling for him.

With a vicious glare, he unbelted his robe, loosened the drawstring of his pajama pants, and came in my direction. "Turn around and put your hands on the bed."

I stood in place.

"I thought you enjoyed me on my back, so you can ensure your cum goes how it's supposed to go."

He stalked toward me, shoving me onto the bed and turning me onto my stomach. "Shut up and just do as I say."

Then he pushed my face into the mattress and pulled my ass into the air.

"Oh, so we are fucking in here. Not in your room where it is my duty to conceive the next heir? Wow, we're breaking all the rules tonight."

"What has come over you?"

"The same thing as always. I hate you."

He jerked my hips up, and I expected him to ram his cock into me, but instead, he pushed away from me.

"You fucking bitch. I hate you just as much."

I turned and saw his dick lying limp.

Immediately, I burst into laughter as if what I saw was the funniest thing in the world, rolled off the bed, and pointed at him.

"Maybe you should go with the idea of in vitro. How do

you plan to impregnate me if your dick doesn't cooperate every time you come to rape me?"

"It isn't raping you if we're married."

"It is when I didn't give you consent, asshole. I didn't consent to marry you. I didn't consent to fuck you. I still don't. It only happens because you hold my mother's and sisters' lives in your hands."

"And what about yours? Don't you care about your life?"

"I don't give a fuck about me. Besides, we've already gone through this. Your threat of killing me isn't going to work. You need me alive to hold on to this family. You have no valid claim to the seat without a true Angelos at your side."

"You still have sisters, don't forget."

"Oh please, Christina and Ariana are seventeen. And in this fantasy where you force one of the twins to marry you, I should let you know that if you think I'm a bitch, you haven't seen those two in action. They will set your balls on fire without spilling a drop of their coffee. And of course, forcing anything on Fi would make you a pedophile. That's a big no-no even in the syndicate world."

"You have all the answers, don't you?"

"Not even close. If I did, I wouldn't be half naked with a man who can't even get his dick hard."

"And who exactly would you be with?"

"Not you." I reached for my robe and shrugged it on. "Are we done, or do I need you to take a pill to make it work?"

He stalked toward me, grabbed me by the throat, and lifted me off the ground.

I clutched at his hand, raking my fingers across his flesh,

drawing blood as he blocked all air from entering my lungs. My mind clouded as my consciousness waned at the edges.

Andraius brought me toward his face, his alcohol-laced breath coasting over me. "I hate you even more than you hate me. All I want is a child, and then we don't have to see each other again."

He threw me on the floor, and I instinctively rolled to the side, ready to avoid a kick. The whole time, I gasped and coughed.

"You don't even know the meaning of hate," I choked out through labored breaths. "And you're the problem, not me. Ask the doctors you love so much."

"If that's the way you want it. Have it your way. I'm going to prove you a fucking liar. And while we're at it, let them do everything. This way, I don't have to touch you. The last thing I want to do is fuck a venom-filled whore. How you got any man to fuck you in the first place is beyond me."

I kept my mouth shut even though I wanted to taunt him more, say all kinds of things that had built in me for years. But, thankfully, through some warped luck of fate, he'd washed his hands of me.

His dream of fertility treatments would never come to fruition. They took time and patience. I'd make sure to draw everything out by months and months.

He wouldn't touch me anymore. The bastard wouldn't touch me anymore. Dizziness engulfed my head as nausea flooded my gut.

Pushing to my feet, I rushed to the bathroom and barely reached the toilet before I let everything empty from my stomach. I grabbed a towel, wiped my mouth, and leaned against a wall.

Tilting my head up, I gasped up at the decorative ceiling through wet eyes. I wiped at them and realized more tears streamed down my cheeks, now flowing free as if a dam had broken.

A sob escaped my lips, and I covered my face with my hands as the heartache and pain of the last few years flooded over me in pounding, overwhelming waves. I'd refused to cry for so long that my body needed to purge everything once I freed them.

I wasn't sure how long I sat on the floor. I only knew that my lungs burned, and I couldn't allow myself to lock away my emotions to this level ever again. It only gave Andraius more power over me.

After a quick shower and a change of clothes, I went back into my room and glanced at the now closed door of Andraius's room. Suddenly, laughter bubbled up from my chest.

I'd let that bastard break me. But it looked as if I'd fucked him up, too.

In my defeat, in my not giving a fuck about anything, I'd chipped away at that man's biggest flaw.

His ego.

I took a deep, almost relieving breath for the first time in a long time. A wave of something settled over me. Determination? Or was it just a certainty that I would get out of this?

Moving to the windows overlooking the front of the

house, I pushed back the curtains just in time to see a fleet of four cars as they drove away from the property.

Most heads of families preferred anonymity when out and about, knowing the less attention they received, the safer. Andraius obviously missed that directive. But, then again, if he allowed himself to become a target, we were all free of him.

Baby steps, Nerine. At least he won't touch you again. Hopefully.

Maybe he'd have better luck rising to the occasion with one of his special lady friends. I turned on my heel, went to my closet, grabbed a thick robe, belted it around myself, and then slipped on plush slippers. Then I moved to the wall next to the fireplace housing the hidden panel for the passageway leading to the library.

I had some studying to do. Online classes and self-learning worked when I'd had no choice, but having one-on-one instruction hands-down was no comparison. The system Lilly had created for me blew away my mind and pushed me to a level I never thought I'd reach.

I still couldn't believe that for the past year and a half, I'd had Lilly as my mentor and hadn't a clue. Then again, over the last few weeks, I'd learned that one of Lilly's aliases was on the most-wanted lists of six continents.

She was such a badass. All the women were.

They were also ultra-feminists and a bit unconventional when it came to getting me up to speed on what they called "fighting the patriarchy." No matter how often I told them I had no plans to take over the family, they insisted I do the crash course they dubbed Syndicate 101. And with Lilly as the primary teacher, there was no getting out of loads of homework assignments.

She wanted me prepared for every possible situation, and her mock trials, as I like to call them, were sometimes over-the-top and harshly realistic.

She'd gone as far as having me reevaluate the coup from five years ago and how I'd handle the situation now.

About two weeks ago, I'd stopped questioning everyone's motives and just accepted the women's quirky personalities and how they were vested in me.

On the flip side, they'd stopped trying to convince me that I'd change my mind about escaping. Instead, the more they got to know me, the more they understood my demons and why I had to take my family and disappear.

Unless a miracle happened, I'd use the escape plan I'd coordinated with my hacker mentor, who turned out to be Lilly.

What happened after I left? Who knew? It couldn't be worse than all I'd endured in the last near five years.

I stepped into the pitch-black tunnel, closed the wall behind me, and let my years of navigating the paths direct me to my destination.

Once there, I felt for the latch that unlocked the opening into the library. From an early age, Papa taught us girls to keep all the pathways that gave access to our rooms locked from the inside of our bedrooms with a special key. This way, only we could get in and out.

Thank God, Andraius knew nothing about any of the passageways. Otherwise, he'd have kept me even more trapped than I'd already been. Plus, I'd drilled it into my sisters' heads never use the hallways if anyone was around, so there wasn't any risk of mistakes. If one of us forgot to close one panel tight, then everyone would learn our secrets.

The moment I pushed the deadbolt to the side, a whoosh of warm air surged into the passageway, and I tugged the wall on its hinge back only enough to fit my body.

The second I stepped through, a hand grabbed my arm, turned me, and pinned me to a bookcase.

"I knew it. You're using the secret passageways to get through this house. That's how you keep sneaking past the team and me." Xander glowered at me, and then his gaze went to my neck, turning his features into a mask of rage. "What the fuck happened to your neck?"

Ten

ander

I stared at Nerine's neck, seeing the distinctive marks of what only came from fingers wrapped around a throat. And from the looks of it, someone had dug their nails so deep that she'd nearly lost consciousness.

No. Not someone. Andraius.

"I'm going to kill that bastard. What the hell was he thinking?"

I stepped back as a throbbing ignited in my temple. I had to pull back the temptation to call in a favor to put a hit on the fucker tonight as Andraius paraded around town with his entourage.

Her gaze held mine as she traced the skin down her throat. "Tell me again that you were keeping me safe."

If she wanted to stab me right now, I'd lower myself to my knees and let her do it.

Would I always be too fucking late to protect her?

"Ang—"

"I told you never to call me that." She dropped her hand and lifted her chin. "I don't need your safe. I'm finding a way without the two of you."

"We have a plan. We're trying."

"It's not mine."

"So that is it? Nothing we said to you matters? What about the fact that we love you?"

Our interactions over the last few weeks had been civil and almost pleasant—no more animosity or arguments. We continued giving each other space and rarely were alone with Nerine. The pressure of it pushed against all the emotions we'd kept at bay.

This whole time I believed she understood, even if she hadn't forgiven us, that we'd left for a reason, that it was either she lived or died. We never stopped loving her and would wait for her in the end.

But now, I wasn't sure.

She cocked her head to the side. "You want me, knowing another man is fucking me? That he is actively trying to get me pregnant?"

I hated the thought of that piece of shit touching her, doing anything with her.

"Why don't you tell me if it is something you want? Is it something you choose? Is it something you desire and enjoy?"

"What does it matter? I'm married. There is no future for me until I escape this marriage."

"Then Theo and I will wait until that time comes."

"You don't even know what escape means for me."

"Do you hate us so much, Angel?"

I expected her to reprimand me about calling her Angel again, but she shook her head and said, "No, I don't hate you. I wanted to, but in the end, I couldn't do it."

"What can we do to get you to forgive us?"

"I'm not sure yet. For now, stop talking about anything but the present. Yes, we have our past. There is no changing that." She closed her eyes, and for the briefest of seconds, I believed she'd let herself break and cry as she'd done when we were younger and allow me to hold her.

I'd been the one she came to for comfort, the one she shared all her emotions with. Theo had been the one to help her think, give her ideas, and help her plot.

"However, you and Theo are my protection. Nothing more. I can't cross that line. Ever. I could be the stupidest fucking person in the world, considering everything that happened. Still, I trust the two of you."

I clenched my jaw and opened my mouth to counter her statement, but she lifted her hand to stay me and continued, "This whole thing with Nyx, Lilly, and Devani is my thing, and I know you will help me. I don't know where it will lead, but it gives me hope. That's all I have for the first time in a long time. I need that."

"We'll give you anything you need."

"Would you let me go?"

She had to be kidding me.

"What are you talking about, Nerine?" Theo asked from his position in the back corner of the room.

The startled expression on Nerine's face made it very clear she hadn't seen him sitting on the armchair by the window.

"I hate it when you do that shit," she shouted at him. "Why can't you announce your presence like a normal person? What the hell is wrong with you? I told you this when we were kids, and I'm telling you now. It's creepy as fuck. You're a grown man. Act like one."

She cocked a hand on her hip and glowered at Theo. Her sapphire blue eyes sparkled with irritation, and a crease formed between her brows. She'd utterly transformed into the girl I'd fallen for in my youth, the fiery viper ready to punch someone in the face.

"Oh, so she is in there." Theo rose from his seat. "I wondered when the real Nerine planned to make an appearance."

"Who the fuck are you talking to? I swear to God, you make me want to punch you."

"The bratty angel with a vicious tongue. Those company manners you kept throwing at us, where you pretended to be nice. We asked you to behave, not cloak yourself in that facade you wear for the public. We want the real Nerine. This mask was starting to get on my nerves."

"I'll show you who's getting on whose nerves, you overgrown jackass." She moved toward him, and at the same time,

Theo stalked toward her. "I'm going to punch you in that smug face."

"Give it your best shot, brat."

I blew out a breath. This was about to get out of hand. I hated being the diplomat. In the past, I'd let them fuck it out, and then I'd get the sweet, compliant version of my Angel, who'd do whatever I told her.

However, since that was nowhere near an option, the Universe had decided that my job was to play interference.

I stretched my hands out in both directions, one shoving Theo back hard, though he came right back at me, and the other gently set against Nerine's chest.

"The two of you need to settle down. I get it. We have too much history, feel too much, and want too much. No matter how much I wish we could, we can't handle this as we used to." I blew out a deep breath and then added, "When the fuck did I become the logical one?"

As if my words sent a surge of energy around us, Theo and Nerine stilled, taking in everything I said.

All our unsteady breaths filled the air, as did the presence of undisguised arousal and need. The buildup from the multitude of days pulsed between us as if it were a living thing.

My cock strained to a painful level, and I had no doubt Theo stood in the same state.

The drive to slide my hand up the column of Nerine's neck, kiss those bruises, ease her discomfort, and then tug her mouth to mine pulled at every ounce of my control.

This woman at my fingertips, so close but untouchable.

The heat of her skin branded me, making me crave relief I knew wouldn't come anytime soon.

The way Theo's body shook as he resisted the same urges pumping in my system gave me some semblance of comfort. We fought the same battle for self-control.

I turned my head, holding his gaze. His pupils dilated.

The draw for him tugged at me as much as the call for Nerine. This complicated mess with the three of us overflowed with loss and need.

Our woman belonged to a man we hated. Because of my stupidity, Theo and I had a boundary between us we couldn't cross.

This was so fucked up.

After another minute, Nerine shifted back, dropping her head and looking away.

Through unsteady breaths, she whispered, "If only I hated you two. Then things would be so much easier. I…I…"

Wrapping her robe around her tighter, she moved to the farthest set of sofas in the room, took a seat on a chaise, and tucked her feet under her body.

She watched us with unsettled cobalt eyes as Theo and I followed her cues, taking the two armchairs near us.

"Answer my question, Nerine," Theo directed when it became clear Nerine wouldn't say anything unless we probed. "And don't be a smartass. You know what I'm talking about."

She narrowed her gaze, and I prepared for more of what had occurred, but to my surprise, she gave him what he wanted. "The escape I want means freedom from this life.

You're engrained in this life. Therefore, you're not part of that freedom."

The hell we weren't.

"You want us to prove our love for you by letting you go?" I asked.

Before she could answer, Theo said, "No. How do we let you go after all of this?" He gestured to the room around him. "I sacrificed my dignity. I teamed up with that fucking loser of a boss. I lost my family. You're the reason for all of this."

"Nothing will bring Papa, Linus, Theios Mik, or any of your brothers back. And do you see me having any credibility taking the seat after what Andraius did to me? I have no power."

"You'll have us by your side," I reminded her.

"First of all, I don't want it. Second, the minute Andraius's body is in the ground, vultures will circle to take his place. And they will use the same methods to force me into another marriage."

"We would never let that happen again." The vein on Theo's forehead pulsed, telling me things were about to escalate.

"Maybe." She shrugged, pursing her lips at Theo, and then glanced at me. "I'm not going to chance it."

"It's your birthright. Your sisters' birthrights."

"As women, do we truly have birthrights? Papa wanted to change things. But he is gone. My commodity is in my genetics, my bloodline. It's my womb everyone wants. I'm nothing but a broodmare for the next bastard who wants to take on the Angelos name."

"Don't talk about yourself like that." I glared at her. "You know that is not how we see you."

Ignoring me, she looked up at the painted ceiling and mused, "If I'd been born a boy, I'd probably be dead, just like Linus. Well, no. Papa would have trained me from birth to run the family, and more than likely, none of this would have happened."

"Where are you going with this, Nerine?"

"Oh, we're using my name. It isn't Angel anymore? I must be getting on your nerves, Theo." She scowled at him. "My point is, without power, there isn't a reason to take the seat. I don't want it. My sisters don't want it. The twins want to go into art and design, and at the moment, Fiona wants to study aerospace. If I get my way, they will have their dreams come true."

"You'd let the family fall?" I asked, surprised by her desire to leave everything behind.

"If it means an escape for my mother, sisters, and me, yes."

"I promise, we won't let you down ever again. We aren't the stupid kids we were before."

She released a deep sigh. "Xander, are you even listening to me?"

"I hear every word you're saying. I don't want you to regret your decisions later." I scraped a hand down my face, knowing agreeing to her decision was the only way to reach any middle ground. "Negotiate with me, Angel."

"Here is my compromise. Promise to let me go, and in return, in the unlikely event someone unseats Andraius in my name"—she smirked as if that statement sounded farfetched—

"the two of you hold the family for the Angelos women. That is, until someone finds us if they can. Isn't there a saying, *no body, no death*?"

I glanced at Theo, and he'd also caught the "that is, until someone finds us" part.

"Are you planning to disappear?"

She lifted a brow and gave a noncommittal shrug. "As of now, it's only a dream. A fantasy about freedom, a life away from the one I know."

"How long have you had your plan in the works?" Theo studied her as he would an opponent for tells, readying for a lie.

"For four years, eleven months, and eighteen days."

Since the day of the coup.

"Why are you telling us all of this?"

"Theo, because the idiot part of me believes the two of you still love me. Now I'm trusting you to follow my wishes. You broke my faith in you once, and I'll never forgive you if you do it again."

"Do you still love us?" Theo asked.

Was he even aware of the unguarded hope he'd revealed in his question?

"I'm not sure what I feel. I don't hate you. I won't lie and say I'm not attracted to the two of you. But love." She released a deep breath, glancing down at her lap momentarily. "I feel something. It's more wrapped in memories and thoughts. A bit of sadness, longing, all the things I want to keep locked away."

I took in her features as she lost herself in her thoughts. We'd fucked up so badly with her. We'd been kids ourselves, following the orders of my father, who wanted only to protect us. Now, I wasn't sure if it had been the right call.

She wanted to leave with her sisters and mother, believing there wouldn't be an all-out hunt for the missing wife and daughters of a slain and beloved boss. Not to mention, hiding five women with features like theirs was virtually impossible. Outside of the fact they looked like replicas of their mother, the Angelos daughters had inherited Theios Peter's midnight black hair and sapphire blue eyes.

"Okay, Angel." A slight curve to Theo's lips said he'd used the name to needle Nerine. "Let's say we agree to let you go. Will you play nice in the meantime?"

"Will you do the same?"

The undercurrent of what she asked had the room going quiet again. The sexual energy the three of us shared never seemed to wane. It remained a constant pulsing beat, sometimes drumming harder and at others, slow and steady.

"Let's agree not to push each other's buttons. We can't afford to fall into those patterns."

Nerine nodded and then focused on me. "And you? I can't have you doing that thing you do."

"What thing?"

She released a frustrated breath and said, "You are my security only, my bodyguard. You aren't my confidant, my counselor. I won't turn to you for comfort. So you have to stop waiting for me to come to you. It isn't going to happen."

Her observation hit me like a ton of bricks. She'd felt the weight of my longing, the need to take her pain and hold her as I'd done in the past.

"I can't change how I feel, even for you. But I hear what you're saying. I know there are lines we can't cross."

"Okay," she whispered, her fingertips drifting over the marks on her neck again, and the rage I felt toward Andraius grew by leaps and bounds.

Instead of letting my mind linger on my hatred for that shit, I asked, "Do we have a deal?"

"On a few conditions."

I leaned forward, resting my arms on my knees. "And they are?"

"Number one. I want access to all information about Angelos operations."

I cocked my head to the side. "You said you didn't want to take the seat."

"For now, I want to know how the two of you are running my family business." Her lips curved at the corners. "Do you honestly believe I didn't know? As Papa said, one isn't a leader if they don't get in the trenches. Andraius doesn't even try to get his hands dirty."

"What do you want with the information?" Theo's curiosity matched mine. "Is there something you're looking for?"

"Whether I take over or not, I have to learn. I can't let others tell me how to handle things and trust they are telling me the truth. This is the plight of too many women in the world."

"Is this another of Nyx and Devani's lessons?"

"No, it's a hands-on lesson I learned over the last five years. Papa trusted me with everything and gave me access to every aspect of his empire. But he never taught his beloved wife the basics of their finances. So when Papa died, Mama went from complete financial dependence to uncertainty. If I hadn't had access to Papa's accounts, I wouldn't have been able to transfer any of the money out before Andraius got hold of the logins."

"I had a suspicion you were the mastermind behind draining the funds into Swiss accounts. How did you know to do that?"

"Papa. He always had a backup for everything." She looked between me and Theo. "I have a right to know how things operate. Papa never got to teach me the full extent of his plans. I'm tired of being helpless. The last few weeks have reminded me of all I let go."

"And you think we are going to do this?"

"I don't need you to teach me. I only require access to the information. Get me that, and the rest is covered."

We were back to her Assassin Squad. "What's the next thing on your list of conditions?"

"I have to make sure you understand. No matter what, we can't talk about the past or what comes in the future again. What we had doesn't exist anymore. I don't want hope."

I wanted to argue. Hope was how to survive. That's how I'd made it this far. I'd made myself believe she and Theo would be there at the end of this.

"And?" I probed.

"Follow through on the lesson plan Devani gave you. I want to learn everything and anything I can to protect myself."

"We may have some issues," I informed her.

"Why is that?"

"Your trainer ordered me to teach you to spar with someone my size. That means close proximity to you. That's a bad idea."

"Oh." She looked in Theo's direction. "What are your instructions?"

"Guns and takedowns."

She frowned. "She's training me like a soldier in her damn organization. That woman is crazy. I swear to God."

"Speaking of," I had to ask. "Want to divulge the name of the organization?"

"Nope." She shook her head. "Nyx said the rule is chicks before dicks. And your dicks aren't on my menu anyway, so that's an easy call to make. So anyway, Devani retired."

"Retired, my ass," Theo mumbled.

"So are you guys going to help me, or maybe one of Nyx's brothers will fill in? She said Tyler is the one who taught her to fight, and he's a very patient teacher."

The head of the Mykos syndicate wouldn't get anywhere near her. I couldn't help the annoyance and jealousy coursing through my body. And when would he have time to fly up here to teach her?

Was Nyx setting her brother up with Nerine for the future?

Over my fucking dead body.

"We'll do it. No one is touching you on our watch."

"Really? But you just said there were issues." She stared at me as if my reaction seemed odd.

"I know what I said."

"Okay, I guess I owe Nyx fifty bucks."

"What are you talking about?"

"I insisted the last thing you'd want to do was add training to your babysitting duties."

"So Nyx told you to do what?"

"She said part of my training was to learn to play mind games. Well, Devani said that part. And they wanted me to try it on you. She said the second I mentioned her brother that you'd jump in and take over my training. I insisted you weren't that gullible, but it looks as if she was right again."

I scowled at her. "Are you for real right now?"

"You walked into that one, dumbass." Theo started laughing. "From the moment we left the Drakos estate, I knew there was no getting out of training her."

"If you're so smart, why didn't you say something?"

"Because it's fun watching you get all pissy."

Dickhead.

Eleven

erine

Maybe this wasn't such a great idea.

Those thoughts ran through my head on a continuous loop as I approached the training room used by all Angelos soldiers for their drills. In the past, I never questioned coming down here. I'd work out and then go about my day. After the coup, things changed. I used the gym in the house and rarely left the house, except during my runs.

Typing in the access code, I pulled open the doors and abruptly stopped.

Holy fuck. Yep, this was most definitely a bad idea.

Theo and Xander stretched at different corners of the room. They rolled their arms and flexed and shifted side to side as if they prepared to engage in some no-holds-barred combat session instead of a self-defense class for me.

Neither wore a shirt, making it obvious how the past few years had honed them from fit boys into toned, lethal men.

As a teen, I'd wanted them with a fierceness of first love and newly discovered passion. Then, everything was new, exciting, and an exploration of desires.

Their passion for each other had aroused me in a way I couldn't describe, and then when they turned it on me, the intensity, the overwhelming nature of it, sent me to places I couldn't have imagined possible.

Now I longed for two completely untouchable people. They represented what I lost, what I wanted, and what remained out of reach.

Logic screamed at me to suppress my desires, that I belonged to another man, even if I hated that man's guts. But my body craved, needed, cried for a touch, a taste, a moment of what it would be just to feel like a woman again.

No matter how much I wished it, the pulsing between my legs never stopped whenever I was around Theo and Xander. The draw they held over me had never waned, even when I wanted to desperately hate them for abandoning me.

Now they'd touch me for the sole purpose of training. An evil torture to remind me of every damn thing I'd lost.

As if sensing my presence, Xander and Theo turned in unison, catching me in their sights. A hum of energy surged among the three of us. My nipples tightened, and my pussy grew slick and wet.

What the hell was I doing?

I released a deep breath, pushing down my arousal, and focused on the end goal.

To leave all of this behind and never look back.

I jumped as the clock on the wall chimed nine, snapping me into motion for my lesson.

I approached Theo, who'd moved onto the padded mat in the center of the room.

"It looks like you're my first teacher in this endeavor." Immediately, I cringed, wishing the words had never left my lips. I'd said something similar my first time with him. Hell, it had been my first time ever.

The need coursing through me reignited, and all I wanted to do was run out of the room and hide.

Idiot.

"Forget I said that. I didn't mean to—"

"Stop talking," Theo said through a clenched jaw as undisguised heat and lust lit his gray eyes. "This is fucking hard enough."

I swallowed, trying to push the desire down. "I'm sorry."

Instead of acknowledging my apology, he grabbed his shirt and slipped it on. "Get your gear. We aren't training in here. There's a better location for what we have planned."

I frowned. "What do you mean? I thought you were going to teach me all the skills of your soldiers?"

"We are, but you need a more private setting." Without looking in my direction, he strode to the gym exit and then nodded to Xander. "Let's go, asshole. The boss wanted us to show his wife the Caves. Let's make it worth her while."

Andraius wanted me to see the Caves, did he? I'd grown up

running its halls. I could navigate every nook and cranny blindfolded. Another secret kept from the piece of shit I'd married.

"What are you two up to?"

"The Assassin Squad wanted us heavily involved in your training, so you will have to wait to learn all the details," Theo responded over his shoulder, not bothering to look toward me, so I fixed my gaze on Xander.

Who sighed, shook his head, and picked up his discarded shirt, donning it as he moved in my direction. "It's been a few years since you went for a visit, Angel. It's time to make an appearance and show everyone you aren't a petrified lamb."

"I know what happens down there. I'm not scared."

"Oh, I'm well aware of your experience of the Caves." The smirk on Xander's lips shouldn't send the quiver deep into my core the way it just had. "However, not everyone knows the depths of the knowledge Theios Peter passed to his heir."

I almost said, *"Or what you and Theo demonstrated to me,"* but kept those thoughts to myself since going down that rabbit hole would only make this mess I lived in bigger and bigger.

But of course, Xander caught the train of my thoughts and whispered, "One day, it will happen again."

"No, it won't. No matter how much I may want it, there isn't a possibility."

"Not now. But one day when you're free."

Free.

The concept of that word made me laugh. Whether Andraius died or I disappeared, I'd remain locked in shackles. No one saw this but me.

The Angelos Angel carried the weight of centuries of tradition, history, and lineage. My death would mean it passed to my sisters, and I'd never allow them to take on such a burden.

"I'll never have true freedom." I turned away. "There are only two choices for me, and neither situation allows the scenario you want to happen."

"Wait and see."

"I won't leave fate in anyone else's hands but mine from now on."

"You still haven't forgiven us."

"When I said I forgave you, I meant it. That doesn't mean I will sit around letting others make my decisions. Those days are over. I'm going to become the Nerine Papa raised again."

"Fine. Let's go." Xander gestured toward the elevators as if I didn't know where they were.

I glared at him and stepped into position next to Theo.

"Want to explain the details of this field trip the boss ordered?" I asked the moment the elevator doors closed, leaving the three of us the only ones in the cab.

Theo angled his head toward the camera in the corner and then stated, "The boss wanted you to see the inner workings of the family operations. You are an Angelos. You need to understand how he runs the business."

"Oh, I see." I lifted my eyes to the camera and stared directly into the lens. "If Andraius wants to frighten me, why is he hiding behind his men? Shouldn't he have the balls to put the fear of God in me?"

If I wasn't mistaken, I might have heard one or both of the men behind me grind their teeth at the taunt I'd thrown at my husband.

"We only follow orders. First, we will go through the halls toward the holding cells and then the interrogation rooms. Last, we will visit the training facilities where we teach soldiers all the techniques used for advanced extractions." Theo kept his tone neutral, but how he gripped the back of his neck told me the last place he wanted to go was that room.

"This was a fucking bad idea," Xander muttered under his breath, sending butterflies into my stomach as images of both Theo and Xander sandwiching me, fucking me engulfed my mind.

We'd been so young and stupid, trying not to get caught by our fathers when we were supposed to prepare for an interrogation. The incident had started as a punishment for going to a party on my college campus without informing my security. It hadn't helped that when they found me, some idiot from my study group was hitting on me and insisting I go out with him.

They'd taken me into that room, stripped me, bound my hands to a chain above my head, and then mercilessly teased me before fucking me until I was within seconds of passing out.

They'd barely managed to get me into my bed and wipe the camera system before our fathers had arrived with the suspect they planned to torture for information.

"It won't happen again. Our history is our history," I whispered, ensuring the cameras couldn't pick up my words.

"You call it history. I call it torture." Theo stalked from the elevator the second the doors slid open.

"I didn't choose this, Xander."

"It doesn't hurt any less." He pulled his phone out of his

pocket and read something on the display, frowning. "Let's go. My workday just got busier."

He strode toward Theo, leaving me to follow behind him.

After a few centering breaths, I exited the cab with my head up. It wasn't fair of them to put guilt on my shoulders, but then again, I'd made it very clear that I had no plans to wait for them.

No matter what I felt for them, there was no point in them waiting for me when a future together wasn't possible for us.

I'd rather them be with other people than in this limbo with me.

God, I was such a fucking liar. Seeing them with other people would kill me, but they deserved better than this.

"Are you coming?" Theo paused, shooting a scowl in my direction. "Let's get this over with."

Cocking a hand on my hip, I matched his glare with one of my own. "I don't need an escort. I'm familiar with the layout of the underground facilities."

"Wrong." Theo's cool tone grated on my nerves. "We've put in a few renovations, and the last thing we'd want to happen is for the boss's wife to get lost. Considering where we are, the fewer problems you cause us, the better."

Problems?

"I'm causing you problems? You're the one who wanted me to see the Caves." I clenched my fists and, from my periphery, noticed Xander take a step in my direction. "If I'm such a problem, as you stated, I can turn my ass around and go back up the elevator."

"You're not going anywhere. The boss gave us orders, and we will follow them."

If he said *boss* one more time, I'd punch him in the mouth.

His gray eyes narrowed as if reading my thoughts, and a smirk touched his lips. "If you punch me, it will only hurt you. I'm faster, and my hard jaw will break your fingers."

"It would be worth it to damage your pretty face."

"Oh, the Angelos Angel thinks I'm pretty. Though my preference leans toward handsome."

"What the hell is wrong with you?" I folded my arms across my body. "You haven't acted this level of dickhead since we were kids."

"Maybe it's your sunny disposition."

Xander stepped between us, blocking my view of Theo, his dark eyes holding mine, narrowing briefly. "Time to table the ire and finish the tasks ahead."

Oh, we'd finish the tasks ahead, all right.

As soon as we left here, I'd message Nyx and tell her the plan to train with these two was off. I couldn't do it. We had too much history. Being this close to them hurt too fucking much.

One minute it was *behave and make it easy. We want to unseat your asshole husband and put you on the throne.* Then the next was this bullshit.

I couldn't understand this head trip. I needed a hard run to get my mind clear.

It wasn't as if I intended for the circumstances of our lives. They had no clue as to how much I hurt inside. They knew nothing of what I'd suffered.

Hell with it. I refused to fall back into self-pity.

Step one: finish this tour. Step two: a mind-clearing run through the streets of Boston. Step three—

At that moment, I caught movement in the periphery.

Focusing, I realized Andraius's head of security stood in the corner, watching us and listening to everything we said.

All the hairs on the back of my neck stood up.

They were acting like assholes on purpose. The way Xander cocked his head to the side and lifted a brow told me he wasn't happy with the direction my thoughts had drifted.

"Why don't you clarify this list we need to tackle so I can let you get back to your real work since babysitting me isn't technically part of the role of those at such a high level in the organization."

"Cut the attitude, Nerine." Theo maneuvered around Xander. "We are only doing as the boss tells us. He makes the decisions. We carry them out. You have an issue, go talk to him."

"This *boss* shit is getting old. Get out of my way. I'll give myself a tour of this place and then go for a run. I don't need you two fuckers as my escorts. As of tomorrow, I want my old security team back. You're fired."

I stalked in their direction, ready to shove Theo to the side. I had no doubt Andraius lurked somewhere in the shadows, ready to pounce on me.

This would have been the perfect time to practice some of the moves I'd started to learn from the Assassin Squad, as Xander and Theo like to call them, but I hadn't mastered any of them yet.

Just as I reached Theo, a hand grabbed my upper arm, hurling me to the side. "Nerine, you will not speak to my men with such disrespect."

So fucking predictable.

"Would you rather I direct my venom at you?" I glared up at him.

Pain shot through my muscles as Andraius's fingers gripped harder. Still, I refused to give him the satisfaction of hearing my whimper.

"Your father indulged you too much. It's time you learned the Angelos way of handling business in the Caves."

I couldn't help but laugh at the stupidity of that statement. "Then you have nothing to teach me since you aren't a true Angelos."

Andraius's lack of initiative to learn how Peter Angelos ran things before he arrived on the scene made him an idiot. Even a little research would have told him I'd seen Papa do many interrogations down here.

Rage built in his eyes, along with a deep-seated desire to backhand me. I'd seen that look often over the years. However, if he acted impulsively, he'd lose the unquestioned loyalty of the people surrounding us. I was the Angelos Angel and therefore untouchable, especially in the Caves.

Smiling, I lifted my chin. I waited, taunted. I wanted him to hit me.

Do it, fucker. Please, do it. Let everyone see the monster I married.

His eyes narrowed, knowing I'd won this round. He then shoved me away, throwing me onto Theo.

Theo steadied me and then pushed me behind Xander as if that would shield me from whatever Andraius planned for me.

"Take her to the extraction room. I want her to watch Xander do his magic with our prisoner."

I knew I should have kept my mouth shut but couldn't help myself. "If you wanted to show me the Angelos way, why aren't you doing it? Papa never let others take on the hard work when he had the chance to roll up his sleeves."

"You want a front-row seat as I wield a knife. Is that what you're saying?"

"I've already experienced this. I rather watch an interrogation."

"Shut up, Nerine," Theo muttered so only I could hear. "Stop agitating him."

I glanced to my side and then at Andraius, not giving a fuck.

Theo knew nothing about what this monster had done to me with his blade.

I'd lived as someone's pawn for way too long. This man planned to hurt me whether or not I played by his rules.

Lifting a brow, I held Andraius's gaze and then smirked before I used the words from the night he couldn't get it up. "Are we doing this or not?"

He shifted as if he planned to lunge at me before he got himself under control. "Gentlemen, let's give her what she wants."

Twelve

erine

"Mama, I'm so happy to hear from you," I said in Greek when I picked up the call. *"I wish you were here."*

There was a bit of comfort in speaking to her in our native language. Growing up, I only used Greek with the elders of the household since the younger generation preferred English. Then when everything went down, I refused to speak Greek with Andraius to spite him.

He'd tried the "I'll only ever speak Greek to you" shit, and I'd acted as if I hadn't a clue what he was saying.

My favorite line to use against him was, "What did you say? I don't understand. It's all Greek to me."

Yeah, I was a royal bitch, but he'd made me into one.

"Cara, if only things were different. Tell me, what have you been doing? I called you on this new number earlier, and you didn't answer. I thought I'd made a mistake. Why do I feel you are sneaking around and may get into trouble?"

In my mind's eye, I imagined her wrapping me in her arms and engulfing me in the scent of her flower and spiced perfume.

Mama was home. The safe place, the love and joy of my childhood, all packaged in one person.

God, I missed her so much.

It had been nearly eight weeks since I last spoke to Mama. I was different now, stronger. Well, I was getting there. I trained in something every day: defense, business, finance. If it wasn't one of the Squad, it was Theo or Xander administering the curriculum.

"It's an encrypted line, just like the one phone I sent you. Only use that phone when you talk to anyone about me or want to have private conversations from now on. Tell the girls the same things about their phones."

After my last conversation with Mama, I'd discovered Andraius had someone bug the phone from her side. And he'd come storming into the library demanding I never talk disparagingly about him to her again. I'd only referred to him as the imposter Angelos, nothing else.

From the beginning, we suspected Andraius monitored and reviewed our conversations, so we spoke in code to relay private information. Only this last time, I decided to test him, and he'd proven me right.

"I'm not stupid. I did notice that you didn't answer any of

my questions. Something is different about you." Mama grew quiet for a moment and then sternly asked, *"What have you done?"*

Typical mom, thinking I'd done something terrible. Technically, I had, but it was for a good cause—our freedom, so there was that. And it wasn't really terrible. I wasn't planning to kill anyone. I only hoped someone else killed him.

"I have found some hobbies to keep me busy." I smiled to myself. *"And made friends."*

"Doing what?"

"So suspicious"

"Answer the question."

"Mama, it's not that bad. I'm learning to protect myself."

She was quiet for a few seconds and then, in a soft voice, said, *"Because of what he does to you."*

A sadness washed over me. I hated that Mama knew. I'd tried to hide it, but somehow she always knew.

"What do you mean?"

"I have eyes and ears in Boston. We true Angeloses still have eyes and ears everywhere. You need to remember this."

"I'm sorry, Mama. I wish I'd been stronger."

"From what I hear, you make his life hell. That's very strong. Are you doing as I told you and using the oils and herbs in case one of his old sperm decides to work?"

I didn't want to discuss this with an audience, especially the two men in the front seat. But hell, they already knew all of my secrets. So I might as well go all the way.

"He hasn't touched me in a few months. He doesn't like to fuck venom-filled whores."

Xander's head shifted slightly, but he kept his face forward.

"Language, Nerine."

"I'm only repeating his words, Mama."

"How will he get an Angelos's child, then?"

"He demanded we start the IVF process."

I could have sworn I heard one of the men growl at the mention of IVF.

"By the saints. No. I forbid it."

"Mama. Nothing will happen until he can provide a healthy sperm sample and prove he isn't sterile. I refused to let them fill me with any drugs to harvest my eggs."

I could still see the rage on Andraius's face when I'd made my declaration in the middle of the doctor's office. He'd been ready to strangle me and probably would have gone through with it if several medical professionals weren't sitting around us.

It also helped that the moron had called in three of the top fertility specialists in New England, and they'd all agreed with the initial findings of my perfect ovarian and uterine health. Which meant the problem definitely wasn't me.

When the one sample Andraius gave the lab returned with a meager sperm count, he insisted it was due to sex the night before. He wanted to proceed with harvesting my eggs, and I told him to shove it until he proved his swimmers were strong enough to penetrate my eggs.

Yeah, totally bitchy thing to say, but I had no fucks left to give anymore.

"Where are you now?"

"In my car, going back to the compound. I had my lessons with my friends today."

"You're talking very freely. This isn't like you. Nerine, what are you doing?" The concern in her voice had me sighing.

"Mama, stop worrying. Xander and Theo are with me. They manage my protection now."

"I see. I don't like this."

"I can trust them. Stop worrying."

Theo's eyes connected with mine briefly in the rearview mirror. Theo's mother, Theia Viola, along with Xander's mother, Theia Brenna, were Mama's best friends. When Theia Viola passed away, Mama and Theia Brenna took it upon themselves to make sure Theo knew he was wanted and loved.

"It's my job to worry. I'm your mother. You can't fall in love with them again. It can't work. It won't work. It's too dangerous."

"Wait. What? Say that again."

"You heard me the first time."

"But...we were careful—"

"Cara, I'm your mama. I have eyes. They loved you in a way that went beyond normal friendship, and I saw you with them."

"Oh my God, did Papa know?" My raised voice got both Xander's and Theo's attention.

"No. Men are oblivious. They see what they want to see. He thought it was them being overprotective because of you being the heir. He thought it was brotherly."

I resisted smirking at that.

Theo lifted a brow, waiting to see if I had an answer about Papa. I shook my head, and both men's shoulders relaxed, which made me want to frown since I knew eventually, Papa would have found out.

"Why didn't you say anything?"

"Until you came to us or became pregnant, I wanted to wait."

"Mama! I can't believe you said that. I thought you were a virgin when you got married?"

"Who told you that nonsense? Why did I ask? Your Papa did —the liar. I swear. That man was an 'always do as I say, not as I do' man when it came to you girls. Do you believe he waited until we married?"

I tuned Mama out as she continued her nonsensical chatter about Papa and their sex life. This was the last thing I wanted to think about—Mama, Papa, and sex.

Yes, that's how my sisters and I came about, but no child ever wanted those images in their mind.

"Do you know the old ladies still talk about your Papa and his reputation before he met me?"

"Oh, Mama. Please don't tell me anymore. No more. I get it."

"You're one to talk. You had two men. I used to wonder how you walked half the time."

I cringed. *"Mama. No. Just no."*

"I got you to stop thinking about your stupid husband, didn't I?"

Unable to help myself, I smiled. *"Yes, you did. I love you, Mama. I miss you so much."*

"Soon, cara. Soon. Things are going to change."

"I hope so. Did the people who brought you the phones teach you how to scan the house with the other equipment?"

Xander's head whipped around, not caring that I knew he was eavesdropping.

"The girls know."

"Mama, you need to learn it. Tina and Ariana are going to college soon. Then it's just you and Fi. You can't rely on them for everything. We talked about this."

"You've become very bossy in the last few months. You remind me of my old Nerine." I heard the tinge of happiness in her tone. *"Don't stop."*

"I'm trying to remember her, too."

"That's a good girl. I like that you have friends."

"Me, too. Bye, Mama."

"Bye, cara."

I hung up and closed my eyes, dropping my head back as a lump formed in my throat. In the last few months, I'd come a long way.

I thought of all the training, the long hours of studying, and the multitude of debates and discussions on topics with four women who'd all had so many more life experiences than me.

They'd also made me realize that resenting Andraius for keeping me from achieving my degree was only hurting me. I had to let it go. Otherwise, he had something to hold over me, and the on-the-job skills the ladies were giving me were far superior to a degree.

Devani ran a multibillion-dollar conglomerate with only a high school education, and what Lilly had gone to school for had nothing to do with her real job as a hacker. She'd taught herself everything she'd ever learned.

This connection and unconditional support were what had been missing in my life, and this was what I planned to give my sisters.

"Okay, we need to talk, so stop pretending to sleep," Theo commanded.

My eyes snapped open as the car came to an abrupt stop in the driveway of the compound, and I stared at two intense faces.

"Umm. What did I do now?"

"That conversation with your mother was fascinating. Did you forget our parents are Greek, and we are fluent in Greek?" The hardening of Xander's lips almost had me laughing.

"No, I didn't. You're my security. You have to pretend everything I said didn't happen. You protect me and my secrets. Isn't that the job?"

"Angel, I swear I'm going to—" Theo clenched his jaw as he cut himself off.

"What? What are you going to say? Smack my ass red?" I lifted a brow. "I haven't done anything wrong. I have a right to protect my family if I find a way to do it. That is none of your business."

"Of course, it is our business." Xander ran a frustrated hand through his hair and then cupped the back of his neck. "You are our business."

"Devani took care of it. Case closed."

He closed his eyes and lifted his face as if praying. "Promise me you aren't doing anything stupid."

"Nothing more than usual."

Theo shook his head. “I swear to God, Angel. You could drive a man to drink.”

“Yeah, well, you didn’t have to fuck a man thirty years older than you for the last five years.”

“You’re never going to forgive us for that, are you?” Xander asked through gritted teeth.

“I already forgave you that night in the library when we came to our agreement. I forgave you for leaving me. I forgave you for staying away. I forgave you for so many things. But I refuse to let you sugarcoat what happened to me.”

“We couldn’t let you die. Fucking Andraius was better than you dying.” The rage on Theo’s face infuriated me.

“Is that right? It’s not called fucking. It’s called rape, over and over again. Don’t try to change the term for it. The first time it happened was in front of the damn priest who forced me to marry him.”

“Angel—”

“No, stop with the Angel,” I shouted. “Tell me, did you two continue after I was out of the picture?”

“You know damn well we didn’t,” Xander exclaimed. “It was all of us or nothing.”

“Is that supposed to make me feel better? How many women you have slept with since me? Don’t you dare lie to me. I know all about Xander, the flirt, and Theo, the coveted gentleman.”

“They weren’t you.” Theo shook his head. “No one could replace you.”

“But it felt good. You enjoyed it, and you got off. No one forced it on you.”

"No one is you."

"No." I lifted my hand, not wanting to hear Xander's plea. "I am tired of having these emotions, all of these feelings, with you two around. Please, I'm begging you. Assign someone else to watch me. It's tearing me up inside. You represent everything I lost, everything I can't have. If you love me the way you say you do, just set me free and let me move on. Fucking let me move on." Tears streamed down my face. It was time to accept the truth. I still loved these men, and it broke my heart that we were always so close but nothing could ever come of it.

"I'm so sorry," Xander whispered, dropping his head. "Please, forgive us. We won't push you anymore. We'll do what you said."

I nodded, wiping my cheeks, and then opened the car door and rushed inside.

I had to calm down. Everything inside me churned. All of this was too much. I had no one that was mine.

Xander and Theo weren't mine. They could never be mine. Mama and the girls were an ocean away. What I wouldn't give to have someone to hold me, hug me, give me some warmth, some comfort.

The best option at this point was a shower.

I took the back staircase, then walked along the landing leading to my section of the house. Just as I turned the corner to my suite of rooms, I crashed into Robert Lavinos, Andraius's head of security.

He steadied me. "I'm to direct you to work in your library."

I really hated this guy. Outside of talking like a robot, he'd stood idly by and found it amusing every time Andraius treated me like shit in public. One of the betrayers, as I liked to call them.

"For Christ's sake, get out of my way. I want a shower after my workout."

"The boss wants you to go downstairs."

"Andraius is here? I thought he had a meeting of importance or something?" I glared at Robert as he blocked my way when I tried to move around him.

"He decided to come home to take care of some business."

"In the bedroom?" I frowned.

If he was covering for his boss, this attempt landed him in the piss-poor-job column. When we first married, Andraius had regularly snooped in my room for things. Luckily, I had all my little nooks and holes to hide something inside.

He hadn't gone back to doing that shit again, had he?

I refused to put up with any more disrespect. That nineteen-year-old girl had long ago died, and now the twenty-three-year-old bitch wife he'd created was the only thing left.

"Get out of my way." I pushed his shoulder, and he stepped in front of me, shoving me back.

Okay, he'd never laid a hand on me before. This was new.

"I'm under strict orders to keep you in your library. So let's go." He puffed out his chest as if his size intimidated me.

Umm. Xander was way bigger than him, and he'd taught me to take someone his size down.

Irritation coursed through me, and a throbbing pulsed in my head.

"If you don't move, I will make you," he said.

All of a sudden, my heartbeat accelerated, and my stomach churned.

Had Andraius learned what Nyx and I had been doing over the last few months?

Robert smirked and shook his head, moving toward me. "You're no match for me. Don't make me carry you downstairs."

"I'm a lot stronger than you believe." I lunged, pivoted in the opposite direction to what he expected, and slid past him, running toward my bedroom.

"You bitch. Why don't you ever listen? This is why the boss has to discipline you," he shouted as he chased after me, his hard footsteps echoing on the polished wood in the hallway.

When I reached the doorway of Andraius's bedroom, I heard the sounds.

Bodies slapping against one another, sex, moans, pleasure.

My hands shook. That bastard thought I wouldn't lose my shit knowing he'd brought one of his women into my house to fuck.

Robert reached me and said with a smirk, "Are you satisfied now?"

"I will be when I punch him in the fucking face."

I reached for the doorknob, but Robert grabbed my hand. Just as I readied to break his hold, I felt the presence of a group of men. Two of them I'd know anywhere.

"Lavinos. Let her go, or the Caves are your next stop." Xander gave his threat in an utterly emotionless way, but his meaning was plain and clear.

Imminent death.

"I have orders to keep her downstairs, sir."

Robert's grip tightened into a hold that may have hurt someone who hadn't dealt with worse. I could handle way more than he could ever dish out. He should know since he'd been privy to countless incidences when Andraius manhandled me.

I'd taken it from Andraius. I refused to take it from this asshole. I hadn't spent the last few months training for nothing. I twisted my wrists, jerked his arm to the side, and shoved him with my hip, breaking his hold.

Breathing heavily, I glared at him. "You will never touch me again. You work for me, not the other way around."

First, shock flashed on his face, then his eyes narrowed. "I work for the boss."

Just as he lunged at me, Xander grabbed him by his hair, hauling him back with a hard jerk. He flailed in Xander's hold but couldn't free himself.

"No, you work for me. I assigned you to Andraius. And I gave you a direct order. Did you forget she is the Angelos everyone protects above all else? If you touch her again, you won't leave the Caves."

He'd barely finished his statement when two men separated from the group that had come up with Xander and Theo. They grabbed Robert and, without a word, dragged him away.

"Did he hurt you?" Theo took my hand, inspected my wrist, noticed the light red marks, and frowned.

"I'm not going to bruise. This is nothing compared to the evidence his bastard boss leaves behind. Those marks last for days or even weeks."

"Jesus, Angel." Theo closed his eyes for a second. "Don't tell me shit like that."

I shrugged. "It's my reality, Theo. Do you understand why I want to escape?"

That's when I realized what he'd called me, and a chill ran down my spine. He couldn't use my nickname around others. I glanced at the soldiers standing behind me. I counted eighteen men, with a good handful being the originals.

That was a lot of manpower for this situation.

"Did you expect a war or something? Why would you bring so many people up here?"

"We were following through on your request." Xander paused. "I was coming up to show them the layout of your security."

I nodded then I turned around to face the door. "Before we do introductions, I need to handle something right now."

Theo set a hand on my forearm. "You don't have to go in there. You already know the situation."

"Oh, I need to go in there. Andraius wants to embarrass me. I'll let him. But remember, everyone who's loyal to him because he lines their pockets is as much a piece of shit as he is."

I opened the door, and if Theo hadn't kept me from taking his gun, I would have shot Andraius right then and there.

"You're fucking her in my mother's wedding dress?"

Thirteen

Theo

The fury on Nerine's face flowed out in wave upon wave. Her eyes burned with rage, embarrassment, and a feral need for violence unlike anything I'd ever seen.

She glanced in my direction for a split second. I immediately shifted, barely managing to keep her from grabbing my gun as she crossed the threshold into the bedroom.

Xander tried to follow behind her, but I blocked his way and shook my head. "Let her handle this. We step in only if he touches her."

"That dress," Xander said.

"I know."

Simultaneously, we turned our heads, not wanting to see any more of the situation in the room.

Nerine's ultimate dream was to have worn the gown all the women on her mother's side of the family had worn when they married their spouses. The dress had passed down for five generations, only changing in design to adjust to the era. So the fact Andraius had pulled it from the storage in the mansion's attic meant he wanted to hurt Nerine in the ultimate way.

This was deliberate. Robert had staged the whole incident with him and Nerine. The fact the fucker had placed his hands on her was just something he wanted to do.

I curled my fingers into a fist tight enough for my knuckles to crack. Once Xander finished with him in the Caves, I'd take my turn.

"You bastard. What the hell are you doing?" Nerine shouted.

"I'm fucking my woman. Get out. Or take a seat and watch how you should take it."

"Take a seat. Take a seat," Nerine shouted. "I don't need to learn anything from you. I'm done with this shit. I'm tired of you disrespecting me. This ends now. I am done with all of you. Get that dress off her, now."

The bed squeaked as if Andraius had moved. "You don't tell me what to do. I gave the dress to her."

"You can't give something that doesn't belong to you."

"I own everything in this house, including you. This woman is having my child, which is more than you can say. She can have anything she wants."

"Is that right? What's your name?" The way Nerine asked

the question had me bracing as if she intended to throw something at the woman.

"Lidia."

"You're pregnant?"

"Yes."

"How many weeks?"

"N...nine."

"Did he tell you I'm the problem?"

"Yes. Andraius said you have weak eggs."

"Why are you wearing my mother's gown?"

"Are you hard of hearing? I gave it to her," Andraius interjected.

"Shut. The. Fuck. Up. I didn't ask you. I want to know what he told you before you put it on. Did he tell you that he wanted to see you in the gown he planned to marry you in once he got rid of me? Did he say that he is the true Angelos, so there is no need for me and that you will become the Angelos bride now that there is an heir?"

"You don't need to answer her. She had one duty, and she couldn't do it. She isn't of any use."

"You don't need to say anything, Lidia. I already know the truth."

"What's the truth?" Lidia asked, a slight quiver now in her tone.

"There is no way in hell that kid is his."

"I'm not—"

Nerine started laughing, cutting her off. "He's sterile. The doctors know it, and so do you."

"This is his child. I swear it." Fear laced Lidia's voice.

"The doctors have tested him every other week for the last three months. He can barely produce a viable sample."

"That's not true. I won't let you talk about me like that before the men."

"Or what? Will you smack me around as you do in front of Robert? Go right ahead. I doubt these men will take kindly to that type of treatment of the true Angelos."

"I'm warning you."

"Remember when I told you that you can't do anything more to me than you've already done? Well, fuck you. I am done with you. I am done with everyone. Go to hell."

Nerine shoved between Xander and me and then turned to the group of soldiers. She scanned all of their faces, pure resignation in her eyes as if she expected an end of some kind.

"Listen up. This boss of yours. The one that keeps everyone nice and comfortable in wealth stolen from everything Papa built. He's sterile, and his dick doesn't work half the time. I hate his fucking guts. The kid that woman is carrying isn't his. And I will never let him claim that baby as an Angelos." She closed her eyes for a moment, taking a deep breath. "If you find me dead by morning, know the bastard in there with his whore did it. And you know what? I'm not afraid. He beat the fear out of me long ago."

She smiled and laughed, shaking her head, and just as fast her face grew hard and angry. "Besides, my blood is the only way his claim is legitimate, and I will never give him a child. Never. I have no more fucks left to give. I am just done. Do you hear me? I am fucking done. That woman will not be in my house when I return, or I will kill her myself. I forgot whose daughter I was, but not anymore. He's called me a cold venom-filled bitch so many times. He's about to learn what kind of cold-hearted, evil viper bitch I can be."

She wiped the tears from her face, lifted her chin to look each of us standing before her in the eyes, and then she shot Andraius the most hate-filled glare I'd ever seen her give anyone.

"I want a fucking divorce. You piece of shit." Turning, she walked straight past us in the direction of the corridor leading to the back of the compound.

Silence filled the space as the weight of her grief and words descended on all of us.

Then, Andraius roared, "Come back here, Nerine."

He charged toward the door, ready to follow her. However, before he could take one step outside of his room, in unison, all the soldiers blocked his path.

"Get out of my way. That's an order."

"You disrespected the Angelos Angel in the worst way," Clay said. "Everyone knows the legacy of that gown. She has a right to her upset. Leave her alone."

"I'm in charge. You do as I say. Move."

At that moment, Stefano, Nerine's original head of security, stepped forward, blocking Andraius from a different side. "You will never disrespect her again."

"Xander, get your men out of my way. I need to discipline my wife."

Before I could stop him, Xander grabbed Andraius by the throat. "Do you mean like this? Isn't this how you held her up, nearly suffocated her, and left your fingerprints dug deep into her delicate skin?"

A group of twenty other soldiers rushed up the stairs and stopped, unsure of what to do. Either they'd heard the commotion or listened to everything going on with Nerine over the hallway surveillance feed.

Andraius grasped at Xander's arm, and the fact no one helped save the asshole meant everyone had chosen sides.

"If you lay a hand on her again, I will break you. She is the true Angelos, don't ever forget." Xander threw Andraius to the floor.

He gasped in air and then said, "She's sleeping with you exactly as she was with the others. That's how she turned you against me. I knew it."

I stepped forward, glaring down at him. "That woman has more integrity than you ever will. Don't you dare play virtuous when you have a woman in the room behind you pretending to carry your child."

"There are consequences for this." The warning in Andraius's tone conveyed he hadn't realized he held none of the cards.

He pushed to his feet and then glared at me.

"Have you not figured it out?" I shifted toward him, letting my body mass crowd into his space. "You can't run your organization without people like Xander and me."

"And you think that dumb bitch can run it?"

"I know she can. And she is far from dumb. She knows the operation ten times better than you ever will. Theios Peter taught her, and while you made us play bodyguard, we brought her up to speed on current business. She'll step right in, and no one will miss you."

"What the hell do you mean by that?"

"I'm saying, start treating her right, or the rebellion you will face will destroy you within seconds." I leaned down, bringing my face closer to his. "And if you even think about making what she believes you will do to her a reality, the psycho they say I am in the Caves will be the least of your concerns."

"It was you." He narrowed his gaze, cocking his head slightly.

"Me what?"

"Who she whored herself to before she married me?"

Without blinking an eye, I responded with, "The Angel never whored herself to anyone."

I spoke the truth. What Xander and I shared with her would never be something dirty as this bastard wanted to make it. Unconventional, yes. Dirty, no.

"So she lied when she said she'd given herself to others?"

"I wasn't there to know what she said to you. And it looks as if you've chosen to believe what you want. We, the original Angelos soldiers, know she has never been nor will be the whore you labeled her."

"Did you forget that all of you pledged your loyalty to me?"

"No, we pledged our loyalty to the Angelos family. Not you, specifically."

"And you think that one of you will replace me by getting rid of me?"

"None of us want your seat. As I stated, treat her right, and we won't have a problem." I stepped back, aligning myself with Xander, who still hadn't gotten himself under control enough to keep from lunging at Andraius if he dared to go after Nerine.

"Stay in your room with your expectant paramour or leave, but do not go anywhere near Nerine."

"And the event at the botanical gardens in a few days. The Drakoses expect us there since she spent the summer working on it with Nyx."

"You'll meet Nerine there per the itinerary sent to you earlier in the week."

"Not everyone in the family is as loyal to her as you believe. Remember, I came into power with assistance." A calculating smile touched his lips.

"True. But that loyalty only lasts as long as you keep all the betrayers happy. You haven't delivered on any of the promises you made them."

"The Drakos deal will accomplish this."

"Which happened because of Nerine."

"No, I orchestrated it."

"Are you so sure? I suggest researching the histories between the Drakos and Angelos families." Xander shook his head.

Instead of waiting for Andraius to say anything, I decided to enlighten him. "Theios Peter helped Drakos ascend to power when his uncles tried to keep him from taking his seat after his grandfather's death."

"And," Xander added, "right before you murdered him, Theios Peter sent soldiers to assist Drakos in a territory war with one of Drakos's cousins. Drakos viewed Theios Peter as a mentor, and you took that from him."

Concern flashed on Andraius's face. "You knew this and said nothing?"

"I'm loyal to the Angelos Family. This deal is best for them. Drakos knows the organization is poised for a hostile takeover and wants to honor Theios Peter by preventing such an action from happening."

Taking hold of my shirt, Andraius jerked me in his direction. I let him, wanting to see what he'd do. The idiot knew that with a single punch, I'd knock him out cold.

"All of these months, you allowed Drakos to play me. I bent over backward to please him." He glowered into my face, the fury almost comical.

Grasping his wrists, I twisted his hands and released his hold.

"Bullshit. You ignored every piece of advice I gave you. Do you remember when Xander and I told you to keep everything on US soil?" I shoved him back and then straightened my shirt. "You made all the decisions, and we all went for the ride. Or did you forget the number of times you informed us that we worked for you and not the other way round?"

"You betrayed me."

It took all my strength not to clock him for his hypocrisy. "I have always remained loyal to the Angelos Family. I have never done anything to tarnish its legacy or its standing for the future. Can you say the same?"

"Andraius, be a good boy and take good care of your baby

mama." Xander stepped up next to me. "We will take up management until the Angelos Angel decides how to proceed."

"The hell you are taking over. I am the head of this family." Andraius shifted as if to charge Xander.

I pivoted to intercept him, and at the same time, Xander moved in front of me, capturing Andraius's throat again in a brutal grip.

Xander shook his head in mock pity as Andraius gasped and clutched at his forearms. "Let me make something abundantly clear so there is no miscommunication. As of this point onward, your access to run roughshod over the Angelos empire ends. You are a figurehead only. Get back in that room and take care of your mistress. Your demotion is effective immediately. Nerine Nicolette Angelos is the true head of this organization."

Xander tossed him through the open doorway of his bedroom. Andraius coughed, struggled to breathe, and slowly managed to sit up as his mistress crouched behind the bed.

"I'll make sure you regret this."

Even after all of this, he wasn't putting the pieces together. I stepped forward, blocking Xander, knowing by this point Xander wanted to kill the bastard.

"If you dare stick one toe out of that door, one of my men will shoot it off. And don't think of escaping through Nerine's room either. On second thought, prepare your things. We are relocating you to a different wing of the house. One used for unwanted guests."

Before Andraius launched into another rant, I turned my back on him. I gestured to three of my men to watch the idiot and run through a standard protocol. Within moments of entering, they would search the room and confiscate all electronics.

Then they would take the idiot to a room on the compound's south wing section until Nerine decided what to do with him. With him cut off from the residential side of the house and locked away in what he liked to call the guest quarters, he wouldn't be able to roam about freely.

"We need to find her before she does something stupid." Xander pulled out his phone, scanned an app, and then scowled, clenching his jaw. "Fucking hell."

"What did she do?" I asked.

Ignoring me, he dialed a number and then barked into the phone. "Your one job was to keep an eye on her. I don't want any excuses. You know damn well she uses the passageways." He hung up, frustration etched all over his face. "I don't know whether to be impressed that she managed to sneak past all the security in the house or pissed."

"Where is she?"

"According to the tracker I snuck onto all of her shoes, she is about five miles away from here."

"After what happened, she went for a run?" I scrubbed a frustrated hand through my hair. "I am going to make sure she understands. She can't do whatever the fuck she wants when her life is on the line."

"We can't touch her."

"To hell with that. After what just happened, we're currently operating in the gray."

Fourteen

Nerine

I raced through the city, desperate to outrun the rage that burned inside me. I darted through alleyways and side streets, my feet leading me on familiar paths to nowhere. Every step I took fueled my rage toward Andraius.

I'd make my way back. Eventually. When I was good and ready.

At this point, I couldn't care less whether I broke the rules about guards and security. I'd do whatever the fuck I wanted.

Yes, Theo and Xander were likely losing their minds, but that was the least of my concerns. Who knew, by morning, Andraius may have a hit out on me, and I'd end up dead.

I had to get this rage out or take the gun I had hidden in

my bedroom and use it on Andraius before he could eliminate me.

I'd done the right thing. I'd ignored his affairs. I never blinked when he openly paraded multiple mistresses before me —more power to them.

But purposefully have me walk in on him fucking someone wearing my mother's gown and then act as if the dumb twat would replace me.

Fuck that shit.

My hands shook, remembering the state of Mama's gown in ruins. We'd hidden it away, made sure no one would touch it, and now—

That crossed the line.

He knew what the dress meant to me. Every fucking person knew the history and tradition of the gown. He'd stolen my dream, stolen so much from me—I hated him with every fiber of my being.

Why had I put up with this shit for so long? Where was my self-respect?

I'd let him destroy it. I had allowed a fucking man to put me in a cage, take away my rights, and then manipulate my mind.

Never fucking again.

Never once had I broken my wedding vows, even when he deserved it. The two men I loved, had always loved, were with me all the time now, and we never acted upon the desires and needs that burned between us.

The bastard had stolen what we had.

A burning sensation filled my lungs, and a wave of

exhaustion cascaded through my limbs, forcing me to stop at a nearby bench. I gasped in heated air as my heart beat rapidly into my ears. Through blurry vision, I studied the area.

Fuck.

This couldn't be right. I focused on the street sign.

Had I really pushed it over ten miles?

I bent over, setting my hands on my knees, my pulse still thundering in my chest.

At least some of the rage boiling in my blood seemed to have settled to a simmer.

Some being the optimal word.

How was this my existence? For weeks I'd trained with Nyx and Devani, studied with Lilly, and believed there was an end to this, but until someone took Andraius down, I was still stuck.

Meeting Nyx, Lilly, and Devani had shown me a glimpse of the future I'd have had if only Papa and Linus had lived—a future my sisters would have had.

The logical part of me understood Papa would have taken some convincing to accept my relationship with Theo and Xander. But in the end, he'd have come around, especially with Mama knowing about it and being on our side.

My lips trembled. There was no point in even imagining that scenario. Life had dealt me completely different cards filled with many painful lessons.

Still, what I wouldn't give for some comfort, a tiny sliver of intimacy and tenderness to release me from the loneliness. This yearning from afar destroyed a little piece of me, day by day.

Fuck. The sooner I found a way to escape with Mama and the girls, the better.

A breeze picked up, and the shift in the sunlight meant it would be dark soon.

When Theo and Xander found me, they would give me hell. I could sneak into the house through one of the secret pathways, and no one would notice.

Yeah, that's what I'd do.

Now to make the long trek back home.

Shit. I probably shouldn't have lost myself in the run. Taking a cab was pointless—with rush hour at its peak, it would take at least an hour or more to get back home. A brisk walk was the better choice.

I stood up straight and wiped the sweat off my forehead—time to follow the same path back to the compound. Pivoting, I stumbled back as I met the unmistakable fury in Theo's gaze.

My heartbeat accelerated, and all I could say was, "Hi."

"You left the house without giving anyone a heads-up." The vein on the side of Theo's face pulsed, and the rigid set of his jaw told me he wasn't in the mood for any excuses.

Before I could respond, he bent, threw me over his shoulder, and carried me to a waiting limo.

"What the fuck? Put me down, you jackass." I banged on his back.

Climbing into the car's open door, he tossed me on the seat, closed the door, and then joined Xander on the opposite bench. He knocked on the window, giving the driver the signal to move.

"Are you two out of your mind? I went for a fucking run."

They only stared at me.

"Are you planning to glare at me for the next hour like that?"

Instead of responding, they continued to scowl at me, anger radiating from them in thick waves.

They both remained silent for five minutes, glowering at me and adding to my agitation.

Fuck this shit.

They weren't my keepers. I'd had enough of these broody assholes. No matter how I felt about them, I'd punch them both in the face using the moves Nyx had taught me if they thought to manhandle me again.

I adjusted my position on the seat, readying for whatever they planned.

"Stop it, Nerine." The order from Xander had me cocking my head to the side, trying to figure out what he meant.

I glared at him. "What the hell are you talking about?"

"We aren't the same people anymore. Even if you don't realize it, you're doing it. It isn't fair to any of us."

Then it hit me.

I'd positioned myself as if they would fuck me into submission. Something they'd done in the past. A game of sorts that we'd played.

How had I instinctively fallen back into that dynamic? Was it the emotions churning through me? Or the anger at Andraius?

My eyes scanned the limo. And all the things we'd done in here flashed in my mind.

I blew out an unsteady breath and leaned back in my seat, crossing my legs before I stared out the window.

"You could have picked a different car."

"There weren't many options available between when we realized you were missing and when we tracked your phone." The weight of Theo's scrutiny continued to play havoc on my thrumming heart.

"I was never missing." I licked my lips and then adjusted the direction of the air conditioning stream to cool my overheated skin. "I needed to go for a run."

Xander shrugged off his suit jacket, laid it at his side, then unbuttoned and rolled his shirt sleeves up, revealing his tattooed arms. Along the sleeve of ink was my name written in Greek. He had another one worked into the design of a dragon's tail that sat over his heart.

Theo had done something similar, except he'd etched my name into the scales of the dragon's back. It had been a secret symbol of our relationship, one we had to keep quiet about because of everyone's conservative views.

He ignored where my attention shifted and leaned forward, giving me that enforcer glare known to scare the shit out of most people.

"During midday, in the middle of summer?"

Too bad his glare did not affect me.

"I had to clear my mind after what that piece of shit did in my house and our over-the-top altercation."

"Clear your mind, is it?" Theo's voice grew deeper, making the hairs on the back of my neck prickle with irritation and causing everything inside me to clench at the same time. "And you didn't think it was possible to clear your fucking mind without ditching your security?"

He kept his cool in all things. He prided himself on it. But then there was me.

I whipped my head around and glared at him. "You aren't my father. You aren't my husband. You aren't my lover. I don't answer to either of you."

"Don't push me, Angel."

"Or what?" I countered, lifting my chin. "And don't call me Angel. I'm not your angel."

"My job is to take care of you, even if you don't want it."

I smirked, not caring about the consequence. Maybe it was the anger riding me at how my life had turned out, or perhaps the arousal coursing through me and the unquenched need I'd felt since these two men walked back into my daily life.

I wanted them to understand taking care of me had nothing to do with my safety.

Safety sat in one realm and care lived in another.

"I haven't had anyone take care of me since before this nightmare began. I handle my own care and needs." I lifted a brow and pursed my lips.

Xander's mouth quirked at the side, catching my meaning, and his pupils dilated into near-black orbs. "Exactly what are your needs, and how do you care for them?"

The hunger in his voice broke the dam on everything I'd shoved away. A throbbing ignited deep in my core, and my nipples hardened.

"Xander, this isn't where we need to go," Theo warned.

Theo's words said one thing, but as he studied me, the

burning heat in his eyes told a completely different story of what he desired.

"Oh no, he wanted to go here. Let's go here."

I knew I played a reckless game with the two most dangerous men I knew. The two men who could ruin me. The two men whom I could destroy.

But I couldn't stop this pull toward them. It drew me. Why couldn't I reach for it? Andraius flaunted his shit all over the place. Why not me?

"Okay then, Angel. Answer the question." Xander picked up a decanter of some dark amber liquid, poured some into a tumbler, and then took a healthy swallow before relaxing into his seat.

"I want to come. That's what I need."

Lust engulfed the cab of the limo, and our breaths grew unsteady.

The throbbing deep in my pussy pushed my desire to an unbearable level, and seeing the hard bulges in their pants pulled at that longing for everything I couldn't have.

I sighed. "Care to guess how long it's been since anyone has held me or touched me to give me pleasure?"

I held their gazes.

Yes, this was reckless. Yes, this was wrong. Everything in my life was wrong.

More than likely, I wouldn't be alive tomorrow, anyway. Andraius would never let me leave him.

Theo gripped the edge of his seat. "We can't touch you, Nerine. No matter how much we want to."

Xander added, "We love you too much to make your life harder."

Did they love me?

Then why had they stayed away? Why not let me know they were still around to give me hope?

My lips trembled, and I shook my head. I would not cry. Tears had no place in my life. "Answer this for me. Why don't I get anything? When will I stop being a pawn in this game?"

"You're not the pawn. You're the queen. We'd give you everything you need if it were in our power."

"What I need right now is one fucking orgasm. Is that too much to ask?" I wasn't expecting an answer from either of them, so I continued, "Nearly five years since I felt anything in the realm of desire. I've been with three men in my life. You two and Andraius."

I looked down at my clenched fists sitting in my lap. "He enjoyed seeing me cry. It made him feel as if he'd won. Want to know what I did within months of our marriage?" I smirked. "I learned to give him no emotion at all. You've heard him say I'm an unemotional, cold bitch. It's better to freeze my soul than constantly see the glee on that monster's face. But you know what?"

After a few long heartbeats, Theo asked, "What?"

I dropped my head back on the seat, not wanting to see either of their faces. "I mourn that girl who felt so much, laughed, loved, and enjoyed life. I was so damn strong, and no one could make me believe otherwise. I miss that girl. I'm tired of playing the cold, bitter bitch. I am tired of feeling dead inside.

What I wouldn't give to feel again, to be her again, if only for a few moments. I'm exhausted from fighting all the time. The old Nerine fought, but she never sold her soul to do it."

Unable to put myself out there anymore, I closed my eyes. I'd hardened myself for the last few years, and being around Xander and Theo cracked my walls. I couldn't afford any weakness in the world I lived in.

It was time to rebuild my shields again. No more falling back into old patterns. I'd focus on my plans with Nyx, Devani, and Lilly.

The men before me were my past, and I had to accept it. Now I needed to use the rest of the ride to rein my body under control and lock away the desires I shouldn't have allowed free in the first place.

"Nerine," Theo said.

Keeping my lids shut, I whispered, "What now?"

"Take off your clothes."

My eyes snapped open, connecting with Theo's darkened gray ones.

"You want to come. You'll come by your hands only."

My skin heated as the melancholy from moments earlier pushed to the back of my mind, and a tingle shot down my spine.

I shook my head. "You don't have to do this. My emotions got to me. It wasn't right to put this on the two of you."

"Angel, we want to give this to you," Xander said, taking another gulp from his glass and setting it in the holder. "We'll guide you, and you'll do what we tell you, exactly how we tell you. You don't come unless we give you permission. Even if we can't touch you, the rules are the same as before."

"You remember before, don't you?" A slight smile touched Theo's lips, easing the knot I hadn't realized had formed in the pit of my stomach.

"You mean I don't get to come if I don't listen."

"You seem to have a problem following directions. It's better to make everything clear." Theo lifted a brow that made me want to smack him and kiss him.

It was as if they transported me back to when I was nineteen and they were twenty-three.

I gave him a dramatic sigh. "Understood." I narrowed my gaze at Xander. "What about the two of you?"

"What about us?" Xander asked.

"Is it all three of us or just the two of you with me?"

They glanced at each other. I caught the longing and pain passing between them.

They really had walked away from each other when things ended with me. Instead of the thought comforting me, it broke my heart.

"Nerine." Xander's use of my name had me toeing off my shoes.

I lifted my shirt over my head and tossed it onto the bench beside me. Then, I slowly shimmied out of my shorts.

Both men inhaled deep when I unclasped my bra and let my breasts spill free. My nipples beaded into stiff peaks, and desire pooled between my legs.

But just as fast, it cooled as I readied to slide my underwear down.

Grabbing hold of my anxiety, I tugged the lace along my hips and let it gather at my feet. "Don't say anything. Please don't."

How would they react to the scars and the word they spelled? They weren't as visible after I'd started the products Nyx gave me, but they were still there. They'd always be there.

I lifted my gaze to theirs.

Theo's and Xander's faces remained blank as they stared back at me, but their eyes gave away the emotions warring inside them.

After a few seconds of quiet, Xander ordered, "Spread your legs and slide those fingers between those lips."

I followed his directive and adjusted my legs to give them a view of my swollen, slick pussy. With a slow glide, I traced the inside of my thighs and then stroked my labia up and down.

"Now, cup your breast," Theo directed. "Pinch the tip. Yes, like that. Harder. I know how much you like it to sting."

I gasped and closed my lids, loving the onslaught of sensation I felt for the first time in so long. I needed this so much, and they were giving it to me.

"Circle that clit. God, you have the most beautiful cunt I've ever seen. Do you know how many nights I've lain awake dreaming about it?" Xander adjusted himself through his pants, and I couldn't help but moan, remembering the feel of that huge cock deep in me.

The way he rolled his hips, knew just where to hit, and pushed me to my limits.

A tremor shot through my core, and I moaned as arousal seeped from my vaginal channel. "Oh, I'm almost there."

"No, you're not. You haven't even slipped those fingers inside that tight cunt yet." Theo shifted as if to come to me and then gritted his teeth, staying in place. "Push three in, baby, and rub that spot inside you."

I plunged three digits inside me, all the while using my thumb to continue to stroke my clit with each thrust. I writhed and whimpered.

My mind clouded, and Theo and Xander continued crooning commands and encouragement.

"Please, I have to come. Let me come," I begged.

"You're not there yet."

I gritted my teeth as my pussy quivered and contracted. I wasn't sure how long I could hold off my release.

"I can't stop it. It's coming."

"Are you sure?"

"Yes," I cried out, sweat dampening my skin. "Theo, Xander, please."

"Come, Angel." Theo's permission and the last graze of my thumb over my clit sent me over the cliff.

I convulsed around my thrusting fingers, soaked in my arousal. Exhilaration and complete ecstasy permeated my senses as if I had fallen from twenty miles high. I could barely breathe, and I had no doubt only incoherent words spilled from my lips.

Slowly I came down and melted into the seat, not caring about anything but catching my breath.

I'd only ever experienced this with these men.

"You're so fucking beautiful." With the rough timbre of

Xander's voice, I opened my lashes, catching the unguarded lust in his onyx gaze.

I licked my parched lips and watched his attention shift to my mouth.

If only I could let this go further, but I couldn't. I'd already pushed it as far as possible.

The haze of lust cleared slowly, but I had to make something clear to them.

"I don't regret this."

I felt nothing in the vicinity of shame or guilt about what happened. Instead, for the first time in years, I had taken something exclusively for myself. Maybe I'd become as selfish and hateful as Andraius, but I couldn't pull up an ounce of remorse for this.

Theo handed me a cloth he'd pulled from somewhere. "You need to clean up."

I wiped my arousal and sweat from my body and then reached for my discarded underwear. In a flash, Theo shifted forward, staying my hands by gripping my hip and pushing me back.

My heartbeat accelerated. "We can't."

"That's not what I'm doing." He skimmed a finger along my abdomen, just below my belly button. "I need to see what he did to you because of us."

I swallowed as the back of my throat burned with unshed tears, and I closed my eyes, turning my face away.

Another set of hands settled on my hips, and Xander's lips brushed my scars.

"I'm so sorry, Angel," he whispered against my skin.

It took all my strength not to slide my fingers into his hair. I shouldn't want more. They gave me more than I ever expected.

"You'll tell us all of it," Theo stated, his mouth replacing Xander's. "Not today, but I will get the full story."

"Maybe." I shifted, knowing I had to get dressed.

"Stay right there." Theo lifted his head, looking in Xander's direction, both having some silent conversation.

I felt the intensity of it, the unsaid undercurrent of the desire the three of us shared.

My heart ached seeing their need for each other. Why they'd made the choice to end everything when I was out of the picture would never make sense.

But as always, they had their reasons.

The second Xander nodded, Theo lifted my leg and tugged me toward his mouth.

"What are you doing?" I gasped.

Xander grabbed my arms, pinning them above my head.

"When you step out of this limo, you will know whatever name he tries to force you to carry, you will forever be ours."

I stared at him and allowed a tear to fall free, not out of pain but pure love for these men.

"No." He shifted my wrists to one hand and thumbed the wetness from my cheek. "This isn't the time for that. You wanted to come. Let's see how many times we can make it happen before we get to the compound."

At that moment, Theo slid his tongue through the lips of my pussy and sucked my clit into his mouth, making my back bow.

"Oh, God."

"Not God, Theo."

A smile touched my lips. "Do you ever get tired of saying that line?"

"Not until you get it right." He grinned back up at me.

I tugged at my hands, wanting to grab hold of his thick mass of dark hair.

"Tsk. Tsk." Xander leaned down as he stroked his fingers down the column of my neck and between my breasts. "You can't touch us."

I frowned. "Why not? We've already crossed the line."

We'd crossed the line the second I'd asked them to make me come.

"All crimes are ours. You can honestly say your hands never touched us."

"That's a technicality."

"Our world is based on technicalities. How do you think so many of us survived the regime change?"

"Then you won't kiss me." I lifted my face toward him, and immediately, he drew back.

He shook his head. "That would mean you would have to lie."

A pang of disappointment hit me, but I understood what they were doing.

They were protecting me.

Then without thinking, I asked, "What about the two of you? Are you off limits to each other?"

I wanted to take back the question almost immediately when I felt Theo freeze and his face lift.

Xander's dark gaze went to Theo's.

A war of emotions passed between them until Theo turned his attention back to me and said, "This isn't about us, it's about you."

I nodded, knowing once Theo made a decision, he wouldn't change his mind.

I gasped as my arms were pulled taut above me.

"Since I know that you can't follow directions worth shit." Xander looped his tie around my wrists and bound them to the seatbelt strap above me.

"This looks familiar," Theo murmured against my inner thigh. "Where have I seen this before?"

"I believe it was on your twenty-third birthday."

"That's right. I wanted Angel cake for dessert." His hungry gaze moved between my legs to my swollen pussy. "I believe I'm going to indulge again."

His mouth descended, resuming his ministrations. At the same time, Xander engulfed my nipple in his mouth.

The onslaught of sensations clouded my mind, and I climbed at an unfathomable speed.

I writhed and moaned into each flick of their tongues and bite of their teeth.

Theo stroked and teased my aching clit, and I couldn't help but flex my legs against his back, urging him closer, silently begging him to move his mouth to the core of me.

Xander switched to my other breast, nipping and flicking the tip. He gave me the edge of pain that drew goosebumps over my skin and drove me higher and higher.

"Send her over, Theo," Xander commanded while continuing to worry my tender nipples.

"With pleasure." Theo thrust his tongue deep into my pussy, licking and making me grind against his mouth.

Less than a few seconds later, everything inside me tightened with small quivers, followed by clenching, a cascade of fiery pleasure sweeping through every nerve in my body.

"Only with you two," I whimpered, too lost in the euphoria showering over me.

I'd barely come down when I heard Xander say, "Now it's my turn. Angel, get ready. If this is my only chance, I will make it count."

The men traded places, and Xander made every microsecond of the ride home count.

Fifteen

ander

Five minutes from the Angelos mansion, I studied Nerine as she meticulously dressed. With every item of clothing she slid on her body, I watched the cool, calm, emotionless mask she liked to don slip back in place.

Yes, it was all a lie. She felt a torrent of emotions under the facade. Hell, the vulnerability she'd revealed to Theo and me spoke the truth, not to mention her loss of control when she saw Andraius with his mistress.

Returning to the house meant erecting those cold steel walls and regaining some of the norms she'd lived with for the last few years. It infuriated me to know her only form of protection was acting like a piece of ice sat in her chest instead of a feeling, beating heart.

This woman loved so hard and felt too much to lock it away.

"You don't have to pretend with us."

She smirked and shook her head. "You have no idea what you're even talking about. I'm being me and accepting my reality."

"What is your reality?" I asked while glancing at Theo, who studied Nerine, assessing her, her words, and her reactions.

He'd remained eerily silent since we'd given Nerine her last orgasm. And no matter how much we wanted to ignore it, our desire, lust, and desperate longing for each other remained a constant presence around us, lingering in the air.

It was as if the moment we'd pulled the last bit of pleasure out of her, we knew this couldn't happen again. Theo's normal operating mode was to grow quiet and brood. At the same time, I maintained an open line of communication with the Angel. However, with him, there was this wall I couldn't fucking break down.

It kept all of our interactions from being one hundred percent authentic.

Now here I was facing the two people who mattered most to me in the world and couldn't get over the stupid decisions I'd made five years ago.

And from the tension I felt brewing, they were about to go for each other's throats at any minute.

This was all I needed.

"The only freedom I will ever have is the one I take."

Theo's eyes shifted to mine briefly, telling me he caught the same cryptic undertones of her words.

Leaning forward, I asked in the calmest tone possible, "What exactly does that mean?"

"I refuse to be anyone's pawn much longer. Either Andraius kills me, or I vanish. Let's hope the former isn't my fate."

Before I realized what Theo had planned, he tugged Nerine across the limo and onto his lap.

He brought his face right up against hers. "What are you and your Assassin Squad planning?"

"Let me go, you asshole." She struggled against his hold, glowering at him.

Fucking hell. In a blink of an eye, they could go from icebergs to molten lava, ready to kill each other.

"Not until you answer the damn question."

"Why would I tell you? I'm a pawn in your plans, too." She lifted her chin as if daring him to kiss her. "You don't listen to me any more than anyone else."

"Nerine, why would you even say that?" I had to ask, feeling the sting of her words. "What we have isn't like that, and you know it."

She whipped her head around, looking in my direction, fire blazing in her bright blue irises. "I accept we have a remembered love, but do you even know me? I'm talking about the woman I am now."

"Of course, I fucking do. Who the hell have we been around for the last few months?"

"Then tell me, what is it that I want most? What have I said I want more than anything?"

Theo whispered, "To escape with your mother and sisters."

"Will you let that happen?" She shifted to stare into Theo's gray eyes. "Will you free me from a life with Andraius and the Angelos legacy?"

"You want us to let you go for a second time? Even after today?"

"Yes." She nodded. "More than you will ever know. He's not giving up his throne as easily as you believe."

Before Theo could respond, the car stopped in the mansion's driveway. Nerine scrambled off his lap just as the door opened.

We'd barely stepped out of the limo when she said, "I won't leave the property, but I want some time alone. I don't need a constant shadow. Is that understood?"

The raw intimacy of the conversation from only moments earlier completely evaporated as if it had never occurred in the first place. Well, except for the fact an immense weight sat like a heavy cloak around us.

"Your security will remain by your side whether you like it or not," Theo countered and then added, "As you stated, if Andraius has his way, you'll die by morning. My job is to prevent such things."

"Follow my traitor husband around then and leave me alone."

I stepped between Theo and Nerine. "We have guards on him, but he has allies, and we haven't identified all of them. Work with us, Nerine."

"You want me to work with you?" Her attention shifted between Theo and me. "Then answer the question I asked before we arrived. Yes or no?"

We remained quiet, neither of us saying anything, only staring at her.

How the fuck could she expect us to let her go?

Anger flared in her blue eyes. "Exactly as I believed. Well, since I am the true Angelos, I have a directive that I expect everyone to follow."

"And that is?" Theo stepped around me and waited.

"I want the Angelos interloper, his mistress, and his possessions removed from my parents' room and placed anywhere but near me." She stalked up to Theo, rage burning all over her face. "You want me to run this family. I'll do it, even if it means running it into the ground."

I grabbed Nerine's wrist before she could move away.

She jerked her wrist and lifted the other arm as if to deck me before I caught it.

I held her hands captive and leaned forward, saying in a low voice so only she could hear, "We did all this to give you back your birthright, not to punish you. We fucking love you."

"All I want is to have a choice."

"Stop thinking like a damn child, Nerine," Theo snapped, moving behind her. "You're the same damn age we were when everything went down. You're too smart not to understand how things have to go."

"Apparently, I'm not since I don't know what you're talking about."

I allowed her to tug her hands free of my hold, and she glowered at us as she cocked a hand on her hip.

"What heir of any family has a choice? Did your father have a choice? Did Drakos? All these months, and you're still thinking like a victim. What the fuck did we do all this for?" Theo gripped the hair on the back of his head.

"Calm the fuck down," I ordered Theo, knowing this situation drew too much attention.

He rarely lost his temper in public and having him unleash it on Nerine in the open meant trouble. Our secrets had to remain quiet, for all our sakes.

And, of course, Nerine couldn't keep her mouth shut. "It looks as if it was for nothing. It is useless talking to you about anything. You don't listen to me. I am finished with you and you bossing me around. Go suck a rotten egg and leave me the hell alone. We are done with this conversation."

She turned and rushed into the house.

Maybe everyone would chalk it up to emotions of her seeing Andraius and the wedding-gown incident.

"The hell you are finished with anything. This conversation is far from over." Theo stalked behind her, following her into the mansion.

Fuck me.

Taking a few deep breaths to calm my nerves, I glanced at some of the soldiers, who all grimaced.

Yep. This was bad.

Slowly I surveyed the men and then internally sighed in relief. They were all part of the originals and loyal to Nerine. They'd kept our secrets and would continue to hold them.

After a deep, calming breath, I asked, "Where's Andraius?"

"We moved him to a more secure location as you ordered," one of the soldiers responded.

"And his mistress?"

"Returned to her apartment."

"Keep everyone away from Nerine's section of the house. I need to defuse this situation before she kills Theo." I shook my head. "I hate playing peacemaker."

"It sucks to be on the other side of the table for once," I heard someone whisper but couldn't decipher who said it.

A few of the men snickered, and I shot them a scowl. "I didn't ask for your opinions."

"I've never seen either of them so volatile," the one who'd answered my earlier questions stated.

"They bring out the best in each other," I muttered as I made my way to the residential section of the house.

Nerine's shout of "You're a fucking asshole!" reached my ears when my foot hit the landing near her bedroom.

Then came Theo's, "And you're a spoiled child who needs to grow the hell up."

I hurried to the room, knowing this would end with her shooting or fucking him, and neither was an option.

I stepped through the doorway to see Nerine hurl one of her boots directly at Theo's head and him ducking and ready to retaliate.

"How dare you call me a child. You have no idea what I've endured."

"You aren't the only one who's suffered."

"Were you forced to marry and fuck a man thirty years older than you?"

Theo stepped toward Nerine, clenching his jaw. "I lost my mother to this life, then my whole family. You still have your mother and sisters."

"Is this a game of tit for tat?"

I had to find a way to get these two under control. Nerine teetered on powder-keg mode, which meant if Theo kept poking at her, there was no telling what she'd do.

And after everything that had happened in the limo, our emotions were too charged to think rationally.

"The two of you need to simmer down."

Ignoring me, Theo took another step in Nerine's direction. "This isn't a game at all, brat. Only a child would say it's a game."

"Call me a child again, and I'll punch you in the face." She smacked her fist against her palm. "Those assassins taught me more than you can imagine. I will fuck you up."

He lifted and then pointed at his chin. "Give it your best shot, Angel."

"Oh, for fuck's sake." I ran to intercept Nerine as she charged for Theo.

Her body collided with my front as Theo's hit my back. I held Nerine by the waist, trying to steady and push her back. At the same time, Theo fisted her hair, pulling her forward, and she reached over my shoulder and clawed at his forearms.

"You're a jackass," Nerine spat. "I hate you."

Theo jerked her closer, sandwiching me harder between them. "Feeling's mutual, brat."

"You two need to calm the hell down before this goes too far." I threw my head back, willing the biting lust surging forward to ease to something manageable, less demanding.

This was how it had always started—an epic fight between these two morons and me standing in the middle.

The energy in the room seemed to crackle, and my idiot cock wanted to join the party.

Breathing through the raging need, I made the mistake of looking down.

Nerine's livid attention connected with mine right as she grabbed my shirt.

"You mean like this?" She jerked me toward her, covering her lips with mine.

Her essence exploded against my mouth, causing every one of my good intentions to evaporate into thin air.

My palm slid up her back, dragging her against me. I feasted on her, knowing the memories of the past were nothing compared to the reality of this woman here and now. She tasted better than the rarest scotch, intoxicating, decadent, indulgent.

She moaned, rubbing her pelvis along my cock, and threaded her fingers into my hair.

This was heaven and hell all rolled into one.

Theo tugged her head in his direction, her eyes fluttered open, and she whispered, "Theo, you have to know I don't hate you."

"It's hate-love, remember?" He leaned forward, biting her lower lip, eliciting a whimper from her before sealing his mouth over hers.

Theo and I walked Nerine backward until we pinned her

to a nearby wall. He continued to worship her, cupping her breasts and pinching her nipples through her clothes as he devoured her mouth.

When Theo broke the kiss and turned his face toward me, I leaned in and then pulled back. We stared at each other. The draw to him remained the same as it had always been. We'd felt it since we were kids, even before we acted upon it.

At this moment, it was his choice. He either forgave me or he didn't.

After what felt like minutes and was probably only seconds, I pushed down the disappointment and dropped to my knees, focusing back on Nerine.

I pulled her shoes off and then worked her skintight pants down her curvy ass and thighs. All the while, I kissed and licked along the skin I slowly exposed. Theo lifted her shirt over her head, throwing the material behind him as he bit and nipped down the column of her neck. She arched into the pleasure-filled pain of his teeth.

"I missed this. God, I missed this so much," she gasped and moaned.

Rising to my feet, I took Nerine's lips. I couldn't get enough of her. I wanted every part of her.

Her fingers drifted to the buttons of my shirt and then trailed down to cup my hard, engorged cock, stroking me through my pants.

God, I'd waited years for this—her touch.

There was nothing like her.

At that moment, a glint of light reflected off her wedding

ring, making me freeze and bringing some semblance of sanity back.

"W—we have to stop." I looked up at her, seeing the confusion and hurt.

"No." She cupped my face. "Please."

I clenched my jaw, and with all the willpower I could muster, I stepped back. "You aren't free. We've already pushed it beyond anything we should have done. You can never be ours until Andraius is out of the picture."

Theo nodded. His flushed face and dilated gray eyes told me he was struggling to do the right thing as much as I was.

She took in shallow breaths, her body shaking.

She braced a hand on the wall behind her. In a flash, Nerine's face grew emotionless, and the mask she wore for the public settled into place.

"Then I guess this is where everything the three of us have ever shared ends."

No, I wouldn't allow this. She had to understand the reasons. First Theo and now her, was I ever going to stop fucking up?

"We're trying to do the right thing," I pled with her. "We aren't rejecting you."

"It's not rejection, I feel, but acceptance. To find my freedom, I either have to disappear or die. In both scenarios, there is no reconciliation for the three of us."

"Dammit, Nerine. Stop saying that shit." Theo got in her face—the anger from moments earlier back in full force. "You will not disappear. Do you hear me? And dying isn't an option. I have lost everyone I love. I will not fucking lose you, too."

She set a hand on his chest. “I don’t plan to die. My job is to protect my mother and sisters. As long as I’m alive, they are safe.”

“Stop thinking about yourself as a commodity.” I glared at her over Theo’s shoulder. “You are the Angelos Angel, the heir to the syndicate. Theo’s right. Stop thinking of yourself as a victim and look at yourself as the viper Theios Peter raised you to be.”

“I am Papa’s viper. You don’t want to accept the version of her that I’ve become. We can’t go back in time, Xander. I can only look to my future.”

“Are you kidding me right now? All we’ve done is for your future.” I gestured to her. “Theo and I played fucking traitors to hold your empire.”

“Is it really my empire if you run it?” She lifted a brow. “I’m a figurehead.”

I countered with my own glare. “Do you think everyone doesn’t suspect who funneled the money out of all the accounts? Or who strategically set up the trust with said assets, making it impossible for anyone other than blood-linked Angelos children to inherit?”

She remained quiet for a moment, then said, “Papa and I had an emergency plan. I never thought I’d have to put it into action.”

“Good thing you did. It has helped keep Andraius in a chokehold for nearly five years.”

“It still doesn’t make me anything more than a figurehead, even if you manage to get rid of Andraius.”

"Don't you remember the golden rule Theios Peter taught you for our world? The reason for so many of our wars."

She pursed her lips. "The one who controls the wealth is the one who sits at the head of the table."

"You are the only one who can access the nearly billion dollars you funneled out of the thirty or so accounts."

"How did you manage it?" Theo asked. "And where did it go? We traced it to multiple Swiss accounts, and then it disappeared. How the fuck do you make a billion dollars vanish?"

"It was Papa's secret. I'm not at liberty to share."

"What happens if you die?"

She shrugged. "I suppose God will judge me, and I'll end up in heaven or hell."

"You are the most frustrating woman I have ever known." Theo moved across the room. "Why is it so hard for you to give us a straight answer?"

"You want to know why?"

"Yes."

"No matter what I feel for you, I will never answer to you. Neither of you is my father or husband, and the being-my-lovers part was out of the question by your choice."

"You will take the reins once Andraius is out of the picture."

"And unseat the two of you? I think not."

"What the hell are you talking about?"

"Believe what you will. Your ingrained loyalties remain with the family. Andraius isn't the head of the Angelos Syndicate. The two of you are. Maybe in the beginning, my spouse muddled his way through things, but the two young men with the business degrees and street smarts took over, and the moron didn't even realize. I can't compete with that. And I don't want to."

"You can't just walk away."

She moved toward her bathroom, pausing in the archway and glancing over her shoulder. "You're right. I can't."

"Enough with this cryptic shit."

"Well then, let me make this crystal clear for the two of you." She took hold of the doorknob and stepped into the bathroom. "I believe our association as anything beyond business is over. As you like to remind me, I'm not free."

"Is that how you truly want it?"

"It is best to do it that way. I can't handle this emotional roller coaster." She dropped her head, closing the door slightly. "I'm sorry. We crossed a line today that should never have occurred. It won't happen again."

"You expect us to pretend it is business as usual?"

"Yes. The two of you are Andraius's right-hand men. And I am his errant wife."

Sixteen

erine

A little before nine in the evening, and almost forty-eight hours after the blowup that caused Andraius's house arrest, I tightened the belt of my robe and pushed open the false wall accessing the library. I craved some time alone, to read, to relax, and to not have a single male around me watching my every fucking move.

With all the traitors who supported Andriaus still unidentified, I understood the high-alert situation we were under. But Xander and Theo were being a bit ridiculous to want to know every detail of my schedule, even when I went to the bathroom.

Telling them they were going overboard only made them

more annoyingly underfoot with them stepping in to be my shadows.

Right now, I was desperate for a change of scenery. It would allow me to settle my nerves and think rationally.

Fucking men.

Yeah, my emotions continued to run the gamut of volcanic rage, depressive sadness, and complete numbness.

Andraius had spent the last two days behaving almost like a model prisoner. Which meant he was up to something.

Everyone knew it, especially Xander, Theo, and me.

When I told Theo to have extra surveillance on Andraius's sector of the house, he grinned and made some comment about me already taking my position as the Angelos. But was I truly?

I hated the fact Theo and Xander had been right. I'd allowed myself to live in my victimhood. But over the last few months, I'd grown stronger and now I would decide what was best for me, my sisters, and my mother.

Theo and Xander wanted me to fight for the family to achieve the results they craved, become the true Angelos.

But would I ever actually be the true Angelos when there were two men who already ran the organization?

I refused to stand as a figurehead only or live under the subjugation of any man again.

This wasn't a pity party for me but an acknowledgment of the truth. The only way to prove power was to demonstrate strength.

My confidence in my abilities continued to grow. However,

fighting off another takeover or coup wasn't something I was sure I had the knowledge to battle.

Through the walls, echoes of movement told me chaos hummed in the house. Soldiers had taken sides, and plans were in the works to see who came out on top.

I had no doubt those who aligned themselves with Andraius waited for an order or sign from him to move. Or they may have decided to abandon ship and look for an opportunity to escape.

The volatility in the air felt thick.

Yeah, the smartest thing to do was to turn back and stay in my room. Where I knew things were secure and no one could reach me.

But then I'd let everything inside me fester into an atomic bomb level of insanity instead of channeling it into something productive. Like the homework I needed to finish for Lilly.

Considering the situation going on in my world, she'd let me pass on my assignments, but at least this gave me an excuse for leaving my room if my wardens caught me.

Frowning, I entered the room and closed the panel to keep the passageway chill from seeping into the warm library. There was no point in locking it since I'd sealed all other entry points from my section of the house and the library.

And just in case anyone decided to annoy me tonight, I had my handy-dandy blade strapped to my thigh.

Keeping a weapon attached to my body that was sharp enough to split a hair in two was definitely a smart idea considering the past few days. It would also come in handy if Theo or

Xander decided to give me another lecture. A slice to their shoulder or neck might encourage them to stay away from me.

For a fraction of a second, the thought of licking a drop of blood from Xander's and Theo's necks sent a shockwave of need and arousal coursing deep into my core.

What the ever-loving fuck?

The turmoil and rage of my life were getting to me.

I grabbed my laptop and took a seat behind my desk.

I set my hands over my abdomen as tremors shook my body. I'd only ever experienced blood once during sex, and it had destroyed a piece of me, left me nearly broken, and I still bore the scars of it.

I'd cover the scars up one day. Have skilled tattoo artists transform them into something beautiful.

No, covering them up meant Andraius won. I would never let the bastard win.

I still wanted a tattoo—a specific one designed by two people long ago. I'd hidden the design away in my childhood bedroom.

I guess it wouldn't happen, though. Because the only person I'd allow to put it on my body was Xander.

He used to ink everyone when we were younger. Art came naturally to him, and somehow it had veered into tattoos.

"If this enforcer thing doesn't work out, I could always open a chain of tattoo shops. I'm sure Theios Peter would lend me the seed money."

"He knows how talented you are. He'd give it to you now. This doesn't have to be a backup plan."

"Nah, I like punching people too much. Just promise I'll get to ink you first."

I couldn't help but smile thinking of the memory. I was a senior in high school then. My classmates loved to tease me and tell me I was fascinated with my too-old-for-me, college-aged bodyguards. Though none of them had a clue I was in a relationship with them.

That was such an innocent time for us. Our biggest worry back then was how we'd eventually break the news about the three of us to our families and the fallout we may face afterward.

Lifting the lid to my computer, I decided to focus and finish my assignments for the lady bosses. The whole process of logging into their system took as long as the homework. The only things they left out of the security protocols were a blood sample and a retinal scan.

Once in the network, I spent the next hour working through the modules to acquire various data packets from locations Lilly had set as my targets.

When I acquired the data drives, she wanted me to relocate them onto a secure network while still connected to the home server. Next, the instructions said to log in using the information provided and review the contents.

As I scanned down the screen, my hands shook. Lilly hadn't been training me. She fucking had me hacking.

Oh my God. I'd just broken into a Bahamian bank's security infrastructure.

My pulse drummed into my head, and dizziness filled me.

That bitch. Was she trying to put a bigger target on my head than the one already sitting on it?

As I readied to close the document, my eyes caught an image of my signature. But it wasn't my signature.

Oh, no fucking way. It was forged.

That rat bastard. He was embezzling money from the family and pinning it on me.

Motherfucker.

I clenched my jaw and decided to use those fucking hacker skills to manipulate the documents, removing any trace of my identity. I also wired the funds into a Swiss account, which would direct wire into multiple holding accounts I'd created based on Papa's directions.

When the time came, all the money would return to the family. But until then, this asshole I married wouldn't get a penny.

I rubbed the bridge of my nose as a throbbing ignited in my head.

Lilly knew about all of this and had never told me.

Why the hell not?

Then it hit me.

She wanted me to learn to take care of myself.

Theo's words about living as a victim and being a child echoed in my mind.

All of these people had come into my life to help me, seeing things about me I couldn't. I fought Andraius out of the sheer fact that I'd given up and, not because I wanted to actually fight him and take back my life.

Okay. I'd shouted my demand for a divorce. I'd better

follow through with it. To hell with the event a few days from now.

I'd go alone. Nyx would probably laugh out loud and clap.

At that moment, a chat window popped up on my screen.

LILLY: Stop stalling and finish up. You're three minutes past the scheduled finish time.

ME: I wasn't aware this was a timed assignment or THAT IT WASN'T A SIMULATION!!!!!!!!

LILLY: Don't shout at me, young lady!!! I will kick your ass the next time I see you.

ME: Apologies, your royal hackerness.

LILLY: Finish the job. You left one spot with your name on it. Clean it out. I'll handle the rest.

ME: Should I learn to do all of it?

LILLY: What I'm about to do is highly illegal.

ME: More than what I did?

LILLY: You have no idea. Plus, these skills take years to master, and people like you hire people like me to do the jobs for you.

ME: I'll remember to keep you on retainer.

LILLY: Smart woman.

I closed the window and traced back through the banking system to find where I missed the connection to me, cleared it, and linked it to Andraius. Once I backed out of all the systems, I enacted the security firewall for my computer and shut it down.

Only someone with Lilly's skill level could break into this thing.

Now for a few hours of relaxation and reading. Tomorrow,

I'd have more than my share of problems to deal with, especially when my beloved husband discovered his accounts emptied.

A chill slid up my spine. Maybe I should have just removed any connection to me and left the money.

No. I couldn't second-guess myself. I'd made the right decision. It wasn't Andraius's money in the first place. It belonged to the family.

The uneasiness in my stomach continued to grow.

I needed to tell Theo and Xander what I'd done.

Fuck. They were at a late-night meeting off property.

I had to keep it together. I had to remember I was safe here. Andraius was on the other side of the compound with around-the-clock guards.

Hell, *I* had around-the-clock guards.

Shit, that wasn't a good example. Mine hadn't a clue where the fuck I was at the moment.

Rising to my feet, I moved to pick up the book I'd started a few days ago. I'd occupy myself with some mindless reading.

I thumbed through the pages, opening it to where I last stopped, and set it on the side table near my favorite sofa.

As I reached to the side to grab my blanket, a hand fisted my hair, hurling me back, and a forearm locked around my throat.

"I learned a secret of yours today. This house is full of passageways. I found one near the fireplace in the room you jailed me inside." His disgusting breath wafted over me. "It led across the house to the kitchen. Then I had three choices. Lucky me, on the first try I found the library."

I tried my hardest to remain calm, even though the barest amount of air passed into my lungs with how tightly Andraius held my throat. I grasped at his arm, tugging and scratching.

I'd forgotten about the connecting hallways from the other side of the house. Why hadn't I checked all the doors? I was so stupid, thinking I was safe and letting my guard down.

I was never safe. How many times would I have to learn this lesson?

"Where is it?"

I couldn't speak, the pressure on my neck too much to bear.

"Answer me, dammit." He jostled my head, digging his nails into my scalp.

"A—air," I gasped.

He eased up, and the sudden burst of oxygen forced me to cough as tears burned my eyes.

"Who did you hire to take the money?"

"What are you talking about?"

He turned me, freeing me from his brutal grasp of my hair, and then shoved me against a table, pushing me back before he pinned me down by my neck.

"I know my money is gone. In this day and age, did you think I wouldn't get an alert the second money left my account?"

That shouldn't be possible—they'd confiscated his phone and computer.

We shouldn't have been so trusting with all the guards. Now it was too late.

"How could I do anything while reading a book in the library?"

"Don't play dumb with me. I know you took your father's money and hid it. And I know you stole my money."

"Stole? Are you accusing me of stealing your money? You are out of your mind. How can I steal money that was never yours to begin with?"

His eyes grew darker and angrier. "You did take it. Where is it?"

He jerked me forward with the front of my robe and dragged me to the desk. "Where is your computer? I know it's in here. Transfer the money back this instant."

The harsh movement caused my nightgown to catch against the sheath of the blade I'd strapped to my thigh.

What was I doing? I'd trained for months to protect myself. Why was I letting this man toss me around and abuse me?

Fuck. This. Shit.

If he killed me tonight, it wouldn't be because I refused to fight him tooth and nail. I'd give him some wounds I hoped and prayed to God that he never healed from.

I remained in place, staring at him, an inferno of hate bubbling inside me.

"No."

"What did you say?"

"You heard me. I am not now or ever giving you anything that belongs to my family."

He yanked me against him. "I am going to enjoy killing you. What you saw in the Caves isn't even close to what I plan to do to you."

"Then you definitely won't get anything. I've made sure of it."

"I will just marry one of the twins. They turned eighteen two months ago."

"Good luck with that. According to Mama, Christina is dating the heir to the Amici Familia. If I die, she gets everything since she is considered the eldest. Even if it is by a few minutes. That's right. My sister broke your rules about staying away from syndicate families."

"You believe that you're so smart. Remember, I don't need you conscious to access your eggs. People live with head injuries for years. Don't you keep up with the news?"

I stepped back, seeing the manic gleam in his dark eye. He couldn't be serious.

"You will never get a single child from me. I will never allow it."

"How can you contest it if you can't speak?" He charged for me, and on instinct, I crouched, rolling to the side.

Andraius grabbed my robe, and I let him remove it from my body. As I jerked my arms free, I fell forward and tried to crawl away as fast as possible, but he grabbed my ankle and kicked me.

Pain shot through my leg, taking all the breath from my lungs. I countered with my other foot, kicking him in the stomach as hard as I could manage.

"You bitch." He stumbled backward, and I managed to slide to my side.

Pulling the blade from the scabbard on my thigh, I held it

hidden behind me. I would not let this bastard win. I refused to let this fucker get any piece of me.

One way or another, this was over.

My death or his. Fuck him. Fuck this whole situation. Fuck fate.

"All you had to do was behave. Be a good wife like Drakos has."

I panted. "Are you kidding me? She's insane, and you don't even know it."

"You're jealous. Now I will teach you a lesson and take back this family." He stormed in my direction as if he had no worries about overpowering me.

And in the past, it had been true.

But not anymore, motherfucker.

When Andraius was within reach of me, I pivoted and jabbed upward. The impact of my blade slicing into flesh reverberated into my wrist, forcing me to release the handle.

A gurgled cry escaped his lips as shock and rage glazed his eyes.

"You'll pay for this." He stumbled forward with outstretched hands, ready to grab onto me.

I barely scrambled out of the way of his fingers grazing my shoulder and slammed into one of the giant bookshelves in the back of the room. Pain exploded on the side of my head, making it almost impossible to see.

Through blurry eyes, I searched the area around me for anything I could use as a weapon.

This couldn't be happening. I hadn't fought this hard for it to end like this.

I willed my vision to clear. Slowly, things came into focus, and I found Andraius desperately trying to pull the hilt of the blade free of his body.

I should stay quiet, should let him speed up his demise, but I opened my mouth. "The blade is the only thing stemming your blood loss. Pulling it out is like popping a cork."

"Shut up," he gritted out. "You want me dead. Why would I listen to you?"

"You die either way. I don't care."

"I will use this blade to cut your tongue out." Andraius jerked the blade free, not realizing he'd caused more damage to himself than I'd done with my initial stab.

Blood oozed from his belly, and he tipped over, landing on the floor. I couldn't help but watch him stare off into the distance, gasping and wheezing as the life slowly drained from his body.

My attention shifted to my hands and the deep red of Andraius's blood covering them. A sense of trepidation and elation filled me.

I finally did it. I finally killed him.

Seventeen

Theo

At around three a.m., I'd barely stepped out of a meeting with a shipping supplier when Xander screeched to a halt outside the building in his Spyder and ordered, "Get in the car."

"Well, hello to you, too, shithead. Do you realize how exhausted I am? I hate these late-night meetings."

"Get in the fucking car. We have a situation." The glare he shot me made it seem like life and death.

What could have happened in the last hour?

I pulled out my phone and saw thirty or so texts and six missed calls. I shook my head.

What the hell could have happened between the start of the meeting and three in the morning?

"They took our phones. You know how shit works with them. I got it back as I stepped out the door."

"Are you going to stand there, or are we heading to the house?"

Sliding into the passenger seat, I said, "Give me the details and cut the dramatics."

"Andraius is missing, and no one knows where the fuck he went. Is that dramatic enough for you?"

"Who was on him?" My pulse hammered into my chest.

"Mason and Josh. They said he never left his suite, but when they went inside to check on him, he wasn't there."

"Where's Nerine? Do we have anyone on her?"

"According to our team, she said she had a headache and wanted to go to bed after a shower. They heard her shower go on about an hour ago and then silence. As far as they know, she hasn't left."

"That means nothing."

"She knows better than to use the passages with everything going on."

"Does she? The is Nerine we're discussing." A thought crossed my mind that had my stomach churning. "He found the passageways. That's the only escape route out of that room."

Xander gunned the engine and dialed a number on his console. "Check every nook and cranny of the house."

"What about Mrs. Angelos? Do we wake her?"

Xander glanced at me. "No. We're almost there."

About ten minutes later, Stefano, Clay, and a group of our

men met us as we pulled into the driveway of the Angelos mansion.

The expressions on each of their faces told me I wouldn't like whatever they had to say.

Clay approached. "You have to come with us."

"Nerine?"

"No. It's Andraius," Stefano answered.

I cocked my head to the side. "Explain."

Clay and Stefano exchanged glances. "He's dead. Murdered."

"You're fucking kidding me." Xander rushed into the house, not knowing where to go.

I followed after him as Clay called, "In the library."

A group of men stood at the room's archway, no one entering, as if afraid to step inside.

Xander pushed past them and surveyed the entire space. I approached Andraius's body. He was sprawled on his stomach, face to the side, eyes wide open, blood pooling like a river around his body.

"Who found him?" I turned to look at the group congregating by the door.

"I did. About five minutes before you arrived," Bran answered. "I followed protocol and kept everyone out until you arrived. No one has touched the body or stepped inside the room."

Xander walked the periphery of the room. "I want the feed for the property checked—every inch of it from this morning to now. I want the names of every last person who arrived and left, from staff to deliveries to business associates. Don't leave a single person out. I want times in and out."

"As of now, no one leaves this property. Lock it down." I pulled out my secure phone and typed in a code, restricting all cell communication from anyone on the compound.

Rising from my crouch near Andraius's body, my attention shifted to the object he held.

The blade.

Not just any blade but one I'd seen before in Nerine's possession.

God, Nerine.

What the fuck happened here tonight?

"Xander. We need to get to Nerine."

Maybe it was my tone, but Xander rushed from the room. I followed behind him, not knowing what to expect when we saw her.

Xander banged on the door with all his force.

"Nerine, wake up."

No sound came. No cursing. No orders to fuck off. The blood in my head pounded.

"Nerine, open up, now! Or we're breaking it down if you don't," I warned, and then not giving a shit, pushed Xander out of the way as I slammed the hinge with my shoulder, busting the lock open.

Nerine jumped to sitting in her bed, fear in her eyes. It was as if she knew what I was about to tell her.

Fucking Angel, what have you done?

Xander moved in her direction and then scooped her into his arms, whispering into her hair, "Thank God, you're safe. I don't know what I would have done if anything had happened to you."

Hallway lights illuminated the room, and Nerine's blue gaze connected with mine.

Something definitely wasn't right. This wasn't a woman woken from sleep. Fear lingered in her eyes and her whole demeanor seemed dazed.

"Andraius is dead, Angel. We've got to get you out of here, now."

She stared at me as if not comprehending what I'd said. "Go where?"

"Nerine, did you hear me?" I asked, raising my voice to snap her out of her haze. "Someone killed Andraius."

She flinched, blinking a few times as if clearing the fog from her mind, and then hunched her shoulders, curling her arms and body around Xander.

"A-are you sure he's dead?" She sounded worried yet hopeful at the same time.

Her body shook as if chills overtook her.

Xander held her close and whispered into her hair as he adjusted his hold on her. "There is no doubt."

She winced when his hand grazed her calf, and I moved in her direction without a second thought.

"What's wrong with your leg?" I tried to inspect the area around her calf, but she swiped my hand away.

"I'm fine. It's nothing." She squirmed against Xander, telling him without words to set her down.

He hesitated for a second and then relented. "How did you hurt yourself?"

"I walked into the end of the bed without looking," she answered with her back to us. "Give me a minute to get changed."

Nerine calmly walked to her closet, pretending her steps weren't laced with the edge of pain.

Her hitting the bed was bullshit. I knew it with every fiber of my being. Clumsy and Nerine weren't words that went together.

Two things gave it away. First, Nerine couldn't look us in the face when she lied. With everyone else, her squad taught her well, but with us, her eyes gave it away. And second, a woman who could navigate the hidden passageways of this house in the dark wouldn't mistakenly walk into her bedframe. She knew this room like the back of her hand. Even in spaces she'd only entered a few times, she remembered the placement of everything. It was a talent she used to joke that would be useful if she decided to become a cat burglar.

Xander switched on the bedside light and shot me a lift of the brow, agreeing with my assessment.

Nerine had been front and center when things went down with Andraius. Was the Assassin Squad part of it?

Hell, no. If those women had any hand in it, they wouldn't have left any trace of evidence for anyone to find. And from what I'd noticed within minutes of inspecting the room, someone had cleaned up, but they hadn't quite mastered their craft.

Which meant all fingers pointed to the woman who currently searched her closet for clothes to wear.

We had to get her somewhere she felt safe to talk to us.

But would she talk to us? Would she trust us with her secret?

Everything from the last few days still sat raw among us. Walking away from her had nearly killed me. The taste of her lips and the feel of her fingers on me was a dream come true. However, we'd pushed the boundaries too many times, and it was better to stop everything than cause her more grief.

Now everything was different.

Or was it? I had no idea.

A few minutes later, Nerine stepped out of her closet wearing thick lounge pants and an oversized hoodie both designed more for the middle of winter than the warmth of late summer. The outfit clashed with everything she usually selected for this time of year. She hadn't a clue that this made it even more apparent that she was hiding something.

I cocked my head to the side. "What the hell are you wearing? That whole get-up is too big for you."

"This isn't the time to question my clothing choices." Her defiant glare prickled at my nerves, but I let it go.

Definitely not the time to pick a fight.

Xander blocked her view of me and gestured to the door. "Once you're in a secure location, we need to talk."

"What does that mean?" she asked, weariness in her question.

She understood what he meant. We'd spoken about this for months. It wasn't how any of us had planned things. Then again, one never knew what monkey wrench fate would throw in our path.

"You have to make decisions," I answered, softening my tone. "Set things in motion for the future."

"You mean the family's future."

"Which includes your sisters and your mother," I reminded her.

"I don't know if I can do this," she whispered, her head dropping briefly as she descended the stairs behind Xander.

"Of course you can." I set a hand on her shoulder, making her stiffen for a moment before she relaxed and covered my fingers with hers, squeezing them.

Then, Xander added, "Anyone who survived the last few years with Andraius can handle anything."

Nodding, she dropped her arm and pulled back her shoulders. "I am Peter Angelos's Angel with a viper's tongue. I can't forget that again."

I wanted to give her proper comfort, to hold her, but this wasn't the time. Hell, I wanted to demand she tell us what happened. It wasn't the time for that, either.

I gritted my teeth as I watched her mask the pain of each step she took down the stairs. It was as if she had trained in the type of body control to overcome the agony.

How often had she practiced this routine after an altercation with Andraius?

We'd left her with a monster, thinking we were making the safer choice. We knew nothing.

Silence descended when Nerine came into view on the main floor. In unison, the Angelos men tipped their heads to her.

The true Angelos now held the seat.

She remained quiet while walking through the soldiers but halted at the intersection leading to the security sector of the mansion.

"I want to see his body." Her words were an order, with none of the uncertainty from before.

I blocked the way to the front of the house. "Why?"

"Am I not the head of this family, Theo?" Her blue eyes held mine, the mask she wore of the emotionless Mrs. Andraius Angelos firmly in place.

"You are."

"Then I don't need to explain myself to you or anyone. Take me to see my dead spouse."

My lips twitched, ready to smirk at her command. But she caught the slight tug at the corner of my mouth, and her gaze narrowed a fraction.

I moved in beside her, with Xander flanking her other side. We strode down the long corridor to the front of the house.

"Where did you find him?" she asked, but her movements directed us straight to the library.

I leaned closer to her. "You know exactly where, Angel."

She abruptly stopped and waited as if I hadn't spoken.

After a few moments, Xander set a hand on her upper back to guide her forward, then dropped it when she glared at him, realizing what he'd done.

"Library."

She slowed her pace and approached the men posted to bar anyone from entering the room. They rose from their seats, inclined their heads, and readied for instructions, keeping their attention on Nerine.

She wasn't even aware of how the organization had immediately accepted her. With Andraius, everyone turned to Xander or me for instructions, and the "boss" hadn't a clue.

"Open the doors."

"Yes, Mrs. Angelos," Luther, one of the men, answered, and followed her order.

Andraius's body came into view. He lay in the same position as when we'd left the room. The only difference now was the pool of blood around him had started to dry and darken.

Nerine studied him, not making any motion to go near him. Everyone remained still watching her, waiting to see what she'd do.

After five minutes of complete silence, she clenched her jaw, tugged the diamond band from the ring finger of her left hand, and dropped it on the travertine floor.

The clang of stone hitting stone rang out all around us.

"I hate him—hated him. Everyone knew it. I'm not sorry he's dead. I wished for it from the moment he put the gun to my head all those years ago." A smile tugged at her lips as she turned. "Luther, it's time to clean up the mess of the last few years."

"What would you like me to do, Mrs—um—Nerine—um —" His face reddened. "I'm not sure how to address you."

Nerine's smile disappeared, and she became all business. "What did you call me before the bastard betrayed the family?"

"What your father called you. The Angel when referring to you and Nerine when we spoke."

"Then you have your answer." She glanced over her shoulder in the direction of Andraius's body. "Since we can't dispose of him like the garbage he is, put him in the refrigerated holding room. Then have my library cleaned up. I'd prefer to have no trace of him in a room I use as my retreat."

"After we investigate his death, don't you mean?" Xander brought her focus to him.

She stared at him. "Someone killed him. I'm fine with it. Let's bury him and move on with our lives."

"No matter how happy you are with the outcome, we must find out who circumvented our security and attacked him in your library."

"No one bypasses your security without detection, am I correct?"

"Yes." The irritation on Xander's face made it very clear the calm version of him had left the building and the one he rarely showed Nerine was about to appear. "Only an insider can circumvent it. Especially for your library."

Something flashed in her eyes as if saying without words, "Are you so sure about that?"

The passageways.

She'd used them to get into the library. But how the fuck had Andraius? There had to be more, ones that weren't on the old schematics of the mansion.

Fucking hell. Why hadn't I thought of checking the room we locked Andraius in for any openings?

Too late to wonder now.

I was a fucking idiot. We'd put her in danger again.

"You act like you had extra precautions placed on this room."

"You like to slip your detail, so I had to find alternatives to alert me when you decided to venture out."

"As in?"

"There are sensors on all the doors, walls, and windows, including noise vibration alerts."

Surprise flashed across her face, and then she pursed her lips. "Well, it looks like the latter was defective since Andraius made it into the room."

"No, he had insider assistance." Xander's gaze swept over the men around him, conveying his intent to question everyone.

We'd always trusted the originals, but now a grain of doubt swept in. We couldn't risk missing anything, not when there were too many unknowns.

"Have you questioned the men guarding his room?"

"They are your old team, Nerine." Xander cocked his head to the side, a crease forming between his brows. "They would never betray you."

Heat flared in her blue eyes, making me want to shake my head. This wasn't the time or place for this.

"Then how did he leave his room without you knowing?"

"I'll find out once I conduct my investigation."

She licked her lips. "Good luck with that. Let me know what you discover."

She circled Xander, and just as she attempted to pass me, I lifted my hand, blocking her path and forcing her to collide with my arm.

"Where are you going?"

She kept her face forward. "To move my things out of the

rooms the dead man over there forced me to share with him for the last five years."

"Not a chance." I leaned down. "Until we clear the house, you will stay in the security center with Theios Alex."

"You don't give the orders, Theo. I'm the Angelos now, or were all those conversations we had you blowing out hot air to fill the time?"

Energy crackled between us, as it always did when she challenged me.

"Have you considered that the intended target for the attack might have been you, not Andraius? Perhaps, he was just in the wrong place at the wrong time."

"Why would anyone target me? My life, my body, my assets are what give others power."

"You think someone eliminated Andraius to replace him?"

She tilted her chin up, her cobalt eyes connecting with mine and her mouth curving a fraction at the corners. "Perhaps. All that matters to me now is that I'm no longer married."

"Are you saying that you're free now, Angel?" I asked in a tone that only she could hear.

A slight flush tinged her cheeks, and she set her palm over my forearm, pushing it down. "My freedom is very subjective."

"Meaning?"

"Aren't you the one who told me to grow up? I'm accepting my fate." She took a few steps toward the security wing, paused, and then said over her shoulder, "You have two hours. No one will ever keep me a prisoner in this house again."

"Our intention isn't to keep you prisoner. It's to keep you safe." Xander defended our actions, but he had to know they were falling on deaf ears.

"What is that saying?" She tapped her lip. "Yes. The road to hell is paved with good intentions."

Five minutes after we received the notification that Theios Alex had Nerine settled in the security wing lounge, Xander and I shut the door to the library, sealing the two of us inside.

Our men knew that until we finished our inspection, nobody would get on or off the property, and no form of communication would work.

I circled Andraius's body and shook my head. "I have no fucking idea how she managed it, but she gutted the asshole."

"Don't you think I know this? Traces of whatever happened between them are covering this room." Xander gripped the back of his neck.

"Traces?" I asked.

"Jackass." Xander jerked his chin, indicating the wall to the side of us. "There is a smudge of something near the opening to the panel for the passageway. It's this fucker's blood. I guarantee it."

Fear filled me. Nerine would not go down for this.

"We need to get it cleaned up. Eliminate anything that ties this to her." A list of tasks ran through my mind, along with the crew I'd bring in to carry it out.

"No shit, Sherlock."

I scanned the room for other spots of evidence. "Someone deactivated the noise sensors for this room. That means he had help getting in here."

Both Xander and I looked up at the same time, and I knew he was thinking the same thing I was.

He asked, "You think one of the originals is playing both sides?"

"At this moment, I only trust Theios Alex, you, and me."

Xander shook his head as resignation washed over his face. "Once news gets out, people will assume one of us did it."

"You and I are clear since we were both in public with allies. She was in the house with him."

"Who will believe a woman with half of Andraius's body mass could gut him?"

"Only one person needs to contemplate it for vultures to circle. We protect her at all costs."

Xander's eyes narrowed in irritation.

At least that was better than the look of defeat from moments earlier.

"That's all I've done since I met her, asshole."

Suddenly a thought crossed my mind, and I had to ask his perspective on this big question now running in my mind. "Are we going to tell Nerine we know or wait to see if she says anything to us?"

"This is her secret. Our job is to protect her, which is what we will do."

I released a deep breath. "We jumped from the pan into the fire."

"At least she is ours now, free and clear."

I shot Xander a glare. He was so fucking determined for the three of us to turn back time and fall into the relationship we'd once had.

It was hard to release the hurt of the past. When everything went down, he still had his parents, his extended family. I, on the other hand, had no one. Xander had no clue what it was like to be alone in the world.

"Keep dreaming. We are no way near close to making that a reality."

Eighteen

erine

Four days.

Four days since I became a widow...since I killed him.

I took a deep breath as I stepped out of my shower into the bathroom of the suite of rooms I now occupied.

This one was triple the space of the one I'd used for the last nearly five years, and ten times more opulent. Everything was designed to exact specifications and brand-new—newish, since it sat here for five years without use and occasional cleaning.

Not a single soul had utilized this section of the house after the completion of construction—well, until now.

I'd moved in the evening everything went down with

Andraius. It was on the renovated side of the mansion, as far away as possible from where I'd spent the last few years.

Papa and Mama had planned to update the entire mansion, section by section. They'd started with new living quarters for them and all their children.

Maybe it was good that Andraius never wanted to stay on this side of the house. This section remained pure of his touch, his stench, his evil.

When Mama and the girls arrived in the next few days, they'd have a place to sleep without the taint of the horrors committed inside the old rooms.

Pulling a towel from a rack, I dried my body before wrapping it around my wet hair. The pain in my calf had finally eased to a dull ache. It was a state I could manage while wearing heels at the funeral in a few days.

Moving before the double sink vanity, I stared at my reflection in the mirror above it.

I wanted to laugh, and at the same time, the desire to cry pushed at the edges. I'd gotten everything I begged God to give me. Except for the escape I so desperately wanted.

And it was time to accept that it was a childish dream anyway. I was the eldest. My sisters and I were the last of the Angelos line in America. If I ran, my sisters and mother became even bigger targets.

I forced myself to study my body and the ugly jagged word carved into my stomach. I had allowed Andraius to win and add to my pain by constantly avoiding looking at them. Never again.

He was dead. He deserved to die. I'd survived. I'd won. Fuck him.

Plus, the cream had faded the lines to lighter shades of brown. Soon they'd be barely visible, and they weren't anywhere near as puckered as before.

These were my battle wounds.

I knew I had a long way to go, but baby steps.

I grinned to myself. *No baby for you, jackass.*

I angled my face to the side and traced the bruises down my neck. They'd turned an ugly shade of yellow-green, something I'd have to continue to hide, at least for another little while.

The fact Theo and Xander had only made one or two passing comments about my choice of body-covering clothing in the middle of a heatwave in Boston meant they suspected.

Who the fuck was I kidding? They knew. Their eyes gave it away. They watched me, scrutinized my moods, and analyzed my words.

Plus, they'd gone beyond the standard protocol of cleaning up the scene and making it seem like Andraius passed in his sleep. Instead, they'd restaged his body at another location far from the house and passed it off as a hit.

Were they waiting for me to broach the subject with them?

Outside of the comments from the night of Andraius's death, they hadn't mentioned anything regarding my involvement.

What would I say to them?

My husband threatened to put me in a coma and impregnate me, so I gutted him.

Out of nowhere, dizziness rushed through my head and bile rose in my throat, nearly choking me.

I doubled over, the towel tumbling from my hair, and purged my stomach into the sink as I realized what he had planned as my future washed over me. He would have destroyed me to have a baby. A child he'd never view with love, only as a commodity.

He planned to steal my life, my legacy, everything from me.

It was all for money.

He deserved to die by my hands. Why had I waited so damn long?

Once I had nothing left inside me, I lifted my head. Tears flowed freely from my eyes, and the color of my skin looked pale and so lifeless.

He had destroyed me.

A hiccup escaped my lips, and I slowly cleaned up my mess in the sink, brushed my teeth, and washed my face. I continued to cry for the broken woman I refused to be anymore.

I'd spent the last four days in a haze, going through the motions, numb and emotionless. But maybe that's what I needed to make all the decisions, take on my new role, and deal with the attention of other "well-meaning" families.

As if I needed any of them to come to rescue me when not a single one of them stepped in to help me when the fucker destroyed my family.

Fuck all of them.

It was time to use my lady balls and take on that role Papa wanted me to fill but I no longer desired.

I desperately needed his guidance, and it wasn't possible.

I missed the numbness that had washed over me after Andraius's death.

Now the floodgates were open, and the pain, the heartache of everything I'd endured overwhelmed me. It was a roller-coaster of emotions, and I had no one to share it with.

One thing I had no problems admitting.

I felt not an ounce of guilt for killing Andraius.

No. Guilt. Whatsoever. He deserved to die.

"I don't regret it," I whispered. "I don't regret it."

I stared at my face in the mirror again just as a laugh bubbled up, and I screamed at the top of my lungs, "I'm glad you're dead, you fucking bastard. I don't regret it."

I screamed even louder, "I hope you burn in hell. You deserved ten times worse than you got. I fucking hate you. Do you hear me? I hate you."

Suddenly, loud banging vibrated through the bedroom door, along with shouts.

First, it was Theo. "Nerine. Open the fucking door."

Then, Xander. "What the hell is going on in there?"

Next, I heard, "Screw it. I'm going through her lounge side."

I barely had the chance to grab a towel and wrap it around my body when Theo stormed into my room, coming to an abrupt stop as he saw me in the open doorway of my bathroom.

His gray eyes heated briefly and then narrowed. "Why the hell were you shouting?"

"Because I felt like it." I charged into my bedroom, glowering at him. "I can do what I like in my suite. I needed to get it out of my system."

"You needed to get it out of your system? Are you fucking kidding me right now?" He ran a frustrated hand through his dark hair. "I thought something happened to you."

Before I could respond, Xander said, "Angel, what's going on? Are you okay?"

"I'm fine."

"Why were you—" He trailed off as he took me in.

Desire prickled my skin, and I tightly clutched my towel to my chest.

Shit, shit, shit. I should have kept the shouting to a manageable level.

"Stop staring at me like that." My heartbeat accelerated, and my cleft grew slick, seeing the undisguised carnal lust radiating from the men before me.

Xander clenched his fists by his sides. "Tell us to leave, Nerine."

I took a tentative step backward, my breath growing shallow, the need building deep in my core. Licking my lips, I stopped my movements.

"I'd run if I were you and lock myself in that bathroom," Theo warned.

I couldn't help but challenge him. It was my base setting. So I asked, "Why?"

"Because we know all the secrets you are hiding, Angel." He advanced toward me.

"You think so?"

"We know so." Now Xander prowled in my direction as if I

were prey, making me swallow to ease the dryness in my throat. "And we cleaned up so nothing traces back to you."

"I have no idea what you are talking about."

"So the bruises on your neck and shoulders just appeared out of nowhere?" He cocked his head to the side. "Or explain the limp you've tried and failed to pretend doesn't exist for the last few days."

"I don't have to explain anything."

"To us, you do." Xander stood a foot from me, his dark eyes cool, almost menacing.

I'd never had this kind of banter with him. Theo, yes. Xander, no.

It was arousing on a level I hadn't expected. Xander had a volatile reputation, but he was the opposite with me, tender and patient. And in the past, he'd been a demanding lover, but never a storm cascading over me like Theo.

This man before me simmered with pent-up energy, ready to burst.

I lifted my chin. "Keep dreaming. I'm the Angelos now."

"Wrong," Theo said, now flanking me from behind. "You'll never just be the Angelos Angel to us."

"We can't go back to the past. I'm not that girl you knew." I peered over my shoulder and then faced Xander. "I'm not even the woman you knew a few days ago."

"No, you're not." Theo's presence, the heat of his body against my back, sent a shiver down my spine.

Xander moved in closer. A flush covered his face, and his dark eyes looked almost pitch black as his pupils swallowed his irises. The throbbing in my pussy grew to a pulsing ache as the arousal between my folds felt as if it was dripping along my inner thighs.

He reached up but stopped when his fingers were a fraction away from skimming my cheek. "This is your last chance, Nerine. Tell us to go. Tell us this isn't what you want. Tell us this thing we have isn't possible."

It was what I'd repeated over and over to them. I tried to convince myself of it. But it was such a lie. These men called to me in a way I couldn't express.

I wasn't married anymore. I wasn't breaking any vows, even if they had been forced upon me.

I could take this, take what they offered.

"Will it make it easier for you if I do?"

Theo's hand settled on my hip, and goosebumps broke out over my skin. "You haven't made my life easy since you were fourteen. I don't expect it to change anytime soon."

"Theo," I whispered, unable to help myself.

Xander cupped my face, bringing my attention to him. "Yes or no."

"You're touching me. Haven't you already made the decision?"

"The choice is yours. We can walk out of here the second you command it." Xander leaned down, his breath coasting over my mouth.

Then at the same time, Theo glided his palm up my torso and over my fingers where I held my towel closed between my breasts.

"What is your answer, Angel?" Theo's hand flexed over mine.

"You know my answer."

"That's not how this works. Xander, put it in terms she may understand better."

A feral light entered Xander's eyes, and a tremor shook my body at the sheer possessiveness I saw on his face. "Who do you belong to from here on out?"

"It doesn't mean you get to boss me around."

Theo's grip tightened over mine. "Say it."

"You will keep your promises to me."

Xander's hold on my face intensified as his nose brushed mine. "How about this, who do we belong to?"

The backs of my eyes burned at the intensity of what was happening. So much, so fast, I couldn't keep up.

My lips trembled as I said, "Me."

"Correct." Theo pressed his body to my back, kissing the juncture between my shoulder and neck. "Tell us who you belong to, Nerine."

Knowing with my following words I'd open a vortex I'd never emerge from, I whispered, "Theo and Xander."

"We've waited a long fucking time to hear you say it." Theo jerked the towel from my body.

Xander's mouth came down on mine as he pressed his front to my naked breasts. He tasted of berries, a tiny reminder of his morning smoothie.

God, how I missed this. The feel of him, the way his tongue rolled against mine. He was all-consuming and overwhelming.

At the same time, Theo pinched and worked my straining

nipples while his lips and teeth grazed down my spine, nipping, kissing, and licking.

The sensations were everything I'd dreamed about and craved for so long. It was as if I was drowning and flying at the same time.

Four hands roamed my body, giving it what it had wished for all these years.

My pussy quickened and contracted, desperate for something to take the edge away.

Theo's fingers glided between my legs as if reading my mind, rubbing up and down through the dampness and to my swollen, aching clitoral nub. He circled and teased.

Then, when he thrust two fingers inside me, I cried out, breaking my kiss with Xander, clutching his shoulder to keep from losing my balance.

"Fuck," Theo groaned. "You're so wet."

"Only with the two of you," I admitted.

He abruptly pulled out, and I couldn't help but cry out in protest. "What are you doing?"

"Suck," Theo ordered, standing and bringing his fingers to my lips.

I stared into his mesmerizing gray eyes, opened my mouth, and then closed my lips around his wet digits. My earthy essence filled my tastebuds.

"You're so damn beautiful." He pulled out and fisted my hair before kissing me in the dominating, owning way he'd mastered years ago.

While Theo feasted on me, Xander walked me backward,

lifting me and then laying me on my bed. Then, in unison, they stepped back, intense want humming around them.

They were so different from each other. Theo was so lean and tall, built like a street fighter, and Xander's body resembled something more in line with a boxer, all muscle and brute strength. Both of them were lethal in their own right. These weren't the men of my youth, my first loves, but ones who'd done things beyond anything the young Nerine of years past could have comprehended.

As if they had planned it, they undressed in a synchronized flow of movements.

First, their shirts came off, revealing honed, sculpted torsos, arms, and shoulders. Next, they reached for the belts of their pants.

Watching their movements was a hedonistic sight that sent wave after wave of blood pumping through my pussy. The muscles of my core spasmed and clenched, wanting desperately to have them inside me.

And soon I wouldn't have to live in the memories of what we'd had any longer.

As if I'd lost sense of time and place, they climbed onto the bed clad in their boxers with their thick, hard cocks a heavy presence before me.

Xander grabbed my thighs, pulling me forward, and Theo spread them apart. They stared at me, slick, open, so aroused.

"God. I've dreamed of you like this. Open, ready, wanton. Ours to do whatever we want." The hunger on Theo's face gave promises of things I'd only fantasized about.

"Stop staring at me and do something."

Xander took hold of my wrists and pinned them above my head as he loomed over me. "Let's get this straight. You're the Angelos only regarding your role in the organization. Otherwise, you are our Nerine. You submit to us. You belong to us. We aren't men you can control. Never have been and never will be. Is that understood?"

This ultra-dominant side of him he rarely showed me aroused me more than I ever expected. I preferred this version of him. Maybe he realized I no longer needed the gentleness of the old Nerine.

I lifted my head, bringing my mouth a hairsbreadth from his. "Crystal clear. But it doesn't mean I won't voice my desires. I do have a mind of my own."

"You can't help yourself, can you?" A smile tugged at his lips a second before he kissed me, silencing my retort.

At that exact moment, Theo descended on my clit, taking it between his teeth and biting down with just the right amount of pressure. My back bowed as a pleasure-filled pain I hadn't experienced in forever coursed through me.

"That's right. Let us hear what only we can give you," Xander growled as he deepened his kiss.

His tongue battled against mine, thrusting, rolling, and tasting all the while.

Theo sucked and teased my pussy. What these men could achieve with their lips, others couldn't accomplish with their entire bodies.

They held my arms and legs captive, giving me no choice but to take the onslaught of their demands.

Heat built in my belly, and my pussy clenched.

"Oh, God. Oh, God." I jerked my arms in Xander's hold, eliciting a chuckle from him as he pulled back.

"Too much for you, Angel?"

I shook my head, the desperate need to come pushing at me. "It's been so long. I need."

"She needs, Xander," Theo said and blew against my pussy, causing a hard spasm to rock through me but not quite push me over. "Let's give it to her."

"Next time, we'll make her wait for her pleasure."

"Agreed." Theo thrust his tongue into my vaginal canal, flicking in and out, driving me higher and higher.

"Theo."

"That's it, Angel," Xander crooned. "Now come for us."

He grazed his stubble along my jaw and neck, then scored his teeth over my breast right before taking my aching, swollen nipple into his mouth.

"Oh, Xander." Immediately, I detonated.

Everything in me clenched and contracted as wave after wave of delicious ecstasy washed over me. I'd waited so long for this exhilaration, this euphoria, this complete bliss with the men I loved.

I was still riding the freefall of release when I felt Theo lift me and heard him say, "You ready for me?"

My brain barely comprehended what he meant until the crest of his thick, hard cock pressed through my wet pussy lips.

My gaze met his, and all I could think was the Theo of before was a boy compared to the man before me.

Goosebumps prickled over my skin as my arousal reignited, and the burning need grew by leaps and bounds.

"Yes," I gasped. "I want you to fuck me. I've waited for this."

A feral glint entered his gray eyes, and he licked his thumb and settled it over my clit. "I get you first, once again. I need to make sure you can take me as easily as possible."

My breath caught, remembering how big he was. This wasn't going to be anything like fucking the asshole. Being with either Xander or Theo wouldn't be anything in the vicinity of sex with Andraius.

"You're enjoying this way too much." I glared at him.

Xander released my arms and relaxed, ready to watch the next few minutes of interplay.

Theo leaned forward, moving his hands away from my hips and clit, caged me with his arms, and then brought his forehead to mine. The menacing and wicked intent I saw looking down at me should have scared me, but it had me ready to tell him to fuck me already.

"If I don't enjoy the moments before I'm about to be balls-deep in the viper that's mine, what should I enjoy?"

I brought my palms up to cup his face. "I suggest you get to the balls-deep part. I won't break."

"You never learn." He thrust forward.

Stars overwhelmed my vision, and a fullness filled me beyond anything I expected.

"Regret not letting me take it slower?"

"No." And immediately, I gritted my teeth as he pushed in farther and I realized he still had so much more to go.

I dug my nails into his shoulder, both wanting to push him away and keep him deep in my pussy. My nipples tightened further, and the pleasure-filled pain he elicited caused me to grow slicker and wetter.

"Did you get bigger?"

"Nope. This is what happens when you play with fire, Angel."

If it felt like this with Theo, Xander would tear me in half. He had an even more enormous cock. I turned my head toward Xander. Humor lit his dark gaze as he fisted said cock, up and down.

"It'll fit. It always has." Xander stroked harder on his erection. "Now, be a good girl and let Theo fuck you."

"Ass—" My retort became lodged in my throat as Theo jolted forward, nestling himself to the hilt.

"No more talking." He pumped in and out in shallow plunges, rolling his hips against my clit with each pass. "I've waited years to be inside you. From now on, be ready for me to fill you up with cum every chance I get."

"You're out of your mind." I lifted my hips to meet his pistoning hips. "I have a syndicate to run, or did you forget?"

"Do you have to argue about everything, even when I'm fucking you?" His thrusts grew harder, relentless, driving my desire to the point where I couldn't breathe.

"Theo, please." I thrashed, jerking on the back of his head and pulling him forward. "I'm almost there."

I arched, unable to shift my body to force Theo to give me the friction I needed to fall over the edge where I hung. His body was too big, and his thrust perfectly measured to keep me hanging, drive my desire higher, and make me crave more.

Bastard.

That's when I realized Theo and Xander held gazes, lust burning in their eyes. They refused to give in to what I knew they wanted. It made no sense, but I couldn't think about it now. I had to come. Dear God, I had to come.

"Xander, do something."

"No." He shook his head, focusing in on me. "I don't think so. You need to work for it a little longer."

"What? Are you crazy?" My nails dug into Theo's neck, and he hissed, gripping my wrists and pinning them to the bed.

He peered down at me. "No matter how much I want to wear your marks, you need to sheathe those claws. For the next little while, anyway."

Understanding settled into me—the funeral, the transition of power, facing all the families.

As if sensing the worry creeping in with his words, he sat back and pulled me onto his lap, his thick cock still tucked deep inside me, and threaded his fingers in my hair.

"You're not alone." The intensity of his gaze gave me a small kernel of comfort.

"I'm not trying to make your life harder with my antics."

A smile touched his lips. "I know. It's your base setting. I've gotten used to it."

I wrapped my arms around his neck and drew him to me. He tasted of me and his natural essence. In his arms was acceptance, comfort, love.

"I believe it's time to have your orgasm, Angel." Xander's hands settled on my hips. "Ride him. Take your pleasure."

Theo leaned back, and with slow, meticulous movements, I rose and slid down on his steely length.

I threw my head back, closing my eyes. The tingle started as a tiny spark deep inside and grew with each lift of my hips. Then when Theo sucked my nipple into his mouth and Xander's fingers stroked my straining clitoral nub, my mind clouded, and my pussy contracted on Theo's cock, first in tiny quivers and then hard spasms.

My back bowed, and I cried out. I gripped their arms, losing myself in what only they could give.

It was glorious, filled with the reminders of the three of us from the past but with the knowledge of the present. Lifting my chin, Xander covered my mouth, drinking in my pleasure as Theo took over the pistoning, keeping my release rolling.

"You ready?" Theo asked.

"For what?" I opened my eyes and realized the question wasn't for me.

In the next second, he pulled out. But before I could beg him to stop, Xander replaced him, and my heartbeat accelerated.

"For this." He pushed in, sliding deep and filling me so completely that I felt as if I'd explode.

"Fuck me." I clenched my teeth and then willed my body to relax.

Xander pulled my legs tighter around his waist. "That's the plan."

"How could I forget you're hung like a horse."

"He's the length guy. I'm the girth one," Xander corrected.

After a few moments, my body calmed, and I stared up at him. "Are we having this discussion now?"

"You're the one who keeps talking."

I narrowed my eyes and lifted onto my elbows, ready to take over, but Theo grabbed the back of my head and placed the soft, velvety head of his cock to my lips.

"Open up, Angel. Filling your mouth will stop any further discussions."

Instead of arguing, I followed directions, took him back, and swallowed a few times to open my throat. It had been so long since I'd done this, only with them.

They'd taught me everything I knew. I'd refused to do anything in this vicinity for the bastard. Even when he tried to force me to do it, I'd threatened to bite it off, and he never pushed again.

"Fuck." Theo's groan and clenching of my hair snapped me back to the present. "I forgot about your nonexistent gag reflex."

I hummed and rubbed my tongue along the vein under his length as I bobbed up and down.

Xander waited until I'd set a steady rhythm on Theo to move again. He started with slow glides in and out, a gentle lulling meant to torment and build my desire.

My pussy quickened, flooding with my arousal and soaking his cock, and my breasts swelled to an almost painful level as my nipples strained.

I gazed up at Theo, who watched me, noticing how my body reacted to Xander and him.

A wicked smirk touched his lips. "Flip."

He and Xander pulled out, and I found myself on my stomach. The next second, Xander pulled my hips back and impaled me on his cock, beginning a relentless assault on my pussy.

"Oh, Xander."

"That's right. I'm about to pummel this cunt. Mark it as mine."

My pussy convulsed at his words.

"Liked the sound of that, did you?"

I said nothing.

Theo moved in front of me, and without instruction, I opened my mouth and continued my ministrations on his hard erection. I worked him with sucks and licks, eliciting groans from his lips.

His hands grabbed hold of my hair, taking away my control and changing the pace to his liking. At the same time, Xander's thrusts grew harder. My pussy wept, and my core spasmed with each pass of his cock.

I needed to come. Fuck, I had to come.

Xander's fingers grazed my clit, and the fire ignited. I moaned and whimpered around Theo's cock as each caress of Xander's fingers along the sensitive bundle of nerves sent a shockwave of unbelievable rapture through every cell in my body.

"Take every drop. Swallow every drop," Theo gritted out.

I nodded, not truly focused on anything but riding out my release.

Moments later, I heard Xander call out my name, pushing into me, the heat of his orgasm pumping into my body. Then Theo's palms tightened on my scalp.

"Look at me."

I peered up into his piercing gray eyes, and in the next second, he came. I drank down everything he gave me, not diverting my gaze from his at any time.

When he'd finished coming, he said, "You belong to us now."

Nineteen

erine

Finally, the day was here.

Andraius's funeral.

I'd wanted it. I'd waited for it.

Now here I stood with an umbrella over my head in the pouring rain under a giant tent that did little to protect us from the leaking canopy above us.

The weather seemed fitting, considering the cloud of suspicion surrounding the guest of honor was going into the ground.

Why the hell had Andraius written that he wanted an outdoor liturgy? I'd never understand. Still, here I was, dutiful wife and giving him his last wishes.

Maybe he'd thought I'd give him a big send-off in the spacious Angelos cemetery where my family members were laid to rest.

Yeah, that was never going to happen.

Hell would freeze over before I'd bestow such an honor on him.

Instead, I'd purchased a large section of the cemetery belonging to his home church and had it designated for him. No matter how I felt about him, he was still considered the head of a powerful family and deserved a proper burial in a blessed area.

It just wouldn't be one sacred to my family.

If anyone thought my actions were questionable, they were all idiots and possessed selective memories of what occurred only a few years ago.

From the moment I'd opened my eyes this morning, I'd known that I had to harden myself for the day ahead, which meant implementing many of the lessons the squad taught me. Principal among them was to show no weakness in front of anyone who slighted me.

I'd survived so much and had grown stronger.

I had to remember society admired men who were ruthless, and when women behaved the same way, they were bitches.

Blessings to all the bitches in the world.

I inhaled deep and then steadied my breath.

All eyes are on you, Nerine. Perform your duties, and don't let even one of them see you sweat.

Representatives of thirty or so families had arrived from around the country to pay their condolences. Even

Andraius's brothers and nephews showed up, which surprised all of us.

My gut told me they planned to determine their chances of filling Andraius's position. They'd hated him with a passion for betraying them. They sought every advantage to muscle their way into the Angelos territory.

Then again, many of the other families here today would do the same thing.

They wanted to see whether the Angeloses were even more vulnerable to a hostile takeover now that I sat at the head of the table.

Assholes, all of them.

I stared into the distance wearing my standard expressionless facade. However, with my sunglasses perched on my nose, no one would know I wasn't paying attention to Father Christianos going through the divine liturgy.

Thankfully, all the kneeling was out because of the nonstop rain.

The wind picked up as the weather eased from a heavy pour to a drizzle.

Being here without Mama and the girls standing by my side felt strange. Their presence would have eased some of my tension and given me the extra boost to build my confidence in this sea of vultures. But as luck had it, being with me wasn't in the cards for them. There had been delays with closing the house, and then unexpected volcanic activity on an island off the coast of Italy had grounded all flights in and out of that part of Europe.

Xander and Theo stood behind me, officially taking on the

roles as my seconds-in-command. They kept our public interactions businesslike to keep anyone from suspecting the depth of what we shared.

Today, I needed them more than I wanted to admit. A slight touch from them would soothe the turmoil churning inside me.

They were my lovers, my protectors, and the only men I trusted. They comforted me on a level I hadn't known I needed. They were my safe place.

But some part of me worried I couldn't give them what they needed, what they wanted from me. Maybe it was the fact things weren't the same level of intimacy as we had before. Xander and Theo wanted each other. I saw it when we were together, I felt it, but they wouldn't act on it. Something held them back. And now it made me wonder whether I would be enough for them.

No, that was my fear rearing its ugly head. I wanted what they offered, and if I took it and something came and stole it away like last time, I'd survive.

I was a survivor.

I shook the thoughts back and refocused on the priest.

It was time to harden up and play the role of the Angelos widow and the new head of Angelos Shipping and Syndicate.

Besides Stefano, who held my umbrella, my row remained empty. And it was probably a good thing.

This position helped me fight back against the figurehead role I knew I'd have to battle. No matter what Xander and Theo believed, no one would respect my position until I met with the local heads and established my presence. Saying I was the Angelos meant nothing when Xander and Theo had run the organization under Andraius's reign.

"Let us pray for Andraius's soul, that he may—"

I tuned Father Christianos out again, not wanting to hear any of his false, loving words and the long-winded sermon about the devil he cared for so much.

Fucking bastard. He was one of the reasons I'd nearly lost all faith in God.

He was Andraius's priest, and his church was not the Greek Orthodox Church of my family.

This man despised me for the woman I was to the core, mainly because I refused to follow what he believed was God's decree to let my husband lead our faith. Which for him meant his church with his rules and principles. What he truly wanted was the Angelos tithing, a lucrative windfall he couldn't get unless I claimed his sanctuary as my church home. That wouldn't happen since I attended regular service with Father Michael at the church down the street from my house.

I avoided being in Father Christianos's presence whenever possible, and the only other religious service I'd attended where he presided was the day he allowed Andraius to force me to marry him. He'd stood there as if everything was wonderful, that I was a willing bride, that he wasn't part of the conspiracy leading to the deaths of so many people.

He'd watched when Andraius took his marital rights, supervising, as he worded it, to ensure consummation. Then he'd held me down when the demon in the casket carved whore onto my stomach. He'd approved it and considered it a fitting punishment for my sins.

I would love to carve *hypocrite* and *liar* all over his face.

"Would you like to say anything, Nerine?" Father Christianos asked, shaking me from my brooding.

I stared at him, trying to comprehend his words.

As they clicked in my head, outrage engulfed my body.

Was he kidding me? This jackass who thought a woman's only place in the world was below men actually wanted me to speak about my dead husband.

The challenge in his dark gaze said all I needed to know. He wanted to push me, put me in my place, make me little in the eyes of all the families attending the funeral.

I sensed Theo and Xander shifting behind me, picking up on my irritation. I slightly shook the hand I held at my side to indicate I'd handle it.

If this was the first battle I faced, so be it.

As a man of God, he wore a cloak of protection, keeping him from retaliation for his part in the coup. But his time in a position of power ticked by just like the grains of sand poured through an hourglass.

During a conversation with Mama, I'd decided he wouldn't die by an order from me or means of any Angelos connections. Instead, we would send information about his dealings to the church's higher-ups and allow them to handle things. Disgrace among his peers was the best punishment for someone like him. To live out his life exiled and shunned was the perfect revenge.

The Angeloses were significant donors to the archdioceses in Boston and throughout Greece. The last thing the church wanted was to look the other way when evidence showed one of their own waded in piles of corruption.

Holding Father Christianos's gaze, I asked, "Are you sure it is appropriate? Aren't you a proponent of a particular mindset on women's participation in religious services?"

He smiled and spoke loud enough for those in attendance to hear. "It is only fitting for Andraius's widow to address all those who came to pay him respects."

Oh, he was diabolical.

He couldn't possibly expect me to wax poetic about the man who killed my father and brother and then raped me for years.

This idiot had no idea what havoc Andraius's widow could drop on his head. But he was about to find out.

I nodded. "I believe you're correct."

Glancing over my shoulder, I scanned the faces of the group behind me.

Concern and worry radiated out from Xander and Theo while the rest of the crowd waited to see what I'd do.

Were they expecting me to fall apart or show them the bitch Andraius labeled me to the world?

I'd do neither.

Stepping forward, I narrowed my focus on the priest and held out my hand. He set the earpiece mic in my palm. Attaching it to my ear, I turned to the crowd and positioned myself in front of Andraius's casket.

Father Christianos remained near me as if he wanted to maintain the position of authority over this situation he'd created.

It was time to shift his paradigm.

I remained quiet until an uncomfortable silence descended around us.

"You can begin," the priest ordered.

I covered the mic and looked directly at him. With my height and heels, I stood at eye level with him.

This fucker couldn't intimidate me, and when it finally registered, a creased formed between his brows.

Maybe it was accepting my change in circumstances or finally feeling that Andraius was no longer a haunting presence in my life. Or perhaps it was my new relationship with Theo and Xander. But I'd never let another man take away my power again.

Plus, using one's height or body mass as a weapon against a woman was pathetic.

It screamed insecure male with little-dick syndrome.

After meeting Devani, I knew size meant nothing when it came to being lethal. She was the deadliest person I'd ever met and barely reached five-foot-two.

In a low tone meant for his ears, I said, "Not until you step to the side. I am Andraius's widow and the only one who can speak on his behalf. You wanted this. Now deal with the consequences."

The look the priest shot me screamed that he'd kill me right on the spot, given a chance. I half expected an argument from him, but to my surprise, he walked away and took a position along the podium's edge.

I focused on the people before me and started, "Everyone

knows my courtship with Andraius was extremely unconventional."

I paused, holding gazes with all of the heads of families who could have helped me when everything happened. Some glanced away. Others remained impassive. I hoped they understood that I had a long memory.

Peter Angelos hadn't raised a chump.

"If any of you are waiting for me to say I will miss my spouse, don't hold your breath. It will never happen in this lifetime or any lifetime. I am happy he is gone."

A slight gasp came from a few people, followed by a bit of chatter, but they all quieted as soon as I cleared my throat.

"He destroyed my family, then tried to tear down the legacy created over generations due to sheer ego and ignorance, and then his stupidity caused his untimely death. Frankly, I'm surprised it didn't happen sooner. I am thankful to the person who committed this act of service. They saved me years of my life. Now I will take the seat Papa intended as my birthright."

My gaze passed over the crowd again.

"Do not assume I am anything like my predecessor. Andraius called me cold-hearted and many other things that aren't appropriate to repeat now. Men who are intimidated by strong women use name-calling and oppression to cover their insecurities. Hopefully, no one thinks to make similar mistakes."

My attention shifted to Nyx, who stood next to Simon. She smiled at me from under her umbrella and nodded her approval.

"A few last things. I will not mourn the man behind me. I

do not need condolences outside of the ones for the many years my mother, sisters, and I lost because of him. I wish him well wherever he is, whether heaven or hell. All I care about is that he is out of my life. Thank you for taking the time to show your support for the Angelos Family."

I took off the ear mic and passed it to Stefano, who handed it to the flabbergasted priest.

The next time I attended a church service, it would be with my sisters and Mama.

Now for a strong cup of coffee to keep me going through the rest of the day.

———

"That was some speech."

I lifted my attention from my phone, where I was reading the latest updates from my sisters, to find Tobias Stratos moving in my direction.

Andraius's nephew possessed the confidence most of the firstborn sons in the syndicate world seemed to have been born with. They knew they were the heir apparent and wielded the power that went with the role.

In Tobias's case, he already ran his family's empire. His father and uncles only sat in their positions as advisers, but he was the force that made all the decisions.

Setting my phone next to me, I gave Tobias my complete focus. "I only spoke the truth."

"Then I have another truth to ask you." He sat next to me,

not asking permission to take the seat, something I noticed annoyed Stefano, who watched us with a keen eye.

"Ask."

"Since you aren't going to mourn your deceased husband, does that mean you plan to move on from him sooner rather than later?"

"Are you applying for consideration?"

He grinned. "Absolutely."

I cocked my head to the side, taking Tobias in. He was around thirty and handsome, with amber eyes and jet-black hair. Height-wise, he wouldn't tower over me, but he wasn't short, and his body tended toward the lean runner type. He held a ladies' man reputation with an array of broken-hearted women who could never keep him long enough to settle down. Or those were the rumors circulating about him.

I'd learned all about him through Andraius's rantings and even more during private discussions with Mama.

I hadn't expected to find out that his family had offered to align our families through a marriage contract for all of us girls with the sons of the Stratos family. I was chosen specifically for Tobias. Papa had rejected it, saying he wanted to give his daughters the freedom to pick their own spouses.

Though to keep relationships on the friendly side, Papa kept the possibility of things open by saying he would allow the Stratos boy to court his daughter when they came of age.

Court us? Were we in the stone ages?

However, in reality, Papa never wanted me or my sisters with the Stratoses. Their family only focused on power and territory and wouldn't think twice about double-crossing an ally.

"Marriage and relationships are the last things on my list of priorities at the moment. I may not even tackle them at all."

"You can't be serious." Surprise and concern crossed his features. "You have to produce an heir. You and your sisters are the last of your bloodline."

Oh, I had to shut this down immediately.

"This isn't a topic you need to worry about. I'll handle it when the time comes. I'm the Angelos, and my energy and focus are on the management of Angelos Shipping."

"Does that mean you plan to ignore the rumors circulating about you?" A calculating glint entered his eyes, reminding me of his uncle and giving me the urge to punch him.

I stared at him. This attitude had to be a family trait. Studying his face, I hadn't realized how much he resembled Andraius.

Now it made sense.

"Why don't you clarify this information?" I frowned. "I don't work in gossip. I'm a facts person."

I gave him my cool, "Are you really wasting my time with this?" tone, which had his posture straightening and making him realize the flirty, friendly approach wasn't working.

"Some say you killed Andraius." He paused, taking in my reaction, but I gave him none. "And others believe you arranged for others to carry out the act for you."

"This is the only time I will ever address rumors. And this is because Andraius was your family."

Tobias waited, watching me.

"When bringing rumors to someone, ask yourself these questions." I gestured to myself. "Do I look like I have the body mass to eliminate Andraius in the location where they found him and then make it home to create a solid alibi?"

"No."

"Now to the second rumor—if I planned to eliminate Andraius, why would I wait all these years for someone to carry it out? And lastly, do you honestly think I'd let him destroy my family's business positioning before acting?"

He shook his head and grinned. "No, you aren't a suspect in my eyes. That is the reason I discounted everything as fanciful talk in society."

"Then why bring it up?"

"To see your reaction."

I gave him no response.

"And to pass on things you need to keep knowledge about, even if it is hearsay."

Oh, he was being friendly, passing on information like we were long-lost pals.

"I appreciate the advice."

A smile touched his lips. "Who do you believe killed him?"

"My men will deal with that situation."

"Are you referring to Onassis and Nephus?"

"Among others."

"I'd watch them. They have the ear of your people. You wouldn't want them to stage another coup under your nose. Don't let childhood friendship blind you to their ambition. You may find yourself as a figurehead only."

I resisted the urge to grit my teeth.

"I hold their ear. They follow my commands. Their loyalty is multigenerational to the Angelos family. They would never betray me."

"Are you so sure?"

"Absolutely."

He rubbed his jaw as if scrutinizing me. "Will you punish the assailants who committed Andraius's murder or commend them?"

He was mistaken if he thought I hadn't picked up on how he kept changing topics. He wanted to keep me on my toes. Very smart.

"You believe there were multiple killers?"

"I do."

"The way I conduct the Angelos business is not your concern."

"He is family, so I have a right to retribution."

"No, you don't. Andraius renounced his Stratos ties."

Tobias rose from his seat. "You need allies in this world you've joined, Nerine. You're playing with predators. Don't ever believe you're safe."

"Is that a threat? Are you telling me the Stratoses plan to position themselves outside Chicago and move into Boston?"

"I'm saying the Angeloses' Boston holdings are weak, and unless they don't want a takeover, they better accept help when offered."

"Duly noted. However, sometimes the deadliest creatures are the ones that look harmless." I rose as I caught sight of Nyx and Simon coming in our direction. "Tobias, I'm sure you know Nyx and Simon Drakos."

As they approached, Tobias's gaze hardened and relaxed as if I'd said something amusing. This was an act I'd witnessed more times than I could count with the man I'd buried today. Interesting, not only did Tobias share a familial resemblance to Andraius, but mannerisms, too.

"You see, I have the Drakoses and Mykoses as allies. Papa made bonds that supersede the grave."

"My offer still stands. Think about it."

I pushed down the irritation. I hadn't heard any offer, more veiled threats. The power jockeying was in full swing, and I hadn't even left the funeral.

TWENTY

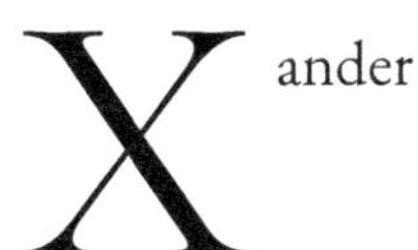ander

"Have you spoken to her?" Theo asked, stalking toward me.

I paused a few feet from Nerine's library and folded my arms across my chest. "Obviously not, since I'm out here and not in there with her."

"You need to get to the bottom of this before the ladies get to the house."

"I know this, Mr. Piss and Vinegar."

Theo ran a frustrated hand through his hair. "The bullshit she pulled this morning is not okay. I would have handled it by now if it wasn't for you."

"No, you would have made it into a nuclear war. Something's up, and Nerine needs to work through it. The last thing she needs is a fight. Your way isn't going to work."

"Then do your counselor, best-friend, I'm-a-softy-in-the-body-of-a-sumo-wrestler thing."

I narrowed my eyes. "You're a jackass. You only wish you looked like me with your skinny ass."

"You keep believing that fairytale. Now go fix it. And remind her that this sneaking-out-of-bed shit has to end. I bet it has to do with whatever that fucker Stratos said to her at the funeral. I knew there was more to it than she told us."

"No, there's more to her withdrawing than a simple conversation or threat from Stratos."

"Well, what the fuck are you waiting for? Get in there."

I shook my head, turning toward the library doors. "Go make yourself useful and check on the ETA for the Angelos ladies."

Instead of knocking, I turned the knob and walked in.

Nerine sat behind her desk in the now-renovated library, her fingers flying over the keyboard of her laptop.

"It's two in the afternoon, Nerine."

She said nothing, keeping her focus on her screen and typing away. She bit her lip, and a crease formed between her brows.

"What are you doing?" I strode in her direction. "You've been locked in here all day."

"Wrong. I signed those shipping contracts after you brought me back the renegotiated terms I'd outlined."

I held in the urge to growl.

Yeah, she'd signed them while barely sparing Theo and me a glance.

Nerine's version of negotiation sat on par with her father's methods. She read through every line and then completely redlined, gutted, and overhauled the contract. Then she expected me and Theo to get the deal finalized with terms favorable to the family's position as much as possible.

What made me laugh was that she thought using hardline tactics would work in her relationship with Theo and me.

She'd had the nerve to tell us, "We will not mix the personal aspect of our relationship with our business one. Is that clear?"

That declaration only ended up getting her fucked nonstop until she passed out from exhaustion in the early morning hours.

"What is going on with you, Angel?"

A line formed between her brows, but she stayed quiet.

I set my palms on the mahogany desktop and peered at her over her screen. "Are you going to answer my question?"

"No," she muttered.

"Nerine, this brat shit is Theo's kink. Not mine."

That made her gaze flicker upward, but she continued to work.

Grabbing her laptop, I closed the lid and put it on a side table behind me.

"I was trying to finish something. Once I finish my work, we can talk about us."

"Meaning?"

"The parameters of our relationship."

Parameters? Was she kidding me?

Something had spooked her, and I planned to get to the bottom of it.

"Ignoring me is rude. So is giving me half-ass answers. Aren't you the one who keeps lecturing me about my Neanderthal ways?" She glared at me, and I continued, "Now tell me what's gotten up your ass."

"You mean outside of you and Theo." A slight flush crept up her cheeks, replacing her frown, and immediately my cock jumped. "Ignore that I said that."

"Why? If I recall, you're the one who demands it."

She licked her lips and stood, setting a hand on her hip. With the long blue dress she wore in the same shade as her eyes and her hair in a messy bun, she gave the image of a disappointed schoolteacher.

Except for the flare of heat in her irises as she reacted to my perusal of her body.

"Keep looking at me like that, and I'll lay you out on your desk."

The desire to lift her hem and eat her pussy until she gasped my name pushed at the back of my mind. Then, maybe the irritation would disappear from her features, and she'd reveal the root of her worry.

She lifted her chin. "Did you forget there is a separation between our work and personal lives?"

"Both parts of our lives are very much entwined." I moved in her direction, crowding her against her desk. "It's you who hasn't grasped the reality of our situation."

I cupped her face, and her blue irises darkened, worry and uncertainty coasting the edges and mixing with the desire.

We no longer had to hide the desire we shared. Well, not in the house, anyway.

"Talk to me. What has you riled up?"

She tried to turn her face, but I held her firm.

"This is moving too fast. I need to get my bearings. I was single for all of a few days before we jumped into bed."

"Oh no, you don't. You aren't going to block us out. The three of us are a set. Always have been and always will be. Andraius is no longer in the picture. You're free of him. He is buried and gone."

"Are you kidding me?" She pushed me away. "A set, my ass. You and Theo refuse to address whatever happened between the two of you. You still want more than friendship and pretend otherwise."

Releasing a frustrated breath, I said, "I fucked up, and he can't forgive me. What do you want me to do? I'd change it if I could."

Gripping the back of my neck, I paced for a second and continued, "Theo and I aren't the topic of discussion right now. We're talking about you and your refusal to see that you are free from the cage of the last five years."

"I swear to God, you're delusional." She threw up her hands. "I'm not free. I'm the Angelos now. I have more on my shoulders than before. You want to know what I was doing?"

I folded my arms, waiting for her to say her piece.

She pointed to the laptop behind me. "I was responding to a message from Tobias since my conversation with him at the funeral wasn't enough to get it through to his thick head. You're lucky I pressed send before you snatched my laptop."

I hated admitting when Theo was right. Stratos was going to be a problem.

"What did you tell him?"

"What do you think I told him? I told him in as friendly a way as possible without starting a war that just because I don't have a dick doesn't mean I can't handle the organization Papa raised me to run. I don't need the help of any fucking Stratos. They're the reason we're in this mess in the first place."

"So, in other words, you told him to take his offer and stick it up his ass."

"I said I was friendly, dammit. My words were curt but to the point. Apparently, I wasn't clear at the funeral, so I had to emphasize that I have things under control and plenty of advisers I trust. And considering the circumstances in which a Stratos murdered my father and brother, I will not now nor ever require assistance from any Stratos."

I closed my eyes and then just shook my head before I started laughing.

"What the hell is so funny?"

"You are more like Theios Peter than you even know. Well, except your approach is a bit more refined. I wouldn't say nice. But more along the no-nonsense business way of handling things."

The irritation on her face turned into a murderous scowl. "Would you rather I told Tobias to fuck off with his offer and that the only allies I need or want are the ones who aren't back-stabbing pieces of shit?"

I lifted my hands as if in surrender. "No, you handled it the right way. But don't expect the dickhead to give up. He doesn't understand eloquent conversations."

"Then you will deliver the follow-up message." She lifted a brow. "I'm sure he will understand your methods of communication."

"Flexing your power?" I gripped her hips again, bringing her body flush to mine.

"I know when to pull out the big guns." She set her palms on my chest, then glided one hand between our bodies to my straining cock, cupping it in her palm. "This isn't the first offer of assistance I received in the last few days, Xander. I refuse to show any weakness. Once I convey a message, the second one will come through my people, meaning you and Theo."

"You don't have to prove anything."

"Of course I do. All of the powerful families are circling and testing me. When we meet at the end of the month, they will all know I'm not someone they can fuck around with."

She stroked me through my jeans in perfect, measured movements, causing precum to weep into my boxers. All these years without her, and now all I could think about was bending her over the nearest surface and burying myself inside her.

"Does that mean you trust us?" I looked down into her mesmerizing eyes.

"Of course I do. It's only ever been the two of you."

"Then what was all that about it moving too fast?"

"I get scared. Worried. I don't want anything to fall back on the two of you because of me."

I narrowed my gaze. "What are you talking about?"

"How have you not heard the rumors? You and Theo have your fingers on the pulse of everything."

I'd heard more than my share of rumors, from Nerine hiring international assassins to do the deed to Andraius dying in bed with one of his mistresses and Theo and I staging it to look like a hit.

"Why don't you fill me in?"

"Rumors are swirling that you and Theo took out Andraius for me because you are my lovers and wanted him out of the way so you could have me."

"That was our original plan," I admitted. "And there is a lot of truth to those statements."

"Can you be serious for a moment?"

"Where did you hear these rumors?"

"The first time was from Tobias at the funeral."

Sneaky bastard. Fucker should have kept his mouth shut. He wanted to see if he could throw her off-kilter.

"Let me guess. He added that you should watch out for Theo and me since we planned to take your seat."

Instead of confirming outright, she said, "I told him I believed in your unquestioning loyalty to the Angelos family."

"Our loyalty is to you before anything else. I wasn't around to protect you before. I am now."

"Others are saying the same things, Xander."

"I like this one. It's not about us taking your seat but about us wanting you." I smirked. "I guess you were wrong about the figurehead bit. It's the power of your pussy that has done your bidding."

"Will you get serious? I don't want anyone to retaliate on you or Theo."

"Nothing will happen to us. Until someone confronts us to our faces, it is all hearsay. And I doubt anyone has the guts to say anything."

"Why aren't you worried about this?"

"Because I won't bow down to cowards ever again. The things I had to do after the coup haunt me more than you will ever know. It went against everything I believed. I failed you once, and it will never happen again."

"You didn't fail me, Xander."

I covered her mouth with my fingers. "I accept the truth of my actions. You forgave me. That's all I can ask."

At least I'd gained the forgiveness of one person in my life. With luck, someday the other one would find it in his heart to accept my apology.

She dropped her head against my chest, and her arms slid around my waist.

We stayed like that for a few minutes before she said, "I never stopped. I pretended to, but it was always there. That was why I was so angry."

Closing my eyes, I soaked in the meaning behind her words. "Is it so hard to say the words?"

She lifted her head. "I worry that if I say them, something will happen to take what we have away again."

No matter how much I wanted to assure her nothing would happen to separate the three of us, I couldn't guarantee it. Believing something like that was impossible, especially after all we'd lived through in the last few years.

"Isn't it better to have said them instead of keeping them inside?"

She lifted onto tiptoes and whispered over my lips, "I love you."

"I never thought I'd hear you say that again."

I hoisted her up by her thighs, gathered the skirt of her dress in my arms, and then wrapped her legs around my waist. She grabbed hold of my shoulders.

"I'm hardheaded. It took me a few seconds to admit I never stopped loving two possessive, obsessive men with insatiable appetites."

I pressed her back to a bookshelf and settled my erection along the damp cleft of her underwear.

"Now that I have you accepting of your circumstances in life, we need to clear something up."

A crease formed between her brows, but she smirked. "Go right ahead."

Instead of jumping into the discussion, I ground my cock against her clit and took her mouth.

A moan escaped from deep in her throat, and she met the demands of my hips with hers.

Her fingernails scored through my hair, down the back of my neck, and across my shoulders. The heat and wetness of her soaked through her underwear, driving up my need for her.

Just when I knew she teetered on the cusp of desperation, I pulled back.

"What are you doing?" she gasped, panic etched all over her features.

"I'm making something clear."

"Please, make it quick."

"You will not hold things back from us. Is that clear?"

She nodded, so I continued, "I am your lover. I didn't kill your husband, and neither did Theo. But you know that."

Fear flashed across her face, and she opened her lips as if to say something. Before she could utter a word, I pressed my mouth to hers.

"You're ours to protect at all costs and keep safe," I murmured.

"Are you sure this is the risk you want to take?"

"Cleaning up a mess is low on the scale of unsavory things my hands have done." I glanced over my shoulder. "The carpet was due for an update anyway. The activities of the other week only sped up the timetable."

"I believe your numerous hours in the Caves have given you a twisted sense of humor."

I shrugged. "Maybe, but you get off on how I handle things in the Caves, so that's all that matters."

"You think so?" Her voice grew huskier and more unsteady.

"I know so." I cupped her through her soaked underwear and slid two fingers past the gusset to her swollen pussy lips, circling and teasing.

Her nails dug into the fabric of my shirt, and she threw her head back, closing her eyes. "Xander."

"Are you sore?"

"A little," she admitted.

I pressed my digits into her channel a fraction, forcing her hips to lift to gain better penetration. "Does that mean your cunt is off limits for a few days?"

"Hell no," she exclaimed as she opened her lids. "I was a virgin, and it didn't stop you and Theo from fucking me nonstop. You aren't making an exception now."

I reached for the opening of my jeans and freed my cock.

Keeping her underwear to the side, I positioned my hard dick at the opening of her dripping pussy.

"I thought you said we were moving too fast and you'd only been single for a few days."

She leaned forward and bit my lower lip, wicked intent on her face. "Who said I wasn't still single?"

I slammed into her. "I did."

"Oh, God," she cried out as her body bowed. "Xander, you're going to kill me."

"No, I'm going to fuck you. Fuck you so hard that you understand you are very taken."

I adjust my stance, positioning her closer to a lamp anchored to a wall. "Grab hold of the post above you."

Her breath came out in rapid pants while her breasts heaved as she reached up, wrapping her fingers around the metal.

I pulled out and thrust back in as soon as she secured herself. I pounded into her. I wanted her to feel the sting on her shoulders from the books behind her. I wanted her to buck into the relentless pace I'd set. I wanted her to drown my cock in her delicious, juicy arousal.

My attention moved down my body to where I tunneled in and out of her fucking perfect cunt. I loved the way her pink and swollen lips glistened and that delicate pearl at the apex poked out from arousal, and how all her cream coated every inch of my cock.

Fucking magical to watch that beautiful pussy taking all of me, letting me destroy her, mark her, give her my cum.

I played on a knife's edge by not using protection, but if she had mine or Theo's kid, so be it. She belonged to us anyway.

God, the thought of her round with my child had my cock growing harder. Fuck, I wanted that more than I realized.

I thumbed over her clit, and she called out my name. Her neck arched, and her hair tumbled free of the knot from atop her head. Disheveled, flushed, lost in the climb to pleasure, the woman was a fucking goddess.

I circled her sensitive bundle of nerves and felt her pussy muscles quiver and contract around my pistoning cock.

"Yes. There. Right there." She bit her lip and clutched at the metal in her hands.

She met each roll of my hips with hers. The rhythm was smooth and completely in sync.

All of a sudden, her body seized up, growing rigid, and her cunt clamped down on me in a vise grip. Without realizing it, she released the post and grabbed hold of me, her back bowed and her pussy grinding against my cock. She worked me with her spasms and squeezes.

As her orgasm waned, I carried her to the sofa and leveraged her on the end. We held each other's gazes as I let my beast out, fucking into her, not caring if I broke the antique furniture. I needed to fill her. Mark her from the inside. This was primal.

Where the hell had it come from?

I knew. It was when Nerine said she was single.

Without thinking, I grabbed hold of her neck. Her eyes widened, and then a smile settled on her lips, no fear at all.

It was time to tell Theo to stop holding back with her.

"You are not single. Is that clear?"

"The world will think I am."

"I only care what you think. You belong to us." I hammered my hips into her, the threads of my release working up my spine as my balls drew up.

"Why does it matter?"

I clenched my jaw. "It fucking matters."

"Fine. I'm not single. I'm yours."

"You're mine and Theo's forever. Say it."

"I'm yours and Theo's forever. Oh fuck, I'm coming again."

Her cunt fisted my cock in a hard spasm, and it was all over for me. My ejaculation shot through me, and I spurted into Nerine in hot, hard jets. I felt the relief through my whole body. There was nothing fucking like it.

I loved this woman, and I could only hope that she truly accepted that we were in this together.

Twenty-One

erine

"Cara, let me look at you," my mother, Delia Angelos, exclaimed in Greek and stretched her arms out when she spotted me under the driveway terrace.

Even with everything she'd endured over the last few years, she was breathtaking. For a woman in her mid-fifties, she could pass for someone twenty years younger, except for her eyes—dark and piercing. She'd seen things and experienced loss on an excruciating level. She was the epitome of strength and resilience. Her whole demeanor radiated those two words.

My sisters rushed from the car, shooting past me and gathering around Theo and Xander, talking a mile a minute.

The fact neither of them seemed fazed by the onslaught

that was the tornado of my sisters made me want to kiss them senseless.

My heart overflowing with happiness, I smiled and stepped into Mama's open arms. Immediately, she wrapped them around me, and for the first time in years, I felt the comfort of the past. It was the unconditional love of my childhood.

My throat burned as tears gathered.

No matter how much I pretended otherwise, there was nothing like feeling Mama's love.

"Mama, I missed you so much." I responded back to her in Greek, closing my eyes and holding her tight, then said in English, "You don't know how happy I am that you're here."

"Things are going to be different now," Mama whispered against my ear. *"Just you watch. You will get the life you deserve."*

"I have big shoes to fill. I'm scared."

"You'll be fine. Just remember whose daughter you are at all times."

I pulled back and studied her face. She lifted a brow, the same gesture I'd perfected. I wanted to shake my head, but I knew better. Yes, I was most definitely Delia Angelos's daughter as much as Peter's.

"I hear you," I muttered.

"I knew you would."

She'd conveyed without words that while I may have taken over Papa's role in the organization, she would still run our family of five. Papa knew the rules and never questioned her authority with us children. Now she expected me to fall in line, and since I had no plans to jump into raising my sisters, more power to her.

However, something told me Mama planned to meddle in my life more than I wanted.

I peered over Mama's head toward Xander and Theo.

They caught the message, too.

I wondered how long she'd wait until she cornered the men for a private conversation.

"Theo, Xander, tonight I'd like to speak with you."

Not long at all, it seemed.

"Anything you wish, Theia Delia," Theo answered in Greek.

Hearing him use the language gave me pause. It reminded me that everyone used to go seamlessly between English and Greek depending on who they spoke to in the house.

We would move back into the norm soon.

Mama's attention moved to Xander. *"Do you have time, Xander?"*

Xander shifted as if uncomfortable with her scrutiny. *"Name the time and place, and I will be there."*

"Excellent." Mama nodded. *"There is much to discuss."*

Yep, Mama Angelos was back in town.

My youngest sister, Fiona, snickered. "Oh, I think you're in trouble already."

Ignoring her, I said, *"Mama, why don't you and the girls get comfortable in the new section of the house before you jump into your routine? I've had the suites readied for all of you."*

Christina slid an arm around my waist. "I'm so ready for you to take the brunt of her attention."

"Thanks, I think."

"Girls, what did I tell you in the car? Just because we are in

America doesn't mean you stop speaking our language. Don't forget Papa's rule, in this house, we speak Greek."

Christina smirked. "What did you say, Mama? It all sounds like Greek to me."

Knowing a head slap was in my sister's future, I jumped in. *"Mama, a lot has changed. That rule doesn't apply anymore."*

I heard some giggles as my mother muttered something about taking the house back from the interloper's ways.

I just shook my head, not bothering to say anything further, to her annoyance.

"Man, I missed how you always knew how to handle her without trying." Christina searched my face with eyes as blue as mine. "Are you okay?"

"I am now that you all are here. I have my family under one roof. That's what I needed."

Ariana approached my opposite side, cocking an elbow on my shoulder. "I'll remind you of those words when you complain about all the noise."

"Honestly, I welcome the chaos. It's been a long time since this house had life."

Christina and Ariana passed each other smirks, and then Ariana said, "She says that now, but in a few days, she'll wish to gag one of us."

I couldn't help but smile. I needed this. My sisters surrounded me, and Mama was being Mama.

"So, Tina, tell me about this boyfriend of yours. Mama said he's a looker."

Her shoulders sagged. "We broke up. I want college and a

career, and he wants marriage and babies. It was never going to go anywhere."

She left off the part where he lived in Greece, and she'd returned to the US.

I led them toward the stairs to the renovated part of the house. "What, isn't he eighteen? That's a bit young to think about the next phase in life."

"He's the firstborn and the heir. You know, expectations and all that."

I nodded.

"In their family, they arrange things early. Plus, I knew it wouldn't last. His mother wanted someone without a 'modern American upbringing' to join her family." She air-quoted the last part.

"Whatever," I muttered, wanting to punch that asshole and his mother for hurting my sister. "What does his family know about modern anything? They lost a catch, if I have anything to say about it."

"I love it when you get all big-sister fierce."

"I'm so over these old-fashioned patriarchal views." I'd dealt with enough of the bullshit from Andraius. "Plus, you need to live life and explore the world, not decide to shackle yourself to some guy you were seeing in high school."

"You are one to talk." Ariana elbowed me. "Didn't you have your life planned out?"

I frowned at her. "What are you talking about?"

"Weren't you shagging two enforcers from the time you were in high school and into college and planning a future with them?"

"Umm." I caught the amusement on Theo's face and then glared at my mother. *"You told them?"*

"I did no such thing. Fi is nosy and has a habit of listening to private conversations. I didn't know she was hiding in the bathroom."

"Fi knows?"

"I'm not a baby." Fiona came alongside me.

"You're still my baby sister."

"I'm well aware of how sex works." She rolled her eyes. "If you only knew half the things the good Greek girls do. It makes us Americans look like prudes."

"I feel like I'm in a parallel universe."

"I told you things are going to be different now. Come." Mama gestured with her chin. *"Show me to my rooms."*

A little after eleven in the evening, after changing into my pajamas, I took the hidden passageways leading to my mother's room. Hopefully, she remembered to unlock the latch from her side. It was how we'd always said good night before our world had turned upside down.

The good thing about this new area, unless opened from a special access point, the hidden pathways behind our bedrooms were only connected to each other. Papa had installed a sliding panel to give him some way to connect to the main passageways. Still, the reinforced wooden and metal door had an old-school style dial lock on it, and Mama and I were the only people who knew the combination.

I was sure if people thought hard and long enough, they'd figure out it was the date Papa had married Mama in Greece, but it would take some time. They'd only ever celebrated the date of their stateside wedding since that was the one considered legal in the US.

I never understood all the details behind why they'd had two weddings. All Mama said was something about stupid people not filing the correct paperwork and making it look like she was living in sin with her mother-in-law.

I loved my *yia yia,* but the woman was a battle-ax, and she'd made Mama's life hard until I came along. Then she'd spent all her time feeding me and left her poor haggard daughter-in-law alone.

As I neared the outer wall on one side of Mama's room, I heard echoes of a discussion. It sounded like the people in the room with her were men.

Oh, the conversation she'd planned with Theo and Xander.

The right thing to do would be to turn around, hang out with one of the girls, and wait for Mama to find me.

But curiosity got the better of me. Besides, one never learned anything useful by being a good girl.

I inched closer. Hopefully, the skills Lilly and Devani taught me worked to keep Theo's stealthy hearing from detecting me. As I approached the section with the sliding panel that opened into Mama's closet, I noticed the wall was still closed.

What the hell?

Mama knew it was our ritual to say good night. The rule was to leave it cracked. She'd broken the rules.

I scowled at the wall.

I wouldn't hear anything from the closet. I might as well go back where I could listen to some of the conversations.

"I trust you two with her. She likes to pretend she isn't, but she is fragile."

"She is stronger than you believe," Xander defended me.

Of course, the guys would indulge her need to speak Greek after what I'd said earlier. I'd forgotten how Mama was modern in so many things but very traditional when it came to preserving our Greek culture, one of them being the family speaking our language at all times while in the house.

Then Theo said, *"If you only knew half of the things she endured, you wouldn't put fragile in any context to describe her."*

Their confidence in me settled the uncertainty I'd felt ever since I learned of the rumors about the three of us.

"I know a lot more than you believe. I have eyes in place, even if physically my body lived in a villa overseas." The clang of decanters told me Mama poured drinks. *"Here, I need to say something, and you'll need this to handle it."*

"If you are planning to tell us to walk away, our answer is no." Theo's direct approach to Mama surprised me.

He was the eloquent one. He used tact and the right words with everyone but me. For me, he took the in-your-face, I-want-to-throw-you-over-my-knee-and-spank-your-ass approach.

My pussy quivered at the thought. Then I pushed it away. If only Theo would do that instead of holding it in. Over the last few days, since we'd reconnected into our unit of three, I'd seen it. The beast was waiting for Theo to set him free.

"I have to concur with Theo's sentiment."

Xander was the dominant and passionate lover. He gave me tenderness, emotion, gentleness. It was what he needed to do. The outside world only saw this beast of a man, all muscles and with a do-as-I-say attitude that took no one's shit. With me, he let down his guard. He softened.

No, he wouldn't allow me to run all over him, and he would force me to answer his questions as he'd done in the library this afternoon. But with him, I could talk to him about nothing and everything for hours.

Theo, on the other hand, kept his fire hidden from the world, rarely unleashing it unless it was on the poor souls who fucked with him in the Caves. However, with me, he pushed all my buttons. He jacked with me for the sake of annoying me. It was a game, foreplay. Domination was part of it, but I also needed to defy and goad him into reacting.

Watching the ultra-controlled, utterly refined man snap turned me on like nothing else.

Fuck, just the thought of it had my pussy contracting.

Why he wouldn't let that side of him out frustrated the hell out of me.

"No, of course, I wouldn't say that to either of you." Mama's words snapped me back to the conversation. *"In fact, that is the last thing I plan to tell you. My aim is to have one of you marry Nerine."*

Was I losing my mind and misheard her? Or maybe she'd lost hers.

I hadn't even been a widow for an entire week. The fuck? Andraius's body was still fresh in the ground.

"She won't marry again," Theo interjected. *"I doubt she ever will, considering her experience with marriage."*

"Are you so sure?"

"Yes."

"Maybe with anyone else. However, she'd change her mind if it were one of you two."

"I'm not following." This time Xander spoke. *"Why do you want her to marry?"*

"I won't have anyone jump in and force her into a situation like the one with the impostor. With one of you, her place is secure. With the two of you, love surrounds her. As the men standing by her side, the two of you will give her the support she never had. No one will think to overthrow her."

"She is more than a figurehead or an ornament while we make the decisions. She knows how to run the organization. She's made more decisions in the last few days than that asshole did in the last three months."

"So quick to protect her, Theo. You'll need to keep doing that when you marry her."

I held in the cough that bubbled up.

"Me?" The shock in Theo's voice was comical, and then my heart broke when he added, *"Why on earth would you pick me over Xander? He's the stable one."*

"Because you need a family more than anyone I know. Xander's family is here. He is rooted here. Marrying Nerine means you can't run away. You can't just one day say 'Nerine and Xander are happy. I'll leave them to live their lives and go my separate way.'"

The room grew quiet, thick with tension, as the truth of Mama's words settled in the air.

A tear slipped down my cheek. Knowing Theo, he would leave if he thought it would make my life easier than to live an unconventional relationship.

"Okay, we need to take a step back," Xander said after a few minutes. *"Before we decide Nerine's future for her as if we are in some prehistoric era, you need to discuss this with her."*

"No, I need to make clear my wishes with the two of you."

"Xander is the better choice. As you said, he has a family. That means Nerine has a line to look back on for her children."

I heard movement and then an angry Xander order, *"Sit your ass back down, dickhead. I'm accepting what we had is over, but you're committed to Nerine. Wouldn't some of those children be yours if your scenario plays out?"*

My mind reeled hearing what Xander revealed in front of Mama. Xander and Theo kept everything about them to a very small circle. The syndicate world wasn't open and accepting of relationships other than those they viewed as traditional.

"I have no family stateside. They are all dead. I have nothing to offer her."

"Do you think that makes a difference to her?" Xander asked with the same irritation prickling at the back of my neck.

Theo being the man he was despite all he endured with his father and brothers was something I admired.

"You know what kind of crap I come from. Someone like me isn't worthy of Nerine."

"Theia Viola was my mama's best friend and gave her life by

taking a shot meant for you. Just because Theios Mik and your brothers became pieces of shit because they couldn't get over her death doesn't mean you forget her. Don't ever say you come from crap."

"She died because she went to hug me. What bullshit is that?"

"Theo," Mama said in her soothing tone. *"She was my friend, too. Believe me when I tell you she would do it all over again in a heartbeat."*

"We also need to get something very clear into your head. You aren't the one responsible for the hit. Uncle Mik was. He went against Theios Peter's orders and went after a group he knew better than to target. All to initiate your brothers into the life."

I remembered the fury on Papa's face when I'd gotten home from school. He'd sat in his office, gripping his hair and shaking his head. He'd raged about how Theios Mik killed an innocent child, the youngest son of a local boss when he'd arrived home in the boss's car instead of him. The boy had been eleven.

"It doesn't change the fact I'm the one they targeted, and Mama died."

"Does it make you unworthy of my daughter? Want to know a secret?"

Yeah, I wanted to know whatever she planned to spill.

"I knew about the both of you and I knew the moment things changed with the three of you."

My mouth fell open. Oh my God. I was still in high school then, a senior in high school, but only seventeen.

Shit, that sounded really bad, now that I thought about it, especially since they were older than me by a few years.

"Why didn't you say anything? About Theo and me or the three of us?" Xander asked. *"I'm sure it wasn't exactly what you wanted for your eldest daughter and heir."*

"I'll address both parts of the question. First, the two of you needed each other. You were best friends, who were more. I saw nothing wrong with it. Not everyone from my generation is closed-minded."

The love I felt for Mama was beyond anything I could describe. I had no doubt she was instrumental in protecting Xander and Theo as teenagers.

"Now to the second part. You made Nerine happy and kept her out of trouble. And we know how much of a troublemaker she is, don't we, Theo?" Mama asked with a humorous inflection to her words.

She wanted to lighten the mood after the heaviness of moments earlier.

He grunted. *"You tricked me into babysitting her. Why didn't you tell me her old school kicked her out?"*

"Because her Papa didn't know. He believed she only used her viper tongue for select purposes instead of at every inappropriate time possible."

"She gave me hell. I wanted to throw her off the nearest bridge."

"And now you love her."

"Now I love her and still want to throw her off the nearest bridge."

"Then it is settled. You will marry Nerine as soon as we can convince her to go through with it."

He sighed. *"Xander, are you good with this?"*

"I was always going to tell you to be the one to make it legal for the same reasons Theia Delia gave."

"I swear, I'm surrounded by conspirators."

"Okay, give me hugs and go to bed. If you can't find Nerine, she is probably in one of her sister's rooms. The girl loves the secret hallways her papa built in this house. I'll never understand why she enjoys walking around in the dark so much."

"This side of the house has them, too?" Theo asked. *"I assumed it was only in the old section."*

I winced. Mama and her big mouth.

That was our secret.

"Oh no. Peter and Nerine insisted the addition have them, too. They wanted ways to avoid people, meaning their security. It was all fun and games until Nerine used the sneaky tactics Peter taught her on him. I can only imagine the trouble she gave you."

"You have no idea," Xander muttered. *"She could drive a man to drink."*

"How did you keep her from barging in here? Your daughter is nosy and believes she needs to be in the center of every conversation about her."

I frowned at Theo's words, having visions of clocking him in the mouth. I wasn't that nosy.

Umm. Yes, I was.

"I kept the latch sealed, so even if she thought about coming down, she'd make it as far as my closet and then have to turn around."

"That was a good call. And thank you for the information on the passageways Nerine conveniently forgot to mention."

Mama laughed. *"Forgot, my foot. We all know she did it on purpose."*

Shit. Shit. Shit.

Mama and her big mouth.

They weren't stupid and had to know I was hiding in the walls or at least suspected.

Those two men knew me too well.

Fuck, I had to make it to one of the girls' rooms quickly.

I tiptoed away from Mama's room, trying to make as little noise as possible. And, of course, the floorboards decided to creak.

Dammit. *Shut up, you stupid pieces of wood.*

Okay, almost there. One more hallway, and I'd be near Fiona's room. She slept like a log and wouldn't even hear me come inside.

I froze as the sound of footsteps vibrated from the other side of the wall. I waited, not daring to move a muscle, in case I gave away that only wood and plaster separated us.

"You and I need to have a discussion, soon," Theo said.

About time they had a conversation. Everything unsaid between them put a barrier in what we all shared.

"Are you sure you're ready for this?" Xander asked.

"Yeah, it's time. The three of us can't work otherwise."

"Let's wait until after the meeting."

"You want to wait? That's a surprise. Why?" The confusion in Theo's voice was evident.

"There are other things on our plate. Just answer one thing."

"What?"

Xander waited for a second and then spoke. "Are we done?"

"Do you really believe that's an option?"

It would never be over for them, for us.

"Where are you going?"

"I need to take care of a few things before I hit the sheets," Theo said.

"Same. I'm sure Nerine is still up. Let her hang with her sisters. Tomorrow's going to be a long day."

I sagged against a wall as relief washed over me.

Okay, back to my room, I go.

Releasing a deep breath, I strolled down the corridor toward my rooms. My nosiness had caused me more tension than was necessary.

As I neared the panel opening into my bedroom, I cocked my head. I distinctly remembered closing the sliding wall since I wanted to keep the draft from seeping into my rooms.

That's when I felt the familiar presence, and the hair on the back of my neck prickled as my heartbeat jumped.

"You've been a very naughty girl."

Twenty-Two

Theo

"Stop struggling." I slid my hand from Nerine's mouth. "Eavesdropping on a private conversation is impolite."

"I have no idea what you are talking about."

"Is that right? Then tell me what you were doing inside this passageway."

"I was on my way to Mama's room to say good night."

"Interesting, since her room is in the direction you just came from. You look very guilty right now, Angel. Want to try for another explanation? How about the truth this time?"

"Fuck off with your guilty." She added a tirade of profanity in Greek and tried to elbow me in the stomach.

I grabbed her wrists and positioned her palms above her

head, flat to the wall. "That wasn't very nice. What would your Mama say about you using that language?"

She bucked against me. "Mama isn't as pristine as you believe."

"Compared to you, she's the Virgin Mary." I crowded her, giving her no space, and forced her to turn her cheek and press it against the side of the passageway with the brick wall. "I know firsthand since I was part of your corruption."

"I should have punched you in the face and asked Papa to assign someone else to guard me."

"You should have stayed at your rich girl's school instead of joining us peasants."

"I got expelled, or did you forget that part?"

"That's right." I brought my mouth a hairsbreadth from hers. "I didn't learn that bit of information until two years into watching you and your bitchy attitude."

"I wouldn't have had the attitude if you weren't such a jerk."

"You liked my jerk side. It got you wet." Releasing her wrists, I slid my palm down her arms, along her waist, and down the front of her pajama pants to cup her bare, slick pussy.

"Keep dreaming." She pushed back, scraping her nails against the brick, and ground her needy cunt against me. "I hated you. It made me want to shoot you."

"Your words contradicted your actions. What's that saying? Oh yes, there is a thin line between love and hate." I pushed two fingers into her heat, pumping a few times before curling them to hit that bundle of nerves deep inside her.

She thrashed, not carrying her delicate skin may have abrasions from her movements against the brick. "Oh, Theo. Fuck. That feels so good."

"Answer this question if you hated me so much. Why did you push it to the next level? You were the one who grabbed me by the shirt and kissed me."

She met each of my thrusts with her hips, her pants erratic as her pussy dripped all over my hand. "It was temporary insanity."

"And what do you feel now?"

"It's still insanity," she gasped, tiny spasms surrounding my fingers.

"If your insanity is ongoing, how can it be temporary?"

"You dickmatized me." She pushed out with her hands and bowed her back. "Just like that. Fuck, just like that."

"This isn't my dick, Angel."

"Shut up and make me come."

"Always the brat. You want to come? I'll make you come." I circled my thumb over her clit while pumping hard and fast, just as she liked it. "But then you deal with the consequences."

"I didn't do anything to warrant consequences."

"That's where you are so wrong. Now scream for me." I pressed down on her sensitive clit, coasting the edge of pain she loved so much without taking it to the place I knew she couldn't handle.

Her body immediately reacted, and she tumbled over into climax, moaning and mumbling noncoherent words.

"That's it. Squeeze down on my fingers with that beautiful cunt of yours."

"Yes, Theo. I love that."

Her orgasm continued to ripple through her, her head thrown back against my shoulders, her body held up by the positioning of my very aroused one.

The drive to fuck her rode me. But first, I had to make something clear.

"You will not walk these passageways until we know this house is safe. Do I make myself clear?"

"You—you don't tell me what to do." Her pussy spasmed with the remnants of her release, making her response so breathy and seductive.

"Oh, but I do. You're not safe. That bastard wouldn't have gotten into the library if we didn't have traitors among us."

"I can protect myself."

I pulled my hand from her slick heat, bringing my fingers to my lips and sucking her essence into my mouth. God, she tasted better than the finest of wines.

"Listen carefully: pretend all you want, but you barely survived after taking on someone who rarely, if ever, trained. Relax," I cooed into her ear when she stiffened. "You are ours to protect, remember?"

"Theo, I—" I covered her mouth with my hand, cutting off whatever she planned to say.

"You don't ever speak of it. Don't let it hit the air. You are the Angelos. End of story."

She nodded, and I glided my palm down from her mouth, over her neck, and to the base of her throat. "Now, back to what I was saying. All passageways are off-limits. And unless you are with a security team, you do not go anywhere."

"I already told you I won't ever be a prisoner again."

"This isn't being a prisoner. This is part of your role as the Angelos. Security is part of the job."

She elbowed me in the stomach, making me hiss. "Bullshit. I doubt anyone ever ordered Papa around like this."

"He understood how things worked."

"I call bullshit again. You think his penis made him smarter. Fuck off with that." She jerked, ready to fight me for her freedom again.

Well, here we went again. The woman would not listen to reason.

"Why won't you make anything easy? I'm trying to keep you alive."

"You are trying to boss me around. I'm not an idiot. This set of passageways only goes from bedroom to bedroom. You can't access anything else unless someone uses the secret access point. Mama and I are the only ones with the combinations to its security lock, jackass."

I gritted my teeth.

She was going to drive me bonkers with all these passageways. I fucking needed maps of all of them and where the fuck they all were and what connected to what. This was ridiculous.

"I swear. Do you want to know who's insane? It's me." I pressed my sexually frustrated front to her back. "Back in the day, I would have gagged you and paddled your ass for being a mouthy brat. Then fucked you senseless."

She stopped struggling and went utterly still.

Immediately the energy changed, and my cock grew harder. I dropped my head to the back of her head. Both of our breaths grew unsteady and faster with each second.

A whimper escaped her lips.

"Theo." The husky way she said my name conveyed so much desire and need.

No. Those thoughts had to remain locked away.

She'd endured more than she should have with that bastard. The last thing I wanted was to trigger a single one of her demons.

I pressed my face into her hair, the craving to give her what she asked at war with the worry this was too soon.

"Please."

"You can't be serious. Not after what you lived through."

"It isn't the same thing, and you know it. The marks you leave are from pleasure and because I asked for them. They aren't because of anger or rage. Your pain is sweet, delicious agony that I fantasize about."

"I'm not sure if I can go to that level with you. Not yet, anyway."

"I'm not delicate. What he did to me doesn't change how I loved sex with you."

"How can you expect me to hunt you in the dark, force you to submit, and then fuck you? What we did before were games with rules we all knew."

"What do you call what happened right now? We're in the dark, and you hunted me, forced me to submit, and fucked me with your fingers."

"That is completely different than what you are asking me to do. I love you too much to chance hurting you."

"Theo." Her tone grew hard. "I'm not saying hunt me through the various passageways of this house, catch me kicking and screaming, and fuck me." She hummed, making my cock jerk. "Though the idea of that turns me on more than you can ever know."

"Then what are you saying?"

"I want you to be Theo with me."

"Meaning?"

"Stop restraining yourself. I want my Theo."

Her Theo. She had no idea who her Theo was anymore. The things I wanted weren't anywhere near sweet. What we'd done in the past was the tip of the iceberg of the things I enjoyed now. I'd explored the darker side of my desires while abroad. I refused to unleash them on her.

She wasn't ready by any means.

"Who is your Theo?"

"The lover that washed over me like a raging storm and consumed me whole."

"I see."

She couldn't possibly expect me to give her all of me to that level. It might destroy her. But maybe a portion of it would satisfy her.

Who was I kidding? This was a temporary solution, not a long-term fix.

"What do you see?"

"You're telling me I'm being too gentle with you. That you like it rough with me since that's our kink."

"You are brutally honest with me. You fight with me. You won't ever take my shit. You don't sugarcoat that I'm a bitch sometimes. And through all of it, you still want me. That's the Theo I fell in love with. That's the Theo I want."

"Are you saying you love me, Angel?"

"You know I do."

"Do I?" I wrapped her hair around my fist and jerked her head back, leaning down and hearing her breath grow shallow. "Say it."

"I love you, Theo."

I grazed my teeth down her neck, and immediately, goosebumps prickled her skin. "Repeat it."

"I love you."

"You want it rough?" I pushed her shirt up, cupping her breast and then pinching her nipple hard enough to elicit a whimper from her lips.

"I want you untamed."

"You're not ready for the games."

I expected a protest, but instead, she said, "That doesn't mean you can't fuck me like you mean it."

"Are you saying I didn't mean it all the other times I pumped my cum inside you over the last few days?"

I kicked her legs apart and pushed her pants down, letting them catch at her knees, forcing her to lose balance and readjust.

"You held back. Be refined in public. With me, you're brutal. You bite, mark, and scare me in the most beautiful way."

Pulling back her hips, I freed my cock, sliding it along the seam of her pussy, up through her folds and then back again.

I released my hold on her hair and gripped her shoulder and neck. A second of worry crept in. The bruises were fading, but they weren't gone, and now she wanted me to put more on her.

"Stop thinking and do it. I won't break. The last thing on my mind is that bastard when your hand is around my neck."

Instead of giving her what she wanted, I dropped to my knees and licked her wet, slick pussy.

"Oh, fuck." She pushed back against my face, and in response, I smacked her ass, which caused her to moan, "More."

This I could give her. I peppered her ass, feeling her skin heat, massaging the muscles under my palms with each pass.

"Harder. I need hard."

"No, it's time for my midnight snack."

I tongued her cunt, pushing into her channel, lapping at her delicious taste, feasting, loving every second of it. I brought her to the edge and then pulled back, keeping her from going over multiple times.

"You're the devil. Let me come."

"Not unless it is on my cock."

She glared over her shoulder. "I want to fucking come."

"And you will come when I'm fucking you with my cock." I thrust two fingers into her, followed by a third. "Is this what you wanted? The taste of pain."

"Yes." Her knees shook, and I wedged my shoulder against her thigh to give her leverage. "I fucking love the sweet agony. More."

"Ride my hand. I give you sixty seconds to make yourself come. Otherwise, you'll wait until my cock rams into you."

"It's your hand. You're supposed to deliver."

"It's your cunt. Make it come."

"I hate you."

I scissored my fingers inside her, and she released a hoarse cry and started to gyrate her hips.

"You keep using that word. I do not think it means what you think it means." I nipped her ass cheek hard enough to leave a mark.

Her back bowed, and she gasped. "That's my line. Only I get to use it."

I bit her on the other side, knowing she'd have matching teeth imprints.

Her pussy quivered and flexed.

A surge of satisfaction coursed through me, and my straining cock wanted me to stop its torment.

I had no doubt precum dripped onto the floor, and the drive to plow into Nerine's sopping heat pushed at me. But I wanted this woman so crazy on edge that the second I plunged my dick into her, she'd fly over the abyss.

"Thirty seconds."

"Shut up. I'm concentrating." She moved up and down my hand, working herself in tiny increments. "Help me. Bite me again. Pull my hair. Just fucking put that big cock in me."

"Fifteen seconds."

"Stop with the counting. It's annoying."

"This isn't my problem."

"Asshole."

"Don't tempt me, Angel. I don't have lube on me, and your puckered opening is calling my name." I feathered my digits inside her. "However, the way you're dripping all over my hand, I wouldn't need anything extra."

"That's it, Theo. That's it." She dropped her forehead onto the stud running down the wall. "I can't without you."

"What was that?"

"You heard me." The way she gritted her teeth had me smiling.

I loved her frustration and arousal. Eventually, we'd work up to how things were before the bastard broke our world apart.

"Time's up." I pulled free of her heat, eliciting a growl from her.

"Fuck, time's up."

Rising to my feet, I gave her no warning before pushing my fingers into her mouth. "I'd rather fuck you."

Her only response was to moan and suck harder on my fingers.

"You like the thought of that, hmm?"

Sliding out of her mouth, I took hold of her neck in the way she craved and notched my cock into the sopping opening of her pussy. "Now, be a good girl and tell me what I want to hear before I give you your pleasure."

She lifted her arm, scraped her nails down my scalp, and then cupped the back of my neck. "I can't without you, Theo."

"And."

She tilted her head up while pulling mine toward hers and then whispered against my lips, "I love you."

I slammed to the hilt inside her.

She instinctively pushed back with her hips and called out, "Yes. Finally."

God, there was nothing like the heat of her engulfing my cock or the way her cunt rippled and pulsed as her arousal grew.

"Didn't the first orgasm take the edge off?" I pumped in and out of her in shallow thrusts meant to torment and drive up the need again.

"Not even close. My body spent too long hibernating. Now, I want you to service my needs every chance I can get. I hope you and Xander are taking your vitamins."

Pulling out to the tip, I plowed brutally into her, forcing a guttural gasp from her lips. "It's more about if you can handle us. Remember, it's one cunt to two cocks."

Her pussy clenched at my words, and I flexed my fingers around her throat.

Her breath grew into rapid pants.

"You dirty, filthy Angel. You love it when we fuck you together." I pounded her, making it so she had no choice but to take what I gave.

"You know I do."

She moved both hands to the wall in hopes of using them to keep her body steady against my assault.

"There is one way we haven't taken you," I said through a shallow breath.

The thought of Xander and I filling her sweet pussy at the same time had my cock growing harder. It was our way of claiming her together.

"I—I know."

"Are you ready for that?"

She knew what I was asking.

"Yes. Once I'm completely free. I have to claim my position before the other families. I want to own who I am first."

"Then you're ours."

"Then I'm yours."

I jerked out of her, turned her, and lifted her a second before filling her again. I set a relentless pace.

"Theo," she gasped, her arms twining around my neck.

"You sealed your fate with us."

"I did that when I was in high school." She leaned forward and bit my lower lip hard enough to draw blood.

However, before I could retaliate, she licked it away and hummed. "Now stop with all the talking and fuck me."

I gave her no verbal response, only adjusted my angle and rolled my hips, giving her the friction she needed to push her right to the cusp.

I held her there, thrusting with the right rhythm and slowing enough to drive a few expletives from her lips. And right when her nails dug deeper than necessary into my shoulder, I sent her flying into bliss.

"Oh, God. Theo."

Her pussy clamped down on me so hard it was almost too much to allow any movement. Her muscles flexed and squeezed, and a flood of her arousal soaked my cock.

I gritted my teeth as the erotic pulsing around me forced my balls to draw up and caused my thrusts to grow erratic. In the next second, her continued clenching sent me over the cliff of release.

Twenty-Three

erine

"This decision affects all of us. I need to know this is something you can accept."

I assessed Mama's and my sisters' faces as they scanned through the folders in their hands—each one containing detailed information about Angelos Shipping, from its finances to its organizational structure. I'd never hidden anything from them, and I never would.

They'd known what I'd done the day of the coup. Hell, they'd watched me do it. But after what Andraius pulled with my forged signature on his bank accounts, I needed them to understand I wasn't making this decision lightly.

After a few minutes, Mama looked up. *"Every day, I see*

more and more of my old Nerine again. It makes me so happy. You laugh and joke. It's been so long since I saw the silliness inside you. That hard shell is cracking away."

My throat burned hearing her say that. I felt the change, too. Not having to hold everything in, not having to be on guard, was so freeing. At least in my home, I could be myself.

"All of this." She lifted the folder. *"It is because of you and what you want and has nothing to do with Theo and Xander. Is this correct?"*

I'd expected this question and prepared for it.

"No, and yes. No, because I feel I have to fix this. I know I can fix this. I'm going to make mistakes. There is no way around it. I don't have Papa's experience or patience, but I'm not so stubborn that I won't listen to advice."

"What about the yes part?" Fiona probed.

Her sapphire gaze speared me like an inquisitor preparing to extract information. She was right. The baby in her had disappeared. I guessed watching the horrors she'd witnessed as a preteen could do that to a girl.

Now she assessed me with eyes so much older than her fifteen years.

"Since all of you know about us, I'll give you the truth. I love them."

"You can't marry both of them. Massachusetts is progressive but not that progressive," Ariana stated.

"She's barely been a widow for over a week. Give a girl a chance to play the field." Christina jabbed Ariana, who shoved her back.

"As if those two would let her play with anyone else."

Ariana glowered. "Do you even see the way they watch her?"

I broke into the twins' argument. "I wasn't finished, so you two can stop discussing me as if I'm not here."

"Sorry," they both said in unison.

Then Christina muttered, "You still can't marry both of them."

"Duh, you're so dumb." Ariana rolled her eyes. "Nerine will marry one and have special benefits with the other. Win-win."

I looked at the ceiling, shaking my head. I'd committed one murder in this room. What was two more?

Mama rose from her spot next to Fiona and strode toward the twins.

"No more talking from either of you. Is that clear? You two are eighteen, and Fiona, has more sense than the both of you put together." Then, Mama pointed at an armchair across from her. *"Christina, over there. Ariana, I'm sitting next to you now."*

They both opened their mouths to say something, and Mama cut them off. *"I said no talking."*

They both gave identical glowers, folding their arms. Christina settled into her new spot, muttering something under her breath, her gaze shooting daggers at Ariana.

"Did you say something about welcoming the chaos?" Fiona asked me with a smirk.

"I have no idea what you're talking about. You must have imagined it." I grinned back at her, then a giggle bubbled up, followed by laughter.

Once I started, Fiona joined in.

Mama chuckled next, and then I heard one of the twins

snort or something, and we all lost it.

For the next few minutes, we allowed ourselves to enjoy the ridiculousness of this simple sibling stupidity.

I had missed this so much. Mama. Fiona. Christina and Ariana.

If only Papa and Linus were here. Then our family would be complete, the way it once was.

Tears welled in my eyes.

As if sensing what was missing, we sobered and looked at each other.

"He would only want you to do this if it was your choice, cara." Mama spoke through the pain that had yet to ease. *"You can still change your mind."*

"Don't I have a responsibility to the family? This is what Papa expected of me."

"No." Mama shook her head. *"You stop that thought now. Have you not suffered enough in the name of this family?"*

"I can't let anything fall on the girls."

"Do you think you are the only one who gets to sacrifice everything for this family?" Ariana jumped up and cocked a hand on her hip. "Pass it to me. I'll fuck a motherfucker up if they even dared to touch me."

I rolled my eyes. "Sit down and shut up. You're going to college. That is what you want, so that is what will happen."

"What about the plan you worked on with your friends?" Fiona asked.

Immediately, my gaze went to the library doors, and my heartbeat accelerated. "I changed my mind."

"So I don't get to change my mind?" Ariana argued. "What

if I want to take up the mantle? You don't get to decide for me."

"Is that truly what you want?"

"Would you give it to me if it was?" She challenged me, with her blue eyes boring into mine as if daring me to lie to her.

Sighing, I shook my head. "No, I will never put that kind of pressure on you. There are too many things to take on that I won't have you carry."

Ariana cocked a hand on her hip. "And now we've circled back to the core of the situation. It's not a matter of whether we want something but what you are willing to give us. Do you want freedom from this life or Papa's seat? Tell us the truth."

I'd been adamant about my choice for so long.

All I cared about was my freedom, my escape, a life away from the hell I lived in, the obligations, the family.

Then all the things Theo and Xander had said soaked in, and maybe some of the lessons from Lilly did as well. Where Devani coordinated my escape plan, Lilly constantly taught me skills based on the scenario where I stayed to run the empire.

"My choice is Papa's seat. However," I added, "this meeting is to make the final decision."

"Are you saying—" Christina paused and then shifted in her seat. "Are you saying that you want us to make the call? If we say we want to go through with the plan to leave, it will happen?"

I nodded. "Everything is ready. All my friends were waiting on was for one of Andraius's rivals to play on his territory to put things in motion. Now, they only need the go-ahead from me."

"Won't they be upset if you change your mind and decide to stay? These people you call friends"—Ariana air-quoted the last word—"are dangerous, and they spent a lot of time and money putting everything together."

"They account for all scenarios, and money isn't a big problem for them."

"Who the fuck are you involved with, Nerine?" Ariana's voice was high-pitched and worried, which wasn't her usual way of handling things.

"Are you really that dense?" Fiona asked in exasperation. "Those women she sent to our villa to debug our house and give us the phones were spies or killers or something. Didn't you notice how they scanned everything and monitored the property? Seriously, they were armed at all times, with something or the other, guns, knives, you name it, they probably had it somewhere on their body. How did you not see that?"

"I had bigger things to worry about at the time, like finishing school." Ariana shot Fiona a scowl.

"I swear, you two are so oblivious. Mama, were they oxygen-deprived during labor? How are the two of you so book smart when you're oblivious to what's under your nose?"

"Fi, enough," Mama commanded.

"Yes, Mama."

I rubbed my temples and stood, stalking over to my desk, opening a drawer, and pulling out a roll of masking tape. "No more talking from anyone, or I will tape your mouths shut."

The shocked expression on the girls' faces may have been worth the headache.

"Now, can I explain why I came to this point before anyone else decides to jump in?"

The girls nodded their agreement without saying a word.

"I want to fix our legacy. I realized how much I truly wanted it over the last few days. I remembered the girl Papa raised and how much I loved learning from him. He made it a game. He made it fun. He taught me so many lessons that I completely pushed to the back of my mind because of my fear." I took a deep breath. "Then, the devil died, and I jumped in. It was scary, and I didn't know what I was doing, but I remembered. It was like Papa was there, telling me about small things and how to handle them. And I figured things out. I want to take my place."

"Cara, have you considered how the other families will behave toward you?" Mama asked, her question more than valid.

"I have. I won't back down and must handle it the way Papa would. I can't show weakness. That means they will continually test me. Meaning you four will have risks."

"That is no different than our lives before." Mama held my gaze. *"I know how the protection works."*

"The girls may not agree to this. They will have to make sacrifices. Christina and Ariana will have to pick universities in Boston."

A crease formed between both girls' brows. They had their hearts set on colleges on the West Coast.

"That is why I said we all have to make this decision. We all agree, or we all disappear, and I leave Angelos Shipping to—" I closed my eyes, feeling the burn at the back of my throat.

Mama saved me from saying, *"Theo and Xander to run."*

I remained quiet.

Fiona raised her hand, and I gestured with my chin for her to speak.

"You would leave them for us?"

My lips trembled. "Yes."

No matter how much I loved Xander and Theo, I must protect my family. They were all I had left. Their safety was all that mattered. One day, I hoped they would forgive me for breaking their hearts.

I hadn't promised them anything. I'd just stepped into my role and done my duty. But deep down, I knew they believed I'd stay, that I'd changed my mind about leaving.

And I had. I wanted this life with them. The one Mama discussed with them last night.

But I couldn't force my will on the girls. They had so many dreams. They deserved every last one of them.

The room remained quiet for some time, all of us lost in our thoughts.

Then, suddenly, Ariana burst out, "I vote to stay."

"Same," Christina said next. "I already applied to schools here, so it's not a big deal."

"Did you get in is the real question." Fiona stuck her tongue out at Christina.

I jumped in before another round of chaos started. "Stop instigating things and tell us your vote."

Fiona shot me a "you should know the answer, dumbass" glare. "Obviously, stay."

We all turned to Mama and waited for her to decide.

"You promise this is what you choose?"

"Yes. I choose it."

"Then we stay."

Relief washed over me. I'd finally get what I wanted, my family and the men I loved.

"I have one stipulation I need to add." Ariana glanced at Christina, who nodded as if they'd had some silent communication.

"Go ahead."

"We want to be involved. You will not leave us out. I've heard about how the Mykos Syndicate operates. Even with the eldest brother running things, all four brothers and one sister have an equal say in major decisions. We don't need you to protect us constantly. Honestly, I'm so over it."

"I second that shit."

"Christina, language," Mama admonished.

This prompted Fiona to defend Christina with, "She's only speaking the truth. What do you say, big sister?"

"Agreed. It makes complete sense." Fiona's triumphant smirk had me narrowing my eyes at her. "Why do I suspect you are behind this line of thought and that you're the one who put it into their heads?"

"Because you're a suspicious person." She smiled. "And you know I'm the smartest one out of all of us."

"And the least humble," Christina and Ariana said in unison, which had them laughing.

Ignoring the twins, Fiona asked, "Now that this big life-altering decision is over, can I ask a question?"

Whatever she had to say, I had no doubt it would be a

doozy—the last few years had changed her from the high-energy little girl to this firecracker of a teen who knew her mind.

I almost cringed as I said, "Shoot."

"So, is it Xander or Theo? Who will be the husband, and who's the side piece?"

I should have expected that.

"Fiona Maria Angelos, that is not something you ask your sister."

Oh no, Mama had pulled out the full name. Fiona was in trouble. It took all my strength not to peek in Ariana and Cristina's direction to see if they were about to burst out laughing like I was.

"Why not? If not my sister, then who?"

Mama closed her eyes, lifted her head up, and made the sign of the cross. *"Lord above, help me. These girls are going to drive me to drink. I don't know where I went wrong with them."*

Around five in the evening, after a quick shower, I stepped into my closet wrapped in a towel. Devani had only given me a few days of respite from my training and then sent a car to bring me to the Drakos estate to reestablish my schedule.

Every muscle in my body hurt, from my toes to my ears. I wasn't sure why Devani thought it was a good idea to fight as if we were in a match to the death. She'd knocked me so hard on the side of the head that my hearing hadn't entirely normalized.

Yes, we had been wearing headgear, and I towered over her

by a good seven inches, but for a five-foot-two woman, she packed a punch.

Her excuse was that I never knew when someone would catch me off guard, and I needed the skills to protect myself. I couldn't argue with her since that had happened when Andraius attacked me.

I glanced at the mirror in the back of the space and angled my face. Thank God, there was only a light redness on my jaw and cheek.

Xander would lose his shit, probably threaten to attach himself to my side, and give me no space. And there was no telling what Theo would do. He'd likely confront Devani or Nyx. That was all we needed, pissing off an ally's wife.

Opening a drawer, I selected a set of workout clothes, slipped them on, and grabbed a pair of trainers. After donning my shoes, I pulled my hair into a ponytail.

Approaching the mirror again, I lifted my shirt and studied my scars. They'd faded so much since I started using the products Nyx gave me, but I could still see the word. Maybe I'd always see it, even if it eventually completely disappeared from my skin.

WHORE.

The lines were all over and not even properly written. He'd done it to hurt, to make a point.

The bastard would never know that every time Xander and Theo kissed over them, as if it was just part of my body they wanted to enjoy, the pain of what he'd done eased away.

Dropping my shirt down, I squared my shoulders. I refused to let Andraius hold the power of his marks over me any longer. It was time to put something on my body I actually wanted.

Stooping down, I slid on my sneakers and then exited the bedroom.

"Good evening," Stefano said the moment he saw me.

He'd returned to heading up my security and was much easier to handle than Theo and Xander. Plus, being around him and my original team felt more comforting than it would have with someone unfamiliar.

No matter how much I wanted to resist the around-the-clock safety protocols, I understood that as I was the head of the family, it was more than necessary, and if it made the two men in my life easier to handle, then why not? Plus, after the discussion with my sisters, I couldn't complain when I would put them under the same kind of protection.

"I'm going to make a quick visit to the old side of the house and then stop in to see the guys in the barracks." I strode through a long corridor and down a short set of stairs leading to a landing.

"Are you sure you want to go down there? It's not something you will enjoy."

He couldn't be serious. Could the originals who knew about my relationship with Theo and Xander have kept the information from each other too?

I glanced over my shoulder, continuing to my destination. "I know what happens down there. I doubt anything can shock me."

"I'm not so sure about that."

It looked as if they had.

"Do you have orgies down there now?" I came to an abrupt stop before he could answer. A surge of anger pushed into the forefront of my mind seeing my parents' old bedroom.

Behind me, Stefano said, "It's over. Remember this. They are only walls."

"I will gut those suites and turn them into something useful. What? I haven't a clue. But I'll erase every trace of that bastard from this house."

"Sounds like a great plan."

Taking a deep breath, I continued down the hall until I reached the blue door I'd used throughout my childhood. I reached up and traced the script carved into the wood bearing my name.

The girl who'd resided in this room knew hope and possibilities. She hadn't experienced suffering or loss. She wasn't naive to the world she'd been born into but wasn't jaded. She'd accepted the role she'd play in her family's legacy.

Parts of her still lingered deep in me. However, her innocence no longer existed. I understood the cruel reality of our world, and the only way to fight was to be the most ruthless one at the table.

I was far from that person at the moment, but I had allies to back me as I built my power.

"Stay here. I'll be right back."

I stepped into my old room and closed the door. I wouldn't linger in here. This place only represented the past. I only needed one thing from a secret location.

Moving to a dresser in the corner, I shimmied it forward and then stooped down. In the back sat a small panel that I slid open, and inside was a black plastic box. I took it out and then opened it.

Smiling, I picked up the paper, unfolded it, and tucked it into my pants pocket.

Less than ten minutes later, Stefano and I reached the barracks, where I could hear the buzzing sounds of a tattoo machine and a group of men shouting at something they were watching on the television.

"This doesn't seem any different than before." I looked at Stefano.

He cocked his head to the side as if in confusion.

"You know that I came down here when I was younger?"

A crease formed between his brows. "I wasn't aware of this."

"I was a notorious pool shark. The amount of money I hustled out of the guys would boggle the mind." I couldn't help but smile at the memory.

"I take it Theios Peter didn't know this information."

"I did a lot of things Papa didn't know."

"If you're referring to your previous relationship with the young enforcers assigned to protect you in high school, let's say I discovered that information over the last few weeks."

"Well, at least you know the true Angelos men are loyal. They keep secrets, even from each other."

He grunted and pushed open the half-ajar door.

The space wasn't anything resembling a military barracks, and I wasn't even sure who had named the place. It was a large warehouse-style open building sectioned off into a gym and lounge with a pool table, a bar, couches, armchairs, and a big-screen television. Near it was a dining area with a kitchenette, and in the back sat a studio set up as a tattoo parlor with a giant sign hanging from the ceiling saying *Barracks*.

I walked around the periphery, taking in the laughter and the normalcy of the environment and how much it reminded me of the past.

I paused for a moment when I caught sight of Christina and Ariana at the pool table.

"Looks like they had the same idea as I did." I gestured with my chin.

Stefano shifted his attention and shook his head. "Those two are a handful. Clay says you are calm and sweet compared to them."

"Maybe I should step up my game. I can't let my younger sisters show me up."

"You've given us more than enough hell for two lifetimes, Angel," Theo said as he approached, his intense gray gaze holding mine and sending a tingle down my spine.

"I believe you need to build higher stamina."

He lifted a brow and then leaned forward.

I adjusted to close the distance between our mouths and then stopped myself.

Theo, Xander, and I had decided to be open about the fact we were in a relationship. However, we kept the affection discreet.

We couldn't chance anyone outside the walls of the Angelos compound learning about us. I had to maintain my role as the widow who was only a month from burying her husband.

The corners of Theo's mouth curved. "Are you complaining about my performance?"

"I'd never do any such thing."

God, he smelled so good, the clean scent of his soap and his natural essence.

"I can make it so every step you take tomorrow reminds you of my abilities."

I pursed my lips and then grinned. "You're on, Mr. Nephus. I dare you to deliver on that threat."

"You're such a brat."

"You love it."

"I do. I most definitely do." He brushed his lips against mine and pulled back. "Now tell me what made you decide to come down and visit with us peasants."

I stared at him for a few seconds, and then when I remained quiet, he probed, "Well?"

"I—I want an appointment with our resident artist."

He gripped my hips. "Are you talking about what I think you're talking about?"

I nodded.

"Then you better ask him if he has space to fit you in." He took my hand and turned.

I tugged him to a stop. "Theo, hold up. You're touching me. And a few seconds ago, you kissed me."

"Xander decided with Tina and Ariana as long as we remained on Angelos property, we didn't need to hide anything. I agreed."

"You took advice from two eighteen-year-olds?"

"Xander did. I agreed with him."

"Don't I get a vote in this?"

He tugged me forward. "No."

"What if it gets out?"

"Will it change your mind about us if it does?"

"Of course not."

"Then, why are we discussing this?"

I clenched my teeth. "You're such a jackass."

"And you love it."

I couldn't help but smile. "Yes, I do."

Theo and I worked our way through a group of people watching Xander work on Garren, one of the soldiers under Theios Alex.

Xander's concentration was absolute. Nothing distracted him when he was in the zone. Right now, his focus was on Garren's upper arm. From where I stood, it looked as if Xander was in the process of completing a sleeve he'd worked on in pieces.

"Hey, asshole, can you fit in a walk-in?" Theo stepped into the beam of the spot lamp trained on Garren's arm.

"You're the asshole, standing in my light." Xander lifted his head with an angry scowl. "Fuck off with you and your walk—"

He locked his attention on me.

Without saying anything, I reached into my pocket, pulled out the paper with a sketch more than five years old, unfolded it, and set it on the counter near him.

"Everyone, get the fuck out of here." Xander stood. "It's time to evacuate the premises."

Twenty-Four

ander

"You heard him. Get out," Theo ordered as I continued to hold Nerine's sapphire gaze.

She'd kept it.

The back of my throat burned with more emotions than I could ever express.

I'd dared her to let me design something for her, and she'd agreed. Theo and I'd spent hours working on it between shifts.

We'd taken the symbols from the Angelos crest, created the sketch to represent the three of us, and then added our names to the images. The design would be laid in black ink with no other added colors, making it stand out against her light golden skin.

Theo and I never believed she'd go through with the tattoo. She just never seemed the type to get one. Plus, Theios Peter and his overprotectiveness with Nerine gave us apprehension about doing anything visible to her that would reveal our secret.

Then she'd surprised us and said she wanted me to ink her on her next birthday. But that day never came since all our worlds changed six months after we'd given her the sketch.

"This is stupid. I don't understand why everyone has to leave," Ariana complained.

"We're her sisters." Christina joined in. "It isn't as if she's getting inked on her ass or boobs. Please tell me it isn't on her boobs."

Nerine's lips quirked up, making me return her smile.

"Nerine," Ariana shouted. "I forbid you to get tattooed on your boobs."

"Noted," she responded, there was no hiding the amusement in her eyes.

Just as the heavy main door of the Barracks slid closed, I heard Christina whine, "That's not fair. Theo gets to stay."

"Those two are like herding cats." Theo approached from my side.

His sentiment was an understatement. The girls had waltzed in earlier in the evening as if they owned the place and made themselves at home. The thought of this space as off-limits for young teens had never occurred to them. Then, when Fiona showed up, we accepted there was no use trying to get rid of any of them.

At least Fiona had had the good sense to leave after an hour. But it probably had more to do with a show she wanted to watch airing tonight than anything else.

On the other hand, Christina and Ariana decided they would play pool and hustle my men out of their money. The girls were good but no way near the level of pool shark Nerine was. But then again, they'd never gotten the chance to learn from their father.

"Did I bitch as much as them at the same age?" Nerine asked.

"Yes. However, we had creative ways of handling you," Theo answered. "Let me lock up the rest of the access areas."

I moved around my station. "You stay right there. I need to clean up and then prepare your chair."

"You don't even know where I want it."

"You'll get it where I give it to you," I called over my shoulder on my way to the sink in the corner of the room.

"Is that right?"

"Those are the rules. They haven't changed." I pulled my shirt over my head, threw it in a basket, and scrubbed my arms and upper body to remove the grime from earlier sessions.

"You're mighty bossy tonight."

"You forget, only with you am I nice. Everyone else thinks I'm the asshole and Theo is the diplomat."

"Are you going to show me your not-so-nice side tonight?"

"Is that what you want, Angel?"

"What if I said yes?"

I looked over to where Theo leaned against a wall.

He'd already set up the station for us, a cushioned seat designed to sit forward-facing so I could work on her shoulder and back.

It was more or less a massage chair, but if angled correctly, it would work perfectly for other purposes.

Taking a towel from a rack near me, I dried my skin and moved in her direction. "You'll get my answer depending on your behavior during our session."

"That's not an incentive to follow directions."

"I can always strap you down. Then you'll be at my mercy. We know that's your kink with Theo, but I'm always willing to play."

Heat flared in her eyes, making her pupils dilate. She liked dominance, and she wanted her men to take from her. Gentle and sweet had their time and place, and this wasn't one of them.

I never pushed it the way she craved it with Theo. With me, it was more about keeping her desperate and making her wait.

"I'm here for an appointment in your chair. The fucking can come later."

"Shouldn't I dictate the order of things?" I asked as I stopped a foot from her. "Especially since I'm the one providing you the service."

"So are you saying you want to tie me to your chair, fuck me, and then ink me?"

"It's a possibility. Or maybe I want to tease you, get you ready to come, leave you hanging, then ink you before I put you to bed."

"You wouldn't be so cruel." Her plump lips parted the

tiniest fraction, allowing her to release an unsteady breath, and her cheeks flushed with her growing arousal.

"Are you so sure?"

"You never leave me unsatisfied."

She was right about that. There truly was nothing like watching her fall apart. The sounds she made, the heat of her skin, the way her body writhed under my touch.

"I can fuck you first and hold your orgasm until the very end of the session."

"You wouldn't."

"Wouldn't I?"

"You'd fuck me in here with all the cameras?"

"It's not as if we haven't bound and fucked you in locations with cameras before," Theo responded to her question. "If you remember, we nearly got caught the last time it happened."

"That was your fault. You're the ones who decided to mark your territory because you got jealous of someone."

"I believe your memory of that incident is faulty." I gripped her hips. "First of all, you lied to your security team and told them that you planned to hang out with one of your friends at her apartment. Then while they waited for you in the parking lot, you snuck out with said friend for a party at a frat house."

Taking hold of the bottom of her shirt, I pulled it over her head and threw it on a chair near us.

"Second, when we found you, that jackass had you cornered, and you looked as if you were ready to punch him." Next, I took off her bra, tossing it next to her shirt.

Fuck. This woman had the most beautiful breasts.

Cupping one in my hand, I pinched the tip. Nerine whimpered and bit her lower lip.

"And third, when you saw me and decided to leave, he grabbed you, thinking he could force you to stay. No one touches you."

I slid my hand up her back and wrapped her damp ponytail around it before jerking her head back. "You will not take risks with your safety. Is that clear?"

Shit. I hadn't meant to sound so harsh.

No matter how many times I thought through it or how hard I tried to process things, the guilt from that horrible day's losses would haunt me.

I'd lost cousins, uncles, friends. Theo lost his family—even if they were shits, they were his family. And Nerine, I'd fucking failed to protect her from unspeakable horrors. And in the aftermath, I lost Theo, too.

All for fucking finals for degrees we weren't ever going to use. I was the one who convinced Theo we shouldn't blow off the exams. Because of me, Pops had arranged the reassignments.

As if understanding the emotions warring inside me, she cupped my face.

"Xander, it wasn't your fault. I was happy you weren't here when everything happened. Did you forget I had Papa order you to take your finals when you second-guessed going that morning?"

"I remember. He threatened to keep Theo and me off all assignments unless we graduated." I closed my eyes for a brief second, remembering Theios Peter's face as he lectured me on my future.

Theo and I were the first in our families to attend college and the first of our generation in the Angelos organization.

"I can't fail you again."

"You didn't fail me. I'd say you saved me. Even more so recently. You and Theo know things and protect me in a way no one else does." She wrapped her arms around my neck, bringing her body flush with mine, then her voice grew stern. "Lose the guilt, Xander. This isn't the time or place for it."

I narrowed my gaze at her, feeling the weight of the past lift. "You're all over the place tonight, Angel. One second a brat, the next so sweet, and now all bossy. I never know what I'm going to get with you."

"At least I'll keep you on your toes." She gave me a smacking kiss and pulled back. "Now, give me my first tattoo."

Before she could move away, I dragged her mouth back to mine. She hummed as I slid my tongue past her lips and rolled it against hers. Her taste was the perfect combination of cinnamon candy and her natural addictive essence.

Wrapping an arm around her waist, I walked her backward and continued to feast on her.

As we reached the bench, I pushed her in Theo's direction, and as if we'd choreographed the move, he swept Nerine into his arms and captured her lips. Theo held her to him, molding his hands along her curves.

I braced my hands on a counter, catching my breath, my body revving with the desire to claim her and make her cry out in pleasure.

The idea was to arouse her and keep her on the edge, not vice-versa.

Best-laid plans and all that bullshit.

Time to focus. The design would take hours. The fucking would have to wait.

"Get her on the chair while I set everything up."

Over the next few minutes, I set up my station and prepped the design onto a stencil for transfer.

"You're going to strap me down. I thought that was a joke."

I peered up from the stencil to see Nerine glaring at Theo.

Instead of having her seated with just her back exposed, he'd tilted the chair forward so she lay flat on it, ass in the air and arms bound to the armrests.

All I could do was shake my head and return to tracing my design.

"I'm going to take any opportunity I can get to tie you down."

"Asshole."

"Keep talking like that, and it's your ass that's going to feel it."

"Promises, promises."

"Enough talking." I rolled my stool into position, and then almost immediately, I regretted it when I heard her hum.

My cock would be in direct view of her face as I worked. The last thing I needed was to have a hard-on for the next few hours.

"On second thought, I will enjoy being in this." Nerine's

hand slid up my thigh to cup me, stroking me up and down through my jeans.

"I think so." Theo stepped up behind her and smacked her ass, making her jump and pull her fingers away. "Now behave, or I'll tie your wrist down, too."

"Don't even think about it."

"Or what?"

She glared over her shoulder. "No sex for you."

"It punishes you as much as it does me."

"I still have Xander."

"Let's get started. Otherwise, this is never going to end, and he's going to end up fucking you to shut you up."

Nerine lifted her head, her blue eyes boring into mine. "Wouldn't it be your cock shutting me up since it's that one in my face?"

"Theo's right. You're a brat."

She smirked and set her head down on the face rest.

Leaning down, I kissed the back of her head, then set the stencil down the center of her back along her spine.

Goosebumps broke out over her skin. "That's the spot where I wanted it, too. It represents us."

It was the perfect placement for the sketch of two dragons wrapped around a figure with angel wings. Now we'd see if she could handle the next few hours.

I clicked on my machine. "You ready?"

"I guess we're about to find out."

Three hours into the process, I had nearly all of the main design inked onto her skin. The shading and details would come during a different session. Nerine had taken to the process better than most people I knew. Even most of those seasoned to the chair squirmed a time or two when a needle poked around near their spine.

Nerine seemed to enjoy the spike of adrenaline that came with the pain. It aroused her. The fact that Theo kept touching her added to the need coursing inside her.

All the lust hadn't made my job any easier, either. Concentrating on a spinal piece with a hard-as-rock dick was no simple task, especially when a wicked woman in the chair kept commenting on my condition.

Thankfully, I'd gotten a small break from her torture. Over the last forty minutes, she seemed to have drifted off into sleep, utterly unaffected by the work on her back or the conversations Theo and I had around her.

Nerine never slept deeply unless she felt safe, and she had no worries with us.

The knot deep in my gut loosened. She trusted me and believed in me. Maybe I should start believing in myself.

Theo moved over to my side to watch as I put in the lines for the dragon tails wrapped around the waist of the angel.

"How much longer?"

"Fifteen or twenty, max." I shifted my focus to his and caught his calculated intent.

My arousal grew, and for the briefest second, I thought he planned to fist my hair and bring my mouth toward his.

Instead, he said, “Let’s see how long this quiet and tranquil side of her lasts.”

“Don’t startle her awake,” I responded, pushing down my disappointment. “I still need to finish this. The last thing I want is to fuck up this design.”

“In that case, I’ll strap her in tighter.”

“The other option is to wait until I finish or ease her to consciousness.”

“What’s the fun in that?

“You’re still the jackass who liked to push her buttons. She’s going to give you a mouthful.”

“It’s the other way round.”

I shook my head. “No one would ever believe that under your public all-business persona lived an idiot adolescent with the need to pick on his girlfriend until she wanted to stab him.”

“It’s better than having your persona of a scary hothead who wants to clear the streets of dumbasses.”

“My way keeps people from talking to me. You have to be diplomatic.”

“Finish up. I need to concentrate and strip her and not wake her.” Theo slowly set his hands on Nerine’s hips and began to remove the remainder of her clothes.

It took him ten minutes since he had to adjust her legs a few times, and I’d never know how she remained in her zonked-out state. She’d squirmed a few times and shifted, but maybe she believed she was dreaming of the touches and caresses.

Finally, after completing all my work, I cleaned and covered up her back.

Stepping away, I couldn't help but smile as I took her in. Her lashes darkened her cheeks, her face so relaxed. That body of hers was incredible, especially her ass. She wasn't the skinny type, a woman her height couldn't be and look healthy. She had curves I loved to touch and worship.

As if sensing my perusal, she opened her lids, and sleep-fogged cobalt irises peered at me.

"You're done?"

I nodded. "I'm done."

She attempted to push up with her arms but couldn't move but a few inches. Immediately, she searched behind her, but the restrictions of her bindings only gave her a limited view.

"Theo, where are you?"

His hand glided up her inner thigh. "Right here, Angel."

"Set me free." She pressed her legs together. "Or I'm going to fuck you up."

Moving in her direction, I stooped down so we were at eye level. "Didn't you have a plan? I thought I heard something about fucking."

Her cheeks flushed, but she continued to struggle. That was when I realized Theo had bound her wrists to the armrests. He meant business tonight.

"Am I a participant or an orifice for your pleasure?"

I leaned toward her. "Have I ever left you unsatisfied?"

"No." Her breath grew unsteady, and she glanced away, so I grabbed her jaw, drawing her attention back to me.

"Don't I make you come at least twice, if not more, every time we're together?"

"Yes. But I want to—" She gasped as Theo smacked her ass, and then she moaned.

"What is it that you want?" I probed. "Were you about to say, participate? I think you forgot what it is to lose control when both of us have you tied down and at our mercy."

Something feral passed in her gaze, and then she smirked. "Do your worst."

"Are you asking me to make you cry, Angel?"

She swallowed as if guessing what I had planned. "You are channeling Theo tonight."

"No, love, this is the side I pull out for you on special occasions."

"Go ahead. Show me."

Instead of saying anything, I fisted her hair, jerked her head back, and covered her mouth in a bruising kiss. I scored my teeth across her lips and bit down, making sure she felt the sting of it. Then I pulled away and stood.

With a small click of my fingers, I adjusted the headrest, freeing up space to stand before her.

"You're going to be my—what was the word you used?" I asked while freeing my cock from my pants.

"Orifice," Theo answered as he moved into position behind her, his palm cupping one of Nerine's beautiful ass cheeks.

"Yes, that's the word. Will you be a good little girl and let me use your orifice?" I stroked up and down my length, bringing the head of my erection up toward her lips.

"Ass—"

Before she finished her response, I thrust into her mouth,

pushing all the way back, holding myself still. She whimpered and made noncoherent sounds but remained in position.

It was cruel, meant to torment her.

"She's fucking soaked." Theo hummed his pleasure while he stoked her pussy with his fingers. "She likes this side of you. I think your best-friend, sumo-wrestler side needs to take a break from time to time and let this version come out to play more."

"What do you think?" I held her angry stare. "Do you like this Xander better?"

I pulled out, allowing her to inhale deeply. "This side can fuc—"

Plunging back in, I gagged her with my cock, pulling her down as far as she could take me.

Tears streamed down her cheeks, and her spit-covered lips stretched so wide they could barely fit the girth of my cock.

"Do you know how fucking beautiful you look right now? You were made for us." I pulled out, only leaving my tip against her mouth.

"Xander, more," she begged, panting. "I'm not fragile. You know I'm not fragile."

"You heard her." I looked up to see Theo naked and aligning his cock to her pussy.

His lust-filled storm-gray eyes locked with mine. The need and desire we refused to act on pulsed between us.

After a few seconds, Theo ordered, "Make her cry, Xander. She wants your darker side."

I wrapped my hand in her hair and pushed back into her

mouth, in and out, in and out. She screamed around me, telling me Theo had joined in, pushing her into orgasm and driving my desire even higher.

Her eyes held mine, begging for more. I gave her exactly what she wanted, using her brutally and forcefully.

As my balls drew up and I knew I'd blow, I jerked out of her mouth, leaving her panting.

"Xander, what are you doing?"

Theo continued to fuck her, but I gestured to him. "Time to switch. I want that ass."

"Oh, God. You're going to kill me."

"You're the one who wanted it. No sweet and gentle tonight."

As I passed Theo, he pointed to the bottle on a counter near me. He was always prepared. "Open up, baby girl. Focus on me now and not the giant cock about to tear into your ass."

"That's not roman—"

"I told you I'd stuff your mouth with my cock to shut you up."

The dynamic between them never ceased to amaze me.

Positioning myself behind Nerine, just taking in the sight of her slick, swollen, glistening cunt had my cock growing harder and my balls ready to burst. I wanted to feast on her, drink every bit of her up, and then fuck her.

At this moment, I'd come on the floor if I wasted any more time. Her mouth had done wonders, and now I hung on the edge.

Grabbing the lube from my side, I poured some over me

and along the seam of Nerine's crack, making her moan around Theo's cock. Then I positioned myself at her puckered opening.

"You know what to do." I gripped her hips and pressed in.

She pushed back against me, with each of my shallow movements in and out helping me go deep and deeper. When I was almost seated to the hilt, I drove three fingers deep into her pussy. Her walls contracted around me, and she released a guttural cry around Theo as he pummeled her mouth.

Her arousal flooded my hand, and I began relentlessly pistoning my cock. I barely grazed my thumb over her clit when she detonated, flexing and spasming around my pumping fingers. The pleasure vibrated through her ass around my cock, pushing me to the cusp.

"Fuck, I can't hold out much longer," Theo gritted out. "You're making me look bad. Come already."

"Not until she gives me one more."

Nerine made some humming noise, a trick to contract the back of her throat, sending Theo spiraling.

"Dammit, Nerine." He clenched her head with both hands and fucked her, using her to take his cum.

Seeing it ratcheted up my need, and I fucked into Nerine like a man possessed. At the same time, I worked her clit and rubbed the bundle of nerves deep inside her, rubbing back and forth.

Nerine pulled off Theo and screamed, "Xander, fuck, you've killed me," and then her pussy muscles contracted and clamped down.

That was all it took.

"Fuck, fuck, fuck." I came in hard spurts, feeling as if I'd lost every bit of my sanity.

Twenty-Five

erine

"Remember, you have nothing to prove, cara."

I held on to Mama's words knowing she meant well. However, today wasn't about proving I was worthy but standing toe to toe with the establishment.

The time had finally arrived when I'd stand as the official head of Angelos Shipping in front of people who'd been Papa's peers and now were mine.

I belonged at the table.

It solidified in my soul after I'd gotten the ink from Xander three weeks ago. I was part of this world, I couldn't run from it, and it was time to accept it.

Plus, I wanted a future with Theo and Xander, and the

only way to have one was to stay here.

"You ready?" Theo asked me as we stepped into the two-hundred-year-old building where today's meeting would occur.

"As ready as I'll ever be. Do you know the players who decided to attend?"

Xander answered, "My sources say nine families, including you. East Coast and New England power players. You're the sole female."

"Get ready. The moment I cross the threshold into their lounge, some of them will run for cover because of all of my estrogen."

"I'm glad you still have your sense of humor." Theo's dry delivery almost had my lips twitching.

"We will remain behind you. Press the button on the ring if you need something." Xander held out his phone, showing me the app linked to the platinum band I wore on my middle right finger with the Angelos crest.

I nodded, not saying anything.

Then Theo said, "You're Peter Angelo's daughter. Don't take shit from anyone. And if at all possible, keep the bloodshed to a minimum. Cleaning up after you is becoming a major hazard of this job assignment."

Those words actually brought a smile to my lips and eased the tension in my shoulders.

"I'll do my best, but I make no promises."

"At least I took her gun from her." Xander patted his pocket. "I don't trust her to keep it in her purse with Tobias in the same room."

"I still have my handy blade."

Tobias was the one I expected to cause problems for me today. Well, he and one other family head, Dante Galani. He was the patriarch of the Galani Syndicate and had extremely archaic views on women and their roles. He'd hated it when Papa announced his plans to pass on the legacy to me and tried his best to convince Papa to change his succession plan when Linus was born.

I had to keep my cool, channel my inner lady mob boss, and take no one's shit. Violence was my last resort.

Deep down, something said I'd have to stab a motherfucker to make a point today.

I hoped it was Tobias. Gutting another Stratos would make my day.

What the hell was I thinking? I was hanging around Nyx too much.

Thinking of Nyx, Simon Drakos would be in the room as well as the Mykoses, Nyx's brothers. I'd have powerful allies at the table, ready to back me.

The doors opened within a few steps of us approaching, and it took all my effort not to comment aloud at the over-the-top extravagance of the space.

Why the fuck would a group of men need to meet in a room that I could only describe as a Victorian ballroom? A giant chandelier hung from a ceiling so intricately designed that it would take hours to study the various scenes etched into the plaster. Along the walls were heavy drapes in deep blue. They matched strategically placed furniture and gave a sharp contrast to the cream-colored walls.

A giant dark wood table dominated one end of the room

with chairs for at least thirty people. And there was enough space behind the chairs for each person's security and entourage.

Only a few seats remained open, the others occupied by various family heads. They seemed to ignore my presence, pretending to engage in discussion of some type or the other, but I knew better. They were well aware of the new addition to their dynamic.

Attendants waited at various spots, ready to cater to the needs of everyone, and a man I could only assume was the room butler rushed in my direction, trying his best not to look exhausted.

His face showed a smile, but the stress around his eyes told me he needed a break or a shot of something strong to take the edge off.

"Mrs. Angelos, welcome."

"Ms. Angelos," I corrected.

He gaped at me and then nodded. "Ms. Angelos. Please follow me. "

"Already at it, I see," Theo murmured.

Xander added, "It's going to be one of those nights. I can feel it."

"I'm sure you'll give me a detailed critique of my actions at home."

"Debriefings are our specialty. Hope you're prepared." Theo pulled out the chair the attendant directed us to. "Remember to use the ring if you feel any threat."

"I'll be fine."

"Promise?"

I released a sigh. "Promise."

"She's not going to use it. Tell the men to stay alert," Xander muttered, making me smirk.

As I settled into my seat, I scanned the faces of those around the table.

Of course, the two families who were my allies sat at the very opposite end of the table. Nico Mykos and Simon Drakos inclined their heads, giving me their gesture of support.

With the looming meeting, I'd forgone my training with Nyx for two weeks, knowing too many eyes watched me. I was no longer playing the role of a mob wife. It wouldn't make sense to visit Nyx as much as I used to do.

I continued my perusal of the rest of the table. That was when I caught Tobias Stratos studying me. Irritation laced his scrutiny as well as lust, a complete replica of his disgusting uncle. He'd done as Xander predicted even after my firm and maybe not-so-nicely worded message. He thought my response was a challenge and pursued another meeting where he offered to help me close Andraius's estate and transfer assets.

As warned, I sent my messengers to deliver a personal *no, thank you*. Neither Xander nor Theo told me what they conveyed to Tobias. They only said they followed through on my instructions, which was all I needed to know.

However, the hostility directed at the men behind me as he glanced in their direction made me believe whatever they'd done left a lasting impression.

"Hello, Nerine."

I turned in the direction of the voice to see Anthony Galani, heir to the Galani syndicate. He was around his mid to late twenties, and from what I remembered, he wasn't a douche like his father. But that may have to do with the fact he grew up on an estate in Maine with his mother and siblings instead of here in Boston with his father, who had no time for children in his lifestyle.

"Anthony. It's good to see you."

He smiled. "I wanted to give you my condolences and apologize for missing Andraius's funeral."

"I'm sure you heard. I don't need condolences."

"I did hear that." Amusement lit his eyes. "You have a refreshing take on your circumstances."

"Refreshing isn't a term I'd expect a Galani to use when a woman joins the ranks."

"You should know not every Galani views things in the same manner. Some of us are more progressive than others. As with everything, it's about timing. Wouldn't you agree?"

I nodded. "Everything is about timing."

His attention moved behind me, and he straightened. "I'd like to give you another apology before we begin."

"For what?" I frowned.

"You'll see." He stepped away with those cryptic words and sat across from me.

Xander came up next to me. "What did he say?"

"He apologized for whatever was about to happen in the meeting."

"That means he's giving you a heads-up that his dick father will pull something. Time to play your A-game. You knew it was either going to be him or Stratos."

"They may team up, so I'm not discounting Tobias. Want to tell me what you did to make him hate you?"

"You did that."

I tilted my head up to glare at him. "How?"

"You're ours, and he wants you."

"Nice try. No one outside of our circle knows about us. Don't avoid answering my question."

"We carried out your directive. That's all you need to know. Time to begin." He moved away as a voice cleared.

I saw an older man with stark white hair and onyx eyes staring at me. Artemis Adamo. Once upon a time, I called him Theios Arte, and I believed he was Papa's friend. Then he hadn't lifted a finger to help us when everything happened. It was as if he watched to see how things played out. I'd resented him for it.

Now, I accepted it was how things worked on this board game. The crash course of the last few months gave me the foundation for my knowledge. Then, I'd jumped into the deep end of the pool after Andraius's demise and had no choice but to utilize everything I'd learned. It was a trial by fire that left me exhausted more than I wanted while at the same time building my confidence in my abilities to lead the family.

Good thing I had three brilliant sisters who wanted to help me sift through the mountain of information my idiot husband had never bothered reading or understanding.

Everything in our world—the Greek syndicate world—revolved around amassing and running territory. Power came from being cunning, strong, and ruthless.

As a female joining this table, most of these men would fall victim to their old-school beliefs and discount my intellect and abilities.

Hell, I'd done it to myself. Not ever fucking again.

"Nerine, welcome to the table. It is remarkable how much you look like your mother," Artemis said, giving me an indulgent smile I'd expect a father to gift upon a small child.

I gave no response to that remark. Yes, I looked like Mama, and she was known for her beauty. However, this was a business meeting, and comments about my appearance reduced my status.

Plus, he'd seen me at the funeral and spoke to me there, even if it was brief.

What the fuck was up with him?

When I remained quiet, he smirked as if I'd passed some test.

All of these were games.

Fucking dickheads.

Artemis then addressed the rest of the room, welcoming everyone, and said, "Let's make this short and sweet. We are here to address any open topics from our last meeting and then discuss the effects of the transition of power following Andraius Angelos's death."

"That topic isn't open for discussion. I am now the Angelos at the table. You have no say in how I run my family."

Dante Galani jumped in. "We have business dealings with Andraius you have no concept of understanding. I say that's the first thing we discuss."

"Let me make this clear again. I am the one here. I know my business. We will speak to those matters privately if you have questions about contracts. Otherwise, discussion of Angelos Shipping or my family is off the table."

"I agree with her." Simon Drakos spoke. "We never question the succession of power when tied to blood. She is the true Angelos. This is her seat."

Nico Mykos spoke next. "I second Drakos. This is meaningless jockeying for power that wastes our time. Galani, accept a woman is at the table and shut up."

"She has no standing here. Those two behind her run things."

"Believe what you want." I shrugged.

Tobias decided to join in. "All you have to do is clear up the rumors."

"I have nothing to prove. Let me repeat. Believe what you want."

"You don't even deny it?" Tobias questioned me as if he were a big brother expecting answers.

I gave him a deadpan stare and then asked my question. "There are rumors concerning you. Something to do with the paternity of your nephew. Would you like me to ask about that?"

Rage lit Tobias's eyes, then cooled, and he nodded. The demeanor of his face changed, and he cocked his head a fraction taking me in as if he saw me differently now.

"You're correct. Our personal lives have nothing to do with business."

Okay, then. I won a round. Or was that two, since I'd passed that test with Artemis?

Whatever. I had to focus.

"We are not dropping this." Dante's irritation grew, making me wonder what was truly behind his dislike for me. "If you can't answer to the rumors, then it's true. You're their whore."

Artemis jumped in. "That's enough."

Using that word sent fire rushing through my blood, and I clenched my teeth. No, this man wanted to wound me, make me lose my calm.

Keep going, asshole.

"No, no. Let him get it all out. I'm sure he has more to add to this tirade." My indifferent tone caused a crease to form between his brows. "This is misogyny at its finest."

My dig seemed to have passed over his head because his following words gave me visions of punching him. "Your reputation is at stake. Are they your lovers?"

"This line of questioning is ridiculous," someone said from the other side of the table.

"We have other things of greater importance to handle." Artemis's patience had run out. "Anthony, get your father in order."

"Yes, get him in order. It may become detrimental to your family's future business endeavors." I let the not-so-veiled threat linger in the air.

It wasn't Andraius he'd negotiated with, but Papa. What he planned to do with Andraius was a renegotiation with terms more favorable to Galani Shipping. Too bad those things would never happen now. And if he kept digging this grave, the contract he made with Papa might never be executed.

Yep, I was that kind of petty.

"Don't think you can square off against me." Dante glared at me as if he could intimidate me. "No one will take her seriously if they question her rise to her seat or her morals. We need to know the truth behind the rumors."

From my periphery, I saw Xander shifting, ready to act. His need to protect me and my honor warred with letting me fight this battle.

"Are you questioning my authority based on who shares my bed?" I lifted my brow, but before he could answer, I continued, "You should answer the same question. I'm not married. I'm a widow, and I can do anything I please. You, on the other hand, are married and have three mistresses." I shifted my attention to his side. "Anthony, did you know your father is giving you another sibling later this year? Isn't that six from his paramours?"

Anthony gave no reaction, but Dante's face grew redder.

"I am your elder. You will not speak to me as such."

"No, I am your equal, and you will show me respect, especially at this table. I can play the same games you can. I'm probably better at it since I'm Peter Angelos's daughter. You remember him, don't you? The man you claimed was a dear friend and an ally."

"You're a little girl who's gained a seat by spreading her legs, nothing else."

"If that's how you feel, then it must mean you no longer need access to Angelos contacts for your next batch of inventory or access to our ports in Cypress. Do you know alliances and rivalries in the US translate to the Angelos family overseas?

One call from me and Theios Rico will shut off all Angelos resources to you throughout Europe."

Surprise flashed on his face, and then he adjusted in his seat as if he were about to get up and attack me. One of his men set a hand on his shoulder, readying to keep him in place.

The movement had everyone in the room adjusting their stances. Theo and Xander moved closer to me, as did the rest of our team.

The whole time, I kept my eyes trained on Dante's face.

"Here is another thing I'll repeat: I am Peter Angelos's daughter. I know the deals he made and the terms behind them. I know everything owed to Angelos Shipping and by whom. Andraius let you get away with many things because he held no real power. He knew nothing about the business. And you took advantage of it. It's a shame for you he died before you completed renegotiations."

"You know even less than him," Dante retorted. "You're weak. You fucked your enemy for years. It took someone else cleaning up your father's failure to give you that seat."

I leaned forward, setting my hand on the table, wanting him to see the fury in my eyes. "I doubt you would have survived one day of what I endured. Answer this question for me. Does it make you feel better about all of your big, strong male insecurities to degrade and insult a woman who is smarter and twice as capable as you?"

Dante jumped up, arms stretched out, ready to reach across the table at me.

I instinctively pulled the knife from the sheath I kept

strapped to my leg, rose from my seat, and threw it, lodging it into Dante's shoulder and making him stagger back.

The next second, the room broke into a chaos of shouts, hands jerking me around, and guns trained everywhere. Xander and Theo had me sandwiched between their bodies, and other soldiers shielded me from the different sides. It was a complete blockade of men and muscles.

"What the fuck, Angel?" Xander set a hand on my waist.

I tried to catch my breath and said, "He started it."

Theo kept his body in front of mine, his gun trained on someone.

That was when I heard Simon Drakos say, "Stand down, everyone. Dante Galani instigated this whole situation when he lunged for her. From where I stand, she defended herself."

"Bullshit. She used a fucking knife," Dante shouted. "She could have killed me."

"Would you rather I pulled a gun? Then you would be dead."

Xander squeezed me. "Not helping."

"No, this is the end of any more conversations about my place at this table. Is that understood?" I tried to push Theo to the side, but moving a concrete wall may have been easier. "Get out of my way, Theo."

"Not until his men put their weapons down."

After a few seconds, I heard Anthony say, "Apologies once again, Nerine. From this moment on, Galani men only answer to me and are no threat to you or your safety."

Theo stepped to the side.

Anthony gestured to my vacant seat. "I'm taking over now. Pops no longer makes decisions for the family."

"The hell you are."

Ignoring his father, he glanced to his side. "Have him patched up and take him home and watch him. Confiscate his phone."

A group of Anthony's men took Dante from the room.

Artemis cleared his throat once again. "It looks like we have two successions of power at the table today. Let's acknowledge it, forget the bullshit from earlier happened, and get to business. The entertainment portion of the afternoon is over."

Anthony inclined his head to me. I gave him the same gesture back, and in some warped sense, I believed I just helped him overthrow his father.

This was turning out to be a weird-as-fuck day.

Twenty-Six

erine

I stared out my bedroom window, utterly exhausted from the day. Two months since Andraius's death. No. Two months since the bastard had attacked me and I killed him. I had a new life. But in a sense, it was my old life. One I'd wanted and didn't want. Not without Papa and Linus.

Then again, if I thought about it. Papa would have had to pass for me to get the title anyway.

What the hell was wrong with me? My emotions were getting the better of me.

Mama told me I was being moody today, but I'd chalked it up to the nerves about the meeting with the families.

Anyway, my bitchy side helped me.

"What are you thinking about so hard?" Xander came into the bedroom holding a crate of some kind and set it on the floor.

"Today. It feels—" I paused. "Surreal. I'm in the seat. I get to be bitchy, and no one says anything."

"No, they say it. You just shut it down."

"What now?" I studied him, and a crease formed between his brows.

"I'm not following."

"What happens now?"

Theo walked in, his intense gray gaze on me. "You tell us. Do you still have the urge to run away? Do you want your freedom from this life? Can you live without us?"

"No," I answered without hesitation.

Both men prowled in my direction, one slow step at a time. It almost gave me the sensation of being cornered and hunted. My skin prickled, and my heart felt as if it skipped a beat.

Xander rubbed his jaw. "Are you sure there aren't more lingering thoughts about leaving us?"

"I'm here to stay."

"Does that mean you're ours forever?" Theo stalked closer.

Arousal pooled between my legs, and my nipples tightened into hard, stiff peaks. My skin burned for their touch. The pull of these men was all-consuming, and I wanted more.

"I've always been yours." When they were near, I set my palms on the center of their chests. "But I have a question."

"And that is?" Theo slid a hand along my waist.

"Do the two of you belong to each other?"

Theo and Xander locked eyes. The emotions passing over their faces brought tears to my eyes.

"It's time to forgive, Theo," I whispered.

He remained quiet, continuing to stare at Xander.

After a few moments, he said, "After you decided it was over, I had absolutely no one. You have no idea what it feels like to be so fucking alone in the world, when everyone else is surrounded by people who give a damn about them."

"I'm so s—"

"Let me finish," Theo cut Xander off. "In one night, I lost everyone I loved. And then I became a traitor to everything I valued to stay alive. It destroyed a piece of me. I had to fucking build a new life on a different continent, pretending to be someone I was never born to be. It isn't something a person can get over with a simple sorry."

"Are you ever going to forgive me?"

I heard the longing in Xander's voice, and it broke my heart. I wanted to fix this for them so much, but I couldn't. This was something they had to do.

"I did that months ago. Just the way you are made it easy to forgive you and fall back into our friendship."

"But not what we were before?" Xander asked.

Theo shook his head before glancing at me and cupping my cheek. "We love Nerine. Focusing on her was safer."

"You mean less complicated," Xander interjected. "You wanted to avoid getting hurt again. I get it. You didn't trust me not to let you down again."

"Could I expect anything else, when the only person I could rely on for the last five years was myself?" Theo shifted his focus to Xander, a crease forming between his brows. "You were my business partner, nothing more."

Xander moved toward him as if ready to shove him. "Are you kidding me right now? I was there, but you made it business. It was like talking to a stranger half the time. *You* did that, not me."

"Calm down, both of you." I stepped between them, trying my best to push them apart and failing. "For all that's holy, you're supposed to talk this out, not fight."

"He needs a punch in the face for thinking I wasn't there." Xander's temper was at ten out of ten, and at this moment there was no reasoning with him.

"You destroyed us and expected me to call you and say 'Hey, life sucks pretending to be the dipshit's lackey. Want to talk?' Not a fucking chance."

And of course, Theo decided to use his calm-as-fuck voice to antagonize Xander. It annoyed the hell out of me when he used it during arguments with me, so I could only imagine how Xander would take it in this state.

"So you chose to screw as many people as possible while you worked your way through Europe wheeling and dealing?"

A calculating smile touched Theo's lips, that made me want to clock him, too. "Oh, so you're jealous that I fucked someone other than you. Interesting. From what I know, you did the same."

"Only after I learned about you."

Okay, this was getting ridiculous and completely off-track. They were both fucking around with everyone.

Assholes.

"The one who needs to be angry about this particular situation is the one who is trying to keep us from beating the hell out of each other."

"Do not bring me into this mess." I blew out a breath and used my arms to push them as far apart as I could. When that didn't work, I dug my nails into their chests, and they shifted.

"Fucking idiots. Now I know why it sucks to be the mediator."

Both of their attentions homed in on me. I looked between them, feeling the calm in the energy between them.

"It does, doesn't it, Angel?" Theo asked. "I do it for a living. And he does it on the regular with us."

"It's utterly exhausting when you two go at it," Xander added, and Theo's gaze lifted to his, something passing between them that I couldn't understand.

"Both of you have to let go of the past or this isn't going to work." They continued to stare at each other, not saying anything. "Answer this, did the love die?"

"Of course not." Xander released a frustrated breath. "I've never hidden how I felt from either of you. He's the one who needs to answer the question."

After a few moments, Theo said, "No, it didn't die."

Then as if I was watching in slow motion, Theo reached across me, grabbed Xander's shirt, pulled him in his direction, and brought their mouths together. I shifted just as their bodies collided.

The kiss was no way near soft or gentle, more on the lines of devouring. It was an exploration of mouths, biting and tasting, while hands roamed and touched.

The sounds they made, especially the groans shot deep into my core, igniting my arousal to a fever pitch.

They were beautiful together, something I'd waited to see.

Xander fisted Theo's hair, releasing a delicious feral sound as Theo stroked him through his pants.

They broke the kiss, pausing, taking each other in. Their faces flushed, their breaths unsteady, and their hard, thick cocks pressing along the inseams of their pants.

My pussy spasmed, making me slide to the floor as the urge to touch myself pushed at the back of my mind.

I was the voyeur in this. A spectator with a vested interest in the participants. And when they came to me after, it would be the three of us, not the two of them with only me.

They reached for each other again, pulling at each other's clothes. First shirts and then belts and pants.

When they were naked, it was like seeing two Greek gods before me, bodies so different, yet absolutely perfect. And those fucking cocks of theirs, long, hard, pointing past their navels, and dripping with precum.

God, I wanted so desperately to touch them, be on my knees before them.

Theo lifted his hand and took hold of Xander's jaw, gripping it. "You piss me off. Don't ever make stupid fucking decisions like that again."

"I've learned my lesson."

Theo slid his palm to Xander's shoulder and pushed, and immediately he lowered, his face right in front of Theo's large cock.

"You know what to do."

"You're an asshole." Xander's tattooed hand wrapped around Theo and pumped up and down, creating a steady rhythm.

From as far as I could remember, Theo took the lead in our dynamic. He was the dominant one, no matter if Xander was a bulldozer enforcer in the outside world. However, there was always this game of push and pull. It added to the arousal, the intensity.

"I am who I am. Plus, you still obey my orders." Theo cupped Xander's head, tugging him forward, then ordered, "Make me come."

Xander opened his mouth, taking Theo as far back as he could. I moaned, unable to help myself, seeing the way they lost themselves in the pleasure. My nipples beaded and my clit throbbed.

They held gazes, completely focused on each other.

Dear God, these men were going to kill me with the sounds coming from their lips.

I slid my fingers between my legs and past the gusset of my soaked underwear. Circling my clit, round and round, I tried to find relief.

That's when Xander cupped Theo's balls and a guttural cry came from Theo's lips.

I knew that face. He was close, oh so close.

Theo fisted Xander's hair and took control of the pace, something hard and relentless.

I stroked myself more, plunging my finger into my sopping pussy. Watching Theo's orgasm build added to my climb to the peak.

"Don't you dare do it, Angel. It's not your turn," Theo commanded at the moment the first spasms ignited in my body. "Now watch Xander take my cum."

I wanted to weep. I ached so much.

"Xander, what the fu—" Theo clenched his jaw, and his hips pumped erratically as he came. "You asked for it. Swallow every fucking drop."

The way Theo worked the last of his release out using Xander's mouth seemed brutal and cruel. But Xander seemed to enjoy it, as if he spurred it on with whatever he'd done.

Theo pulled out of Xander's mouth, his cock still semi-hard, even after an orgasm. Xander's, on the other hand, looked as if it was about to explode at any second. Veins bulged from the sides and the flared bulbous head seemed to pour out precum.

"On the bed." Theo motioned with his head.

Xander stood. "I get on my knees for you, and you can't do the same for me."

"Later. Right now, she wants a show. Let's give it to her."

They both looked in my direction.

"I can't argue with that decision," Xander responded.

The back of my throat burned. I loved these men so much. It was etched deep into my soul.

"Come on, Angel." Theo offered me his hand. "You'll want an up-close-and-personal view of this."

"I can see perfectly fine from here." I narrowed my eyes at him. "The only reason you want me close by is to keep me from taking care of myself."

"That, too."

Rising to my feet, I strolled toward him. His pupils darkened as I neared, and a shiver slid down my spine. The ache deep inside my pussy now seemed to pulsate in painful waves. It was a constant reminder of my unquenched desire.

Taking hold of my fingers, he brought them to his lips, kissing my knuckles. “Settle him on the bed, Angel.”

“You’re a tease, Theo Nephus.”

I led Xander to the bed, pushing him onto his back. His cock strained toward his belly, thick and hard, arousal coating his skin. I wanted to lick it off. I wanted to taste him.

But this was all Theo and Xander’s show.

The second I shifted, a wicked light entered Xander’s eyes, and he clutched my hair in a tight grip, pulling me to him and covering his lips with mine.

I tasted both Theo and him on my tongue. It was a heady mix that pushed my need higher and higher.

Xander gasped and arched, breaking away.

Theo fisted Xander’s cock, pumping it from root to tip. His stormy gray gaze locked with mine, and a devious smile touched the corner of his lips.

“I didn’t say you could kiss her.”

Through gritted teeth, Xander said, “You didn’t say I couldn’t kiss her either.”

Theo’s grip tightened, making Xander hiss.

“Sit back and enjoy the show,” Theo told me. “Your turn will come soon enough.”

I scooted back against the pillow, watching the way Theo’s hand moved up and down. My pussy clenched, and my nipples pebbled. Moaning, I cupped my breast, desperate for some relief.

"Remove your hands."

The order had me frowning. "You can't be serious."

"Do you want to come?"

The challenge had my heartbeat accelerating.

"Asshole," I muttered as I curled my fingers into fists and held them by my sides. "Well, get on with it."

Theo ignored me, his attention homing in on Xander before he moved closer to him without releasing his movements on Xander's cock. The way they stared at each other was hot as hell.

Theo leaned down and slid his tongue along Xander's neck, then followed it with bites that had him arching. Theo licked, sucked, and bit a trail down Xander's shoulders and chest. Goosebumps broke out over Xander's skin the second Theo scraped his teeth over his nipples. Xander's arms shook as he held them to his sides. They had these rules between them.

Xander's cock wept with precum, covering Theo's hand as he kept up the steady rhythm meant to torment.

Theo's game.

He loved to hold us on the edge, leave us right near the cusp of going over, until he was ready for us to come.

I ached so badly just watching them, and Theo wasn't even touching me. I could only imagine how Xander felt.

Theo lifted his head and raised an eyebrow as if he'd heard my thoughts.

Bastard.

He slid lower, adjusting himself between Xander's knees. He lowered and then engulfed Xander's cock.

"Fuck," Xander cried out, his eyes clenched tight and the veins along his neck bulging.

Whatever Theo was doing to him with his tongue and mouth, Xander was in bliss. It was as if he could barely breathe.

Watching these men together overwhelmed the senses. They brought forth an indescribable level of arousal.

I pressed my tights together, but it only made the ache worse.

Theo lifted his head, holding Xander's eyes, and commanded, "Come," before taking him deep again.

In the next few seconds, Xander jerked, bucking his hips up, and groaned as his orgasm washed over him.

These two were fucking beautiful.

Twenty-Seven

Nerine

"Now it's your turn Angel," Theo said as he lifted his head from Xander's cock.

My pulse jumped as Theo and Xander moved apart, homing their attention directly on me. There was an unnerving gleam in both of their eyes.

I tried not to squirm as I leaned back against the headboard of my bed, taking in the two naked Greek gods staring at me. They both had swollen lips I couldn't wait to kiss and bodies I ached to touch.

I'd waited so long to see them together again. I'd never get tired of it. I loved it.

The bond they shared was built long before I came into the picture, and it made me so happy to see them finally break that wall down between them.

We were truly three again.

Xander licked his lips as if he'd read my thought about kissing him.

The shameless tease.

Their focus remained on me, not averting in the slightest.

What were they up to? This was more than sexual. It was as if they planned to pounce on me like predators.

"Why are you two looking at me like that?"

"We need to settle something so there is no confusion later." Xander crawled toward me in unison with Theo.

Whether fully clothed or undressed, these men were an indulgence for the eyes.

"And that is."

Theo glided a palm along the inside of my leg until he reached my knee. "You're marrying us."

I sighed as a twinge of sadness hit me.

If only that were possible. Wife to both of them, taking their names. Well, in my case, they'd take mine. Our children would take the Angelos name.

Oh God, we'd have children one day.

A longing bloomed deep inside me unlike anything I'd ever experienced. This wasn't about genetics but about our love.

"Legally, it doesn't work that way. Considering our lines of work, we need to avoid prison."

Xander lifted a brow. "On the books, Theo gets the title. However, you belong to both of us."

My attention shifted to Theo, who watched me with an intensity that had my heart drumming an erratic beat.

"Is this what you want, Theo? Do you want to marry me?"

"I've never questioned my desire to marry you."

"Then what's the problem?"

"There isn't one. This discussion is to clear up technicalities. You good with it?"

"Are you asking me to marry you?"

He shook his head, his lips curving. "I'm not asking. You're going to marry me. I want to know if you'll give us a hard time about it."

I rolled my eyes. "Of course I will. That's my normal operating protocol."

He came toward me, fisting my hair and tilting my head back. "Good to know. One more thing."

"Go ahead."

"You're married to both of us, and sooner rather than later, we will make it public that the three of us are together."

"Let me guess. I have no say in this decision, either."

"Fiona was the mastermind of that thought process," Xander informed me. "She told us how she wanted things handled in her family. You may be a figurehead, after all."

"If she still wants it when she's older, I'll hand it to her. But something tells me Ariana and Tina want in on the action."

"Are we about to enter the era of the Angelos sisters?"

"Let's get them out of puberty first. I'll think about it after that."

"Now, back to marriage." Theo's fingers flexed in my hair for a second. "Xander, get on with it."

Xander stepped off the bed and walked over to his pants, taking something out of his pocket. When he returned, he took my left hand and slid cool metal onto my finger. I couldn't help the tears burning the backs of my eyes. Their ring was all I ever wanted, never Andraius's.

"I want children. It's not your womb I want. I'm not that fucker."

"I know this." I couldn't help but smile at Xander. "In a few years, we'll have a houseful if that's what the two of you want."

"I hope you remember your words when you're pregnant nonstop." Xander ran a thumb along the column of my neck.

"Stop talking and kiss me."

"Always have to have the last word." Theo tugged me forward, taking my lips in a devouring kiss.

It was a claiming, filled with the emotions of the promises we'd just made. When Theo pulled away, out of instinct, I turned to Xander, capturing his mouth with the same uninhibited need.

We tasted and savored. It was an intoxicating mix of sensations playing over my skin. Four hands roamed my body, touching everywhere and nowhere near where I wanted them most.

My skin heated and burned, already so sensitive from watching them. The need for these men consumed me.

All of a sudden, a realization hit me. The restraints deep inside no longer existed.

I pulled back, as tears streamed down my cheeks.

"What's wrong?" Theo asked, concern all over his face.

"I'm happy. I can move about and feel without worrying. After five years, I'm finally free."

Understanding lit his eyes.

"You freed yourself. Don't ever forget that," Xander said.

I loved these men. They were mine—my lovers, my future, my family, and I was theirs.

"Shower. That's what we need after this long day."

Xander carried me into the bathroom, where he and Theo undressed me. By the time we neared the shower stall, I was nearly out of my mind from the teasing touches and sliding of fingers.

At least they were suffering as well. Their cocks jutted out, so thick and hard, so ready for me. The urge to drop to my knees and lick the precum dripping from both their tips called to me. I wanted to suck, taste, and enjoy them as if I were double-fisting lollipops.

"You'll get our cocks, but not like that." Theo ran his thumb across my lower lips. "We'll give you the pleasure and the pain. You'll beg for it to stop and never stop."

My nipples ached, and the throbbing deep in my pussy grew to an almost unbearable level. The desperate need to come pushed at me, and we'd barely begun.

Xander reached inside to turn on the multitude of shower heads. The room immediately filled with steam, adding to the desperation building inside my overheated body.

These men were so fucking beautiful and turned me on in a way I couldn't comprehend. Whether it was with each other or me, every movement, every look, every touch was a delicious torture.

"You're teasing me."

"Of course I am. Fucking your mind is as important as your pussy."

"You've been fucking my mind all night." I grabbed the back of Theo's head, pulling him in my direction.

His gaze darkened, but instead of giving him the kiss he expected, I bit down on his lip and drew blood.

A growl erupted from deep in his throat, and he held his mouth over mine, letting me taste his blood. Our tongues dueled, and my need grew by leaps and bounds.

"We're vampires now?" Xander asked a second before I fisted his hair and brought his mouth to mine.

I couldn't care less that he could taste Theo's blood on my lips—we'd already shared his cum.

"If you want true blood play, I can give it to you." The huskiness in Xander's voice sent spasms deep inside my core.

To have both my men feed every one of my dark desires was everything I could dream about. But after Andraius's handiwork on my body, could I ever let anyone bring any blade against my skin? Even if it was for pleasure?

Eventually. If it were one of my men.

"Not yet, but when I'm ready. You'll do it over the scars."

"It won't change them. That's not how it works. It's about desire, giving you that edge of pain that makes you float."

"I know. Gaining pleasure from something that caused me excruciating agony is the best healing, don't you think?"

"One day. When you're ready." He leaned forward, retaking my lips. "Now it's time for our shower."

Xander lifted me into his arms as if I weighed nothing and carried me into the multiple streams of water. Theo followed behind us.

Xander set me on my feet, and I tilted my face to the water.

The heat seeped into my skin, calming and soothing. And just as fast, my body ignited with sensation as two sets of hands washed me, my hair, body, every part of me.

My men surrounded me, engulfing me with their presence, unique scents, and sheer beauty. They were so different from each other, each magnificent in their own right. They were both honed weapons, built to protect and fuck like madmen.

When their mouths and bodies joined in the ministrations, it was almost too overwhelming. I couldn't think, only feel. My skin burned as if on fire from their scorching kisses. Each touch, tease, and bite sent me to an edge I was desperate to tip over. And they hadn't once touched my pussy.

This was so evil, meant to drive me mad, to keep me hyper-aware of them.

Theo's teeth scraped down my stomach. "Oh, dear God. Yes."

I threaded my fingers into his hair as he lowered to the floor, continuing his delicious, wicked torture over my mound and lower to graze my clit.

Xander glided his hand between the globes of my ass and slowly worked two fingers inside me. I pushed against him, loving and hating the situation at the same time.

Theo lifted my leg onto his shoulder and licked my pussy, tonguing my entrance and then circling my clit. He glided a palm up my thigh and thrust three fingers inside my throbbing channel.

"It's too much," I couldn't help but whimper.

Xander chuckled in my ear. "Never too much. This body is built for us. "

I was so full, no way near how it felt to have both of them in me, but the stimulation of their thick fingers inside me had me writhing. Their wicked hands worked my body, my breath coming out in short pants, and heat bloomed in my belly as everything clenched inside me. My mind clouded with a euphoria I couldn't describe.

"Oh, God." I raked my nails through Theo's hair, unable to control myself, so lost in the spasms rocketing inside me.

Spots burst behind my eyes, and the sensation of falling cascaded throughout my body.

"Theo, that tongue. What are you doing to me?" I reached up. "Xander. Please."

I had no idea what I begged for, but I needed something. They had to know what. I was losing my mind with need.

Xander pulled his hand from my ass and Theo freed his fingers from my core. I whimpered, hating the loss of their touch, the extraordinary feel of having them so incredibly deep in me.

Without warning, Theo spread my thighs wider, and Xander positioned his cock at the entrance of my pussy and plunged in with no mercy.

I couldn't help but scream, tossing my head back.

"That's right, let everyone hear how your men pleasure you." Xander pummeled me while Theo held me stretched open for him.

"Let me see your eyes, Angel. Watch me watching Xander fuck that beautiful cunt of yours."

My lids snapped open at Theo's command. The sight of his

hunger pushed my desire higher. All I could do was take the overwhelming pleasure pushed onto me.

"She's so fucking tight and slick."

"Let's see if we can make her even tighter." Theo's mouth dived down to my soaked pussy.

He stroked and teased my clit and just when I was about to scream, he slid that wicked tongue away. But then I felt the wet heat of him where Xander fucked into me.

Theo teased and tasted both Xander and me. It felt so good, the sensation exhilarating and just on the cusp of overwhelming.

"If you keep that up, I'm going to come before I'm ready," Xander gritted out.

Theo lifted his head, giving Xander a smirk. "No, you're not. This is all about her right now. You'll have your turn again later."

"Then keep that mouth from fucking with my cock."

"If you insist." Theo's lips returned to my pussy. He took a long swipe with his tongue, purposely lingering where Xander fucked into me, and moved up to my clit, sucking it, right before he gave it a slight bite.

In the next instance, I bucked and begged as another release cascaded into me.

"That's it, Angel," Xander murmured into my hair as he thrust in and out of me and worked my breasts and nipples.

The shower poured over us, cascading in streams and filling the area with steam.

The onslaught of sensations pushed me to an almost unbearable level, making me want to desperately beg them to stop and threaten them with death if they ever stopped. I couldn't get enough. This was what it truly felt like when two men worshiped the woman they loved.

Heat and quivers bloomed deep in my core, and my legs weakened. I reached back, clasping Xander's neck as my other hand clenched harder in Theo's hair. His dangerous tongue continued to lave my sensitive bundle of nerves and feasted on my pussy.

Theo continued to torment Xander with small grazes of his mouth. This game was one I loved so much.

Heat bloomed deep inside me and the walls of my pussy quivered and flexed around Xander's pistoning cock.

"Come, baby. Come for us again," Xander whispered into my ear.

With the next two strokes of his thick, hard cock, I detonated, screaming my pleasure. Pure, unadulterated ecstasy rocketed throughout every nerve in my body. It felt as if a kaleidoscope of color exploded behind my eyes.

How was this even possible? I went years without coming, and now this.

Theo stood, holding my thigh in his large hand and cupping my face with the other. He sealed his mouth over mine in a searing kiss. All the while, Xander continued to shift in slow, tormenting movements deep inside me. It was as if Xander and Theo were determined to keep me hanging in a state of sheer bliss.

"Remember that we've got you," Theo said as his hand slid away from my jaw.

Opening my eyes, I stared into his dark gray gaze. I heard

the familiar click of a bottle and then the press of a cock along the tight space that Xander currently occupied.

Oh God. They were going to take me at the same time. We'd done this in the past, a thing we'd worked up to. It was the deepest level of sexual intimacy we'd shared.

I remembered the heat of them, incredible sensations.

"You good with this?" Theo asked, leaving himself poised.

I held his gaze and did not hesitate to say, "Yes."

Xander lifted me against him, taking all my weight, and Theo notched his thick, bulbous head inside me. The sensations of fullness that burst through me felt almost too much, too intense. And for a split second, I wasn't sure I could do this.

"Breath, Angel," Xander cooed. "Relax."

"I'm trying. God." I threw my head back. "Those dicks of yours are going to slice me in two."

His thumb circled my clit, and a tremor shook me, allowing Theo to slide in further. I whimpered as he stretched me and seared me from the inside. It created an addictive mix of delicious pain and desperate need.

I wanted to run away and beg for more at the same time.

A head trip at its finest.

I held onto Xander's and Theo's arms, letting them rock against me. Lifting my face, I noticed how intensely they stared at each other.

The intimacy of this, the lust. This was who we were.

Theo and Xander moved together, sandwiching me between them and sealing their mouths together. Their passion was a livewire to my senses. It was an all-consuming kiss, owning, possessive.

My nipples strained harder. Fuck, this was hot. Then in unison, they turned their heads toward me, taking my lips one after the other, biting, sucking, tasting.

My pussy contracted, and a flood of desire coated their cocks.

Xander muttered as my spasming walls clenched around him, "You need to fucking get all the way inside her. This is torture. I won't be able to hold it back this time."

Theo pushed in farther, using shallow thrusts. "This isn't as easy as you think. You can control it."

The shower poured onto us, the drum of the many showerheads adding to the intensity of everything happening with the men holding me.

"Xander, kiss me, again." I lifted my head, and he met me, letting me focus on him and the tingling exhilaration building within my cells.

Without realizing what I was doing, I began to gyrate against them, the movement so delicious. They were both deep in me. They pulsed. I felt the heat of them. Their torsos pressed so tight against my body and each other.

Their lust was more than evident in every caress, sound, and breath.

"You ready, Angel?" Theo asked, his voice thick and laced with so much desire.

I nodded, and the men began to fuck me. It wasn't a hard-and-fast pounding but a measured and slow process. They filled me to capacity, stretching me beyond normal. I needed care, and they gave it to me.

A slow seduction, a building of my desire. Fuck. These men knew what they were doing.

With each plunge, they worked as a unit to keep a steady rhythm. The way they played my body was beyond anything I could imagine.

"It's almost there. I feel it." My clit throbbed, and a clenching heat took hold of me.

I moved along with the men, needing the extra friction. They pumped in and out, in and out. We were a unit, three lovers who trusted each other.

Xander reached between Theo and me and massaged my clit, right before he pinched it. That was the thing I needed to shoot me into bliss.

"Yes. Thank you," I cried, tossing my head back and forth.

My back bowed, and I couldn't think, only feel. I was in an unending loop of pleasure. It rolled and rolled. I barely registered the men roaring their releases. All I felt was my pussy continually contracting and quivering, my body and mind completely lost in the pleasure.

I knew if I died at this moment, I'd die happy.

Twenty-Eight

Theo

I jarred awake, feeling as if I'd emerged from deep water. My muscles ached as if weights sat heavy over every inch of my body.

What the fuck?

Immediately, dread crept in, and everything inside me sensed the wrongness in the room.

No, no, no.

Nerine.

I whipped my head to the side, regretting the wave of dizziness.

She wasn't there.

The sheets were cool to the touch. How long had she been gone? That's when I noticed something near Xander.

What the hell?

I jumped up, caught my balance, and crawled to Xander's side of the bed.

My heartbeat pummeled into my ears as I focused on the used syringe next to Xander.

Instinctively, I rubbed against my neck and felt the slight lingering ache.

I reached over to the side table to turn on the light but pulled back when I realized no power lit any corner of the house. There was always a dim glow somewhere, from the windows to under the doorways.

Shit. This was not fucking happening.

"Xander, wake up." I shoved at him, pushing down the drowsiness still pumping in my system.

When he remained stock still, my hands shook. No, I would not fucking lose him, too.

I rubbed my eyes, trying my best to clear the haze. I had to get it together.

Checking for Xander's pulse, it beat strong, giving me a short bit of relief.

I staggered from the bed, grabbing clothes and putting them on. I searched for my phone and realized it was gone. In fact, all of our devices were gone.

Jesus. This had to be a professional job. I never slept this deep, and how the fuck had they gotten through our security?

Would the Assassin Squad do this? Nerine had spoken of

wanting freedom, and they were the ones with the means to make it happen.

No. Nerine had put away her plans to leave. She wouldn't lie to us. We'd planned our future last night. She was the one who decided for us to marry sooner rather than later, even though I suggested we should wait a few more months.

Moving into the closet, I pushed back some of Nerine's clothes and found the safe. Opening it, I grabbed some backup phones.

I checked the devices, and none of them had signals.

Whoever did this had tech skills beyond any average motherfucker.

Gripping the back of my neck, I reached into the safe and pushed through the false wall encasing in the far right of the enclosure. Thank God for Xander and his paranoia.

I pulled out flashlights and his encrypted satellite phone. Turning it on, I released a deep breath as the screen lit up.

I dialed Clay, who patrolled the properties near the port tonight.

"Sir, we've been trying to get through, but all lines are dead, and access to the house is restricted. We assumed you put the compound on lockdown."

"No. I have no idea what's going on, but you need to get here now. Whoever it was drugged Xander and me. We need to account for the Angelos women."

"They aren't there?"

I blinked a few times. "I just came to. I'm going to search. The house is too fucking quiet."

At that moment, I heard the distinct sound of something

crashing and knew it was Xander stumbling off the bed and knocking things off the side table. Whatever dose they gave him was probably a hell of a lot stronger than mine.

"Xander is conscious. Let me check on him. Call in our forces. Assume we are under attack. Contact Theios Alex. He'll know how to coordinate everyone."

"We assumed he was at the compound. No one can reach him."

"Fuck." I gripped my hair. "Send someone to his house. Check on them. Report back and get your asses here."

I hung up, grabbed the flashlights, and went to the bedroom.

The churning in my stomach pissed me off to no end. This was bullshit.

Whoever gave me this drug needed their head bashed in.

Xander braced his hand against a wall. Fear burned in his eyes, and the firm set of his jaw made it obvious he was doing all he could to keep hold of the panic welling up inside him.

"Tell me this isn't happening."

"I can't. Our nightmare has come to life. Xander, Theios Alex is missing."

"The fuck he is. I talked to him before we went to bed. Mom and Pops were at home."

"I sent a team over to check on them. Right now, we need to find Nerine and the girls." I tossed him a flashlight and his pants. "You take the passageway to Fiona's room. I'll go down the main hallway."

He nodded.

We went through every bedroom, with no sign of any of

them. All their things were as they had left them the day before, nothing out of place. The only thing missing was them.

Our men were alive but lay unconscious all over the place, all drugged.

The sat phone beeped with an incoming message, and as I read it, my heart sank.

"What?" Xander saw my face.

"Same MO for the security at your house. All were knocked out, and the cameras were disabled. Your parents are gone."

Immediately, Xander pulled out his phone and sent off a series of messages, his face a mask of fury.

"What did you do?"

"I'm getting Drakos involved. We need help. I can't keep fucking failing everyone." Xander's anger radiated out from him.

"This isn't on you. It's a coordinated attack on us."

"We need to keep looking."

We continued our search through every possible corner and passageway, but hope dwindled. Then when the team arrived, the power reconnected, nearly blinding us with the lights.

"The library," I shouted, and Xander and I ran toward it.

If I found her in there, I'd tan her ass so red for scaring the shit out of me.

Xander and I slammed through the doors and came to an abrupt halt.

There on the sofas were the unconscious forms of Theios Alex and Theia Brenna. They lay on separate couches with blankets over them as if they'd lain down for naps.

We rushed to them.

"Mama, wake up." Xander lifted her limp form.

I checked Theios Alex's vitals, hearing his shallow breaths and weak heartbeat. He opened his eyes, shaking his head.

"I had no chance, too many of them, too organized. Planned—I'm sorry." He passed out as the drug took effect again.

I stared at Xander, but his attention was on something behind me.

"Turn around," he said through gritted teeth, not letting go of Theia Brenna.

His body shook with waves of anger unlike anything I'd ever seen from him.

Instead of doing as he ordered, I asked, "Is she breathing?"

"Yes, barely. With Mama's heart condition, they could have killed her."

At that moment, Stefano and other soldiers rushed into the room.

Stefano went directly next to Xander. He was a trained paramedic and could help Theia Brenna.

"I've got her, sir. Let me help." Then Stefano gestured for someone to help Theios Alex.

Xander and I moved out of the way and turned in the direction where Xander focused. There, on Nerine's desk, sat a large cream piece of paper with red writing.

Xander grabbed my arm and warned, "Don't touch it. I want to check it for prints."

"It won't have any. Everything here is too professional. They targeted her. All of us."

Xander's fingers curled on my arm in a brutal hold. "The only way they could have gotten past our security was if they had help from the inside. I thought we'd weeded the traitors out."

"I don't know what to think right now. We have to find them." I clenched my jaw. "I'm going after whoever did this. She's our everything."

We moved closer to the desk, and instantly my world shattered.

Mr. Onassis and Mr. Nephus,

Did you honestly think there was a happily ever after for the three of you?

Especially when your enemies circle nonstop and each plans to take you down to make a point. Do either of you know who your enemies are? Not Angelos's enemies, but yours?

Yes, we know all about the Xander-Angel-Theo throuple. We've known about it since you were youngsters.

FYI, we aren't the only ones who've known about it. You weren't as discreet as you believed.

We commandeered your most prized possession before others could implement their plans to take her.

Your Angel's life and the lives of her family are in your hands now, gentlemen.

Run her empire. The two of you are the standing Angelos now. Remember the rule, no bodies, no deaths.

We will notify you when we are ready to return her to your keeping. However, looking for her may result in her death.

Finding her will guarantee her death.

Now, here is something to think upon. The Angelos bloodline is worth billions. Yes. Billions. Peter Angelos was a ruthless man and made deals that netted him well. Your Angel's signature is needed to cash in on all of them.

And guess who his partners for these investments were?

That's right. Think of our procurement of the Angelos women as protecting our assets.

They are safe and protected, and they will want for nothing.

As long as you keep your distance.

Congratulations on your elevation to the roles of the heads of the Angelos syndicate.

"Who the fuck are these people?" Xander looked at me.

I shook my head. "Whatever it is, this isn't only about her. It's about us. How are we connected to everything that's happened?"

"I don't know. One thing I do know is that nothing is going to stop me from finding Nerine. Fuck them for thinking they can threaten me and believe that would keep me from searching for her."

"Good luck hiding five women who look the way they do and act the way they do from us."

Get ready for more mayhem, suspense, and steam as Theo and Xander search for their Angel.

And let's see if they can handle Nerine's deception the same way she handled theirs.
Preorder the next book in the series - > *Sin and Deception*

Want to learn all about Devani and Lilly - Dive into the dark depths of New York with book one in their series with *Dangerous King*.

Do you want more of Nix and Simon? Get their story in *Master of Fortune*
Or
Step into their indulgent world of Vegas from the beginning with *Master of Sin*.

The End

Books By Sienna

Rules of Engagement

Rule Breaker

Rule Master

Rule Changer

Politics of Love

Celebrity

Senator

Commander

Gods of Vegas

Master of Sin

Master of Games

Master of Revenge

Master of Secrets

Master of Control

Master of Fortune (Nix and Simon)

Sweetest Sin

Intrigued By Love

Street Kings

Dangerous King

Vicious Prince

Deceptive Knight (Lilly and Rey)

Ruthless Heir (Devani and Sam)

Violent Delights

Claim

Defy

Own

Sin and Lies

Sin and Betrayal

Sin and Deception (Oct 2024)

Sin and Redemption (March 2025)

Collections

Reckless Rome (A Cocky Hero Club Novel)

Take Me To Bed (2019)

Meet Me Under The Mistletoe (2021)

Nightingale (A charity anthology in support of Ukraine) - (2022)

Darkly Ever After (An Organized Crime Anthology) (2022)

RARE Melbourne Anthology (2023)

About the Author

Inspired by her years working in corporate America, Sienna loves to serve up stories woven around confident and successful women who know what they want and how to get it, both in – and out – of the bedroom.

Her heroines are fresh, well-educated, and often find love and romance through atypical circumstances. Sienna treats her readers to enticing slices of hot romance infused with empowerment and indulgent satisfaction.

Sienna loves the life of travel and adventure. She plans to visit even the farthest corners of the world and delight in experiencing the variety of cultures along the way. When she isn't writing or traveling, Sienna is working on her "happily ever after" with her husband and children.

Sign up for her newsletter for notifications of releases, book sales, events, and so much more.
http://www.siennasnow.com/newsletter
contact@siennasnow.com

www.ingramcontent.com/pod-product-compliance
Lightning Source LLC
Chambersburg PA
CBHW060632310726
48982CB00003B/750

* 9 7 9 8 8 8 5 3 5 0 2 0 4 *